Candia McWilliam was born in 1955 in Edinburgh where she was educated until, at the age of thirteen, she went to school in England. After leaving Girton College, Cambridge with a First, she worked for *Vogue* magazine and later as an advertising copywriter until her first marriage, in 1981, by which she has a son and a daughter. In 1986 she was married for the second time. She lives with her husband in Oxford. *A Case of Knives* is her first novel.

Critical acclaim for *A Case of Knives*:

'. . . very fresh, very sharp, and as memorable as a nightmare. It is a brilliant and distinguished book, and the start of something new. I was astounded by it.'   *Peter Levi*

'Full blown, exploding with intrigue, suspicion, violence – and love . . . McWilliam creates indelible characters'
                                                    Publishers Weekly

'A fiercely clever book'   *The Standard*

'A very striking first novel indeed'   *The Times*

'This writing is so extraordinary that I am tempted to call it an opera. It is a high and extravagant style, voluptuous, avid and epigrammatic, passionate and risky'
                                                    Sunday Telegraph

'Immaculately written'   *Elle*

'A clever and ingenious first novel . . . Candia McWilliam has the mark of a true novelist'   *The Scotsman*

A CASE OF KNIVES

Candia McWilliam

SPHERE BOOKS LTD

Published by the Penguin Group
27 Wrights Lane, London W8 5TZ, England
Viking Penguin Inc., 40 West 23rd Street, New York, New York 10010, USA
Penguin Books Australia Ltd, Ringwood, Victoria, Australia
Penguin Books Canada Ltd, 2801 John Street, Markham, Ontario, Canada L3R 1B4
Penguin Books (NZ) Ltd, 182–190 Wairau Road, Auckland 10, New Zealand

Penguin Books Ltd, Registered Offices: Harmondsworth, Middlesex, England

First published by Bloomsbury 1988
First published in Abacus by Sphere Books Ltd 1989
1 3 5 7 9 10 8 6 4 2

Printed and bound in Great Britain by
Richard Clay Ltd, Bungay, Suffolk

To my Father and my Stepmother,
and for my Mother

My thoughts are all a case of knives,
    Wounding my heart
    With scattered smart,
As wat'ring pots give flowers their lives.
    Nothing their fury can control,
While they do wound and pink my soul.

George Herbert, 'Affliction (IV)'

LUCAS

I

I needed a woman. Or, better, a girl. A woman would be too set in her mould. I required for my purposes something unrefined and eventually ductile. I would perform the smelting and hallmarking myself. I wanted the pure substance I obtained to be worth my effort. I was thinking in terms of ingots, not of pigs.

I have found out recently of women, that, although they are less than pigs to me, since I do not have to eschew the devouring of them, as I do of pigs, to some these fleshy creatures are precious and worthy of the assay.

Occasionally I see in the street a man whose bearing tells me he has endured many of the same privileges and ostracisms as I, and read many of the same books; we have what is called a lot in common, yet we care to remain separate, poised, attentive and distant above our secret parishes, like birds of prey. Our quarry is shared, and our romantic hunger common. We require, like policemen or vicars, a beat. What we hunt is monsters who will turn on us, victims who will show themselves panthers and Calibans; they may be meter-readers, good husbands, fine fathers, but briefly, in the dark or the excoriating snowy brightness of under ground, they are to me, and to these other well read, civilised, gentle men, everything we have wanted. I have never woken up in the bed of someone I have made love to; nor has someone who has made love to me woken up in my bed. The people I have seen in that touching, crumpled state of waking up have all been my patients. One cannot feel violence towards a person one has seen asleep.

But then there was Hal, and he changed the regular, discrete, unadmitted quarterly satisfaction of this essential service in my life.

It was clear at once that I could not forbid this boy my home, nor deal him banknotes just out of the lamp-posts' sight.

When I first saw him, I was thirty-nine and he twenty. He was entering a chemist's shop in St James's Street. The Palace looked on, a toy fort full of courtiers. I saw at once that he was not to be picked up. Even in St James's, there is provision for that sort of thing. I fell in love with him as I looked; the sensation was of sinking, without end. As I sank into the sight of him, I caught on nothing. I saw he had no archaeology. He was simply what he appeared to be. My past is full of bones and ghostly shapes traced in salt and acid. I saw he was an untroubled English boy, his past a simple matter of roots and earth.

My appearance is elegant. I wear conventional clothes. I have been told I look like a man who has had at least one child. Whether this is on account of my profession, I do not know. At any rate, it has been useful to me.

In the chemist's, this young man and I each purchased a wooden bowl of shaving soap. I said, to the assistant, but of course to the young man, 'I find the floral soaps leave you with the blue cheeks of a baboon.' He smiled – did he even shave? The respectable shop fronts were dark but festive as we walked up the street, as though khaki cigars and chestnut hats and dusty-shouldered green bottles were emblems of love.

But that had been six years ago and now I needed a girl.

Here, I thought, she was, smiling, her back to a tall looking-glass, her arms athwart the marble mantelpiece. A woman with her back to a mirror is a rare enough thing, one who will keep her hands still almost unique.

I even felt something of the twinge of recognition which is a presentiment of intimacy. Housemaid's memory, Tertius calls this, meaning the realignment of recollection so its nap lies smooth with the velvet of sentiment and comfortable untruth. His snobbish name for this emotional editing has its source in the frequent employment of the device in detective novels. When his Lordship is found dead on the library bearskin, the housemaid remembers that his Lordship always was funny about bears, never could abide them really. When you come to like someone, you recall the first meeting dignified by time's paragraphing; they were not drunk, they were recently bereaved, their orange sombrero was a welcome note of colour at the funeral. It is far easier to reorder memories than to admit to repeated errors.

I was struck by this girl. She appeared to meet all my superficial requirements. Classical beauties draw to themselves light, their faces pearly in any room. This girl drew to her face and arms not light but colour. A painter will tell you these are the same thing, but at first glance they are different. Light is all take and colour is all give, at least until you look again. She flashed colour like a witchball, bright not pale. There were some pearly girls in the room, and they would surely wear better, if kept in padded cases and held close always to scrupulously soaped flesh, but they were not to my purpose.

Had she held, balanced on her lifted face, a disproportionate sphere, glowing like ectoplasm, she would have resembled one of those Art Deco lamps which have twice been fashionable this century. She had the uselessly sportive length of limb, and the base-metallic glow. She appeared covetable without being unattainable; had auction houses dealt in young women, she might have been picked up quite reasonably at a fairly popular specialist sale in Geneva, with invited bids. She was listening far too attentively to an old Greek three-quarters her height. She looked down her face to his, and moved her features in response to his. The thick brows of the Greek beetled; her thinner eyebrows flinched. His eyes, the red-brown of prune flesh, gave a warm leer; her blue eyes hid behind mauve lids. His grey jaw jutted; she tucked in her chin like a dove. Unless she really was horribly shy, this submission was unconvincing, and gauche in one so big.

Her clothes were not those of a shy girl. She appeared not to realise her size. Unless she learnt soon that her little ways would sour and leave her, like a pale old cheese, on the shelf, she would be wasted. But if she grew into herself, well, then, she would be the perfect picture for the frame I had in mind. In her appearance there was something unEnglish which appealed to me. I was pleased to see this combination of confidence and unease; it is a suggestible compound.

The girl seemed also to have big breasts. I wanted that, too. It was, perforce, to be a full-length picture.

I sought our hostess. Anne was upstairs in her fur cupboard, shivering. There was no sign that anyone had been with her.

If it is possible to admire a person intellectually for their storage system, I did Anne. Her clothes cupboards were tall lozenges of space, obscure and cool. So all cupboards might be described, but hers were a cathedral of sartorial labour, its craftsmen Siamese mulberry tenders, French button piercers, Amazonian crocodile skinners, small men pulling shards off beetles in jungles below warring helicopters, men in palazzi weaving fields of cloth from dreams of past power. The guildsmen of bonded beauty all contributed to her cupboards' satisfaction, and, unlike Nana, the end of all this endeavour was not the pleasure Anne might give men, or the money and power she might gain from this pleasure. She was like the bibliophile of pornographic books. She had all these lovely things created solely for adornment, yet her pleasure was in their contemplation more than in their employment. She told her clothes like a miser, but dressed almost invariably in immaculate constructs of no definite colour.

From the east of her cupboards came the glow of sequined dresses beneath stoles of chiffon; there was a lady chapel of underwear sewn by nuns. Anne's own faith, as far as I could tell, was the limiting of chaos by external control, the absolute control of passion by ritual. Anne kept her clothes in an order logical and convenient, ready, like a soldier, for any contingency. Her cupboards were a thesaurus of social possibilities. I would tease her by inventing absurd putative events and making her select clothes to wear to attend them. She could always do it. We played in her cupboards like children.

Both Anne's houses contained their air-conditioned armoury of skins, muslins, wools, and the braced infantries of shoes. Each item bore a card which was inscribed with the date and place of its last wearing. I once asked her whether she notched the satin heels of her evening shoes for each conquest. She replied that she had her conquests made into coats. I was not sure whether she had lovers.

This evening, I sat with her in the gloom among the furs, the coldest part of the clothes-cathedral, giving a faint winter smell of naphtha and gauze-bagged dry flowers, downy buttons of immortelles, with their petals like small fallen pointed fingernails.

The furs were shouldered with shawls of chiffon to prevent chafing. These capes looked, on the congregation of sleek or brindled shoulders, pitifully domestic.

Anne was not vain. She had short light hair which lay where it was placed, a creased face with prominent cheekbones, very pale blue eyes, and an expression without guile. She was thin, not slim, and never wrinkled her nose, swivelled her hips or licked her mouth before or after telling a lie. So far as I knew, she had never told me one. Her posture was that of a sailor; she was always braced against some greater force, hooked to a chair, set against a wall. Her skin and hair were of a similar light brown, which grew more differentiated in sunlight. After prolonged exposure, her skin would darken to the colour of soft brown sugar, and her hair lighten to the colour of caramel. She was always neat, but she pushed her sleeves up from her wrists. She had thin feet and hands and the eyebrows and gaze of a boy. She had no greed but I sometimes worried that she was easily bored. I despised this, but she never seemed to be bored by me, so I was mollified. She was never bored, she said, at Stone. Stone was home, the house of her dead husband.

'Lucas, come in at once, take a pew.' Anne would adopt phrases, use them for a time in a voice different from her own to show she was joking, then forget to highlight them in this way, so that they became assimilated into her speech.

She had no blood which was not Scots, but often her speech was like that of those anglophile continentals who have tellingly twisted our tongue, somewhere between E. F. Benson and the War. I enjoyed seeing askance looks as she spoke.

I hear this, although I am not English. I hear also the diction of expatriates, speaking as though they are reading aloud the fourth leader of a four weeks' late airmail *Times*.

I put on my camp, shopwalker's voice, to disarm her.

We sat in the aisle, between the gowns and crusted capes, she on the floor, I on a set of library steps Anne used to reach her hat-boxes, white drums above us. Her gloves prayed in flat pairs above the silent drums. Above them, the air conditioners rarefied the air, charged it with ions and emitted it once more.

'What's new, Lucas, I haven't seen you in an age.' We had seen each other only the day before.

I had no intention of allowing her to know, although she was probably my best friend, that today had been a hinge in my life. She looked at me. Her eyes were as blue as eggs in a nest. She had a very nice face. Momentarily, I was tempted to tell her of my plan.

To control myself, I concentrated very hard on the fabric of one of the hanging dresses.

'One too many, dearie?' asked Anne.

'Annie' (I did not like doing this; she was shrewd enough to hear the wrong note), 'Annie, could you introduce me to someone?'

'I hadn't realised there were any who were quite your toolbag here, dear, but, why, yes of course, though you must realise that it could be no better than a pig, whoops sorry, in a poke.'

I do not like the type of woman who habitually fraternises with homosexuals, though of course this sounds as though I do not like my own female friends. What I mean is women who seek to join in, to nudge, to use argot, to be all but men. They invariably claim also the privileges due to them as women, the softer flesh.

I become cold when this line is crossed. My lawyerly rectitude of manner stiffens.

'It's a girl, actually, Anne, the tall one being talked at by Leonidas. Have you any idea who she is? And please don't tell me the only reason I am interested is that she is really a boy. I've seen enough, I mean she is showing enough, to make it quite clear what she is.'

'I know,' said Anne, serious now the subject warranted it. 'Aren't those clothes terrifying? But there is something there. With care, I think she could learn to dress.' She spoke of this capacity as though it were as necessary as walking yet as magical as transforming matter into gold.

'Why is she here? Who is she?'

'Why do you want to know?' The jealousy was not sexual. It was the jealousy of sculptors over an untouched block in which each sees different things. I gave the most evasive reply I could.

'It's to do with work.'

'Lucas, darling, you're not getting spare parts from the living now, are you? Did your X-ray eyes tell you a particularly fine pair of ventricles pumps beneath those breasts?'

I am a surgeon; I do not perform transplants very often, but it is surprising how even the most intelligent prefer to believe nonsense about something they do not understand. I specialise in the repair of the small hearts of babies and children. A new heart is about the size of a matchbox. Of course, I attend to adults too, but I must admit that the bulk of the fame and the money has come from the little ones.

'I can't say, Anne, I will when I can.' Could she really not penetrate this false mystique, indispensable to the professional man?

'Oh, Lucas, that's fine, I'll tell you, but she's newish on me too. I met her a fortnight ago at home.'

'Met her? In your own house? Annie, do tell.' Ask a person to tell and they are back with their childhood and its plain little codes of decency swapped, a peek for a peek, an eye for an eye, a feel for a feel. Traded secrets are part of the old code. She looked down.

'Tertius brought her, without asking. George and George were angry till they saw her and then they fell about to make her little messes on dishes and diddle in her vanity case.' George and George were the butler and the footman. One was married to the cook, the other to the chambermaid. Or were they all brothers and sisters?

'Where did Tertius find her?' Old Tertius, older than me, living in Albany, cataloguing his frames, pinchbeck, ormolu, palisander, gesso, what could he want with a young woman?

'Apparently she's broke, she went to a vernissage, mostly for something to eat, got picked up by one of those wide-boys with a line in new masters of frigates in the spume, and, to cut a long story, woke up in the chambers opposite Tertius's. She rang his doorbell to ask where she was, and when at last he heard he gave her an egg flip and took her on as the lady who does. And she does very well.'

'Does she need to?' I was interested. Particularly in Anne's world, one was unlikely to find young women willing to take the job of charwoman to a total stranger. 'Is she foreign, without a work permit?'

'No, she's English, as English as you or I.'

I am the son of Polish Jews and Anne makes much of being a Scot. I left it alone, because I wanted more information and even the most fair-minded women are distracted by anything they can possibly take personally, which includes objectively truthful correction.

'But no money.'

'No money.'

'And family, what about that?'

'Not much of it.' As though it were a dry good, measured out like haricots or gems.

'Name?'

'Not a name name. Rather the sort it would be better to drop like a hot cake than simply drop, if you get me.'

I hate the idiom, to get, loathe it, but I did not say a word. I dream sometimes of faces close to mine screaming, 'D'you get me, d'you get me?' and I wake up afraid. The expression seems to push the breath of another hard into your own lungs.

'Still, tell it me,' I appealed to Anne.

'Cora Godfrey.'

'Cora. Miss Godfrey. Or does Tertius call her Mrs Godfrey as an honorific?'

'Tertius seems very fond of her, Lucas, though it can hardly be anything remotely under the blanket.'

Tertius had damp unrequited feeling for boys in shops and long dry passions with very old multiple duchesses. Once a week, a man of upright bearing came to help with the dusting of the stock, and I imagined that, even were Cora Godfrey to dust all day, the upright man would have his place in Tertius's timetable.

'So, she's gerontophile, clean, what else? How did she get on at Stone?'

'Not a foot wrong, even the boot on the other foot in a way, a bit too good, trying too hard. Very careful with everyone, fetching and carrying for Tertius without being proprietary, asking me about the garden, knowing not to ask about Mordred, not jumping every time drowning was mentioned, and eating too much, attractively, as the young should. She did not roll her eyes about when Tertius got tertiary, nor did she fail to mend the cistern in the bachelor's bathroom which I break as a trap for newcomers once in a while.'

Mordred Cowdenbeath had been Anne's husband; it was said that he had been found by Anne, his gun at his side. She had told me one evening that this was not so. By definition a crime, but a crime of passion, she had said, and slipped the oyster into her mouth as the tears slipped out of her eyes, trebly fluent salt.

II

I t is not that I believe in a good breakfast as you might believe
in telling the truth, or in assisting the blind over roads. I believe
in it as Anne believes in her cupboards. At least I have cut into
the day and seen it unaddled. I like my life to be as pitched as a
piano – with nothing lax and slippery to mar the tone, skew the
hammers, slip between the snug keys. Before Hal, there was my
curricular keyboard, the black notes of nocturnal jarrings struck
only in timely order, when a sharp or a flat had been scored by lust.
This plain upright opened into a grand piano with Hal; love opened
up my ordered life.

It is not the case that a pianist must have long thin fingers, nor
is it so of surgeons. What each requires is a broad palm, a wide
stretch, and fingertips whose supply of neurones makes of each one
the finder of exact destinations. I have hands like that. In other
physical respects, I do resemble the surgeon of the nurse's comic-
book dreams. I am tall, dark, sad-eyed with a mien combining that
of television intellectual and Dracula. I move quite naturally in a
way conveyed only by the most swaggering and self-indulgent
portraitists, Sargent or Boldini. I am etiolated but masculine. Until
puberty, I looked like a tall, modest girl. At eighteen, I grew
shoulders like coat hangers and rose to six foot four inches. Women
fall in love with how I look. I frequently see women fall in love. It
happens in hospitals; it is a form of gratitude. My looks are wasted
there. The mothers with their repaired babies weep and embrace
my fat and unpoetic-looking colleagues quite as much as they do
me. The other women who fall in love with me are an inconvenience,
sometimes worse. My looks feed fantasies which are not my own.
The only real satisfaction I gain from how I look is the occasional

mean one when an oily boy realises he is being crushed by expensive flesh, finer than that of any girl he can ever have. A solace is that Hal likes the way I look. He doesn't love it; he doesn't have the lover's sponsorship of my beauty. He is content that I pass in most surroundings unrecognised for what I am.

My breakfast is unfaddy. I take porridge as a poultice if I am not operating in the morning. It keeps me warm. If I am operating it undesirably insulates my nerves. At the weekend, I have one (jugged) kipper (no smell) and during the week one egg.

I like a lot of mild coffee, brewed very strong; I dislike drinking it from thick china, or china with a raised pattern. I am fussy about what goes near my mouth and I don't feel that embossed china can be very clean; I hate the knock of china on teeth. The teeth of spinsters on teacups in the consultants' secretarial office is the most voracious noise I know, when I am jangled after a long performance. Naturally, I don't have bacon.

My father sold it, though, in his last shop. 'Cooked meats, speck, schink, rauchfleisch, tongue, back, belly, green, or there again nice cheeses . . . ' He would lift the bare-faced rind-stockinged hams and slice pink wafers from them, to fold in greaseproof, wrap in sugar paper and bag up only when all the purchases were assembled in soft white bags which were twopence the hundred and melted if anything leaked. Eggs came in bags, impossible to carry, even if there were no children, no other bags, no other shops to visit. At first the small shop in Clerkenwell sold little; it was just after the War and there was not to be for years the Esperanto of pimentos and the snobbery of refrigerators. Our first refrigerator ran on kerosene and had no name. Soon afterwards, with the last puff of Empire, came our Icecold Monarch. We bought our first car, a grey Consul, years after food rationing stopped; its name too smacked of victory, martial success and ascendancy, soon to fall away. We had sold the shop in Clerkenwell and even our most loyal customers could not make it to Bayswater to hear my father intone, 'Nice olives, nice breads' – that 's'! the profligacy, the delicious excess! – 'nice butter salted or unsalted . . . ' Nice was a particle to my father; he never was quite at home in English, save with food, and then he used the language as his larder, cooking up sentences with happy gusto. His last shop was tall and thin, sausages hanging down six feet from the ceiling. Sugar balls in cellophane and strings of chillies hung in ribbons, and the shelves went right to the top of the shop. There was a smell of candy sugar and burnt coffee. My father, a small man but born tall, hooked items down with long tongs, tender as a gardener dead-heading a high rose. (That 'items' gives me away; 'garment' has on occasion unmasked some of the boys I grew up with, politicians or lawyers now.) Of course, they were ambitious for me, my father with his height taken from him and my mother impaling receipts in her kiosk at the back of the shop. I was well mannered. They had sacked a boy who had flirtatiously cut just two inches of the soft brown hair of the fat daughter of a regular customer with the knife he used to slice citron peel and angelica. I worked in the shop, and I worked at night. I think my bookishness then came from sex. It had that fanatical energy.

Not sex itself, perhaps, but things, for an adolescent boy, congruent. Sex is the brutal adultese for romance. I felt ennobled and powerful as I worked over books I could remember and forget swiftly, serially, as examinations required. My father and mother had diluted my Jewishness. Sometimes, now, eating or working with the *haute juiverie* of this country, I regret this; but I see that I could not be so polymorphous, so accepted, had my parents not to some extent diluted my flavour. I had no brothers or sisters; till they died my parents protected themselves from my unmarried state by saying I'd better wait till I was a qualified doctor, a GP, a consultant, a professor. He had owned a printer's with a staff of a hundred and she played a piano with a raspberry-pink shawl and a vase like a silver cornet, the pinks for ice-cream, on top of it. I had seen the shawl and the vase, so I knew. They brought out little else. Polish is a difficult language; if it is your first tongue, you lament in all others; all sentences, said Polishly, sound sad. Mr Borzecki and Mr Sapietis would come monthly to make merry with my father. Mr Borzecki had a watchmending business with two dusty ostrich eggs in the window, each on a silver rest shaped like an eagle's foot. Mr Sapietis was a Serb who made models of big cats in clay, fired turquoise; they were briefly popular in the 1950s and Mr Sapietis was miserable because he was bereft for that short time of being misunderstood. He had no fingernails for the clay to stick under. They had been taken from him. When they made merry, these three old gentlemen sounded sadder than ever. Their wives ate cakes, little tubs of short pastry filled with sour cream, a pistachio nut or a green *glacé* cherry on the top. Those green *glacé* cherries tasted differently, I swear, from the red ones.

The only line my father could not move was green cocktail onions, in the winter of 1959. For one vinegary week, we ate them with our potato and fish, little glass peas; the rest my father sold to a joke shop in Bloomsbury. My mother, who read in her kiosk women's magazines illustrated in brush and pen with waspied ladies preparing for Ascot or for cocktails, made a remark about this which my father did not understand: 'Those onions are eyeballs for highballs,' she said. Even had my father possessed so advanced a grasp of English, he would not have used it to say such frivolous things.

They appeared devoted, though I wonder whether that matters. It seems important to us, now. Running from a dark town in flames, hiding in haystacks from bayonets, knowing the list was shortening, that it could not but bear their names, concealing their child, swallowing an egg – raw indivisible luxury – did they enquire whether they liked, loved, desired each other?

My parents lived by mutual loyalty. That I recollect the green onion *facétie* shows it was a rare lapse from their blessed unalarming days of quiet retailing and lugubrious retelling; it was a rare hint of a small skittishness in my mother, a little willingness to participate in their new country. He did not get that far.

I saw her touch him once, after I qualified. She wore black lisle and black wool and worked with staining purple carbon paper and dusty cured meats all day, but she smelt of vanilla. She was, like many wives of thin men, fat. They were both crying. For that whole day I felt no guilt about my parents. They drank coffee with cream and pulled shiny red crusts from the plaited loaf to dunk; the bread was egg-yellow inside. A row of these loaves, some sprinkled with poppyseed, lay on the floury counter of the shop. In our back room some asters, brown themselves, were in a jug, with black seeds of pollen fallen on the table. We could go straight into the shop from that back room.

We celebrated my success, weeping and eating sops of bread, and serving when our customers came in; to some I was displayed, a prodigy. They had always known. At a quiet time, my father slopped a very little of his coffee on his serge trousers; my mother took a small knitted cloth, and, systematic as a mother cat, dabbed and rasped till he was tidy. The mark had been perhaps the size of a little coin. She hung up her cloth after rinsing it, washed her own hands and flicked his left ear with her left hand, he sitting, she over him. She flicked it in the same cat's manner, as though she found the contiguity of their separateness an acceptable source of comfort. We were not demonstrative habitually, but for tears, lavements and festivals and beatitudes of tears. We cried together, not alone.

I slopped my coffee, too, more than twenty years later, the morning of Anne's party, when Hal arrived in time for breakfast. He had not often done this. All signs of intimacy between us were kept to a minimum. I had trained myself to expect nothing, so that I could, when it came, be surprised by joy.

'Lucas, I must speak.'

'Sit down, I'll make your tea.'

I am a coldish man, yet with Hal I am all uxorious attention. I lay trays with cloths for him. I know that he can endure neither socks with nylon nor deodorant with zinc, so I ensure he has neither, though all too rarely do I see or touch the places they are worn. He has his tea, orange pekoe, in a mug with honey. Is there no end to the refinements of profligate peacetime? My parents had the same bedspread all their lives. They would as soon have changed each other as the spoons they used. Hal sleeps half the night under only a sheet; the other half being spent, he assures me, beneath four blankets and a counterpane. He leaves me at the changing-over point. I lie and listen to the riderless horses led by one man return to the barracks at Knightsbridge. I doze. I hear the fishmonger's lorry.

'Lucas, I'm twenty-six, I'm starting to be successful at work, I've got a house, both my lodgers are leaving to be married, and what am I doing?' I knew this tone, discontent disguised as responsibility.

'My dear, you are the king in a cabbage-patch, go out and conquer nations.' I was concentrating, wifelike, upon his reaction to his tea.

'I've been feeling stale recently, negative.' This phrase did not have Hal's own unoriginality to it.

'Who've we been listening to?' I realised too late that I sounded shrill.

'Don't bother patronising me. Lucas, will you try for once to think of me, just for once?'

23

His tone was brattish; I must let him alone and resist my impulse to insulate him.

'The thing is, Lucas, I want to settle down, to feel above board, clear, out in the open.'

I could not keep silent. 'Live with me,' I said.

'Oh God, Lucas, I want to get married. Married to a girl. You know, one of those things with two of one and one of the other, one of those things with dressing tables.'

It was then that I slopped my coffee. It honestly was not so much marriage – that is a superstitious tic to which few are immune – but – *dressing tables*. How dare he? 'Dressing tables' was a code in our language; it stood between us for mess, screech, defilement, menses and powdery purses, habitual censorship and unnaked faces. Or so I had understood. Hal did not help me with the coffee spreading on my fine expensive suit.

'Well, Hal, I see, how nice. Have you anyone in mind?'

'No, since you ask.'

This sleek flaxen boy was bored with his toys. I would find a doll for him to break to save my own heart breaking first.

III

I chose Cora because I wanted a wife for Hal quickly and she appeared to be the most available girl in the room, a room which I could fairly assume would contain people to some extent already vetted. I could as well have gone to the outpatients' clinic of my hospital or to the supermarket, but my day had not brought me to these wife-nurseries. I was still acting with the decisiveness of a man taking the most direct means of saving his own life. I had not worked out how I would introduce them, how I would counter-suggest Hal into marrying this one (if, after a period of courtship, I did in fact want her for Hal), or how I would direct the denouement which would bring him, wounded and gentled, back to me. If there was another reason I selected her, some sympathy between us, whether I had some presentiment of intimacy, I simply do not know. My experience as a pimp is limited; as an undercover marriage broker non-existent. I sought the most direct way to make her trust me; I tried to make her like me. This is not my style. My patients revere and need me; to have boys who actually like you do you satisfactory violence is impossible, and I am sufficiently complacent to believe that friends will come to me without effort, when they know me; I am not sugar-coated. I do not know how to flirt, if that is the scarf-twitching sort of Noh play Tertius goes in for, and as for flirting with women, even the thought of it makes me feel the grave embarrassment I suffered when I first saw that Hogarth painting of a flushed couple in silks and ruffles and shame, his groin a flayed lapdog among the gay satin stripes. I decided to rely upon the manners which had been so useful in the shop; I am ashamed to say I did realise my height and appearance would help. Would she see the silver hook?

'Good evening,' I said. Leonidas had gone, I imagined, long before. She was talking to a man with a very small mouth and no pupils to his eyes. He made no response and left her side as I arrived, swiftly absent like a fish. She was still standing before the mirror. In it I saw the fish-man, just leaving. I saw a great deal of her back, and, unlike Dracula who cannot see himself in the mirror, I saw myself, standing over her. She had shoes – part of the ensemble which was so terrifying, according to Anne – which were raised on platforms. The toe of each was a snake's head. The strap which kept each shoe attached was the snake itself, a green, glittering, padded spiral, clinging to her leg like greaves. Each snake had a rather straggly red tongue. I felt I must say something about these shoes. Did she wear them as a charm?

'No,' she said.

'No?' I said.

'*No*, I do not know what snakes signify, *no*, I do not have an apple in my pocket, *no*, I am not a charmer.'

'That's clear,' I said. 'But who are you?'

'Cora Godfrey,' she replied. 'And you are Lucas Salik.'

I enjoy, no, I thoroughly do not enjoy, a sort of folk hero's part in the newspapers. Within their fifty-word gamut they find titles for me. No paper is innocent. The expensive newspapers say, 'Heart Knight's Vigil', 'Surgeon Through the Needle's Eye', 'Aesculapius' Sword Hangs over Tracy, 4 days'. The papers which are read by people who fold them small to do so, thus ensuring they can read only four uppercase letters at a time, emphasise, reasonably enough, the parents' pain. 'AGONY OF HEART-MUM JOAN', 'DEATH OF HEART MITE BEVERLEY', 'BIG-HEARTED LITTLE ANDY' . . . Children, the smaller the better, and death baulked or death triumphant. Recently it had been 'K for Drama Doc', 'Sir Lucky, say Heart Mums'. And still some of the babies live and some of the babies die, and I drive a quiet blue car as long as heart-mum Brenda's garden.

I was going to begin one of those sentences which are puffed full with otiose words, when I noticed in detail, for the first time, the rest of her dress. I do not know more than what I have learnt from Anne of women's clothes. Cora Godfrey was wearing a baby's nappy, tied not as is usual at the waist, but at the bust. She wore a length of cloth tied in a knot over her bosom. From either side her body was clearly visible. There was a knot at the back too. I wondered wildly for an instant if she wore a clamp on her umbilical cord. I was happy to see she was wearing plain white knickers. But I was not happy that they were visible. About her clothes, something must be done. The length of cloth was white, but sequined intermittently. She sparkled in her horrible chiton.

She was not uncomfortable, it seemed, in this conversational pause. She held a glass but did not drink from it. She looked at my face, then at my hands. She dropped her gaze to my shoes and waited for me to speak.

'I gather that you are doing for Tertius, lucky man.' I thought I might find out whether nights in strange men's flats were her tone. I wanted flawed, not rotten, goods. 'How did you meet him, actually?'

'I think you know. I got picked up at Cam's by a villain from the lilac Honours list. Completely revolting except for a Renoir in the loo. The worst thing was the endearments as he heaved away. What he wanted was love. Disgusting.'

I felt that she was either drunk or possessed. She did not know me and she was making her reputation hostage to me. I could not see why she spoke in this appalling way. She put her glass on the mantelpiece; on the piers of the fireplace were two deep-bosomed doves, in the bill of each a ribbon in bas-relief out of the pure marble. I wondered how this hussy could have struck me earlier in the evening as dovelike.

'Ask men about themselves, so here goes. Did you always want to be a doctor?'

'I wanted to be something secure and remunerative and my family had left everything in Poland.'

'I think doctoring comes in genes, doctors marry doctors, have little doctors. Doctors are respected as priests almost.'

I felt hocus-pocus on the way. Did she want to know something about holism or some dreary witchcraft for the dilettante sick? I began to speak.

'I like the mechanical nature of medicine. It is why I have chosen not the magical zones of lymph and gland, but the engine, the pump, the heart.' I had started to speak to her as though she might begin to understand what I said.

'I imagine,' she said, 'that a doctor is not troubled with the feeling he does not exist. Other people tell him all day that he does because they need him.'

The only son of people who might very well have stopped existing, not merely have considered themselves not to do so, I thought her remark intense and trivial and indicative of a sort of shaman-respect which has corrupted many decent doctors and made them ponder uselessly on their 'personal role' in the families they treat, and such rubbish. But increasingly Hal made me feel, though I would not admit it, as if I did *not* exist. He even debased the doctoring part of me; he had said one horrible night that it was an excuse to get inside the bodies of people less fortunate than myself. The next child I operated on died eventually, not of heart failure, but of an infection I had not the pathological facilities at that time to have identified. In the end, the tiny refrigerated cadaver was flown to America.

I remembered that this girl was not a baby, as her clothes suggested, nor a grown-up woman, as they revealed, but that elvish thing a girl, a sort of social axolotl, equipped only with rudimentary gills for breathing the fiery air of adult life. She was managing fairly well with me considering that the glimpses I had of her were not, as they would be to most men who chose to converse with her, a welcome substitute for conversation.

'Let me ask *you* about *yourself*,' I said to her, not expecting the reaction I received. Her skin was thin, pale. Her colour came to its surface. Again I thought of some pale gasping reptile, its organs visible.

She looked for a moment desperate, as though she could not find her breath, and then, gracious and unconvincing as a child acting, she said, 'And whereabouts in London do you live?'

Why was I bothering with this gauche creature? Because of her gaucheness?

'If you say that you will tell me a little about yourself, I shall show you "whereabouts in London I live". Are you hungry and have you a coat?'

It was eleven o'clock. A young woman who would do this, repair upon request to the house of a stranger, was surely a weakling at best, a tart at worst.

'As long as you are not looking for someone to clean for your next-door neighbour,' she said.

We left, observed, I think, by Anne, and, oddly enough, by the fish-man, who did not appear, after all, to have left. I had exerted no charm, no pressure. My one effort to bring the girl forward had been decisively rebuffed. Either she was perfect for my plan, egoless, pliant, or she was reckless to the point of stupidity. I could see no other reason for the docile way she allowed me to place her in my car and take her to my home. I could, after all, have been going to drink her blood.

She did have a coat. It, like the dress, was a piece of cloth without hook or eye, button or hole; it appeared to be a plaid, or simply a length of cloth before the tailor has begun to pin and chalk. It was, like its wearer, unbegun, but shot with a suggestive, shifting, metallic glimmer.

IV

When we arrived at my flat near the canal, I got out of the car first and opened the door for her. We had not spoken much on the journey, because she had opened the glove compartment and taken out the Bentley maintenance book. It is a hardback manual; mine is as old as my car, that is twenty-three years old, three years older than Cora Godfrey, I had ascertained. She did not read the illustrated parts of the manual, or the log, but what could most nearly be read as continuous narrative. It was as though her eyes needed to absorb some print. The open pages on her lap were sometimes obscure, sometimes mauve-white with sodium street light, once (at Hyde Park Corner) a tabernacular red as we were halted, and then, as we slowed down along the canal, the less chemical glowing yellow of a light more like that of gas.

I let her into my flat with none of the feelings which must have attended almost every other such broaching in her life. The kitchen, where only that morning I had first understood the imperative necessity of a Cora, was to the right, the drawing-room at the end of the hall on the left. My bedroom was first on the left, a spare bedroom between it and the drawing-room. A large bathroom and a dressing-room abutted my own bedroom, a smaller bathroom the guest bedroom. My flat is on the first floor, second floor and attic. The attic I use mainly for books. The second floor is one enormous room which is always approaching perfection. It is ballroom, study, cave or retreat, as I will. There remains no trace of where the dividing walls once were, unless you lie looking at the ceiling in a high evening light. Then you see them; it is like terrain under snow. The walls were painted for me by a swart little flat-painter from the Opera, with a sort of cod Vuillard, which I love. It has no theme but happiness. Sometimes he comes and puts more in; the picture's promiscuous domesticity can take any abundance of detail, like a good bourgeois French table food. The colours are the blue-greens, fuming lavenders, orange-yellows, viola colours (*not* pansy at all) and delicious pink-browns which blush and blanch depending upon where you stand. Against one wall is a bath on lion's feet. It is not large and I have not permitted the *jeu d'esprit* which you might anticipate. No warm-hipped girl is stepping out for ever on the wall behind. But visitors to my room say they see her. One or two tricks I've allowed. There is a screen in the Chinese style which 'disappears' into the wall, and I like, in season, to have bowls of quinces and jars of japonica about the room, such as are seen in the painting. The smell of quinces, and their grey fluff, going in to that tight flower-end, are pleasurable to me. The bath is plumbed in. I use it often.

I took Cora, of course, into my drawing-room. It is a fine dark-green room whose white curtains are lined with heavy crimson blanketing – a secret unless I choose to draw the curtains close before sundown and then the room takes on a meaty, private, autumnal brown, and I can take the covers off my watercolours. These appear at first glance to be architectural elevations of naves, of domes, of proscenia; they are early dissections of the heart, painted with marvellous observation from the life – should I say the death? – by an unknown painter who was surely risking his own life by doing so. They have a diagrammatic quality which is not at all repulsive, rather satisfying and abstract. There is nothing of butchery to them.

'Can I get you anything?' I asked my nearly naked guest.

'If you wouldn't mind, I'd love something to put on, and a bite of something to eat.'

'Most adults, when they go out in the evening, have provided themselves with those things, or have made arrangements to do so in the case of nourishment.'

'Let me explain,' she said, saucy hussy. 'I dressed like this in order not to have to what you call make arrangements in the case of nourishment, and now I am here, it appears to be a house which must contain at least bread and cheese and I am certainly not properly dressed to eat *à deux* with a distinguished older man at home.'

'But in a restaurant, or with a less distinguished man . . . ?'

'I could hardly have taken a change of clothes in a grip to the party.'

'But why wear it at all?'

'You mean, it's as good as wearing nothing?'

'I didn't say that, no, but yes, I suppose that is what I could be said to mean.'

'Money,' she said. 'I get bolts of cloth with flaws – seconds, you know – and tie them up in different ways. I daren't cut them into shapes or make definite holes for my legs or head to go through because then I'm limiting my options. It's very cheap.'

'But, Cora, forgive me . . . '

'You're going to say it looks it, too. I am sorry. Now, have you some trousers and a jumper and some food?'

It was midnight and I had a – female – pirate aboard. I went into the shadowy grey of my room and through into my small dressing-room annexe. It is papered with faint and faintly lewd toile de Jouy of blue-grey; a girl plays the cello, a man the flute; a grinning dog in a ruffle watches this pastoral of *onanisme à deux*. It is pretty, womanish even. I found a grey jersey and some plus-fours and some long woollen stockings. On second thoughts, I took a pair of garters, too, the kind with wool flashes. Tertius had given them to me when he discovered I shot. He is a snob with the concomitant love of over-correct dressing.

'Put these on, I'll find a little supper and then you must please tell me all about yourself.'

I put her in the spare room to dress. It was where Hal slept. I longed for him to colonise it, but I was sure she would find no trace of my loved one. He could be tidy as a spy.

We re-met in the drawing-room. The big breasts were no less conspicuous for being wrapped in grey wool; my plus-fours were plus-sixes on her, in spite of her height; and the shooting stockings gave her the soft rusticity of a huntsman in the ballet. The garters the facetious child had used to hold up her hair which was abundant and of poor quality. She sat up straight, the book she had been reading snibbed between the cushion and the side of her striped chair. She had brought another chair and a walnut caddy-table into a mealtime group about her. On the table I placed my tray. It bore no traycloth, but a plate of charcoal biscuits, a pat of white butter, some salt, some radishes, a log of ashy cheese, a can of anchovies with their key and a head of celery in a vase which looked, plain clear glass in ornate golden stand, like a retort from a rococo laboratory. To drink, there was milk or water or pale tea. And she would have to *ask* for those – and then I caught myself. I was thinking churlishly of this girl I had invited to my home, who very possibly thought her frame would have to contain me later in the night, whom I in fact was contemplating kidnapping, and whom I was treating almost as offhandedly as I treat the passing boys. I offered her champagne, and of course she requested milk. I gave myself champagne. The bottles stood together on the tray as though for an art class to paint, thick white and thin green.

'Do this, would you?' I said, again as abrupt with her as with one of my sweet louts. I was behaving to her as men will to women, not as I do; I am courtly as a rule, what is called old-fashioned. I handed her the flat nugget of anchovy tin and the key for opening it. We ate them stuck into the runnels of the celery with unsalted butter and extra salt. I fetched two large cloth napkins and she tucked hers into my grey jersey.

But in order to hobble this kid for my panther, I must find out about her.

'Are you English, Cora?' I asked.

'I am not from your social class,' she said. 'I'm a bit flashy to fit in, what with my size, and a proper tall girl from the shires wouldn't do that. She'd wait around till someone came along who would give her a son so she could pass on her height like a parcel containing a bomb – don't drop it, pass it on, only unwrap it if you're a man. When I realised it was an asset I started learning how to use it, but I do get these lapses and that is when it is very nice to eat high food with a very tall man in his tall flat.'

I was delighted by her insecurity, so raw that she would be entirely tractable.

'And your job, Cora, what do you do or do you only clean for Tertius?'

'I do a number of small jobs, none of which is more important than any other. You could say I mark time but, lacking the cousin in Asprey's or the father in the City, I'm an unsubsidised subsidiser of the subsiding upper crust.' She was extremely nervous.

'You talk a lot.'

'I read a lot.'

'Why?'

'I'm gathering honey for the shining hours to come when I have earned my stripes.'

'Stripes?'

'Take it as you will. As a worker bee, or a beaten wife.'

'Do you hear the terrible things you say? I could have gathered from your callow lineshooting this evening that you were a whore, a drudge or a masochist. I am sure you are none of these. I think you are just a young thing awaiting your vocation, and, just as your brothers have no war, you have no arranged marriage, no baby for your fifteenth birthday.'

'There is something in that. No brothers, though. These radishes are good. The jobs I do are all part-time. It adds up to more than full-time. I came by them not through ambition but through a need for cash and an incapacity to say no. I work packing executive toys in a basement, I work laying out a magazine made of advertisements separated by prose which must not contain fewer than three references to teeth per article. I sew frogs filled with millet seed and pass them on for smaller frogs to be stitched into their arms and on Saturday mornings I serve at a restaurant where it is good to be seen. I also work in a charity shop. I like that, quite. I am of dependent means.'

'I assume you are educated.'

'I read a lot.'

'What did you read?' I asked this touchy girl.

Slick, out it came, before she thought, 'Greats, but I fell out, fell not dropped. I just did not have the graft. But it's given me all sorts of itches because I half understand such a lot. Medicine's the worst in a way because you have a derivation pat like that and then it's not the ligament which joins the foot and the ankle at all. So I've the illusion of comprehension and no understanding at all, like those awful clever children with swollen heads who understand fission energy and can't get out of the burning snug when the telly explodes.'

'What is your ambition?'

'To be good. To be a good wife.'

I liked this, of course.

'And what is goodness to you?'

'My husband's interpretation of goodness.'

However appallingly this equipped Cora Godfrey for life, it equipped her well to be Hal's wife. Hal had a loose interpretation of goodness, if he thought about it at all.

'Cora, have some champagne and then let me drive you home.'

She padded off to the kitchen – women always find the kitchen, it is like the rapacious hermit crab finding the soft flesh of the previous occupant of its new shell home – to get a clean glass. She required no exchange of confidences from me; now I had her in my house the quick-talking party girl with opinions was gone and I had a pliant geisha. She did not obviously react to what was a clear statement of intention not to ravish her that night.

She was evasive about her family. She was a town girl, a university town I guessed, or cathedral; I did not want to clutter myself with intimate knowledge of her provenance. I did not care to burden myself with what would be, in effect, should Hal have her, associations-in-law. She invariably neutralised too acidic a remark with an alkaline one. I wondered whether she had been brought up in some nonconformist creed, or one of those British sects. I hoped so. There would be more manipulable guilt and reflex torments with which to rein her in.

I drove her to the villa she shared in a far northern limb of the Crown Estates. It was one of those pretty houses where you may not hang out your clothes lest it distress the monarch. Indeed, these crescents have an unurban appearance, as though built as tiny farms. We agreed, Cora and I, that she should keep my clothes till we next met, which, I assured her, we would. I had put her two bolts of cloth and her stiff snake shoes in a bag, which I handed her.

I watched her watch me till I was out of sight. It was eighteen hours since Hal had told me he wished for a wife. Once home, I washed up, and finished the champagne. I toasted myself in the mirror of the drawing-room; in its golden pediment a tired but friendly enough lion pulled two boisterous naked golden men in their chariot across an Arcadian landscape. 'Cora, our complaisant wife,' I thought, and went satisfied to bed. I looked into Hal's room and blessed his shade as I did always when he was not there.

V

It is time for me to try to describe the years between my first sight of Hal and the announcement at breakfast six years after that. So far, I am aware, I have not suggested that Hal is an agreeable person. Of course, it is not necessary to be agreeable to be beloved, but I must try to convey what power it is that he has over me.

When I seek my bad boys at night, or in zones where it might as well be night, I am hunting out not so much a particular way of looking, as a certain deportment. It is not what the unaroused analytical or aesthetic eye would find beautiful; it may well have an equivalent for what is called a 'normal' man in flossy hair, gross breasts and a trashy lasciviousness which he would deplore in his own house, and would prefer not to see after it had served its use. I am not ashamed about this, though it is trite. There is conformism in pornography; I can see this is so between bouncy-chested girls and their leather-limbed boys on bikes. But why should husky window cleaners and big scaffolding climbers strut and swell in a way as satisfactory to me and men like me, as, no doubt, it is to their wives? Are they conscious of the connoisseurship which goes into the contemplation of their singlets, their jeans, their donkey jackets, their laced yellow boots fudgy with cement? I am not speaking of the pretty boys with their aping of workmen's clothes. I like boys and men who would think all the foregoing words sick; intermittently, this is bringing me to admit, I like the company of people who mistrust and dislike me. I must like the tarnished-metal smell of my own fear. In a straightforward way, I like the healthy appearance of men on building sites and other places of urban endeavour; there is something too much of Socialist Realist posters in country toilers. The country men do not seem to be so inviting of the subtitling my senses give the gritty teabreaking knots of navvies in the street or over my head, calling babel to girls on hot afternoons. I am not what Tertius calls a cruising queen, in a state of constant heat. I know that there are those who see in every demolition site a seraglio, for whom a visit from the heating engineer is full with erotic promise. I simply feel, about four times a year, drawn to something which is not of the life I inhabit, which is not controllable, ordered and poised.

All I can say is that I, almost on principle, eschew most theories about this type of thing, and after it is over I must say that I feel no shame about myself at all (I have never coerced anyone, though I cannot make out my appeal for them; can it honestly be money? Once or twice I have even thought it must be something so simple as novelty or curiosity – like going on safari), no shame, as I say, and a perfect absence of complication. This absence is like grace to me. Then the complications reaccrue, I behave well, I deal with my multifarious acquaintance, I save lives and have to let them slip, I live my life with Hal.

That is, I do not live my life with Hal. He lives in his flat in Westminster and I live in my flat by the canal. Our two ménages are not a maintained fiction for the sake of propriety – they are the case. Hal and I are not lovers. Sometimes, as though it were an accident that we found ourselves together, or as though he were in a sleepy stupor, Hal will let himself loll against me. Sometimes he has let me tousle him about. Occasionally, utterly passively, Hal has allowed me to deceive myself into believing I am as much to him physically as, let us say, his own hand. No, less than that. After these unreciprocal episodes, which have too much, to my taste, of deceit and mock horseplay to them, Hal is invariably unkind to me, treating me as though I were a seamy old man having soiled an *ingénue*. He is nastier to me the more nearly he has been completely pleasured but I cannot resist. He touches me rarely, and always with a semblance of accident. He has a celibate's seductiveness, as though his chastity went before him into rooms like a cat, treading the laps of old men, winding about the legs of young women, sitting heavy on the shoulders of women old enough to be his mother, showing its lifted tail to boys his own age. He sleeps sometimes at my house, otherwise in his own flat, where I have never been.

When I say that my life opened like a grand piano, I do mean it. Let me first describe his appearance. In the chemist's he *was* Englishness to me, his hair in a pale lick over a face without a wrinkle. He had none of the fat rubicundity to be found in fair Englishmen. His hair was silver blond and heavy; it fell at the back of his head into a V and shaded below that into paler grey-blond feathers. At whatever angle his face was seen, it was edged with light. His skin had no soapy shine, no visible pores, but a matt down, a bloom without shine or variety of texture. Could that cover him, that surface too fine to perceive with the naked eye? I imagined that, magnified many times, the skin of this boy about whom I as yet knew nothing would reveal itself of a preternaturally orderly pattern, minutely tessellated honeycomb. Like most people who blind with their beauty, Hal looked as though he would not understand a word of what, with a constellation of similar dazzled thoughts, was turning in my head. Romantic intellectuals ascribe to the beautiful not cleverness but a wise vision. Usually what the beautiful have is . . . beauty. His features were regular and slightly flat. When men want to imply that a girl's face would look fine beneath their own, they say 'kittenish': there is something inviting about very slightly mongoloid features. Hal's eyes were blue, his lashes black with surprising blond ends; his upper lip was square and had at its left corner a flat coffee-coloured stain. He was about six feet tall and very thin with bowed thighs. He was wearing a pair of jeans, thin-skinned brown shoes, a creamy jersey and a white shirt whose collar was roughly turned up, for warmth it appeared, to support the muffler he wore, a plain pennant of clear blue tied like a stock. His jacket was old, outgrown, patched. The clothes told me that he was not in the Forces or the City; perhaps that he did not work at all; that he was a gentleman. He was stowing a navy and white spotted handkerchief in his pocket. His long legs were clothed in that pale cotton blue of old outdoor paint and salty days at the seaside. I just saw him at that high turning tide of beauty between boyhood and manhood. He had still the child's look of self-absorption, but he moved like a swift adult, a man with much to do, all the time in the world to do it, but so much energy that each movement was compounded of force and ease.

It was he, so young he was, and so respectable-looking I, who spoke when he saw we were buying the same shaving foam; not, as

I said before, myself. I lie in my memory, wishing to protect him; but he was innocent and the innocent need no defence. He said he had to collect a painting from the framer in the concealed yard behind St James's. I had never seen this hidden part of London, so from topographical curiosity (so he thought) I accompanied him, and in return offered him those formal, rather deathly gardens behind Mount Street, with their benches donated by Americans, and 'some lunch in Scott's'. That 'some' was important; its implication of equality, that we were both simply men in need of food at an hour when food was customarily taken.

We sat at the bar and ate sandwiches and drank Guinness. Immediately, I felt we shared much. He was quick to demarcate groups. He could identify types. There were some flushed Irishmen drinking 'more pop waiter', all one word, for a race run that day; there were the lawyers up at the bar; there were the quiet men who sell pearly treasures over their oysters and use the restaurant as the counter of their shop; there were men in royal blue suits with clammy-lipped women eating fish in sauce and drinking pink wine.

Hal came from Dorset. Hal Darbo, he was called. He had three brothers. Their names Saxon, Norman, Roman. He was working in property. That explained the jacket, which he very properly referred to as a coat. He had to look right for selling country properties today; tomorrow it might be a suit to wear and a church to sell – 'suitable for conversion', as he put it, not smiling, though English was his first tongue. We finished our pudding (I had a savoury, my unassuageable Dead Sea thirst for salt made raw with love and black beer), I gave Hal my card, and I walked to the hospital singing like those inflamed men you see falling off the pavement in university towns, once Horus Professors of Arcana and now spinning drunks, the tuned brains awash. I am sure if I had been run down that day as I danced to my work, my blood would have run gold.

Hal telephoned me a week later. For a year or so, I dared not touch him, save by rationed accident. I remember each of them that year, the touches; before I had even questioned him about his private life at all, I imagined he liked girls. Most 'older men' protect themselves with this over their boys.

My left leg touched his right knee at *Rosenkavalier*; he was tapping his foot, or began to just as our legs touched, and the friction made me stupefied with him, so that I could see only him, not the stage at all. All brightness came from that singing wedge of warm dark to my left which contained his face. That November I touched his hair with my left hand by the timberwolves' enclosure in the zoo; he had said he liked wolves. I replied, 'I can hear them from my flat in the middle of the night.' He was so guileless that he replied, 'Well, I'd love to do that.' When I touched his head, I looked in that trice at my hand on that silvery hair, sugared with gold. I imagined that if I took the hair in my mouth, it would diffuse like spun sugar. There was my hand, each white metacarpal with its black hairs.

And the other times of touching; in my car, at my home, after the first time I fed him there, when we reached simultaneously for the wine (he was not falsely diffident in his acceptance of hospitality), and in winter in St James's Park when we rescued a poor frozen bird and put it in one of those boxes where they wait for the warden – 'Who probably eats them,' said Hal, and I was sad he should be cynical, for I felt it showed the world had perhaps already been unkind to him in some way. I remember looking out that day over the lake. The air was blue, the earth white, the lake black, clear and solid. Frozen in by her flat pink feet was one of the pelicans, droll and the more pathetic for that drollness. In the clear air you could see the targe of her eye. It was as flat as an heraldic device; were there drops of blood on her breast?

In that first year, I so longed for him that lacing my shoes became an allegory of love. At the same time, my work extended in range and variety – what some might call hubris. I found even the smallest and most faulty organs full of good omens, as I read the small entrails between the green drapes. I was full of the spiritual energy of unanswered desire.

I did not long for him at that time in the simple, direct way I longed for the passing boys. I should have hated to shock him with any touch other than paternal. I felt I was taming him, gentling him down. During that year and the next I was like a lover separated by a sea or continent from the beloved. I attempted to make myself dear to him in small daily reconstructions of the best of myself – letters, telephone calls, tangible thoughtfulness – for his pleasure. I was not constructing a false self; loving him made me good. I thought of Hal and his well-being. We were seen together only twice in that year, once by Anne, who said that he was made to be gift-wrapped and left it at that, and once, I assume, by some poodlefaker of Tertius's, because Tertius mysteriously revealed himself to know a little about Hal and myself.

There was obviously no mistress in my life, surely Hal observed this? His set appeared to be a carefree group of young people, all having shared fun. Most had fallen into that dreary pocket of premarital cohabitation which can, I am told, appear so glittering to the young person whose alternative is fierce serial passion and a happy animal scratching of any itch. Nowadays the pram in the hall is a new erotogenic tool. Many of his friends lived already in large London houses, filling the servants' quarters and nurseries with flowers and wine and friends. Being the children of the rich, they had proper silver and real glasses without obligation of fidelity to their sleeping partners. Hal dined out a great deal, and went to the cinema, so I did not see very much of him, unless there was a specific outing; I feel this must have been his diffidence. He may have reflected that I was a very busy man with an entirely separate life; he may have thought about the whole thing very much less than did I. At my age, of course, I could not easily be assimilated into his circle.

I decided to introduce him artfully into mine. I made him a life member of the London Library half-way through our second year (I am quite certain Hal did not think of the year thus). This was selfish, I do admit, but I felt like the older party in an arranged marriage, aware of the pending contract while the spouse-to-be plays marbles in the sun.

He does not very much care for books. I, unforgivably selfish, thought that everyone must care, very much. I had gathered from his talk that he was not very widely read, but I, again, made the mistake of referring this observation to myself, thinking that what had kept him from books was the possession of brothers, just as what had kept me from the company of other children was my books. The London Library, of which I did not become a member till rather late in my life, has always seemed to me like a continually flowering garden. I like the shady *piano nobile* and meccano walkways and stolen teas; I love the storage racks which you can pull out and spin flat. I like the confirmation that others think, that thoughts are being trimmed and fed and watered and that books, their compost, are tended, turned and replenished. To Hal it was dark and full of dull people sitting still. I had thought of our meeting for drinks in summer, of the gravid erotic silence of libraries and how he would emerge and see me in a new light, or, better, a new darkness.

Membership of the London Library is non-transferable. Hal's is of no use to anyone. My hospital is linked with one in Westminster and sometimes it would have been convenient to dine at Hal's flat, or even to sleep there. But what had not been spoken between us in now over two years made this impossible. I saw him sometimes in restaurants, but his timetable was very different from mine. He and his friends would take meals in the middle of the morning or at dead of night. 'Property' did not seem to get in the way. They read newspapers and ate breakfast in night clubs. I did these things at home. When I did glimpse his 'pack', I was jealous. He would not acknowledge me. He was a king among his courtiers and I not even the joker. I do not think his friends ever noticed me. The only places where there was a possibility of crossing were the very expensive Italian restaurants which are favoured by models, male and female, or the Connaught where some of these children, Hal's 'set', were to be seen softening up a parent behind the screens. In one white-tiled basement, I saw a group of Hal's friends order steak and red wine. They were all white in the face and their wrists showed. They spat out the meat once they had chewed it white; the wine they drank till they were sick. Anne was with me. 'Very slimming,' she said, and she ordered sweetbreads and three types of green vegetable and a jug of water with our wine. When it came she said an old Scots grace: '"Some hae meat and canna eat, and some hae nane that want it, but we hae meat and we can eat and so the Lord be thankit." Begging your pardon, dear,' she added, 'but thank God too that we don't know those ghouls. Think, Alexander would have been one of them, maybe.'

So, how could I introduce Hal to Anne? In the third year of my love, I began to resume my visits to other shiny white-tiled places underground. There was even a regular boy, but in a way that is a danger and blunts the edge. I think he was drawn at that time to what must have been very evident in me. Deep in love with an indifferent Hal, I had advanced hyperaesthesia. He was a nice enough, lazy enough boy, and it took very little at that time to hurt me quite a lot, so he kept face with the wildest of his friends without upsetting himself by having to do anything very rough. I jangled with uncomfortable lust for Hal.

Anne's clothes gave the opportunity, and it was easy and pleasant when we at last all met at her house. Hal was like a boat with the wind behind him among those bolts of silk; Anne had a high old time with him, dressing him up in her clothes. I would not allow her to paint his face. I could see her classifying him incorrectly. Of course, many of her acolytes were young men who worked in the service of clothes, men of the cloth of her particular church, but it made me hot to contemplate that she thought my sexless Hal just such a Cedric or Alun. So much of my own physical life has been to do with harshness that it astonished me, when I saw Hal's neck coming from the neck of one of Anne's gowns, a vatic grey purple, that neck almost without an Adam's apple, to know I wanted only to protect it. 'Such a little neck,' I said to myself, and felt weak with paternal tenderness, as though I were sending him to war.

Anne was loyal. She did not see Hal alone, though he would have liked this. She did collect and drop the young and it was a conferral of prestige to be in her train for a time, a graduation in style.

Tertius and he seemed not to get on at all well and I left it at that, in a way a little relieved that Tertius's worldly way would not spoil my Hal.

We had no routine, but there were things we did together which I am sure he did with no one else. We went to church, for instance. Each Saturday we chose a service from the newspaper, and, if I was not working, we went either to Sung Eucharist or to Evensong. My Jewishness is not offended by such excursions. I very much care for the music. Sometimes, I induced Hal to come to one of the City churches at lunch-time for some organ music. I love the swell, the sound so unlike that I produce from my grand piano. The music of the organ is like that of the sea; the church becomes a shell conveying the beating and soughing into the little shell of the ear. Hal seemed to like these outings.

We went to the sea itself in winter, and in autumn. Not many people would wish to take long pointless outings with someone with whom they were not in love, but Hal often initiated them. He loved docks, shipyards, piers. Chatham was the favourite. For the last four years before Cora, we went often. There is a figurehead with flaking rouge at the side of the Admiral's House, and no flag on the flagstaff. Hal is patriotic in a highly coloured way and I am moved by this. It was not always easy for me to get away from the hospital for a whole day, but when I did, it was to the sea that we went.

I cooked for him, the sort of food he would not find in his restaurants. I cook with precision and invariable success; I do not talk about it during or afterwards and I always wash up. This is a rare combination which I have from my mother. I make very good bread, in batches, which I give away. I do observe Passover, and bake no bread for its duration.

I taught him about his own country, of which he was ignorant. I should have loved to teach him of Europe but he went abroad with his jetsam crew, usually to destinations involving no demands on his brain. 'Not a holiday otherwise,' he said, and he went off to another island with a beach or country with a coast.

I myself hardly believe that I have known him for so long and established so deep a bond with another person, for deep it is, despite its ostensibly thin substance. I have wondered whether this is what keeps me so preoccupied with Hal; he is in flight from me and might transform himself, if I grow too close, into something other, not a beast, not a tree, but a white indifferent flower.

What kept the power between us fairly balanced were my seniority and Hal's need of me, which appealed to me at all times.

I understood him; I knew that when he was unkind, it was for a reason, and that when he was apparently cold it was because he felt too much.

Hal is shy. Over the past six years he has learnt from me many of the characteristics which should, in one of his breeding, be innate. Yet it took me to teach him to read, to dress, to walk in his capital city, to take his spoons and forks in order and not to hold them as pencils. I am puffed up with pride when I see him as he should be, at ease anywhere. It is odd that he needed to be taught, but I think that this must have to do with sending these boys away to school so young. So few of them have parents who share a name, let alone a bed, how can they learn a coherent manner and easeful grace? And the television, I suppose, saps the springs of action so that the poor brutes mistake the natural thirst for knowledge for a hypernatural thirst for experience. Those of these boys who go to university seem to use it rather to regress and to soak and to dip their flies in amber; perhaps I was more of a university to Hal than university would have been.

Hal was the one living person who needed me, I felt, on the morning he told me he needed a wife. I had not thought of it before; he was so much my angel that I had willingly allowed myself never to reflect upon tomorrow, lest he fly.

VI

I had decided in the week before I telephoned Cora to introduce
my love and my lure at a dinner party, which I would give at
my flat. This would appear to Cora to be courtesy, maybe even
interest on my part, and there could be no harm in that. Hal, no
doubt already seeking his wife from among his jackals, would be
smitten with her. I was almost certain I knew how to ensure that.
I would whet his appetite by making it clear, after some encounters,
each choreographed by myself, that I did not approve of Cora,
meanwhile polishing her at my own leisure as I had polished him.
But I would not be polishing her, as I had him, to be my adornment
and stimulation, but to be so smooth as to be simply a convenience,
Hal's and my modest handmaiden and ultimate licence, the suave
hoop which would at last bind us. I could not bear that someone
else might have him. That someone must be chosen and created by
me for Hal, and Cora had shown herself to be as suitable as anyone.
Besides, I was in a hurry and I did not meet pretty biddable girls
of a type attractive to Hal at the Hospital.

Hal himself was the most difficult guest to trap for dinner; I
secured him by making sure that Anne was free. Anne would come
to dinner with me in any circumstances, no matter how difficult it
was for her; this was part of her loyalty. She would cancel a sword
swallower, a Chancellor, a Maharajah and a performance artist to
eat sandwiches in my big room. She would come if she was ill or if
she was being fitted. She had come from several lands to hold my
hand, even, when my parents died, to hold my head. On each
occasion she was always perfectly accoutred. This will often pick
me up from my sadness; it is a pleasure to see consummate tact at
work. The black terrors recede when confronted with the conscious-

ness of Anne's decision to wear grey or beige, or mushroom, pleats, pads or peplum.

I telephoned Cora Godfrey.

She sounded very surprised and rather odd.

'Oh, Sir Lucas,' she said, 'that is a relief. I thought it might be someone else.' Which meant that she had also thought it might be me.

'Please just call me by my name. Might you be free for dinner next Thursday, or is this at very short notice? I have a few friends for dinner on Thursday.'

'I'd love to, it's long notice and I'll bring your clothes.'

She was nervous, gabbling.

Hal would not care for her haberdashery-department dressing habits, I knew, favouring tailored hoydens with shocked hair. I took a plunge taken as a rule only by royal patrons and worried mothers.

'Cora, I know so few young women and I love to go shopping with Anne Cowdenbeath. Why don't you come with us, this afternoon?'

'This afternoon is the charity shop, but, no, I mean, it's sweet of you, but I couldn't possibly afford, and if you were suggesting . . . I couldn't . . . '

'No, I see that, but let me worry about that, and please cancel the charity shop. Isn't there another girl behind the counter?'

'There's Angel.'

'Angel?'

'She's the power behind the thrown-out. That's what she says. I'll ask her.'

'You have given your answer, then?'

'Provisionally for this afternoon and unprovisionally for Thursday.'

'I shall telephone you again in half an hour. Until then.'

To persuade Anne to change her afternoon for me was simple. I had no duties at the Hospital that day. Cora settled Angel, whoever she was.

I collected Anne after lunch. She wore a mauve coat and skirt whose dull planes were smooth as metal. The geometry of her blouse gave her a breastplate, so she did not look soft and divided like a bird or a woman. She looked as though she might have a clock for a heart.

'What is this, Lucas? I can perfectly well tell you are laying some plans.'

'I just happen to like this girl. I think she is amusing and, as you say, that there is something there.' If I showed merely a collector's interest, Anne would not be able to perceive my motives. After all, *she* had collected Cora at first.

'You like her so much that you want to deck her? Lucas, it must be for another reason.'

'Deck her *out*,' I said. It was pedantic, in character, and it obscured the scent.

The cream paint on Cora's shared cottage was blistering; the capitals of the porch columns were starting to split. I could see down into a basement kitchen. It was dark but full of gilt. Gleams of copper, brass and dull gold reflected the afternoon sun. An enormous drinking vessel stood in the middle of a large table, whose cloth was blue velvet. Leaning in one corner was a pair of boots, very long. A sword with a jewelled hilt lay on the floor. Each of these things looked too big for the room. There were bars across the window and dark ivy grew there. I saw all this as we waited for someone to answer the bell. I was expecting some damsel in samite by the time Cora appeared.

She was looking perfect for Hal. I had proposed an afternoon which was not necessary, or would not have been, had I been able to tell her truly of what I was doing. But that truth would have dashed my plans and killed all magic, so I, rather sharply, indicated the car. I was angry with the poor girl for reasons she could not help; now Anne and I were going to have to waste our afternoon and our money just to make sure that Cora arrived at dinner in a week's time looking just as she did now, and not as she had when I first saw her. Today the too large features of her face seemed glazed with some powdery layer which made them more controlled-looking. She wore a sort of sailor suit, but much too small, in navy blue. Her legs were skimmed navy blue, very sheer so that the colour showed only where the profile of her legs turned. Her hands were long and clean and her hair under some restraint. The shoes, thank God, were not snakes.

'I hope you don't mind, I've got my thrift-shop clothes on today. I wear them to show our customers what really great stuff there is if they look. This is mostly Girl Guide uniform with sailor's buttons.'

48

'It's lovely,' said Anne, turning round to smile at Cora. Cora had set herself along the back seat. She had put the bag, which must, I assumed, contain my clothes, on the floor. I had noticed Anne noticing this bag.

'I've got to go shopping, anyway,' said Anne, 'so would you very sweetly both just come along?'

Women like Anne do not mean by shopping the exchange of money for some other commodity. They mean the placating of their hunger for another day. Money does not appear. Alterations of an invisible yet crucial nature are made.

We began in a corsetière, so old-fashioned that the photograph of the monarch was in sepia, tinted with the icing pink and green of poisoned cakes. The attentive yet disembodied nature of the assistants made it not at all improper for a man to be there. I was able to see no hint of flesh as Anne was fitted behind the curtain. Cora sat on a little chair next to me, and wandered off after about half an hour. I heard women's voices, intent, expert, nurselike. I almost went to sleep, until I heard the whisk of Anne's curtain and saw on the wall of the compartment where she had been a battery of what appeared to be light engineering tools; some of them looked like my own instruments, glistening hooks and clamps and pins. There was an alterable metal hoop, like a sieve without the stiff bowl of veil; it looked like a speculum for a huge but frail mammal. I also saw a bunch of what appeared to be pale onions, but soft, as though one of Anne's modern sculptors had forgotten them from the handle-bars of his soft bicycle. These onions, though, were not plump and shiny and alive but the grim pink of institutionalised femininity. I realised that they must be prosthetic breasts and I wondered if Anne needed them. How little I knew about what clothed the skeleton. How much about what it housed. We left together, Cora having mysteriously reappeared.

'For women's clothes, London isn't really the place, but it is wonderful for men and for unmentionables,' said Anne. 'Did you like that basque lacer?'

'I got them to use it on me,' said Cora. 'The very grand one with a pleated mouth told me there are girls who come and get laced tighter and tighter. Very popular with husbands, she said. Less so with lungs, I guess, but then – one's got two of those.'

'Spare me,' I said. 'And what is a basque lacer?'

'The sort of giant boiled-egg decapitator at the back of my booth,' said Anne. 'Do you believe in trepanning, Cora? We might go sometime if you've a moment, I've a friend whose life it changed. She can go up and down stairs entirely unattended though she still cannot deal with horizontals, they're too committing, she says.'

Anne was certainly teasing Cora with some malice. I opened the door to allow the tall girl into the back of my car and reobserved her shoes. Over the high blue heel of each something hung, and on the smooth blue leather that capped each heel something was written. The left heel bore a tiny red telephone receiver and three figures; I knew what the right would bear – a tiny red telephone and four figures. Had I not noticed, I wondered in horror, were her ankles linked with a stretchy coil of red telephone wire?

'Shoes,' I said to Anne.

'Lucas does admire your shoes,' said Anne. 'Are they to tell the world you are engaged?'

Of course, I was cross, but forgave her when she continued, 'I just do need some more slippers, Lucas. Do go on, Cora, and let's get you some too.' This was kind and rescued me from feeling compromised. Anne of course had slippers for a thousand and one nights.

In the back of a men's shoe shop were lasts for both of Anne's feet. While Anne went behind yet another curtain, Cora sat among a pile of silvery grey slippers. They looked like the perfect wear for a cat burglar. She took off her prostitute's shoes. In haste, the novice shoe votary put them away in a box. Cora put on pair after pair of leaf-grey slippers until she found some snug enough. I had not seen her in flat shoes since she had worn my socks in the night. The canting of her body changed; her hips went forward, her hands towards her pockets, her shoulders back. She looked less English than ever, but still had her awful bag which looked like the severed hump of a dromedary stuffed with waste paper, and her earrings, which, I now noticed, pursued the telephone motif, being small but unmistakable telephone booths.

'May we have a black pair and a grey pair of the slippers and have you any ready-made shoes for ladies?' I asked the young man with his soothing confidential manner. He was like a pimp provided by the state for municipal health reasons. He knew about younger ladies and older gentlemen. He may have recognised me. Two days

before, there had been an article about my latest operation; opposite
it was printed the photograph of a girl whose only garment had been
a fishing rod and her own hands. Her caption had been 'TWO
THAT GOT AWAY'. 'My' caption had been 'BIG-HEARTED BIG
KNIGHT'.

We bought a pair of navy-blue shoes for Cora which were unre-
markable in all but price. How did she feel, being treated as a pet
or as a child, by people she hardly knew?

Cora and I crossed the road and entered the glass corner of
Fortnum and Mason's Fountain. Anne continued her game of hunt
the slipper. At the table next to us a couple transparent with age,
she in velvet and marcasite and he in a town bowler hat, each
wearing a grey coat, faced each other over a shared quarter-bottle
of champagne. Her hat resembled a black cat which had swallowed
a squeeze-box. She was beautiful and wore pince-nez; blue veins
stood out on their hands, which were linked. These veins were all
that moved. Two pairs of gloves lay together on the table.

Cora ate nothing and drank two glasses of iced tea. The once
compendious and prolix menu had dwindled, the splendiferous
blonde Irishwoman had disappeared. No wonder, when one saw
the changes. For Anne I ordered a chocolate ice with chocolate
sauce, and for myself crumpets with salt and a pot of tea. Anne and
I had spent hours here during the twenty years we had known each
other. Overnight, it seemed, the Fountain had changed. The only
way to react to the frosted glass facelift was to ignore it. Plastic
oranges bobbed in a tank in the corner. Gone were the watery mural,
the sugary illicit atmosphere.

'My God, what has happened here?' cried Anne, when she
arrived, carrying a thin paper bag. No one responded, so deep is
the English teataker's terror of lunatics. So Anne spoke up. Two
Americans forking plywood *mille-feuilles*, at the table on the other
side, facing the lacy grey couple, looked uncomfortable.

'Anne,' said Cora, and tugged at Anne's mauve sleeve to pull her
to sit down. At the same time, she indicated to her that the old
woman was trying to get her attention. The grey-coated woman
moved her head very slowly, with its strange hat; it was as though
Nefertiti's bust were being rotated by a rapt Egyptologist. She
caught Anne's eyes with her own and then mouthed, making not
even a breath of noise, 'My husband is blind. Do not make him see

the change.' The silent head rotated back among its pale goffering. Her eyes once more faced the witty, sightless gaze of her companion. Anne ate her ice-cream. I saw Cora looking at her with envy and greed, the face I have seen from time to time on my patients as they watch their visitors eat the grapes they have brought. While there is still that greed, I do not despair of an energy to sustain life. But Cora was not an ill girl, just a vain fit girl who had decided not to eat. When Anne laid down her spoon, Cora seemed relieved, as though she had feared that her own hand, in spite of herself, might lick out to take the sweet brown ice.

Anne raised her head to me and said, 'I hope you like what I've got here,' and she indicated the thin bag. 'It's for Cora.'

She unpacked from this narrow envelope of paper a wool suit. How had it been packed so flat? A white fall of tissue paper, volumes of it, was all about our feet, landing with the sound of flexed wing feathers.

'It's a real one of what you've got on, and, frankly, I don't know if it's as nice, but let's see, shall we?' Anne's voice was barricading itself against a patronising tone. It would not be kept out.

She picked up the jacket and shook it by the shoulders as you might a child who is going to sing his party piece. She looked at it with proprietary pride. Inside the neck was stitched, by two loops of ribbon, a very small gold chain, to take the feather weight of the jacket, during, perhaps, some meal taken in mime with other women clad in sumptuous modesty. The wool of the suit was the blue of a starling in sunlight. Its buttons were as considered as those on an expensive gramophone.

'It is exactly what I have always wanted,' said Cora. 'And now please take it back, or I shall always want more, and never be able to relax with you. When I am very old I shall still be in your debt, and who knows, I may have become wicked in order to satisfy my need for hand-hemming. I'll be' – she gave a smirk and blushed, and yet did not stop herself – 'hooked, on the needle, kind of thing.'

'Worse things happen, Cora,' said the serpent Anne to our unfallen Eve.

'I can't afford it,' Cora said, 'in any sense. I just do not dare to start accepting things.'

'Very well,' said my naïve sophisticated friend, 'but how do we pack it up? You should know,' she went on, 'you work in shops.'

I was embarrassed for Anne. Did she honestly not understand about other people and money and the infected bondage of obligation? I think she was innocent on that afternoon, and simply wanted to spoil Cora, and then wanted to hurt her when the girl rejected the gift.

Did we appear, from the outside, to be a family, two parents and their leggy daughter?

'Who is Angel?' I asked, trying to save us all from embarrassment, while Cora ineptly folded the blue wool and creased tissue paper. Her face was red, as though she had been hit. I saw the old couple full with years and moderate in their ways and I felt sad for Anne. What could be making her behave in this way? She looked suddenly up as though she heard something. It was twenty past five, when angels pass.

'Angel is great. She wears weird clothes and she's wound up in a lot of causes.' This lazy language was in Cora insolence. She was showing Anne and myself that she was alive and young and needed nothing more than her body to give her fun. Hal does it to me, often. I think of my father who spoke English hardly at all and the closed firework-box of his Polish growing damp over the years. But Cora's feelings had been hurt, I imagined, so I persevered.

'Causes?'

'Yup – you know, animals, all that, comets, rhinology . . . '

'She's a kidney expert?' I tried to make a joke. I failed.

'No, the nose being, you know, symbolic of the rest of the body. Each bit having its own bit of the body.' She was still sulking. She was leaving herself as few words as those poor newspapers. I considered momentarily the congruence of circumcision and nose-bobbing and held my tongue. Where in the nose was the heart?

Where, for that matter, the tongue? 'It gives you a whole new outlook on noses,' said Anne, in a doped religiose voice. As she said it, she squinted wildly, and held her hand on Cora's wrist, and they both laughed. Anne looked as though she had closed a drawer on a cache of rusty knives.

'But the main thing is animals, with Angel. She likes them better than people. She thinks they should be free to run their own lives. She says a hare is better than any rabbi.'

I took this as a reference to that form of spiritual superiorness which entails promiscuity and sententiousness in equal parts.

'How did you meet?'

'Oh, in the shop. We even do vegetarian dog-food.'

'Is it popular?' asked Anne. She had many characteristics of the conventional British woman. She loved animals in a straightforward way; this involved feeding her dogs on what dogs eat.

'Not for dogs, but it's cheap, and a lot of people buy it for themselves. There are people poorer than you know,' Cora said, rather wildly, not addressing me, not daring to address Anne, truce being too recent. Somehow my money was meritocratic, I supposed.

'I know someone who's going that way,' said Anne.

Whether she referred to vegetarianism or poverty, I doubt if she knew. They were remote, exotic states.

'There's a lot of it about,' carried a voice.

It was Tertius.

VII

Tertius was misleading to look at, but when he spoke he left no uncertainty. At the dinner party, he sat between his old friend Anne and his cleaning woman Cora. I had not particularly wanted him to be present when I introduced Hal and Cora, but he had ensured that things fell out thus when we had bumped into him. He had been delivering a frame to Cam's just opposite Fortnum's, a very little frame, he had said, but chased silver and what *is* chaste nowadays?

Tertius was a pantomime queer. He was too old for camouflage chic; I refer not to the fashion for wearing army drab, but to the fashion for appearing to camouflage among the heterosexuals, which was, I must admit, what I wanted for Hal. A fat man, Tertius had the red hair which announces its ubiquity at neck and cuff and ankle. His bottom had the mass, in its invariable grey flannel trousers, of a tired old circus elephant's. He had huge shoulders, even for his size, and all his clothes were covered with checks, squares, dogsteeth, tartan, plaid, shadow-paning, windowpane or other designs playing the not many variations on ninety degrees. I had seen rooms shatter into a mosaic of squares once Tertius entered, as though dividing into those grids used by painters of fresco and mural to control their matter. A flower placed in his buttonhole would, you felt, marshal and bevel its petals to squareness. It was nothing so clear as that Tertius the seller of frames saw everything, as it were, through a square or rectangular frame; it was that he was so strong a presence, so colourful and so vivid a sight, that curves lost their importance wherever he was, confronted with his bulk and squareness. He re-emphasised perception, shook it up and squared it up. Perhaps the only thing which might have reasserted curvature in his life, a Fat Lady, was not at all what he wanted.

I liked him for his campness and his explicitness. He was what I was not, for certain. And then, he was what I was.

My mother would refer to people who were kind all through as 'fat souls'. Tertius, I thought, was a fat soul. He was certainly a fat body.

We began with a cold soup of red fruits. Using sour cream, I had written the initial of each person in their soup. With those same perfectly steady hands I had that morning reinforced the interventricular septum in the heart of a small brown baby. His mother had lost two boys already from the same cause, after the same operation. She had three daughters, cursed, I thought, with perfect health, looking at their flashing-eyed father as he visited his wife and son that evening. The little girls, in pastel trousers and long tunics, had come the night before and laid their heads against the side of their mountainous mother as she watched the baby boy. Perhaps some of their life penetrated her pyramidal form. The whole family wore woolly cardigans. The father, with his astrakhan hat, moustache and blue eyes, looked particularly compromised by his cardigan. The sternum of his little son, like a bird's, would soon, I knew, be safely enfolded in canary cable stitch. God send it keep him warm. The small girls were so respectful of their parents that not even their hair was disobedient; it just receded, at the end of each silken pigtail, to a point where it was no longer visible, at the tunic's hem.

I had chosen with care the balance of guests to make our dinner party up to eight. I wanted no one to outshine or to show up Cora. It was as though I loved her myself, with such care did I consider her and exactly how she was. I had selected a couple who had married late and who loved each other, an advertisement for the married state. He was a rich man whose hobby was cancer, his main luxury giving money to conferences on the subject in countries like India, which had their own special cancers, dictated by climate and way of life, cancers related to the carrying of braziers or the consumption of fish. She had been a nurse. She was pretty and tired and since her marriage had become a garden historian. He would help her file plants by colour, on the floor of their music room. He had index cards made for her in every colour there is, including sixteen different greys. They were called Daniel and Flo Bayley and he was her dream come true; I doubt whether he had dared to dream, since he had no hands. He wore false hands, ungloved, so unhorrific, and his metal fingers were eerily deliberate in movement. On account of Daniel's hands, I had avoided cooking anything too fibrous, but I will not make those tone poems on a gout of sauce either. It was a stew with dumplings, each dumpling filled either with an apricot or an almond, and flecked green like mossed eggs. After that, a salad and small potatoes, to absorb the gravy. I find it hard to talk and eat salad, but, as I had anticipated, this did not inhibit my eighth guest. Her name was Dodo, for Dorothy, and I had chosen her for her swift smallness, calculated to show up Cora's grand scale and her latent wit. Dodo bound books. Nerves and the passing years had made her preen and namedrop and assume. Tertius, Anne and I all knew her and knew she meant no harm, but I wanted her to be at or near her worst that night and she did not disappoint. Her face looked like those eighteenth-century carica-tures which you turn upside down to discover what they could be. One might imagine poor Dodo as 'the week preceding Matrimonie and its aftermath'. Dainty at first glance, her face was coarse; it was not easy to look her in the eye, the nakedness of her desperation was such, and her scrub of unshining curls was not the texture of the hair of the head. Dodo seemed never to close her mouth. She had bracelets of flesh at wrist and ankle, and was very thin in between; she moved as though her waist were a single ball and socket joint, with none of the dip and swoop which must as far as I can see be something to recommend women. She did bind books very well. 'Like an angel,' said Tertius, 'the Recording Angel.' Certainly, her work looked to me serviceable and unlaboured. She had a friend of dim dazzling beauty who had enjoyed a season's fame with a copy of Brillat-Savarin bound in the skin of a tanned goose with inset into it a garlic-tooth of ivory and a gilded rosemary sprig. Dodo, painfully whimsical in life, did not affront the page with this chicanery.

Hal sat opposite Cora and between Dodo and Flo. He wore a plain grey suit, a white shirt of silk, with his initials sewn upon it at the left breast, and a pair of black velvet slippers whose shield-shaped toes were each decorated with a forkful of gold thread, his initials, as though his feet were members of some club. He was without a tie.

I was dividing my attention. All my motor activities were concerned with the meal; all my thoughts were occupied with Hal and his reaction to Cora. My eyes were drawn to Hal, as they always were; but today I had to conceal this. The means I found was to observe Cora. To see her seeing Hal for the first time had been to feel lightning conducted. I had introduced them – 'You two know each other?' – and left them for a moment. She stared at him as though it would pain her gaze to cease, and so it was throughout the meal, though they did not speak much.

Dodo spoke to Hal about things ostensibly objective, their burden her own unmixed relief and sense of independence at not being obliged to spend time with men. Or even a man. None the less, her indiscriminate voracity for anything, not disqualifying a tapir, for company, was clear. When Hal responded, in, reasonably enough, objective vein to this talk, he became useless to her and Dodo began to talk over him to Flo, who lived for the company and ease of one man, and had probably never reached the tapir-state, finding quiet monogamy pure cream after the chalk and water hospital life. Their childlessness was a warmth between Daniel and Flo and went unpitied among their friends, which is rare since people will wish children upon the most wretchedly mismatched couple, perhaps to make themselves feel that their own broken nights and fractured ambitions are no more than the price of being human. Dodo invariably wore clothes covered with that small sprigging with which the wallpaper of an attic room will conceal misplaced pipes, bulging ceilings, and botched plastering. This suggested, as did her stiff motion, that her entire body was an artificial mechanism beneath the too pretty cloth. Why did she not just out with it, like Daniel with his hands like kitchen utensils?

Dodo was a Catholic; she lodged with a Kosher family who did not like her to use the telephone. I used to think that this must be relief to her, since she would not feel obliged to pretend to have friends, ringing up no one, like a child. It was food laws, I am certain, which were the barrier to her using the telephone. Perhaps she had been eating prawns in her room? Her landlords charged her next to nothing for rent, and were not avaricious.

We came to know Dodo because she had been at school with Anne, a fact which Anne remembered when we required in a hurry someone to bind a series of essays as a *Festschrift* for the Galenic scholar Gilbert Marjoribanks; blue and silver and very plain, it came. The immeasurably thin paper edge at the top of each page was lightly stained, and when the book was closed you saw why; there was a moonlit marsh with a flight of geese; pages making the soft released purr of wings above the marsh banks. Dodo could do with stamp and die and leather all she could not do with her own self.

'It's completely secluded,' she was saying to Flo of her room at the top of a smallish and busy house in Archway. Flo lived in a quiet yellow rectory by water. 'So there at last I can just be little me.'

'How do you do that?' asked Flo, who had no poetry and had not considered being anyone else but big her.

'I mean I can relax at last.' The implication was that Dodo could take a recuperative bath in peacock-egg albumen before being whirled off again, if, of course, she wished to be.

'The great thing about those snatched moments is the freedom to read,' she continued, as though books were forbidden to book-binders, as Tertius tells me love of great pictures is to art dealers. 'And how I love to read. At the moment I am on one which tells you how to . . .'

I rescued her, coming to take her plate.

Daniel, being kind, said to her, 'Do go on, Dorothy, or may I call you Dodo?' He had turned from Cora to whom he had spoken through the first half of dinner. He had not asked her about her work, either with perfect instinct or with the understandable egoism of a happily married man who has all he wants and finds himself being asked all about that self by a pretty, younger, woman. He put people at their ease, so they talked well. His hands and his fine head discouraged do-good flirtation to make up for the hands. He was funny. Yet Cora's eyes often lifted over the table to Hal, whose mouth was just mauve with the soup, so that his eyes were heightened to the bright blue of stones. In fact, he looked, so vivid was his clothing, as though he could, like Dodo's paper, have been touched with paint. Cora, like a mother, had managed to keep her attention on him, while seeming to give it all to Daniel, who was now listening to Dodo. Dodo's gestures and near tearful cheeriness suggested to me a thyroid condition. What would Daniel be seeing there? Not a cancer, certainly. Nothing so faithful. She was made for transitory relations, even with illness.

I returned to my place when I had made sure that everyone had their cheese and dry biscuits. I had put a bowl of preserved green almonds on the table, with a silver fork, and a bowl of shaggy peonies was flanked by a flat glass bowl of lime jelly, whose smell, as it melted slowly among the candles, was like a woman's perfume. To go with the jelly, made with a calf's foot and twelve sour green fruit, was yellow cream in a silver jug. Tertius and Anne had been talking together in a way which, to my irritation, I could see titillated Hal. They spoke of people and of places which were public knowledge, but which were, at any rate to Anne, private fact. Very many of the people they discussed were related to her. She did not see Tertius's over-enthusiasm, being innocent in that way. He was watching her as some men will a car which they have been allowed to drive for an afternoon. He even began to show off on his own account.

'My new friend,' he was saying, 'Angelica Coney, she does so much for charity.'

'If you admit she is your "new" friend you must have met her an hour ago. I've never known a nine days' queen like you,' said Anne. She was not angry with Tertius. She did not like charity as practised by her class, and was irked by his borrowing of it. 'Dressing up to feel better about people who can't dress up.' 'Do it, but don't say,' she would state. I suspected she did it, but I did not know what form it took.

I watched these people, two of whom I could say I loved. I sat at my end of the table and saw to my right Anne and Tertius, he red with wine and she by now white with smoke, laughing. Were they happy? He was satisfied and greedy, his personal life was regulated as library membership. She was almost certainly not happy but had world enough to make others so.

Opposite me, Daniel was flirting with Dodo. Happiness made him free with charm. I could see her assembling, from this crippled handsome married man, a romance, which she, selflessly, for Flo's sake really, since Flo would never really get another chance, not really, would turn from, to bury herself once more in her books on Tarot, chick peas, tantra and the old lie, something for everyone. I turned my head to talk to Flo, plain and regnant. What I then saw was what I had wanted – Hal talking to Cora, his pale head inclined over the white and black and silver to her dark one. Her mouth was as loose as though he had only just let it go. I was as jealous as sin.

VIII

At midnight, Tertius left; he was drunk. He said he would drive Cora home, but this made Daniel offer to do so. His car had been adapted to his hands. The head of the gear stick was a gel-filled knob, so that his metal fingers could have purchase. Cora said goodbye to Anne, smiled brokenly at Hal, and came to stand next to me in the cold doorway.

'Thank you *so* much. Perhaps I could do something for you?' and she kissed my cheek. She did not have to strain up to do so, as most women do, but gave a little lift because she was wearing her grey slippers, no snakes or telephones.

Would Hal stay with me? If I could have my desire that night, it would be to sit and discuss the evening with him. I miss this joy. My parents had it. They gave it to me.

'Well, that was a good enough feed, Luke,' he said. He spoke to me in this caricature of buddyspeak for Anne's benefit, as if she had not thought out the nature of my love for him.

'It was lovely, Lucas,' she said. 'And now let me stretch out.' I saw that she had decided to stay, that it was with her I would have to go through the evening. I did not mind so much.

'I've got to ease now, Lucas, in fact, as I said I'd meet a couple of friends. Who was the tall one in the great clothes anyway? I could favour her.'

I felt as though I had to eat the tip of my own tongue, cut off. In choosing the girl for Hal was I cutting off my nose to spite my heart? I thought I was ensuring that he went to someone whom I could make certain was a cypher, so that I could keep him all mine.

'She's a friend of mine, actually, she's been up to Stone,' said Anne, saving me and saving Cora the slur in Hal's eyes of having been procured by me. 'And now off you go like a nice boy please.'

She was sparing me pain yet I could have slapped her for it. I knew that had Hal stayed to talk he would not have stayed to sleep with me, yet I said to myself that I was angry because I wanted to trail more bait towards the gingerbread house of marriage to Cora.

'Well, you two look set fair for a cosy and I must fly,' he said, putting his hand into the silky dark tunnels of his greatcoat's arms. He buttoned up. Dressing, the fastening and knotting and tying and lashing, the closing of gaps, must be for a child the first test of dexterity unconnected with the body's feeding. Hal pulled from his pocket a pair of black leather gloves; he inserted his hands and pulled at the wrists to install every digit. They moved like crabs. 'I'll ring you,' he said. 'I'd like the big one's number.'

He left the flat. I followed him out into the hall, its cold floor the colour of brawn. There was a lavatory smell of disinfectant, no longer the warm scent of my safe flat.

'More your turn-on out here, is it not?' said Hal. He had not done this before, directly referring to how I spent my lust for him on others. I was shocked, and then told myself that it was after all quite natural for a young man contemplating marriage to be sickened by my life. If only he would let me explain.

'Hal, darling . . . '

He opened the outside door and looked at the mounting clouds, high in the sky. His hair streamed straight. The low barges on the canal swung at their moorings. The water reprimanded the sides of the canal.

'Lend me an umbrella, please, would you, and thank you more than I can say for a good evening,' he said, like a boy leaving a children's party. I gave him my best umbrella, shining silk, shining wood, shining metal, taking it from the tall stand by the door. I hooked it over his left forearm, insinuating it and letting its ferrule hang against his side. It is not normal after six years to perceive in such detail each chance contact with the beloved; we should by now have been rolling and pulling each other like dough, familiar, easy, certain of sleep.

'Goodbye, Hal, have fun tonight.'

'I shall.'

I watched him down the street. The canal receded towards the main road, which was still bright with life. Along the pavement, Hal made a tall trapezium with the black stick at his side, moving towards the false light.

'I took some whisky, do you mind?' said Anne. She had replaced the pieces of cloth I hang over my heart-watercolours, and was sitting against one end of my sofa, with her feet upon it. At the opposite end of the sofa I seated myself with the drink she had poured for me.

'How's Hal?' she asked, enabling me to reply as much or as little as I cared. Did I want to say everything?

I did not reply at once and she, insulted by silence, said, 'Is there something going on with Cora?'

'With Cora? That suggests a liaison.'

'It's normal, Lucas, the only thing I can't fathom is why you chose her.' So Anne was telepathic, she knew that I was making this match for Hal; what a mess of explaining I was relieved of.

'I mean, after all this time, I'd have thought it might be easier with . . .'

'Oh Anne, it's not easy at all . . .'

I thought, forgetting the bleaknesses and humiliations of the past six years, of all I had relished and shared with Hal, the recitals and sea walks, the years of his youth and my prime. Thought is too slow and too unvoluptuous a word for what was more like the swell of a note in music, resonating long after it was inaudible.

'Isn't it easy, Lucas, darling? You can hardly be surprised, I suppose, since she is so very young.' It is not often that I detect coquetry in Anne. She is rich enough not to play, and confident of her ugly face and clothed body; but at the word 'young' she had curled both hands about her glass as though it were too heavy for one wrist, and lifted her eyes to my face. She showed me her eyes under the fringe as though hypnotising me.

'Don't you think she is the right age? Why on earth not? I'm keen for it to be someone I can train and prune,' I said.

'People aren't hedges, darling, you can't do topiary on them. Or, if you do, be prepared to find nests in the branches, like the old man with his beard.'

'But a hedge is exactly what I want, do you see? I want a hedge against the future, against getting old alone, I suppose, and, without being too coy . . .'

Even Anne is not innocent of a woman's need to talk about babies.

'You quite fancy a nest in those branches,' she interrupted, 'don't tell me, and that's where the youth is especially advantageous, and you a medical man . . . All eggs in one sound enough basket. But how are you on breaking the eggs to make the omelette? On cutting the mustard? On making bacon? Or is that offensive to you for dietary reasons . . . ?'

Anne was crying. She must have been drunk. I know whisky does make Scots lachrymose. I had not specified to myself that I would like Hal and Cora to have children, but Anne had instinctively led me to see that this must be one of the reasons I had not gone mad when he said he was going to get married. I would like children, to leave my money to, of course, and to vindicate the expense of Hal's seed on Cora. But that was far in the future, well beyond the marriage which was at present my concern. And here was my dear old friend wiping her nose on her brocade elbows, hugging her knees, shaking. I assumed she must be thinking of her one child, wilfully sucking up his death.

'And the other thing is, Lucas, love has made you lose your sense of humour. God Almighty, a hedge against the future, will you listen for a moment? One minute it's all privies and privates and now it's layettes. The first thing you'll do I suppose is drop all your old friends? It's bound to do you no end of good professionally as well. Most doctors are whited sepulchres anyhow but at least it's swabbing the sister in the bloody chamber not trunking a dumb ancillary worker down among the kidney bowls.'

For the second time that night I was shocked. I considered my life organised, separated like a shell into chambers. My colleagues at the hospital knew me for a talented professional man with no private life. The tabloid newspapers had supplied me with a knightly character, and hinted at no errancy. The boys, I was almost certain, knew me as nobody, just another randy man hiding beneath the sheep-belly of class and decency. Hal knew I went to what Tertius called cottages. And Anne had known, but never said a word. She had kept a seemly silence. What was the source of her rage? Is the vanity of all women affronted by any man who will not desire them so that they may – sweetly, reluctantly, fragrantly, lingeringly – reject him? Not Anne. It must be the thought of drowned Alexander which was making her cry. I do not as a rule trust centripetal grief, all tending to one source laid down long ago, but I could see that the voluntary deaths of her husband and her son could not go unconsidered. And then, she must be menopausal. I do not care to think about that. Perhaps she, whose one child was dead, was jealous of Cora, who carried the pods for more children than her years might give her time to bear? I would comfort her.

'My dearest Anne, are you sad because you can have no more children? Don't wipe your eyes on your brocade, it must scratch.' She was blubbering. The golden threads of her jacket were webbed with mess.

I leant to take her in my arms, a magnanimous thing to do since I would be gummy with tears when once she was comforted. Up came her hands, soft fur at each wrist. She hit me, right, left, so I could feel each cheek burn with the imprint of a hand. She was severely discomposed. Could I, as one must with an hysteric, hit her? I did not. I laid her back against the cushions of my sofa, lifted her feet and pulled them out from her body, so she was completely stretched out as though for sleep. She was shaking. I must loosen the tight frogged collar of her jacket, and cover her with something warm.

I fetched from the arm of a chair a folded Kashmiri shawl. It will pass through a wedding ring and is light enough to lie in the air. I placed it over Anne, pulled it over her pretty shape and enveloped her feet. I knelt at her head and bent to unhook the fastenings at her breast.

'Is this to practise, or to get back at me for my cheap crack about bacon?' asked Anne in a normal voice, not the pleading whelp she had been using since the tears began. 'Either way, my darling, you may have developed a taste for it at this late date, but I prefer it nowadays with people I don't love.'

'Are you mad, Anne?'

'You are mad; concealing, dreaming, plotting, keeping every-thing from me,' she said, the hysterical tone returning.

'What can you be saying?'

'All this getting married stuff, I'm just so upset you couldn't tell me. I thought we had it so clear between us, no secrets but the linen, and that's clean enough since we both go to outside contractors, and now you tell me you're getting married because you want respectability and a washing machine and little ones. And you are insulting me twice; once as myself, your friend, by not telling me your plan, letting me help, and twice as a woman by callously choosing some chit – for strictly eugenic reasons. And now, come to think of it, a third time, Lucas, you brute, by thinking you can wreck our happy closeness by committing sort of friendship-incest just as a boast to show me how well you are getting on with female anatomy.'

'Are you drunk or hallucinating or is this a product of indigestion?'

'You wicked cold fish, I am sober, I take no drugs, and you are a good cook, as you know. That'll come in handy since I'm sure little Missy has never chopped a liver in her life. Just hearts.'

'There is no need to talk of Cora like that. Besides, she is, or do you forget this, *your* friend?'

'And you select her from my menu as your personal feast. Do you think that pleases me? Moreover, without including me. I would have been the Marquise de Merteuil for you, you know that, Lucas. Besides, you can't but be an amateur when it comes to choosing eligible young women; I would have helped you there. I am after all disinterested.'

'Your exhibition this evening leads me not to believe that.'

'Speak straight, Lucas, since you are determined to pretend to live so.'

'Anne, there is a misunderstanding. I think that there may have been one since last week. But before I explain to you, let me ask you. A fearful thought has struck me. Are you in love with me?'

'Why do you ask?'

'It seems the only explanation of your behaviour this evening. We have always been easy together, and now this storm. I thought we were close.'

'That is exactly it, you oaf.' At least she was not snivelling. 'No, I am not in love with you, but you are being obtuse if that is the only reason you know for violent jealousy. You must see that it is a shock for me to hear that you plan to marry. It is usual for eminent homosexuals to equip themselves with wives in order to continue with their upper worldly life of contribution and exposure, but I would like to have known. As to being in love with you, it's not that, but I'd have thought you more canny and more likely to be happy if you had allowed your marriage to be chaste and expedient, and what could be more suitable than a quiet wedding one afternoon at a Register Office to a widow of substance and position, one whom you have known for twenty years? Perhaps I do sound like a bitch in the manger, but you appear to be choosing a sweet enough young girl with lots of It and none of anything else, and you have no use for It. I am also miffed by the suggestion that I am past bearing a child. I am not. So, if you were to want children as much as you think you do, we could have one, or two, and it would be balanced, rich, clever and the apple of our eyes.'

I was curious. 'So *not* chaste, if expedient.'

'We could steel ourselves. Even, with your connections, do it in vitro,' she laughed. 'We could call it Ming.'

Weak jokes leave a bleak little silence. It would take time for me to trust Anne as I had before. Was she as objective and sensible in her absurd proposition as she was pretending? I thought not. But I must, before I made her an enemy, explain to her that I required Cora not for myself but for Hal. Perhaps she would even help me, though I must realise that losing Hal would leave me so to speak undefended, should Anne really want to marry me. Was it even so impossible an idea? As a plan, it had everything in its favour. But, though I was willing a comparable arrangement upon Cora, I could not feel honourable about living in that closed vice called an open marriage with Anne. I had wanted, before her unpredictable outburst this evening, to laugh out our last years with each other, cackling in the wardrobe, choosing clothes in which she might rise up at the latter day. I thought now that we would lose our domestic ease if we married. Her money would ease the chafe of marital practicalities, but then married people as a rule have the rosin of sex.

I began carefully. 'Anne, it is not I who am mad, nor you, though I did think earlier on that you were. We have just been misinterpreting each other. I wish, in a way, I must say this, though it may wound you, that you hadn't made your gallant proposal. It would have been better unsaid. But I see that I was ambiguous. What were you thinking in the Fountain at Fortnum's?'

'Why was I so rude to the little witch, do you mean? Because, if I must admit it, I couldn't buy her with the suit.'

'What for? You must realise that *you* are more likely to desire her than I?'

She looked surprised. 'I wanted her to show she was nothing, so that she would be unimportant in your life. I am your female friend, you don't need a little sugardrop, you've got me, all the best traits and none of the muddle. Or so I thought.'

'I must say, I was quite pleased she didn't accept your generous public lobotomy, because what I require from her is just that moral keel, and little else but big breasts and long legs.'

'How refreshing it is to meet a man who is unafraid to admit he is a pig. And you are going to marry a girl because she's got a big keel. All the better to support the angel's wings, I suppose, when she has to rock the cradle and ignore your periodic late returns from a night-time operation, or should I say dog fight?'

'Annie, the great thing I have learnt this evening is that you are a vile mixture of malice and stupidity. You are also blind.'

'Thank you. I'll get myself another drink.'

I let her pour the whisky, walk over to the mirror with its golden lion and the standing men in their chariot, check not her face but her clothes, and return to the sofa. I could not see how she had been so obtuse. Then I realised. Hal was not for her the centre of the world. She was the centre of her own world, and I somewhere near it. Hal was there, but he had his place in the cosmogony, somewhere between Bayreuth and guipure lace for importance. Living in a denatured universe, without husband or son, she had come to trust only herself and what she could control; she had allowed me to come close to her and I had introduced a vagrant pull into her orbit, a new, unignorable moon. Poor Anne.

'Cora is not for me. I want her, and have since your party where I first saw her, for Hal. On the morning of your party, he told me he was going' – and now *my* voice went out of control – 'to get married, but he had no one in mind. All he admitted to wanting was breasts and legs.'

'Oh, darling,' said Anne, and had I not been afraid of her feelings for me, just in those raw hours, I would have lain on her comfortably undivided bosom. 'Oh, love. And it's you who wants the moral keel.'

'I thought it as well.'

'Why is that? Surely you haven't noticed an insufficiency in Hal?'

'I can't argue over Hal now, Annie, please, so don't be ironic at me.'

'And who wants the babies?' she asked.

'I hadn't honestly thought of them until you started. I'm in the early days, they aren't married yet, after all, but when you spoke of children I rather cared for the idea.'

'You rather cared for the idea. Lucas, no wonder you have to go and get violated by Nibelungs, you fool, this is life, the thing which even you can't sew back into leaky bodies. You have let a dragon out.' The note of management, of knowing better, which I fear in the voices of my ward Sisters, crept in. 'No harm done, though, nothing has happened, after all. You can't ensure they will like each other, let alone marry, and surely if Hal suspected that you were calculating this match, he'd run.'

'Leave it to me, Anne, please, after all Hal is mine.'

'He is not, nobody is yours, Lucas, not even those little unborn cherubs. Do you know how crazy you are? You are experimenting with human flesh. You are doing something which, if it were surgical, would be as repulsive and unnatural as . . .'

'Transplanting the heart?' I asked, pleased with myself, but on edge.

'As obscene as what you tell me it is cheek in Gentiles to mention.'

'Was Mrs Bennet guilty of that when she planned for her daughters' future?'

'Do not be disingenuous, Lucas. A natural desire for one's child's security is not the same as finding a hale consort for your catamite.'

'That he is not.'

'No. He is something worse. If he were that, these complications would not be facing us and half your life would not be lived in either the baleful light of illusion or the dark of rough trade.'

My whole mien discourages criticism. There is a perfect control about me which deflects fault-finding. I am conscious of it because I forged it, link by link.

'It's true, darling. If you lived openly with a boyfriend, there would be no fear of discovery because there would be nothing to discover. But then, I think, and I must be quite careful here, it wouldn't be as thrilling. Also, if you did live with him, you might see him as he is, not the prince in his tower.'

'So, what do you suggest I do, Anne? Forget it all, let him cut loose, lose my last six years, have no one to live for?'

'Oh, you great self-pitying thing, who have I to live for, for instance? We live for life. Not for another person. Or at any rate no person to keep us in a sufficient state of misery to endure life. Did your mother and father suffer for you to suffer? They did not. Come into the sun. If I can do it, you can do it. You commit idolatry with Hal. Why not settle for a godless universe if you cannot find a true god? He is a golden bullock. I'd be happier for you living in open sin with a wet fishmonger than this mawkish abdication from hope for the sake of a puppet queen. We have not spoken of this before because I had not wanted to hurt you, but you have gone too far and now I can't stand by and see you throw a perfectly nice girl to your pet puss. You have drawn his teeth, Lucas, but his claws are there in the paddy paws. Poor little Cora will just be left like a mouse after the cat has played with it, only the skin and spleen left. How dare you do it, Lucas?'

'I shall do it, Anne, and you will help me. I am sorry to use desperate measures but I must have your co-operation now. I have told you what I intend to do. In the end, you may come to see I was correct.'

'What, when you and I, in the cere and yellow, see Hal, by now in the fullness of his years and for once at home and upright, dandling little Hal, Cora mysteriously absent, in the home for battered wives? *Please.*'

'Anne, you told me about Mordred, do you remember? You would gravely dislike anyone else to know. I love you, I am not in love with you, and I ask you to permit me to blackmail you.'

'Good of you to ask,' said Anne.

I had won.

IX

The tiredness after that night brought a sleep without dreams, until just before I awoke. There is a vivid crack of bright dreams just before waking up. Whether it is the red of one's eyelids being interpreted by the brain I do not know. All dreams have to do with love and death.

My dream was of Anne. She and I were fighting over Hal, who was dead. He was not decomposing, but rather flowering. When we pulled at his flesh, it came away, but in drifts and bunches. It was like dismembering a man of petals and fruit, an Archimboldean harvest-festival man. At length, we were tired, and settled among the fruit and flowers to eat. We ate meats brought to us by Cora, who wore no clothes. Anne and I were dressed for a Presbyterian Sunday. She wore mittens of grey lace and her little hands were clawed. When I awoke I was afraid, but pleased when I remembered that I now had an accomplice. I had made Anne swear that she would not include Tertius in my plan. He has a wagging tongue in a small world, with its four corners, trade and sex and money and class, enclosing a formal maze. To introduce a girl into its geometry would be to forfeit entry, and Tertius was not only my friend; he was guide in the maze, the one who told me in what shade next to seek ease, and who held the other end of the thread to tweak me back when I was lost.

I had the false energy of hangover, but my crapulousness was not from whisky but from the gambler's fear; had I loaded my dice so heavily that I would be caught? I left a note for Concepçión, who came to wash up for me before her day of sluicing Embassy kitchens began. She earned from the Embassies perhaps a sleeve of one of my shirts a week. I gave her the equivalent of a couple of cuffs beside. I liked her boy, who sat and played wherever he would least disturb his mother. He did not like the Hoover, which he called Dog. One day he called me dog and I spent the following morning thinking of ways to win him back. In the end, I chose a box of that coffee toffee the Dutch eat. He put a cube flat in his mouth, flat hand to flat cream face, and Concepçión said, 'How nice.' She washed the boy's hair in dishwasher liquid, she told me. It did shine like black china.

I left for the Hospital. Driving a car before the streets have begun to smell and while there is still pink in the sky is a pleasure. Some women lick their lips when they see a significant car in their mirror, women with coats like troika rugs on the passenger seat beside them, and red nails, and dogs like wigs.

There were seagulls in Hyde Park and deserted groups of green deckchairs. There was an air of recuperation, London treating itself gently before a new day. Cities, more than the country, hold crevices for the irrational to gain a hold, but London was showing a bland face where the spores could not, at any rate in this clear dawn, settle. I wondered how the child with the new part in his heart was. I looked forward to seeing him and his family. At least I was blameless in their respect. No one could accuse me of manipulation save in its literal and curative sense.

The flower man in Belgrave Square had put away his ugly blooms. No more guilty husbands till nightfall.

When I arrived at the Hospital, their flower counter was just opening. We do not encourage visitors to bring flowers. They occupy nurses and vases. Those flowers we do sell are serviceable. Some are not real. They last, are undemanding of maintenance, and do not rot down. Sometimes when I see a patient presented with one of these sterile bouquets, I see through his flesh to the pacemaker or to the plastic valve or reinforced nylon aorta and, according to my mood, I feel gratitude or fear on account of these miraculous or intrusive inorganic spare parts. Like the husband who sees his new bride remove wig, nails, padded brassière, I begin to wonder whether in the end I shall be left not with a living body but with a machine, a pump and some tubes.

I like to arrive early at the Hospital. Any who have died in the night have been taken away in false-bottomed stretchers, the new batch of nurses take over, once again in love with the job, full of tea and bread and jam; the Hospital is winning. The dark adversaries are at bay.

Hospital life is absorbing; it may debilitate you in the end. To care is impossible, not to care is impossible. Those patients who stay for a long time come to live by hospital time. They quaver for their supper at tea-time, they need the circumscription, they are dependent upon the hectoring way of the nurses. They are afraid of the violent profligacy of choice in the well world. They live in a valetudinarian, half-lit world where all decisions are taken by another. They are children, with no need to pubesce. To believe in the hospital is essential for the patient or he will not mend. Not to believe too much in the hospital is essential for the patient, or he will not adapt to the bright day his well body should now be fit to inhabit.

And then there are the mages. That is myself, and my fellow consultants. Not all have my newspaper notoriety, though the men who give babies to the childless are worshipped in this way. This is understandable; it is after all primitive magic as well as microscopic science of life which builds and shelters these new lives. Those of my colleagues who are given this type of adulation are touched and troubled by it. What they do is misdescribed, made misleading and to them couples come for whom the hope of hope is not even to be hoped for. They come from Anchorage, from Lima, from Dunblane. I have been lucky. My surgery is not arcane and has little of magic, though the heart is like the moon in our minds, and even more so in the shrunken mind of the narrow-vocabulary papers. The moon is made of green cheese, the heart of soft-centred chocolates in red velvet. The moon is for June, to spoon under at the prompting of the heart. The moon takes all women in its tidal tug, the heart has all the best lines. When the first foot was set in the dust of the moon, its silvery disc, the lozenge of love, was not pulverised. Minds baulked at the conclusion of literal events. The first transplanted heart, tucked in by the archetype of all heart-throb surgeons, did not hurt the romance of the idea of heart. It is a soft pump of muscle, but do you not wear it, with no incongruity, upon your sleeve? Does your heart not come into your mouth when you see the whore's heart cut out by her brother? Heroes are great-hearted, hearts are for lovers, knaves, tarts and queens. The heart has its reasons; it is a lonely hunter. All life returns there repeatedly, and at the end, having reddled the blue gallon of blood for the last time, the great heart breaks.

The heart is an emblem we understand. It is proof love need not be literate. So the meaty seat of my professional endeavour is rich in metaphors. It stands for all we beat for against the tide of what is sure. To consider all this in the servicing or repair of a faulty heart would be as rash as to drive a space rocket on champagne and a driving licence. Professional men must not reflect too much; we delegate this to our universities. The trick of living is to travel light, and too much thought will put wings on your cap perhaps, but set your ankles in stone. If lawyers gave to law the equal balance its practice and philosophy require, no judgement would ever be made. Draco's bloody stylus would still, ineffably slowly, be approaching the set wax. Seeing illness, sooner or later, we must act, and thought, the instigator of action, is also its great enemy.

I am a man of thought become a man of action.

Hospitals, then. Most people will tell you, as though revealing something quite exclusive about themselves, that they hate hospitals. I love them. Hospital was for me what university had not been. I at last was able to leave home. My parents would not have understood my leaving home while I was at university in London, so I cycled daily from Bayswater to Bloomsbury and took my meals with my mother and father. My first hospital was in Buckingham; even my mother realised that this would make it impossible to share our evenings and our food. It came just in time, for me. My mother had begun to ask about girls. I think she was relieved enough that there were none, in case I should be distracted from my work. Perhaps she imagined that I did all the courting I needed in the refectory or lecture hall. In fact I went to the cinema once a week with a dark medical student named Douglas Hardiman, who wore the same jersey for four years during which it grew tighter over his belly. His flesh raged. Once inside the cinema, we would separate. Douglas would look about till he saw a girl as nearly alone as possible. If there was no single girl, he sat next to anyone female whose flank was undefended. After the film, there would be either Douglas alone and with a story of sally and rebuff, or Douglas with a girl who might even accompany us on a subsequent trip to the cinema. They would not last longer than this, on account of Douglas's approach, which was an impassive but violent molestation, his face staring ahead at the screen, his hands working like a person trying to get inside a corpse for warmth in a snowstorm. Outside of the cinema, as far as I could see, he could not look at his victims. He was compelled to talk, and to talk about medicine. He was drawn to discuss all that, in the early 1960s, was not pertinent to the wooing of girls. He would glaze over in cafés – the Rumble Tum, the Digest, the Tom Tom – and give monologues on lesions or fluke. The clear beauty of the function of the eye, or articulation of the hand, became in Douglas's mouth meat and juice and gore. 'Ooh, isn't he morbid?' these girls would say to me, hoping to stir into action the dishy friend of the mad boy talking carnage in the warm coffee-steam. But I liked these cinema outings because I could do what he was doing, in a stealthy way, with boys. Where he paddled and dipped and unhooked, I stared and tested and occasionally found my eye met. Assignations were made, and one afternoon I discovered that there was an end and a means to them which was neither lonely nor procreative. I never wanted to stop. I do not know whether Douglas knew. I was mooning, desiring and not daring to pursue; Douglas even followed the plots of the films, so simply physical was his quest.

My first hospital brought my first happy sex. In the white laundry, among slapping towels, tents of sheet, eight osier chariots full of dirty white linen, and the rolling surge of industrial washing machines, the slippery floor gritty with fragrant blue Daz and my eyes stung with bleach, I embraced and was embraced. I was old to be learning, and my joy was great. The smell of hospitals, which is fearful to many, is mysterious and delicious to me. The hospital was the first world beyond my family. It was disciplined and self-contained; the first institution discovered after the family is laid down for nostalgia, and the glamour and function of hospital are blended for me into something for which I feel what could almost be called patriotism. Their glamour offers me something resembling that which hotels offer the homeless rich.

As I grew into a real doctor, then specialised and became a consultant and at length a recognised plumber of the heart, so I became more dependent yet on my hospitals, though no longer dependent on them for love. I could not be. My success had stripped me of the anonymity which had made things easy before. I was not tempted either to try to find my first paradise again. Just as public school boys move on to their clubs, I moved on, without losing the tingle of danger and indulgence I had enjoyed. In Turkish baths, in plain tiled lavatories, I remember the sluices and laundries in which I had first been happy.

The hospital where I have been for some years now was built as a small foundling hospital. It has grown four times; once, when a philanthropist commissioned Norman Shaw to add to its modest single block. He added long windows set in a tall façade of stone; pendant from each window is a small false gallery, faced with tiles, in eggy blues, greens and sunlight yellow. There are twelve windows and each set of tiles depicts a different illness, succoured by men and women dressed in long green robes, much as we appear, in fact, though the intention is pre-Raphaelite. Conspicuously absent are heart-disease and cancer and the new Pink Death. Brain-fever and tuberculosis are there, and infant death. No cure for that, but the panel parallel shows a slim woman with a furled armful which may be a baby though it looks like a small adult, standing up as present and correct as the Bambino. At the upper corners of each of these glossy tablets is a tile showing a snake bandaging a meaty iris stem, the flower signifying the Trinity. This part of the Hospital is called the Trinity Wing, which makes me think of a wounded dove – a Holy Ghost – winged, as it flies over, by a bad shot. I enjoy Christian iconography; it is like roadsigns, an attempt to find a language which will show all nations the way, without taking into account that what is St Mark to one man is a bored old lion to another.

The next two additions were made in the 1960s. They are buttressed with spindly steel and their surface is hubbled and the yellow of coarse sand. The buttresses are as awkward as the legs of drinking giraffes. None of the windows in this part of the hospital is without its niggling draught. Inside, the optimism of that decade has allowed the architects to waste a great deal of space. There is a wide hall with a gorilla-sized mother and child carved from granite. I have not seen less living rock. It feeds out its own cold, which it retains all year, intensifying in winter. The only thing about the sculpture which is on the human scale is held in the hand of the monstrous child. It is a ball, or a fruit. This part of the hospital is where the children are treated, and many of them touch this ball as they come and go, so it is sometimes warm. Single mittens are put there, until they are paired up, or lost again.

The remaining addition to the hospital is 'my' part. It adjoins the original building and is devoted to disorders of the heart. It is not large but it is efficient, containing two theatres. Because it is not large, there are not so many corridors, which patients fear. Seen from outside, the building is an upright creamy tube, with a sloped roof, whose window is a single ox-eye. The body of the building is pierced with what look like arrowslits. Artificial light is a constant requirement. We have two generators. The theatre in which I most frequently operate is in the top room. Because of the height and angle of the window, you cannot see out, but I have looked up to see stars from there, and dawn breaking. Every part of this modern cylinder is in use. Insofar as this is possible, there are no corners to contain dirt; unlike most followed-through architectural theories, this does not seem to be foolish and is handsome. It is also appropriate, as the building and my department were endowed by a man whose fortune was made from the manufacture of cleaning agents 'good at reaching corners'. Only once the patients are mending in health does this cornerlessness present problems. The furniture of convalescence – sofas, chairs, the television – is incongruous in the circular rooms. Occasionally, I wonder whether I should ask Tertius to have one of his designer friends make appropriate, curvilinear, furniture, which I shall give to the hospital. Then I reflect that coin is both circular and more appropriate.

I took the lift up to the ward, having been to the consultants' room in the main block. I was greeted by many nurses, each busy with something, as though in a diorama of a well-working hospital. I sometimes feel like a performer, with great longueurs between performances, while my juniors ensure that what is real – tests, readings, turning, dredging, wiping, feeding – all go on. They fill time. It is only once the patients are asleep, and the nurses begin to knit and quietly talk about husbands and children, that the truth comes out again. Life is dense with empty space.

The little brown boy was asleep. When I see the very small children with tubes in their noses and arms and sides, they look like puppets on transparent proteinous strings. To mediums, that is what we are. Geneticists know this too, I suppose, as we dance about on our helical threads. The boy was about two, but in that prim bliss of baby sleep he looked younger. His mother appeared to be praying. In fact she was helping a grumpy old man, who had come in from the adults' ward, with a crossword clue. It was one of those crosswords which are called 'quick'. The old man was in a dressing-gown with a badge over the breast. The crest was not familiar; it must be that of a chain store. I imagined he had six months left to him of life. He had a vile temper and did not enjoy the visits of his wife. One of the nurses had heard him crying at night. He had told her he did not want to die, he loved life. Each day, he made the newspaper last. He would call the more gullible nurses over on a pretext and then say, 'Dreadful, isn't it, shouldn't be allowed, crying shame,' and show them the photograph of the naked girl in the paper to make them blush. Then he would scuttle off to the bathroom to shave. He disliked many things, which gave him a sort of firewatcher's vigilance. That he was currently doing the quick crossword with one of the things he most disliked he had not noticed. He fawned on me, with a menacing servility.

'The opposite of white, Doc, even I can do that one, that's another one done. I do not mind telling you this lady is not bad at this at all, are you, love?'

'Another question right away please, Mr Mallard,' she said, handing him a squashed paper bag of fried plantain discs. She seemed incurious about the child. I think she felt that as long as she was there, he would be safe. Perhaps she had once momentarily left the bedsides of her other sons, and saw their deaths explained in that.

'All's well that ends blank,' said Mr Mallard.

'Well,' said the mother, and I wondered what her house looked like inside and if she let her girls play outside in the street.

'Eh?' said Mr Mallard. 'Too deep for me that one. Not at all bad these sweets. Taste of banana.' Then, perhaps feeling he had been too nice, a bit womanish, he continued. 'Bastards, the lot of them. It all began with that star in the East, of course, if we hadn't of had that we wouldn't of had years and decades of rule by rag heads, front wheelers, left footers, and how's your father.' But for the possession of his pension and his precious ill health, Mr Mallard would have been one of those fierce invertebrate drinkers with red eyes who free associate at bus stops and have scabs on their faces and wet trousers. As it was, he was ill enough to live in hospital, like a rearrested criminal.

'Sit down and get comfy, Mr Mallard,' said the mother of the sleeping child. She searched in the bag at her side and brought out a tissue and a Jaffa Cake. The tissue was mauve.

'Your nose needs a good blow,' she said, 'and then you can have a biscuit. You like these don't you?' She was speaking to the old man.

It is a mother's wish, I observed, in my own mother and in all the mothers who come to guard their children in the hospital, to feed her child. While her sleeping boy was having glucose dripped into his vein, this woman was feeding Mr Mallard. The baby had eyebrows which met, like a man's. About the room were people making the best they could of the conditioned air, false lights and dim colours of the hospital. By now it was legitimate visiting time and the tippling of barley water and handing over of gifts from home had begun. It was the nurses' job to send Mallard out of the children's ward. They had allowed the mother in her synthetic silks to stay because of 'the history', as it is called. She was also a great keener, and this is very bad in hospitals. When they sense hysteria the patients get insubordinate and plot against the staff whom they suddenly see as enemies. We have a room where parents may sleep. On its wall is a crucifix, in tooth-coloured plastic. Christ has a foppish smile and His feet are crossed as though spatted. The hole in His side looks like a buttonhole.

'Prithee, undo this button,' I thought. There are those thoughts which are a refrain, which you do not intend to think, yet which you think daily. They are automatic and not especially illuminating. I think of these words when I operate and am close to the distinction between living and not living, just a breath. I also think it just before the act with my boys. But when it seems most pathetic to me is when I am operating on a child. Silly word as button is, it is the right one. It stands for life, and the child's death leaves a hole you cannot mend. You may stitch it up, but it will always be clear that something has been there, and is now gone, something round and essential for security.

I spent the early part of the afternoon making sure that the theatre and the nurses I required were prepared for that afternoon's operation. We began at three o'clock and stopped at eight. I like to keep an atmosphere with none of that tension which is shown in hospital-television. I like a sober neutrality; there is a beefiness in my colleagues, especially obstetricians, which is not suitable. Today's patient was a girl of about Cora's age. About her wrist was a plastic bangle, which said, STEEL, Dolores. She had been born with a heart murmur. It had recently worsened. If you have, as I do, an italic hand, you will write in that word murmur exactly what the electro-cardiograph does not show when it is registering a murmuring heart. Instead of the regular up and down of the beat, mur, mur, there are pauses.

When we had finished with Dolores Steel, my last shift male nurse said to me before he left for home, 'A real heartstopper, that bird.' There are those who do not think as we do.

He noticed nothing strange in his own word. When I was clean, I took the lift down to the hall, said goodnight to the porter who was reading a paperback bent back on itself, and got into the safe interior of my car. It was a rainy night. I closed the door, heavy and snug, and turned on my lights. Only as I turned out of the gates, and the first sweep of the windscreen wipers began, did I see the letters written across my windscreen in red grease. The writer had taken care that I should be able to read the letters in sequence from inside the car.

'WE KNOW,' they said.

Petrol is a solvent for grease, so I used a little from my emergency can and spoilt my handkerchief. It was the first time my handkerchief had been covered with lipstick.

X

The next days were busy for me. Because I had the central worry of Hal, with its new matrimonial turn, and then the natural and necessary worry of my work, I did not wonder very often who 'knew', or what. I was surprised, like most owners of sumptuous cars, that the attack had not been more permanent and damaging.

I had spoken during the week only once to Hal, when he rang me, as he had promised, to find Cora's telephone number. He telephoned just as I was beginning my late supper after operating on the murmuring heart of Dolores Steel. He was calling from somewhere where there was a dull and regular beat, with occasional rattlings. It sounded as though he was not far from a battle at sea, the distantness of the telephone and yet its closeness to my ear giving the absent yet carried quality sound has over water. I gave Cora's number to him and asked him how he was.

'Better than for a long time. I think I could be seeing my way to sorting things out.'

I do not believe he thought of speaking to me in the way I thought of speaking to him.

'Goodnight, Hal, stay well,' I said, meaning it as a father will mean 'Take care' to his child.

'And you,' he said, taking it as an impersonal injunction he might as well have been giving to a man who had sold him a razor.

I ate my boiled egg with pumpernickel and capers. I like the scourging taste of things kept in vinegar. In my refrigerator are jars with vegetables held like specimens in the clear liquid, cucumbers and cauliflowers like seaslugs and heads of coral, and hydras of dill suspended above. I keep small pearly corn cobs and lotus roots

82

which show an Islamic flower when you slice them, and a jar of beetroots, as small as I can find. Concepçión must give these to her boy, I think, because his cream-yellow hand is sometimes stained pink if I come home early. Children like vinegar; a physiologist of the tongue may say that the distinction between sweet and sour is the last to come. Does that make me a child?

A week after the dinner party, Cora telephoned me at the hospital. At first, I was not pleased. I need to sequester the chambers of my existence. Then I recollected that she was to marry Hal, and I welcomed her call. Perhaps Hal would take to telephoning me at work.

'Lucas, if I may call you that, Hal said I could call you there, I do hope it's all right, it's two things, really. Would you join me and Hal for supper tonight, I'll cook, I'm sorry it's such short notice, Hal said you wouldn't mind, and could I perhaps ask you a favour?'

Anything, dear Miss Nothing, already using his name to touch like a girl with a tiny diamond, anything you wish, if you will remain so besotted.

'Of course, Cora.'

'If I came to see Dolores this evening, could you possibly give me a lift home? I'll do all the cooking this afternoon.'

'Dolores Steel? Do you know her?'

'Pretty well over a time, and I'm sure she needs visitors. Her friends, well, the sort she has now, wouldn't go into a hospital to save your life.'

Could Dolores Steel be a Christian Scientist? Surely it had said Church of England on her papers? I was not curious. She was a girl whose small features and long limbs were noticeable to the younger doctors. She sat up in bed, black hair over her breast. She did not read, she ate only fruit, and she wasted time. She asked questions all day, about the hospital, its history, its design. These poor men wanted to touch the one wound of her body which was not penetrated by a high-hung tube. I was not surprised she had no visitors. But I was pleased that Cora was showing herself a soft-hearted girl and a loyal friend. I thought of my old age; would she tuck me in a rug as my mother had my father?

'Of course, I'd be delighted. Why don't I help with your cooking a bit? I'll bring some surprise from the market by the hospital if I can.'

This was unlike me, and I surprised myself. And Cora, who replied, 'That is sweet. So shall I meet you by Dolores's bed at half past seven?'

'An assignation many would covet,' I said, referring to Dolores, gallant, pompous and wrong, for do not all women hate to hear of another's desirability?

'Thank you,' said Cora, and put down the telephone. She had taken the fool's gold of flattery for herself, as they will.

I spent the morning going through the notes of my current patients. Many of the babies had never been well. Glancing at the notes of Dolores Steel, I saw that her heart specialist had been for two years someone called Hardiman. It was Douglas, I was almost sure. This surprised me; I knew he had wanted to be an osteopath. I looked again, as the notes were unclear at this point, and decided, prompted more by interest in my own life than in his, to ask a colleague about this. I asked my assistant, who wears a single pearl in each dark brown ear, her biro in her stiff black hair, and who has never once been late, to ask John Payne to call me. In spite of his alarming name, he is a gentle man. I think he is as good a surgeon as I am, but the newspapers have not found him photogenic. He is a married man, twice; the blond issue of each marriage plays in two separate frames on his desk. The two latest children play in a silver frame behind glass; the former babies, now with children of their own, sit like propped sandbags in a folder of red leatherette. That may be his worst secret; John Payne is a blameless man.

'Lucas, what can I do you for?' He makes these jokes. At weekends he shoots pheasants. I imagine him, more at ease with the farmers, joking, a bit too red in the face, and a bit too blue in the joke. His wife would look well with a dog, both trained to pick up what another's skill has brought down.

I asked him about Douglas Hardiman.

'Published a paper no one liked, ahead of its time but dotty in its way, or dotty-sounding. He contended that the spine was a sort of allegory for the rest of the body. It was called "The Myth of Atlas", something like that. He was found a bit wanting by the big guns and he went into high dudgeon. Only to resurface in, ha ha, sort of low dungeon, you could say.'

'John? Go on.'

'He got a conshie fit if you can call it that and went off to work in the Queen's Service, if you know what I mean.'

He was not asking me if I knew what he meant, but I relied upon my foreignness to pretend I thought he was. 'What do you mean, John?'

'He got himself seconded to H.M. Prisons, and treated them all for their knocks and blows, stitched up their mailbags, that sort of thing.'

'Did he work on hearts after his break with bones?' John's puns were affecting me. No word in English is free of the body, often impolitic.

'Good one, Lucas. I think, d'you know, he did. Not like us, but I think he has made a study of congenital irregularities. A bit of a weirdo, though, very anti the knife and for the exercise of the heart.'

'That sounds like Douglas. I wonder, does falling in love exercise the heart?'

'Lucas, that isn't you trying to tell me something I ought to know, is it?'

'Thank you, John, I hope I didn't disturb you.'

'Pleasure all mine.'

Had Dolores spent two years in prison? It must be coincidence. After all, I take my car to be serviced in Wormwood Scrubs, but that does not mean the mechanics are taking metal files in to the inmates daily. That spoilt girl with her chocolate eyes could not have survived prison.

At a quarter past seven, I left my room and collected the small package of shopping and a bunch of flowers I had bought in the market. I had a gauzy swarm of painter's sorrow and a long spill containing five white anemones, wall-eyed, without the black centre of coloured anemones. The white flowers, like white oxen and white horses, looked like emblems of unfallen times. I took the lift down to the adult ward. As I passed the children's ward, I saw the family of the brown boy. I saw the crossed legs of the daughters. A nurse was giving the boy a drink. His parents observed him as though he might break, as though they saw the drink trace through him. An enormous bear in jogging clothes crowded his cot.

When I arrived at the bedside of Dolores Steel, Cora was already there. She was seated and her hair was full of rain. So, she had only just arrived. She cannot have been very enthusiastic about seeing her old friend.

'Good evening, Dolores, how are you feeling?'

She must have been feeling very much better because she turned to me with an expression, more a grimace, of what looked like strong antipathy. On her dainty features, which had the enamelled prettiness of a ballerina's, this looked like a rictus of photogenic, intense, forced pleasure, what a rapist may imagine he sees in the victim's eyes. She reached to her bedside table and took her spectacles, which she put on carefully, lifting the black tines of hair away from her ears. She continued to look at me; I felt grateful for her spectacles, as though they were eliminating the worst of her gaze. She said nothing at all, but picked up a brown ball from the counterpane and nipped it with her teeth. Then, with the concentration of one peeling layers from their fingernail, she removed the skin, with its silver pink lining, of what must be a lychee. She put the jellied fruit into her mouth.

'Hello, Lucas, I've brought Dolores some fruit as she doesn't eat much else. How are you? Have you had a busy day?' said Cora.

I liked her for her dull little question, and her wide open face. Dolores was cracking and sucking at the fruit with her fine fingers and huge eyes like a lemur. On a green hospital plate on the pale green bedcover a pile of shiny stones and spirals of husk was growing. Poor girl, her body was so slight, it hardly lifted the bedclothes.

'Aren't you the lucky one tonight, though?' came the voice of John Payne. He stood and rocked at the foot of Dolores's bed. 'Two gorgeous ladies,' he said. Had they been nurses, he might have said, 'What a lovely pair.' But he knew his game, and these girls would never be in his season. I introduced Cora to him. 'Who are the flowers for, Lucas?' he asked. To ask that was to know they must be for the invalid, and I handed the blank-faced windflowers to Dolores with as little grace as possible. It is not professional to give flowers to one's patients. A Sinhalese doctor had once given a bag of sweets to one of 'his' mothers and the nurses expected the baby to be striped, Tooting and Kandy. But John had made it impossible not to bunch the wraith in the bed. He was looking at her like a dog. There is an acrid type of woman, invariably thin, who whips men in. The men read in the malice and sourness of these narrow bitches some delectable painfulness, biting or scratching, I do not know. Dolores was looking at John with the same pointed antagonism she had directed at me. It was as though she disliked us on principle.

'They won't live,' she said to me of the flowers. They would not, now she had cursed them.

'I remember you love flowers, Dolores,' said Cora.

John took his eyes from black-haired Dolores and turned to Cora. This evening she was hiding inside a tent of loden cloth. Her very white neck and glowing face made the china witch in the bed look more deadly. Her eyes were patched about with colour and she wore boots which curled like mangoes at the toe. These were pink and red and silver, and at the front of each, as though they were small Greek boats, were eyes.

John looked at this Tyrolean scarecrow with boats for feet with pleasure, and I felt the air lose some of its charge. He introduced himself, and Cora herself, and then she said, to him and to Dolores, who had been rattling in her hand a handful of pits like a maraca, 'I must go now, do get well soon, Dolores, I'll come and see you again soon, goodbye Mr Payne.'

'I'll come down with you,' I said. I did not want to, on account of John Payne and what he would now think of my exercised heart, but I was tired of the black spell of Dolores's bed, and how otherwise would Cora find the car?

'Goodnight,' said John Payne, reassured to see the animals leaving, as God intended, two by two.

Cora had no parcels. It was a blue night without stars, cold. I opened the door on the passenger side to let her in and put my things at her feet. She fidgeted a little.

Only when we were moving along did she say, 'Your shopping leaked, I think.'

'What?' I was not concentrating, though I had been pleased to notice she did not hum or talk during the music from the car tape-machine.

'There is something on my seat, I think it is meat.' I had bought that morning three bulbs of fennel, some smoked eel and a horseradish root.

'What do you mean, Cora? Here, let's stop, it's a red light.'

I see viscera very frequently, but in the place where they belong, inside the body. In the light Cora's coat was brown, but her hands were a light red, marked with darker brown. Matted and textured like the coat of a drowned dog, and big and lolling, in her long fingers, was the long tongue of an animal.

She did not scream, but she took my evening paper from beside her feet and began to wrap up the tongue. The paper said, 'LITTLE AHMED STRUGGLES FOR LIFE'. There was a photograph of 'my' family, in their cardigans.

'Are you all right?' I asked. 'Would you like to get out? Do you feel sick?'

She made no reply. I feared an ululating female scene.

'What shall we do with the tongue?' I asked.

'Press it,' replied Cora, and I saw it in my mind like a juicy flower between the pages of a book. 'Shall we go? The light has changed.'

'Please don't tell Hal,' I said, 'he hates mess.'

'Hal hates mess, does he?' said Cora, collecting even now information about her loved one.

'I am sorry,' I said, after some time. We were approaching her house. 'I can't think what it is about.' I did not seem to be able to think at all.

On the doorstep of Cora's house, I waited for her to open the door. She was taking a long time. The basement light was on and the room appeared as usual to be awaiting at least Prospero. A thin animal, with white elbows, eight of them, was on the floor. It had two white eyes at its centre. They were moving up and down. I felt cold as though my blood had stopped reaching the edges of my body.

'Do you feel better?' asked a tall girl with pale blue velvet breasts and a long butcher's apron.

'Than what?' I felt well but very empty.

'You were sick,' said Cora, 'and you fainted. I'm lucky to be so big. I put you here.' We were in a white and blue room.

'*I'm* lucky,' I said. She gave me some tea. It was dark and sweet and reeked of rum. The room smelt of mast.

'If you feel better, would you like to start cooking? Hal's coming at half-past eight but he is always late.'

I replaced the visor of chilliness I keep about my face. I did not want to be told about my love by this fat girl.

When I had drunk the tea, I felt better and followed a noise of singing to where Cora was cooking. In a very big saucepan was boiling water. It was scummy, but smelt faintly of sausage-making day in my parents' shop. The tongue, I guessed.

'There was a note,' she said. 'It says "THEY CAN'T TALK". She looked interrogatively at me. I had no reply, and felt ashamed.

'What had you been going to make?' she asked brightly. She seemed to have taken my jacket off so all I needed to do before cooking was roll up my sleeves.

'Fennel fritters and eel with horseradish.'

'On you go, I shan't interfere,' said Cora. The kitchen was wallpapered with the jocular paper which was popular before everyone knew about ratatouille and holidays, when shops like my parents' proliferated. It repeated a design of flasks and wine bottles and yellow onions.

I am fond of unthinking regular activity. I like to chop and dip and slice. She left me to myself. I found the flour and eggs and ice. I even found some sour cream. I made my batter in a jug, and each fritter but the first came out like hot syrup spilt in ice, a frozen gold splash, lacy. I recollected my mother making these fritters, and I made, as she had made mine for me, Cora's copperplate initial in the smoking fat.

'Eat it while it's hot,' I said, and put salt on it for her. I put the other fritters to keep warm. She had the dazzled look of a child on a snowy morning and she bit it as though it were going to be very sweet. I was hungry.

'What did you make this afternoon?' I asked this girl. I could have been anywhere but here, with my peers, or with my hulking inferiors. I felt that I had sunk a degree or so off my dignity. I did not know how to put her away from me. Anyhow, in the end it would only be to pull her back into Hal's and my charmed circle.

'Cold chicken and ice-cream and wafers,' said Cora. And, God, hospital food to eat, I thought.

But she seemed to be busy in her kitchen, and not fussing. There is a type of English cooking which is loveless. It is a factual sequence of unattractive nourishment in which nothing is what it appears to be and everything causes atrabiliousness. It restores the dear dead days of rationing, I think. If Cora had prefaced her menu with tomato soup, she would have made a paradigm of this type of food. I am sure the Royal Family eat that food.

If I was not anticipating my supper with any pleasure, I was longing to see my darling. So it is odd that, when he arrived at nine o'clock, I felt edgy. That must be what women do, give you a cow's warm company, then kick you just as you settle to milk them.

Hal was untouched by rain and he spun like a man in a spotlight, throwing out his arms from the elbow and talking as fast as a jackpot. It was clear he knew Cora's house quite well.

'Hi, Lucas, long time no see, and how is it at the hospital then? In Gloria and Dick's room then, Cora? God, I'm hungry. I could eat an army.'

'Gloria and Dick?' I asked.

'They are the couple who live in the basement,' said Cora.

'Hence the sets and props and all that. They work at the Royal Opera,' said Hal.

'That shelf up there is all hat steamers,' said Cora, and she indicated a row of metal shapes, some like buckets, some like cones, and a small one like a pewter-coloured skull, about which I enquired.

'It's for smoothing out bald-pate wigs,' said Cora, 'so people's heads don't look worried from behind.'

'Do you like opera, Cora?' I do not usually listen to the answer to this question. Those who do are tedious and those who don't are ignorant and opinionated and tell jokes about inflated tenors and bouncing Toscas.

'More as I get older,' said Cora, and I liked her for not wanting me to think anything in particular of her. 'What,' she continued, 'would you like to drink?'

The three of us crossed to the room of Dick and Gloria. Cora had laid the table plainly. It was very white in that damascene room and the gypsophila hung above its vase as though it might at any point disappear, like gnats. She brought the crisp fritters and we dipped them into the horseradish. We dropped the eel into our throats.

'Sold this fantastic property out of town today. Pool, sauna, paddocks, the works, and a heated cellar for turtles too. For soup, you know. I mean, would you believe?' said Hal.

My parents had told me of pre-Revolutionary palaces with tanks below for turtles, but each generation is surprised again, and how touching he was in his discovery.

'Doesn't that come into *The Grand Babylon Hotel*?' asked Cora, and Hal scowled, then reached across the table and wiped his hand on the upper part of her breast.

'Best thing of all, fishy fingers,' he said. He did not realise, in his artless compliment, that I had been responsible for this part of the meal. The cold wine set fair in my head and I felt smug that I was able to feel a tactician's satisfaction when I saw him touch her in a way that suggested they were intimate. Cora left the table. Her face looked turned, as though she had tasted something bad. I imagined she was off to trail some watercress over the slabby chicken. It was fortunate I had brought so satisfying a first course.

'Getting on?' I could not resist asking Hal. I wanted to hurt myself before another could.

'Getting off,' he replied. I wondered how he liked this cosiness, which he had been at pains to avoid with me. It must be different with a woman.

I went to find Cora. She was wedging the now pale tongue into a tin. It was steaming and the room smelt of boiled socks, instead of herbs and butter as it had.

'I just had to nip out to peel it, and I nearly forgot,' she said. 'I hope this doesn't happen again.'

I was so soothed I had forgotten the early evening.

'Sit down, Lucas, or, even better, take this.' She gave me an oval pottery bowl. Upon it, its skin thin and brown as strudel, was the cold chicken. Half carved, in lines straight like harp strings, it sat in a pool of white and green. Between the flesh and the skin was a layer of this same marbling. Cora brought a bowl of green noodles and a dish of salad of those tomatoes shaped like the muzzle of a boxer dog. It smelt of fresh oranges and red wine and was drizzled with sugar.

She carved like a man, I could see that from what she had done already, but when it came to offering more, she asked Hal to carve. Not me, though I was senior, but Hal because he was her lover.

'Have you been to see . . . ' began Cora.

'Don't let her start, Lucas,' said Hal, and Cora, blushing, looked down. I, his not-lover, was often treated as the enemy, but where there was a girl we were linked against her. She was feeding us well; tonight was the sure fanfare to the overture of what I wanted. Why, when I should be feeling as though I were watching the champagne break on the prow of a ship of the line, did I feel equivocal? Was she not after all the right girl? It must be the tongue in the car. *Who* couldn't talk?

Hal was pulling at the legs of the bird, and he dug his spoon into its cavity like a sexton.

'Wake up, Lucas, she's not that bad,' said Hal, and he clicked his hand before my eyes, as shocking as a flashlight. 'Been sleeping badly?'

'I have, in point of fact,' I said. 'I think it must be the change of season.' The season is always changing, but I did not want to admit to having been alarmed by a lipstick scrawl, and I could hardly tell him and the girl I wanted to mate with him that I was undergoing a painful gestation until at last they married. It felt like that. I was pregnant with Hal's future.

Half of that future, or the nominal half, Cora, my zombie, took away our plates and returned with a fez of smoking, pale yellow sorbet. The smoke was the smoke of cold breath in the warm room. Inside this chilly cream were rimed cranberries. The wafers were of that sort which snap like unsafe ice.

I regarded my plate. Hal and Cora faced me through the flowers. I took a spoonful. Cranberries are celebrated in America, in malls and boulevards and marts. There are landscapes of them. Cranberry liquor in milk is a good head start for a life of hard drinking. They are a sour fruit, and sweet, and their colour heightens to the pink of monoxide-poisoned blood as they grow transparent in the pan. They jostle for closeness like snooker balls, but can never touch all over, as nothing spherical can, as our corpuscles even cannot. We are infinitely divisible. What can touch us, ever, all about? When I am host to this pointillist perception, I am nearing danger.

I was drunk. I kissed my future, he and she, goodbye, and drove home with the motor co-ordination of a medical man who is disobeying the law.

XI

'C ould we take a spin down to the docks?' asked Hal. His voice was not clear. He must be telephoning from one of the sites he was selling.

'Which ones, Hal, and when? I am committed every day after today for a week.' This was not true, but I had not heard nor seen him since the lamplit evening in the opera-room half a month before and was starting to crave him. Autumn was here, and the hospital was preparing itself for Christmas. It was dark early enough for me to *cinq à sept*, a Tertiusism, at four o'clock, straight after a long morning operation. I was getting lazy, often went to the same place.

John Payne was watching me for symptoms; my own feeling of expectancy about Cora and Hal may have looked to him like the preoccupation of love. He was friendly to me now, as though I alarmed him less. Dolores Steel had become well; this meant that she had reached a steady plateau of malice and sulk. The nurses were pleased to lose her and did not enjoy the bag of rambutans she left for them, like torn-off tigers' ears. I did not miss her, but I had dismissed any suspicion that she could have been in prison. Anne had been away, seeing her aunt Oppie in the Carse of Gowrie. The aunt soothed Anne. She farmed soft fruit and small potatoes and remembered the golden days of Sapphism with pleasure and sadness. She took her name from the rhyme which goes:

> Artifex and Opifex,
> Common are to either sex.

I did not know her proper name and had met her only once, for tea at the Stafford Hotel, where she had asked the maid to pour into a teapot the milk and sugar, to save effort later, exhibiting hereby both practicality and imagination and their direct opposites. She dressed in fawn, tan, buff, and her clothes were the shape, too, of envelopes, with a little deckling of lace at the lifted chin, and perhaps a pale mica window of blouse underneath. She did not accommodate the opinions of others, she did not see the need for it, with the result that people agreed with her, all save Anne, who was treated as heiress to this infallibility.

Hal replied to my direct telephonic questioning, rare for him. 'Today is great. Would the tank make it to Chatham?'

I was already planning, and replied, 'That would be perfect, just before the winter. I shall collect you . . . '

'Don't bother with that, I'll come to you right away.'

I had forgotten that I could not go inside his flat, and would have to wait outside in the car. I respected his containedness.

When he arrived, he looked pale to me, and there was no brightness in his face. I wanted this, but not until they were safely spliced, when he might have had demonstration of women's strength-sapping. The pretty birthmark on his lip was clear honey on the white face. For the first time, I saw a growth of beard, like splinters, on his chin and cheek. Even the soft hair looked less bright. It must be the absence of the sun.

'Car going all right?' he asked. He sounded nervous and bored.

'Job going all right?' I asked. I would not give him a bouquet for a bunch of stalks.

'As you see,' he said.

'Much of the car's working is internal too.' I could not stop myself.

'About that . . . ' he said. Like many people who will not ruminate, he was trapped into introspection in the passenger seat of a car.

'Yes, Hal.' I kept from my voice the breaking hope that he was going to blurt out that after all it was not marriage he wanted, but love, and that with me.

We were leaving London, making for Kent. For this day it would be nice to be away.

'I'm in love, Lucas,' he said. He spoke as though he were testing the words in his mouth. He spoke as though he were reading the words of another man. I realised how much it must cost him to tell me this, and was moved. There was no music in the car, and outside were the heavy brown fields of Hal's own country, the land of married men and regeneration of history less recently interrupted than my own. In some fields, spring corn was starting to show; it would be reaped, perhaps at the same time as Hal married, strong and straight. Englishman's bones would make terrible bread. It would not rise. Polish ones would cause the bread to rise like Jacob's ladder.

'Tell me, darling.'

He did not react to the endearment, which I had fed myself as a cachou.

'I love Cora.'

I was so relieved that I was almost pleased to hear him say he loved another, not myself. Now I would not even have to feign dislike to secure him on her hook. It was moving fast. I overtook a field of cars, my heart leaping. We were approaching the hop country, with its leaning staves like a struck camp.

'Do you want to marry her?'

'I'm not asking you. I'm telling you,' he said. 'And I've done the same to her.'

He made it sound like a single action, not the beginning of a changed life. But I did not care; they would be happy, then unhappy, and the weak world would give them their caging freedom, and there I would be, the keeper with the keys, waiting for Hal, at the door of his open marriage.

'Are you happy?'

'As a hatter,' said Hal.

'Why do you care for her?' I was pleased with this soapy phrase.

'She's beautiful, she's sweet, she'll be a wonderful mother, and she loves me.'

The grey air was full of unfallen rain and the horizon was thickening as we drove seaward.

'Children, Hal, so soon?' I was still unsure what I felt about this. When they split, would any child stay with Cora? Could I bear Hal's child not to live with me? I do not know many well children. Perhaps they are not so agreeable as sick ones. 'My blessing goes with you always,' I said. The inside of the car, its walnut and leather, were apposite for this conversation. I felt like a parent, a trustee.

My thoughts turned to money. Cora had none, according to

Anne. Hal's family were landed, I knew, but had they cash? I felt that it was immodest to speak of money so soon after we had disposed of the nature of Hal's love for his Cora, so I said, 'Would you like some music? Why not find something you care for? And take today as a holiday, Hal. It is the most important decision of your life and you deserve a quiet time.'

He was passive, seeming still a little tense, and he was cupping and uncupping his hands as though catching and releasing a stream of small birds.

He pushed into the machine what was already in it, not concentrating. The Commendatore was calling Don Giovanni to the feast. Through a fissure in the melody came the beat of unavoidable Hell. The voice was low and could not be refused. Giovanni tried his worldly charm, his excuses, circumstantial irrelevancies. But you cannot refuse a man of stone with a heart of stone. He just will not take no. I am afraid at this part of the opera.

The tape fell silent. There were two clicks. A voice, unsexed and didactically narrative, rather in my own manner, said, 'Lay open the chest cavity, or, in the case of a pig, the thoracic cavity, taking care not to tear the skin, since, in the case of most laboratory animals, re-use is possible . . . '

It continued. I recognised the words because I had written them, in a paper, designed for a general audience, on vivisection, which is necessary, or so I feel, for my research. I think it is fatuous to deny this; one of my several quarrels with the idiots' papers is their reporting of the question.

I pressed the button to eject this recording of my own words. I did not feel they were suited to this hymeneal day.

'What happened there?' asked Hal. He looked perkily interested, like a boy train-spotting.

'I know you aren't mad about opera so I added a little interest.' I am not good at jokes. This one changed nothing. 'I don't know, Hal, to be honest, perhaps I recorded *Don Giovanni* over my broadcast on Righting Animal Wrongs.' The voice was nothing like my own. My accent is very English.

'Maybe you did. Do you get a lot of weirdos barracking you? I never asked, but there's quite a bit in the papers at the moment about animals.'

This was untypically personal. Hal was asking me about my life.

I wondered whether to tell him of the red words on the windscreen and the loose tongue on the seat. I did not want to spoil his day. But thinking of these things did alarm me. I had read of attacks on laboratories, on farms, even on graves. Beneath a grey photograph of two cutely mismatched animals, a pussy and a rhino perhaps, with its lightweight headline as full of double meaning as that below the uddered girl some pages before, would come an article, incoherent and sometimes directly contradictory of yesterday's doctor-as-dragon-slayer article, describing the vile conditions and advanced tortures imposed upon animals. Inconsistent, but aphrodisiac to that sense of outrage which sells papers. I had seen facing-matter in those newspapers which came from two sets of premises. If people with those views met, they would not face each other save to fight. But the monster which buys and consumes these papers has not ideas but digestive juices, there to help it soften and digest neutral nutritious facts. I saved human lives, was ridiculously fêted for this, but I had also and indirectly been the cause of the death of many animals. Had someone made this link? If so, why were chops and steaks and sides not being burnt like books on street corners, huge barbecues of dissent? Why was I being singled out? As well put rattlesnakes in the boots of one single leather-wearer. That, of course, would be barbarous to the rattlesnakes.

It is abstraction which sets us over the animals. We live in the more than here and now, our memories hold more than modified and relearnt reflexes. Or so I feel, and must feel so that I do not go mad in my work, at least not until God, our great abstraction, bends down into my cage in his white coat and clips to me wires to still me as he makes ready to investigate my heart.

It was Hal's day and he must be treated as a bridegroom.

We parked the car outside the main gate of the dockyard, and set off first for lunch. I would have made an autumn picnic if I had had more notice, with some game perhaps, but now we had to go to a pub. I did not much feel like meat. The bar was full of seaside references. There were pictures made of stuck-down shells and net bags of glass floats. We ate two fishermen's platters. 'I wouldn't mind a "Sailor's Plate",' said Hal, and I liked him for noticing the roundabout genteel language, and mocking it. His face wore almost a leer; I thought that the interrupted Giovanni must have upset him more than he would admit. I hoped the lunch would not be the main part of our day wasted, inside instead of out in the last of the light. My temples felt as though they were nearing each other, as we sat in the gloomy bar. The dartboard was the right breast of an enormous mermaid, cut from polystyrene. What we ate was a drenched palette of pink shrimps and a squeeze of oily yellow. You could imagine these assemblages being made as therapy by old sailors, six crescent squeezes of pink, a puddle of red, a wormcast of yellow, the lettuce-green rag and that's two more done. We drank Guinness and Hal looked about him with that touching undimmed boy's interest.

As the day was growing cold, we walked back to the yard without lingering. What I loved best about Chatham after the *Victory*'s dock was the terrace of sailors' houses behind the Admiral's House which stood alone looking out to the estuary. This terrace was small and each house built for a midshipman, his wife and their family; even the stove-in greenhouses had finials. The squint washing-line poles were cast iron and handsome as weathercocks. The back gardens were ragged now, but they must once have given the homelocked sailors a taste of the earth, potatoes and leeks and neeps after all those captain's biscuits and dried fish like stiff vests. Each of the little houses had its fanlight, small and pretty, the houses smiling behind them, each with its proper approach, a gate, a path, and a knocker. The modest fans gave a touch of grace. In the gardens of a few, Michaelmas daisies, tenacious as wire, were not yet subdued by weeds. Late butterflies took in the last sun on sparse buddleia.

We progressed, each knowing perhaps that we were unlikely to return together without Cora for some time to the same places we always enjoyed, in the same order. Hal was not speaking much, but he looked about him all the time. We lifted up our heads to look at the grey webbed timbers of the great dock which had seen its last ship. I knew Hal's family had ties with the navy and I wondered if he felt that British sense of insular romance when he watched the sea. I could see only one ship and it looked like a square rock, far out. As we turned back from the sea, I asked Hal if he would like to go in to some of the buildings. At first we just looked round corners into high stores. Carved at the back doors of what looked like warehouses were initials and drawings and some dates. The accomplishment of the lettering suggested that there had been a time when things were lovelier, more orderly and more careful. I thought of the sailors queuing for their guns and carving deep into the stone, standing with their seven-creased white legs, waiting to embark. I felt terrific sentimental lust. I wanted Hal because he was a boy setting out alone. I was sure other Hals must have carved that same name, digging with a marlinspike into the lee wall of the store, and I wanted to have their closeness with each other, with Hal. He made me feel landlocked by my Polishness. I was awash with self pity, an island in it. The feeling was not unpleasant. The cold wind, the seagulls, the dipping cranes and bare flagpole combined to make me feel pity for myself, no longer daring, young, combatant. The saltness of my face was for my youth, lost in effort, and Hal's youth, to which we were saying farewell today.

I pushed against a door in a high building and it gave, into a hall of light, the size of a pasture. At first, I could see nothing but white, as though I were looking up on to snow. We were in a sail loft. All colour there was clear. The colours were the unobscured tints of heraldry, intensified by the white, as are the clothes of skiers. I could see no one, though I heard singing. I started to mount the ladder which led up to the highest rafter where the head of the vastest sail was made fast. These sails, though empty of wind, were hanging smoothly still; at their widest, they settled into glaciers of folds. I signed to Hal to come up, but he did not. I followed the singing, and turned a corner behind a swag of sail. I felt as though I were going backstage. A row of trestle tables receded from me, and the backstage impression grew. Six old women were bent over six sewing machines. A wireless played. The women were humming; the song was about love and rose gardens. I wondered whether they were the wives or widows of sailors. Over the table of each woman was spread her work. They were sewing flags, or rather pennants and ensigns, for these were rare work. One woman was fixing wings to a red dragon, another finishing the golden dots on the withers of a smiling pard. The hair of the old women and their spectacles were the only patches of half tone in the room. They might have been the imprisoned daughters of a king, stitching, stitching, stitching, in a fairy story. The black and gold machines purred. I was sorry Hal had not seen this.

'Seen a ghost, dear?' asked an old woman with pink hair. She had the voice of a parrot, among these parrot colours.

'Good afternoon. No, I'm sorry, I am lost and I was enchanted with what I saw when I came in here.'

The old women set up that ribald cackle you will hear them exchange after confidences. They were refuting what they took as a compliment to themselves. I think they were suspicious of me with my posh accent and my long overcoat. I was not like an officer, but I spoke like one. My patronage was not naval, jocose. I was foreign. They did not know how foreign.

A woman, her puff of hair mauve, who was sewing a spiky red lion passant gardant on to a yellow flag, said, 'Turn up the radio, June, dear.'

She had not seen me. It was time for me to go. We had no meeting ground. I wanted to give them all tea, to buy them all hats, to flatter them till they bridled. I wanted to rest their hands and legs and see them sitting in chairs with their feet out and their stockings down eating ices from tubs with little spades. I wanted to kiss them and cuddle them and show them a good time. I wanted them to be as sloppy as they liked, to leave the Christmas Club, to stop washing the front hall, to let their husbands go hang, to stop saving vouchers. I wanted to take off their glasses and give them back their eyes and deck them out, yellow and red and blue and green, and shower them with gold.

They wanted me to go away.

When I found Hal, he looked warmer and quite easy. His eyes were clear and he seemed in higher spirits. Darkness had come, and the cranes were lit, red and green, port and starboard. There were not many lights in the place, two in the Admiral's House like calm eyes, and the high single light of the sail loft, not too big a window because sunshine would bleach colour from the flags, before the wind and sun might have them.

'Did you find something nice?' I asked Hal.

'I found a place where they make ropes,' he said. 'I saw one being made. It was a mile long. It had a steel heart. It holds things together and can never break.'

'Nothing cannot break,' I said, and minded having said it all the way back to London.

XII

I f anything, my having constrained Anne to be on my side had made us closer. It takes a good friend to lay down principles for your sake. I had, after all, blackmailed her. She was quite clever enough to agree under pressure and then to work in a subtle way to undermine Hal and Cora. I wondered how she would take the engagement, now it was a fact.

After the day at Chatham, I asked her to come and see me. The trees were almost empty and I had seen Hal and Cora together on several occasions. What impressed me in Cora was her meekness, her desire to please. She had begun to dress in a womanly way, as though she might have a unicorn on a lead outside. She listened charmingly to Hal when he spoke. I had told him after lunch one day that I would help financially with the wedding. He looked so surprised I was touched. Surely it must have crossed his mind, no matter how lapped in love he was? It made me diffident about confiding in him the main point of our meeting. I was again giving him lunch in Scott's, to salute my own sense of symmetry. All that autumn I was making festivals of this nature, disengaging myself from the first phase of our love. I spoke quietly, to save Hal's dignity, and said, 'And, Hal, I'd like to get you a wedding present.'

'Just not mats,' he said.

'I thought a house. Where would be up to you, but my one proviso is that it is not a poky bargain with views to a kill. And if you have children, that is, when you have children, there is a sum settled on them. Up to the limit of gift tax, I have done the same for you.'

I did not like couching it in these grey terms. Money is just a token of other things after all and they could buy for themselves with all this a ton of ortolans or one fine emerald or an education for ten sons. My money was the product of work and I wanted it to be spent in play. I had my father and mother's shop money, I had magnified it with my diligence and I would have no children. I wanted to buy with it love for me and for the generations to come an insulated future.

'That is good news,' he said. 'I'd been wondering about where we'd live. The thing is, I've come to see everything as a good investment. That is big of you Lucas,' he said, looking straight at me like a man who is appreciative. 'I am very appreciative. Let me give you lunch.'

I was touched. Did he remember our first time here? I saw his face. Only recently had it begun to age at all. The blossom colouring was settling down and his thin body was filling. I did not very much like his tie. It was narrow and black and shone like a fish.

'D'you think he'll be kind to her?' asked Anne, later, in my upstairs room; a painted man in pantaloons played his lute close by.

'For a time.'

'That shows more knowledge of the beast than you've ever had, or do you mean if he is too kind for too long you'll put a stop to it?'

We were pushing between us a tray of matzos and cheese. Hal had told me of an uncle of his who had so hated Jews he kept a tin of matzos in the front hall to discourage any Hassid who might be peering through his letterbox. I am fond of the testimonial on the packet. I like Anne to see that I am an aristocrat too, one of the chosen race, and, moreover, not careless as her lot are but careful, so careful we can tidy seas, half to one side, half to the other. Anne wore some leather with the grey glow of caviar. I do not like women dressed like this.

'What a staggering ensemble, Anne, darling,' I said in my Tertius voice, and as I said it I felt found out.

'Revolting, I know, but I'm in a little fix, really,' she said. She liked fixes. They filled her time and her erupted heart.

'Tell on, dear,' I said, hating Tertius as I used the phrase.

'I've had rather a delivery recently, you see, because my poor fur man is ill, or not him at least, but someone must keep the wolf from the door.' She looked shy and lit a cigarette.

'His name is Mr Virtue, I don't know what his parents' name was, and he lives in a house about half the size of this room.

'It is his child, you see. The papers have organised for the child to go and get done in hospital in America and they've forgotten travel and accommodation, never mind Mama and Papa and three sisters.'

He was, who would have doubted it, a Polish Jew. The child was ill. The story came out.

'What do you mean, done?' I asked.

'Oh Lucas, you know how I am, I never know real things, but it's not your sort of stuff or I'd simply have put the boy your way.'

'I'm delighted you say that. What is up with him? I am surprised it can't be dealt with in this country.'

'He got burnt.'

'Burnt?'

'He came into the workroom and they were steaming a female coat.' She could not eradicate details like this; she would have been a fine identifier of corpses, recollecting the colour of their eyeshadow. 'The heat is to make the fibres lie, and he got burnt. The papers don't want to say how he got burnt, but they got committed to him when they saw his little melted face, and so I'm doing a big order quick so Mrs Virtue can go with the boy. But we've got to keep it quiet or I would just hand over the money, without question. I have known Mr Virtue since Mordred introduced us and the child is a sweet boy. Now he is bald and his limbs are held akimbo by his shrunk skin. So that's why I'm dressed as a Hitler Maiden.'

My best friend said that to me. I was pleased that she was quite free from fear as she said it. I let the sentence lie, and be buried, with many others. I wished to leave its grave unmarked.

'The thing is, the papers started to make a fuss about him before they realised what his father did. A reporter saw him at his weekly physiotherapy place and took along a photographer on spec the next week. It was all perfect bleeding heart stuff and Mrs Virtue hardly speaks English so they didn't gather why the child was in such an awful way. Once they found out, it was too late, but they are desperate at the paper to keep it dark about Mr Virtue being a furrier. They show those girls with their wobbly fronts in marabou scanties but they can't come clean about the skin trade. Animals are big circulation, and so are tragic tinies. The paper didn't mean for it to become such a big thing but when people saw the picture of the child with his lovely eyes looking out of a squashed bag of face, they kept on sending in money, as though they had to pay for their unburnt children, and the paper has discovered a man who mends faces and bodies. Not just a wrinkle smoother, but a man who repairs people after wars and spillages and secret fallout. What I can't bear is the thought of people getting mended just to get broken again. At least with a child, there's some hope of a real life to follow. But I can't think where they will take the skin from. It's so patchy, the notion that they will tidy his face and arms by plundering his legs and back; can't things be made good without spoiling other things?'

'There is some talk of artificial skin, but it could not grow with a child. Surgeons of the interior can be a little snobbish about this type of thing. But disfigurement is a wound as severe as any other.' I said I was chilly on home ground.

'Cora is scarred,' said Anne.

'Anne, what do you mean and how do you know?' I did not like the idea of Hal touching a scarred person. Yet I was pleased, for any imperfection would at length divide them. Hal hates mess, as I said.

'Oh, Lucas, it is nothing terrible. I should not mention it at the same time as the poor Virtue child. I only glimpsed it when I took her shopping with you. Her chest is scarred, as though a string of small pearls had slipped down between her breasts under the skin and stuck there. It is raised. It makes your fingers want to touch it, like scabs.'

'Not appealing.'

'Not unappealing.' She broke a biscuit with one hand, flat, as though to do so were a skill. It was like watching a woman throw a ball like a man. 'This room, Lucas, it's not finished, is it?'

'That's the point, in a way. I don't know that I ever want it to be so. I like it to change and shift. When they come and paint a new clown or a tub of bay or a far away tempietto I am refreshed. It's a bit like a family, but without mess.'

'There is no family without mess.'

'You say that. The English upper class is infatuated with its own sense of cousinage which in the end ties down the individual like Gulliver. And I suppose because your own close family has been nothing but mess.' It is because I am a stranger that I can speak the truth.

'And thank you for those few kind words.' I cannot bear the way they glove their grief in little jokes. Instead of being direct she was 'guying', a great conspiracy word of the inhibited British, the reaction of someone repressed and humble, a landlady perhaps or an undertaker. 'Thank you, I'm sure,' she said, on firm ground, being a housekeeper, settling her feathers, taking no more offence than was commensurate with her position.

'Tell me about Mr Virtue,' I said. 'And why not have a plum?' I pushed the bowl of blue fruit to her. They were quetsches, the kind which cleave neatly under the teeth, not those sweet English bolls of wetness, the colour of their faces.

'The Virtue family live at the Elephant and Castle. Every day Mr Virtue goes to his shop in an alley off a mews behind Bond Street. Some of his ladies he visits at their houses. The reason why I've got this rather awful stuff from him is honour. The sort of thing he makes for me takes ages and he had these in stock for what he calls passing trade, the people who go and buy Rolls Royces for cash and sneak away to Spain one day just before the knock at the door. But he would not accept a loan because of any scandal. I like him because he loves what he does and he tells you about it in detail. I could listen to a mortician describe his trade as long as it was in sufficient detail.'

'Some would say that is exactly what Mr Virtue is.'

'I don't think about that.' The list of what Anne did not think about included it seemed to me almost everything which actually preoccupied her. This is another trait they have. I do not know whether I admire it. I envy it.

'Did you have a good time with Oppie?'

'Very. She thinks she has bred a new strain of yellow raspberry and wants to call it Winaretta. But she does not live in the past. She has plenty of young friends. What they like is her bossy ways. She seems to have all the experience without telling you about it or forcing it on you. It seems to share out infinitely like the loaves and the fishes. We went fishing too, out at sea. No herring came, because we women were on the boat. You can be sure if we had hit a shoal it would have been because we were on the boat too. One night we did plash-netting at the seashore and got very wet and caught a lot of flatties and weed.'

'Flatties?'

'Skate, plaice, those ones with their eyes in the back of their head and their mouths like a face against a window. The ones with bones down the edge. If you leave out a night-line for them you can come in the morning and find three one inside the other like Jiffy bags.'

'Where should I get a house for Hal and Cora?'

She faced me, blue eyes in her shocked plain face. 'Do you really want it to fail immediately?'

'I want them to have a decent start. A house will go some way towards providing that,' I said.

'If you have to, can't you at any rate allow Cora to think that Hal has bought the house?'

'I had intended that, yes.'

'And then she can find out later?'

'Or not.'

'Short of buying the house next door, I can't see what more killing thing you could do.'

'Forget, Anne, that I am I. Think of me as a bank.'

'Hal does,' she said.

'That is beneath you.' I will not have these remarks tearing into my life. Anne suffers from prudishness about money, where Hal is refreshingly straightforward.

'Lucas, get them a nice big house with lots of room for babies and a garden so Cora can land on something soft when she jumps.' All promotion of Hal and Cora's love affair to the outside world, Anne liked to show me what she imagined were her real feelings about it. I think she must have been suffering from jealousy of Cora, about to begin married life with beautiful, and not dead, Hal.

'Are you at *all* pleased, Anne?'

'I am pleased that you have what you want. I don't love many people, but I do you and it is selfish I suppose. If you wanted human liver for breakfast, I think I would bodysnatch for you. Of course my conscience jabs me sometimes and I wonder where it can all end, but this is what you think you want now and I cannot, not being God, see what it is you really want. If I could see that, I would be very pleased to miss out this step. But as you are determined upon it I am now going to forget my reservations and hurl myself into wedding preparations as though Cora were my daughter.'

'Not Hal your son?'

'You may award yourself that privilege. Have you met the Darbo parents? It is a funny name is it not? Sounds Hungarian or pretend, a sort of mistranscription of something grand. The kind of thing an actor might give himself once he's mastered' – she made appropriate gestures – 'the plum in the mouth.' She was sorting plumstones into pairs. She had two, and the lone stone which she pulled from her mouth, point first. Fine, for a rich man.

'I've not met them. They have land.'

'So does Mr Virtue, so do I. There's land and land. I prefer the starry sky. I shall be very interested.'

'Cora's only real insistence about the wedding is that it be soon, and Hal wants that too. It is hardly as though gratification of desire were the motive for this, but I am of course of the same mind,' I said.

'Lovely,' said Anne. 'The sooner the better.' She appeared enthusiastic for the first time that evening. 'When shall it be?'

'December the sixth, in just over a month.'

As we sat, the pale faces of the painted figures glowed in the deepening darkness. When Anne left, I felt as tired and as satisfied as a man who has taken hard exercise and eaten a dish of meats. I felt like a ringmaster who has induced the lions to form a circle and dance sedately bearing in their teeth a silk ribbon with no beginning and no end. I sat until the room was dark.

CORA

XIII

I was looking for a man. Until I saw Lucas Salik at Anne Cowdenbeath's house in autumn, standing taller than anyone in the room and looking as clean as mint, I had been smug about love at first sight. Like burglary, though, it must be something which comes to you at last. Perhaps I had been too old too young and had this shock coming to me to teach me that all my monkey tricks were no good at a real tea party. I knew it was love because it was painful and the pain was about my heart. Even as I put my head in the noose and jumped and danced, I knew too that I was swinging not only for this man but for the chance of a father. Not just because of his age, but because of the purity about him and the air of difficultness, I became aware that I was going to lose time to this person. When he looked at me, I saw that he recognised something, too, as though a current of just stirring air were moving blue paper to orange flame. I was leaning against a mirror, my back to it, and a short man was printing out words from his mouth to my bosom. He chopped with his hands between sentences and even his eyelids had hair. I watched Lucas Salik, whom I recognised in fact as well as with my heart, since I had read articles about him and knew that he was a friend of Anne's. I saw him leave the room and felt lustreless immediately. In the end the Greek left and I learnt that love in its early stages is self-reflexive and to do with vanity. Had Lucas Salik remained in the room, I would have been surrounded by men. His presence made me feel royal. His absence left me wretched. The only reason I stayed at the party was that Johnny returned to speak to me and I can never shake him off.

If I could ever have shaken him off I would not be in this muddle, I suppose. What I minded about the whole thing was the time limit.

I have always kept procrastination as a solution; if you conceal the worry, something will turn up. I was almost certain that it is justifiable and normal to treat time like this; it was only once you were old that time was measurable. As soon as I could, after my orderly childhood, I had concentrated on squandering time, spending it on anyone, purposely not acquiring a profession, absolutely not cultivating my own garden.

Johnny was stupider than I, and for a time I idealised him for it. I felt it made him more moral, since he had only one view of things. I allied this in my imagination with his breeding, to compose a *beau idéal*, the kind of young man who has won wars. I ignored shortcomings in Johnny because I thought I could see that they were streamlinings. Who needed all these extra apprehensions and desires? They had done nothing for me but get me into terrible trouble. I had now managed to do exactly this. I had got into trouble and Johnny was the father of the growing gun-butter inside me. Another soul for England. Of course, I could not tell him, or he might do the decent thing and we would be imprisoned with each other on his acres with our child. I wondered, would it keep its fish's tail? Johnny was like a fish or a half-human being specially adapted for underwater life, pale, pupil-less, gilled. He swam well and his rather beautiful voice uttered phrases as round and empty as bubbles. The words he used were round but empty, as though he read mostly the magazines you find in aeroplanes. He had mastered the stirring potential of cliché. This is not to say that his own feelings were not deep; they were, but beneath them lay things deeper into which it would be perilous to enquire, great invertebrate squids of gloom and voracious pessimism. But when I met him, I saw, romanced by his gold hair and his lineage, buried treasure; not the gold-digger's ducats, as you might imagine, but unpolished jewels and fallow pearls. I thought I could free him into light and air, forgetting or, worse, ignoring that a sea creature cannot live outside its element. And now, through my own stubborn will, writing a fiction with my own days, I had managed to do the most undreamlike and incontrovertible thing imaginable. I must find a father for the child, and one who will never show up poor Johnny, who must not be touched by such things. Best of all would be a father who would not realise that the child was not his own, a blond and slim man, like Johnny himself.

I did not tell Johnny. This particular deception is a form of theft, but I was saving myself. He would find the sea-woman he deserved and I would try to teach my child to walk on its feet without a pain like knives shooting up its legs. I do not remember what Johnny talked to me about that evening at Anne Cowdenbeath's; in order not to rush at him with the truth, I was looking at small specific things about the room – a painting, a small square of serge green, glowing from it a single canary with legs like twigs. A girl stood before it lighting a cigarette, the sharp flame showing her profile which was as formal as though it had been bent from wire, and the profile inclined to it, that of her husband, the face of a man who has lived outside and among animals. Most of the people were older than I was and I could see girls in their thirties talking reluctantly to each other and smiling as though for a flash camera at men. They had begun to see into the fire. On an adjustable piano stool lay a white cat, small and long-haired. It appeared to have no bones but it flexed its claws as though admiring them from time to time. Both its upper and lower whiskers were abundant and they turned away from each other so that the cat, which in fact had no expression, was apparently frowning like a stylised Chinese warrior. On the piano beside it lay a can of chocolate sardines. Groups of three people would break and re-form regularly, as though that number only could sustain the preliminaries of conversation. A girl who looked like Tobias's angel talked loudly without stopping. The man whose marriage she was remodelling looked tired and attractive and was smiling with snail eyes at a girl whose hair was the green and yellow formal shape of a large pineapple. The room smelt of white flowers. My height gave me to see why. Circlets of asbestos impregnated with scented oil rested upon each light bulb. I could also see the circles of baldness starting on men's crowns. I felt slightly faint, whether from hunger or pregnancy I did not know. I imagined all the bow-ties in the room taking flight like a flock of butterflies. On whom would they really alight? Would they flit from husband straight to wife? I suspect people not of more fidelity than they practise, but of more contentment than they profess. Of course, there were in the room people who were not married and people who would never marry, and those male couples who were most married of all.

I knew that Tertius was a homosexual. He did not have to tell me so. Perhaps if I had stayed at university, I would have known more about this.

Tertius made sure that I knew about him – not, I think, because he was wary of my falling for him, but because he liked to talk about it. I suspected he was miffed by the legality bestowed upon his special taste since his younger days, the thrill of alluding to them being tempered by it. He touched upon his habits frequently in speech like a blown old beauty revealing her share certificates. Though I guessed that Tertius had not ever been pretty, he was forceful, and still many of his visitors were handsome. He had a visitor once a week who must have been in the army with him, I think. They shouted a lot when they were together. I liked cleaning Tertius's chambers. Albany was a surprise to me; I had dreamed of London like this. It was orderly and safe and something interesting was always happening; in streets this may pass unnoticed. In Albany it is shared, collegiate. Albany felt like a university attended by a very superior selection of ghosts, just such clubbable, entertaining and personable intellectuals as I should distrust because they are the jujubes in the shop window, and I outside, staring in, like poor Keats. But I prefer association to participation, it favours quick changes.

As the taller and darker figure of Lucas Salik returned to me, so the slighter, fairer figure departed, with the balanced and opposing movement of funicular cars. What had Johnny been saying? I would have liked to think his departure linked to some fight over me, which Lucas had won, but I suspected it was to do more with his recognising Lucas and fearing that he would be shown up by him. I had no idea what Lucas Salik's personal life was; it was ridiculous to think I could pertain to it in any lasting way. Anyway he was not blond and I had, very soon, to be married to a father for my fair and growing baby.

I would not allow myself to have a fatherless child. I would not do it; I am not independent in that way. As to any other future for the child, adoption or death, I could not do it for the ghosts I would let into my life.

I knew that I had a very short time in which to seduce Lucas Salik. I would then be able to contemplate what had happened for the rest of my life. It would be my last freedom. The only way I knew to do this was by making it clear that I could easily be had.

The sad thing was, I wished to be for him a nun, a virgin, a daughter, but the only way I could be sure to make him swiftly mine, and then almost certainly lose him, was to speak to him like none of these, but like a slut. At Stone, there had been talk about him, but none of it personal, as though everyone there knew him too well to ask questions.

When he said to me, 'Good evening,' I was delighted by the restraint of his manner. It suggested the discipline of works and days which I admire and cannot reproduce. I wished I were not dressed in trash, but quiet as a nun, so he could see me as no one has, calm and not trying. Instead, I behaved like a tramp, showing all the cards at once, drawing attention to my snaky shoes, accosting him with sex.

We introduced ourselves. He seemed, which pleased me, to have asked about me already, since he reacted not at all when told my name. Most people remark upon a name, any name; not to is to acknowledge an uninterest so complete as to be rude. In my life, I have thought up charming reactions for a dishonourable roll of silly names. When I called him by his name, I liked its taste. All the time, I was just liking him more and more and not very much liking behaving like Salome. He seemed at least to be scrutinising my body. I stared at him and what I saw made me want to drown. I felt as though I were growing younger, cleaner, further from my husk which was saying ugly and provocative things. I must stop myself before I did in fact insult this tall gentle man from whom I wanted only love. I turned the talk to him with an audible shift of clumsiness, and there passed one of those conversations which always cause regret later. It was pretentious and consequential. Most often, I have these conversations with men or women on whose abstruse and well-tilled field I have been trespassing; they gracefully conceal their surprise that I should need to inform them about what they know best. I flounder, my tongue thickens, and I feel the disuse of my brain like a cloth turban worn inside the head. If only someone would take it out, wash it, iron it, and embroider order and variety upon it.

At last, it seemed to work, and, stultified by my conversation perhaps, he suggested that we go to his house. He would think I was trash, but perhaps in the anonymous night I would be able to smuggle into his ear the contraband emotion I was carrying, growing at the same time as the – unrelated – child.

What I felt was not what I had felt for anyone else, but then, I was very young. Two things, I think, made it so monstrous in scale. I had given myself so little time, by conceiving this child, to be simply myself with one other. And then there was his age, and, allied to that, his publicness and profession. I wanted the touch and understanding of this doctor-saint. I did not know of any other coin but the ready one with which to buy his touch. He was also beautiful; from my childhood, I had admired height and darkness and the look of suffering. There had been adults, even when I was four or five, whom I would wheedle into pushing me on the swing, or taking me to catch minnows; what had been between us was frail, flirtatious, unbegun, diffuse, without dirt. This man was the conclusion of those handsome decent men pushing me in the rust-scented swing park or carrying my net and jamjar by the water.

He drove me to his flat. A sentence with little promise but of seediness. But I had to read something in the car not to shake, and the streetlights seemed like banners put on just for us. The traffic lights scribbled at the car windows. I felt we were touching, because we were in the same enclosed space. Air which touched his hair was touching me also. As we drove by the side of the canal the turning trees, under the street, were in gold leaf.

Once inside the house-sized flat, it was easy to behave like a hussy. I felt as though I had come off stage. He, in his own rooms, grew. Each piece of furniture and painting seemed placed to frame his beauty. There was no trace of a woman. I knew he had no wife. I must see his bedroom. I wanted to lick his mirror, to crawl over his sheets, to eat his clothes.

I was hungry.

He sent me into his spare bedroom to put on the clothes he gave me. The room was tall and striped with white on white, the pelmet hung with grey tassels, and the curtains looped over grey hooks. It was like a tent before Agincourt, not that of Prince Hal but of the Dauphin. There was a sterility to the room, no signs of recreation, not so much as a tennis ball. I opened a drawer but it made a noise and I did not want him to know I picked and pried. Men do not do this prurient investigating, or, if they do, not where you wish them to. If you put all your ribbon and gauze underpinnings in a drawer and scent it with boxes of creamy soap and a scatter of photographs, they will not look. What they will find is the blistered pan and the grey-footed stockings, the things their mothers have taught them to fear. In the drawer of Lucas Salik's spare bedroom, I found a square of unshiny grey paper cut to fit the drawer and, at the back of that drawer, beneath the paper, a box of razorblades, which I left. To carry that as a memento of my great love would be not only uncomfortable but misleading. Most of my friends would buy those razorblades in boxes only for chopping up lines of drugs. I wanted to watch him shave, but I knew nothing so intimate would pass between us. I was here for the least close intimacy convention permits, loveless sex, the lovelessness not unilateral. I undressed, regretting my scar as I do perhaps more often than I do anything else, and then in the same phrase of thought telling myself I am lucky it is just that, and put on the clothes he had given me. I smelt them before I put them on, lavender and mothballs, and went out to find him. Tears waited behind my face.

He was not in the drawing-room, so I looked for a book, remembering not to choose it simply to match my clothes like a woman in Firbank. The danger then is to look for a book which you think will impress. In the end, I took a book to hold, that being really all that I needed. I held it and I regarded it and I do not know anything about it, now, years later.

Our conversation, when he arrived back with the sort of food it is easier to eat outside, I attempted to keep reasonable, unprecocious and also completely open to the fact that we were about to do something without consequences. I was sorry that he extracted my near university career from me; men prefer to have flings with girls who won't think, and Greats are incontrovertibly thoughtful.

'Cora, let me give you some champagne and I'll drive you home.'

Thank goodness he was beginning to behave like the wolf at the door. The shadows around his eyes were the colour of mushrooms. He did not sit up, but along, making of his whole length a lap. His mouth was pink, red blood seen through white skin. I was familiar with the business about driving back. Would we engage in the inevitable combat at his elegant house or at my harem, with washing over the bath and Dick and Gloria shrieking? I hoped it would be here; then I would be able to remember the entire occasion, without having to relocate it afterwards in my memory.

In his kitchen I opened the fridge. I do it automatically, like reading letters. I was too excited really to concentrate. I wanted to keep all my observation for later. The cold air from the refrigerator and its hum restored to me some calm. I took a glass the shape of a sconce and returned to him. He put his own glass and mine upon the floor and poured lackadaisically and incidentally, a bronze man in a fountain. He did not look either at the tilted bottle foaming into the deep narrow glass or at my face. Could he be nervous?

I spoke gently to him. Perhaps he liked the illusion of chastity in his girls and I had gone too far beforehand. I sipped and slipped out sweet words.

We were obviously to do it at my house. I could understand that. Why should he sully his own? It was a long drive, but fast, and I felt pleased with the certainty I had that his trap was closing round me, that soon I should be nothing but a thing in his clutches. I felt like the fox, who, we are told, having enjoyed the chase, gives in to the teeth and the rending. I had not believed that the fox feels like this before, had even been to meetings with Angel and Dolores, but now I was keen to have my mask and my brush cut from me.

'Goodnight,' said Lucas Salik on my doorstep. 'Why not give me my clothes when next we meet?'

I watched him till I could not see him any more and then I watched where he had been. It was six hours since I had first seen him. It was nearly eight months till my child was due to be born.

XIV

When he telephoned me, I was not expecting to speak to him. I was thinking of him, but I had not prepared my voice for contact with his. I did not fear that he would fall short of the perfection with which I had endowed him, but I knew, as time passed, that I would grow fatter and slower and that I should have to hide from him. None the less, loving him had made me perform all actions with care and conscientiously, as though he were watching me from a star above. I knew nothing of his daily life, so I could not imagine him locking up his house or greeting his colleagues or pulling off the surgical gloves. I could imagine him only in the most fanciful and unreal way. I allowed myself to picture him taking me from all the muddle and worry, not in his already improbable car, but on a caparisoned horse or in a boat with wide sails. I let myself do this partly to fill the dreaming my body was dictating to my mind. Perhaps other mothers dream of the child. Will he have the father's hair, will he be a doctor? There was at the moment only one doctor for me, and only one healer.

When the telephone rang, I thought it might be Johnny. I could no longer remember how the child was conceived, but I feared he might wish to remind me. How do fish reproduce? Isn't it all quite vague and haphazard and impersonal? Had I perhaps left a sac of eggs behind a plant in a restaurant, and he absently slipped past it on his way to somewhere quite else? It was astonishing that a child could be the product of such a nothing. Most of all, it was sad, for human children should not be conceived thus, and I needed a father for the baby, about whom to think as the foetus grew, so that the child would receive not only my jolting worries but a nourishing flow of thoughts about the man who would shelter it. At the moment, the child was being fed an indigestible diet of wild dreams and dreary panic. It would be wicked to deprive the child of Johnny, at this rate. Was it anyway wicked?

When Lucas Salik asked me to dine with him, it was as though I had stopped falling through bottomless air to nowhere, unsupported, my ballast my baby. I was at once slung safe from a large steady balloon, moving at a stately pace over green fields. I could even see my own shadow again. I was once more real. Time reassumed shape, stopped being something to be killed. Two things about the telephone conversation were awkward: he proposed buying clothes for me, and he made me change my afternoon's work at the charity shop. Clothes implied a liaison through time, which could not be. But it was a thought so tempting that I allowed myself to admire it, rather as though he had offered me a cat. There was the same suggestion of shared life. It was like planting bulbs, like conceiving a child. It was not to do with stimulus and boredom, like my friends' amours. I let myself think of him and me in a shop, choosing unobtrusive clothes because he did not want other people to see me decked out vulgarly. I had thought of this person constantly since meeting him, but I was glad we were not to spend the afternoon alone. Finding words and assembling sentences in his presence was not easy. I am not inexpert at it, all my life I have talked too much to too many, but he lost me my tongue.

Since first meeting Anne Cowdenbeath, I had liked her. We met at Kew Gardens. I was alone and she was with Anto Cranley, a redfaced fat man with unamiable blue eyes and small hands and feet. He was the author of a scurrilous train of novels called *The Stations of the Crossed*, and he had about him an air of fresh scandal, though all I knew was that he was good at cricket and idle in other ways. I had watched him cook meals involving immeasurable quantities of very extravagant stuff, which he would combine and reduce to exact reproductions of favourite dishes otherwise easily to be found in a tin. A morning of peeling, dicing and deseeding effortlessly tracked down oval tomatoes and liaising them with double cream and salmon coral would result in an orange liquid, thickish, sweet and comforting, indistinguishable from tinned tomato soup. Every pan and tool would have been used, and Anto would be exhausted and nervous until extravagantly praised. I would indulge him, go to specialist shops, find fresh bass or corn meal or white saltless butter from the barrel, and then, while the dreadful clattering from the kitchen was at its height, I would speculate about what he might produce – fish fingers, perhaps, or saveloys, or baked beans. How Anto knew this well-dressed woman who was looking at the cacti with disapproval, I did not know. I had known him since he picked me up in Hatchards.

'I don't like the way cactuses just sit there,' said this woman to Anto.

'No. But what do you expect? Roots aren't made for walking.'

'They don't have roots, Anto, I don't think anyway, and you are being obstructive. You know what I mean. They are stolid and their flowers are arbitrary. Like hats on the wrong person. They have none of the poise and short life which is so nice in flowers.'

'Hello Anto,' I said. I had been looking forward to the Temperate House since I too do not much care for cacti, but love instead the sweet damp warmth and the light through banana leaves.

'Anto, won't you introduce us? So this is the light at the end of the bushel.' She grinned at me, which women do not often do, grin I mean, and even less do they grin at me. She gave a great deal with her face, keeping no secrets; it was an open face, not pleated with vanity and self-consciousness. It wore no make-up. After that first meeting, she had asked me to parties and to dinner and once to her house in Scotland, where I went with Tertius, before the party where I met Lucas Salik. We had not become close, but I had come to like her and to respect her. She was not like most women, who mark stages in friendship with increasing revelation and confidence. With Anne, there was no creeping, clinging, vegetable advance; she was just there, crisp and placed and rootless as the cactus flowers she disliked. Not that she was without family, but she was without very close family, and this seemed to disinfect her of her past, as though she had wilfully sterilised her memories, instead of carrying their complicated odour as people do. It was as though the past were an appendix and Anne was better off without hers, bearing not even a visible scar.

It was strange to observe today, with Lucas, that she was without the plain grace I had grown used to in her. The presence of a man will often knock askew women's friendships, but this was a shock because Anne was not, I had thought, like that. She was brittle, patronising and eventually rude on that day, and I felt wretched. I was sure I had done something. All I could imagine was that she must love Lucas. Who would not? It was hubris to imagine that I, new to their grown-up, ordered lives, could storm him. Of course, he would prefer a woman of the world. Why should he degrade himself with a raw girl whose years were still unshaped? I felt fonder of Anne, the more badly she behaved. It was like a huge oversight in grooming, as though she had left off her blouse. I felt I could see her more intimately. The worst moment was when, already a little weak with a childish self-pity from watching Anne wolf her sweet brown ice-cream, I had to find a way of refusing a present she had bought me. It was a blue suit, it was a bribe, it was a humiliation. Or so it would have become had I taken it. As it was, I did not, and a blue suit it remained. It had shimmered with temptation, its cloth as subtle as the skin of a snake.

It even distracted me for a time from looking at the dark head of the man who just once, before I became a wife and a mother, in that order (or was I a mother already?), I wished to love me. I felt him watch me all the time as though he were weighing me up, and this pleased me, though I wanted him to be so close that he must cease assessment, appreciation even, and just breathe me.

But I was still acting. I've learnt that my speech can put men off. The big vocabulary and qualifying give an impression of arrogance, and, worse, unsexiness. It is sexy to be stupid. If there had been more time available for me and Lucas Salik, I should, of course, have allowed words to find a companion volume for my bookishness, but I had no time.

If there had not been the certainty of eating dinner together in the same week, I might not have found the strength in my colonised body and besieged heart to behave properly. The reward for my good behaviour was the arrival of Tertius, who joined us, looking very interested. Perhaps it was his clothes, but he had the air of a betting man who sees two trainers and a horse and senses a few tips to be had.

For a round man, Tertius was all angles. I don't just mean the repeated checkings of his garments. He was touchy and opinionated. He had firm but short-lived opinions and did not care for people to disagree with him. Perhaps what he welcomed really was the chance to be put out when people did disagree with him. This was necessarily often because of his changeability. I did not think that he changed his opinion because of deep convictions or considered argument, but really because he was bored. Other people were the meat of his conversation, not, you felt, because they interested him as problems or because he was fond of them, but because his attention span was so short that only the inexhaustible but unpredictable swivels of human behaviour could keep him amused. I imagined he might go out like a candle without air if there were no gossip for him. In the manner he talked, he read. There were books with broken spines all over the floor, unrespected. He came to life when there was what he called a bit of meat in the book, just as he stopped coasting in conversation when he felt the approach of a stimulating feud or taking of sides. His chambers were dignified but, until I arrived the morning after a torpid night of paying with my flesh for some veal and six prawns, they were squalid. The few rooms, darkly painted, with handsome ceilings, were a muddle of splendour and dog-ends. Nothing had its place and the telephone was always in a drawer or under the carpet. Apart from a few 'fine pieces', by definition impermanent, since Tertius, a natural dealer, would sell any of them to the right person, the possessions were few but deployed so carelessly, all open, or ajar, or splayed, as to suggest profusion. Dimly lit, the rooms could give an impression of richness and lavishness, but the daytime, until I brought order, revealed a tinker's lair. I was not sure why Tertius liked me. It cannot have been just the dusting. He could have got a boy to do that and given himself that pleasure. For everything about boys, Tertius would say, and especially watching them, presumably while Hoovering as much as while doing anything else, was superior to its counterpart in girls. This is not an exceptional view – in Tertius's world it was the only view, an iron rule – but so much did he like to talk about it that I occasionally suspected he was an exhibitionist, and that he liked to have me there to shock me. Why else, after all?

After tea in Fortnum and Mason, then, Tertius turned to me and said, 'Cora, love, there are a couple of little tasks I'd be so grateful if you could do for me before tomorrow when I've rather a big fish coming by.' I said goodbye to Lucas and to Anne and we walked to Albany. Tertius was shrewd and I did not want him to see the opening of my heart to Lucas when we parted, as though it were being drawn from my body into his, on a thin, excruciating wire.

On our return, Tertius gave me a few unarduous chores. I washed his pots which were on the top of the stove. He did not wash up between meals, so a pot stained blue with red cabbage could be left with a rime of coffee grounds and a small Gainsboroughian thicket of cauliflower. The stove top had when I first came been syrupy with varnish.

'Like this do we?' asked Tertius, and his red head and a tie like a dangling lamprey appeared round the kitchen door. His malmsey butt body was clothed in russet and heather checked tweed. In his right hand was a mirror. It was a hand mirror, and it was a mirror not a looking-glass, a dull but polished moon of metal with a spindle shaped handle seemingly just pulled from the same piece. It was so simple that it suggested the actions required to make it – the beats to flatten the metal, the pull on the appended silver, the immersion in cooling water to set it. The impression it gave was that it would, whether by magic or euphemism, show to the person who looked into it their own self beautified.

'It's lovely.'

'It's yours.'

'No Tertius, I've already been tempted today.'

So he extracted from me the story of the suit. I found ways of not mentioning Lucas too frequently, to avoid exposing myself, and also to keep him clean, as it were, to avoid mentioning him to this clever but degenerate man, so different from himself.

As I left Albany, it was completely dark, and cold.

'You should have taken it, you know,' said Tertius. 'After all, you could never break it. No bad luck.'

I left, full of the superiority of one who has refused blandishment twice, spent a time scrubbing, and knows herself to be the repository of love for a good man.

The baby gave a kick, or was it my heart? Had they changed places?

XV

By the Thursday of Lucas Salik's dinner party, I was blown with thoughts of him. I had so little information, most of it from glancing reference or tabloid newspaper, the one too sketchy, the other too heavy-handed. But I could sit for hours turning my head like a sunflower to thoughts of him. He was a continent to me; I could have made charts of his eyes, maps of his hands. My perceptions were distorted by pregnancy and by obsession. I felt like Alice, so extremely did the scale of things swell, or shrink. In my dreams, I was walking over terrain which was Lucas, he was carrying me safe in his hand, he was wearing me in his buttonhole. In the day, I seemed suddenly to grow, to knock things over with my monstrous limbs, to have such heightened senses that the powder of another girl on the tube would nauseate me, the smell of flowers make me weak with maudlin grief. I could not read newspapers without crying. Every tale of gallantry or misery made me shake. The simpler the story, the deeper was my response. I was becoming the perfect tabloid reader. I left Tertius's chambers drunk on the delicious raspberry smell of Windolene, arrived home weeping after seeing the headline 'PLUCKY LITTLE AHMED – MOTHER'S VIGIL'. Moreover, I could not stop myself.

I was possessed.

When Lucas answered the door, I felt momentarily appeased by the sight of him and then discontented that we were not to be alone.

'Lucas might have a surprise for you,' Tertius had said. Had Tertius guessed? Had Lucas actually confided in Tertius, who was after all his friend in spite of their different ways of life? Did he care for me, then? But make it soon, oh God, for then I must find the man I am to marry.

I could smell Lucas's clean skin as I came in. I felt a completely pleasurable relaxation, a sense of subjugation, like a deer settling in a patch of shade so cool that it does not matter if the striped coolness is actually a tiger dormant. I delivered myself to him.

'Have you met? I feel sure you must have, Cora Godfrey, Hal Darbo.'

Was I imagining the proprietary tone in his voice as he introduced me to this blond, slim man, perhaps twenty-five? I wondered briefly how he knew Lucas and then, I thought, *A blond, slim young man, perhaps twenty-five*, and I concentrated all my attention upon what fate had offered me as a potential husband. I arrested my floating, blissful, besotted, pregnant, diffused self, and clapped myself in the stocks of reality. The main obvious physical drawback was that this Hal was a creep. His meat-eating laugh and raucous accessories told me as much. He was like a boy who will become an old woman without seeing manhood. His looks were good, but not fine. He was made to be seen from far below, like a mannerist boy on a distant ceiling, all swagger and codpiece and painted eyes. He wore just a very little mascara. Had I not been pregnant, I probably would not have noticed, but I could smell the creosote in it. Lucas, very busy with plates and tureens and glasses, none the less watched us as much as he could, so I made an effort for him as well as for my child's security. I am good at looking rapt and thinking about other things, and this evening I did better even than that. I looked rapt and thought about the same thing. This Hal could not be entirely awful or he would not have been here.

'So,' he said, 'what brings you here?'

I did not reply, 'I came for a chance to glare at a man whom I have fallen in love with but cannot have since his colouring is not congruent to that of the man who somehow fathered the foetus I am carrying – look no hands.' Besides, he continued speaking.

'Not from London, are you?' Most people who live in London are not from London, they come from other islands, other continents or far-flung suburbs.

'No, are you?' I asked.

'I know it very well, but no, my family are from Dorset.'

This is code for, 'I and my ancestors know who we are, we have lived in the same place for generations, we are people of substance, we pick fruit from trees our forebears planted.' If it is true, it is finer unsaid. He was like a man polishing his watch to show that it is gold. He proceeded to wag before my gaze, which he hoped would be hypnotised, the fat gold watch of his pride. We got on perfectly well. I kept my eyes open. I saw him notice my breasts which were bigger than they usually were because of the baby. He could not see my son. I could feel him pricing my clothes like a salesman. I wondered whether he was an actor.

'No, estate agent for my sins.'

I love 'for my sins'. It is a way of getting through a boring conversation. If you stick it on the end of the baldest statement it has a portentous ring which strikes a pompous gong. At least on the evenings together I would be able to identify, bring down and tag this boy's flights of vocabulary. But now I would not tease, but lure.

'You must see some lovely houses.' I looked at him as though he held the key to heaven.

'There are some fine homes,' he responded, 'but a lot of them are dogs. Still, you can do wonders with the particulars.'

Incredulous, I took part in the conversation which translates 'leaky windowseat' into 'conservatory with view to water garden'. It is a game for dull car journeys to unanticipated destinations.

But how could I mind? I was in the house of the man I had fallen in love with, fallen like an apple. At dinner I was placed between Tertius, who was ribald and easy, and a delightful man called Daniel whose artificial hands were like silver crabs. As Lucas cleared away the soup plates, which had contained a dark red soup, I looked up to see Hal Darbo staring at me. He looked like a drag queen, with his soup-lipsticked mouth, but I knew he was a last chance and I sent over into his eyes the long beam like a searchlight which says, 'I am really interested in you, you remarkable, rare, creature.' His eyes returned a look which seemed to say, 'Accustomed as I am to receiving that information, it is acceptable from you and we might yet come to some accommodation though it is always a dicy business until contracts are exchanged.' I felt, which was mystifying, that he was approaching me with something of the same calculation with which I was attempting to acquire him. Even in these earliest exchanges it was clear that he was prompted by something more willed than desire.

Various remarks he made struck me, for my sins.

'I never use Barbados,' he said, and not during a course when we could have been taking sugar.

'A couple of hundred ks, I tell them, or they think they're in shantytown.'

'Not a bad cook, Lucas, when he pulls his finger out.' This was a bray.

And so on. By the time Lucas set upon the table a glass bowl of shimmering green jelly, I was sure that Hal Darbo would ask to see me again, and my plans were laid, though I could envisage no elevation of the edifice whose foundations I was laying. I felt cold when I considered what I was actually doing, taking steps towards a decision I could not but regret. If I married, I would have to stay married, but in the time available I would be unable to find the double of Johnny with all the qualities I admired in Lucas. I was using secret knowledge as an excuse for ruthlessness. I was committing, if not a sin, a dangerous manipulation which could not be without its own consequences, in the name of my child. I had seen women take small ruthless actions on their children's behalf before. In the name of the little ones, atrocities are quite possible.

But in those days, I could have argued myself into committing almost any crime to see the dark head of Lucas Salik.

When I looked up at him, towards the end of the meal, taking my eyes briefly from those of Hal Darbo, I was so far advanced in the deliquescence of love that he appeared to have a halo. What I saw in his sunk eyes was wonderful to me. He was jealous. He looked as though he had stepped into an acid bath. He blazed, white and black, his halo the street light outside, blazing beyond the window, which, being of old glass, took and reinterpreted our solid lives like water. I looked into the black window where we all floated and settled, the colours drained of brightness, our faces white, the most real things the cold silver and green and transparent glass of knives and forks, bottles and glasses, paraphernalia more enduring than we who used it. When I said goodnight to Lucas, I wanted to cut a hole in his side and re-enter it, to be a rib of Adam.

I was driven home by a man with no hands, my heart belonging to a man who was a mender of hearts, and within me was growing another heart, not mine at all, but never quite not mine. These grotesque anatomical tmeses touched my dreams through a thin sleep.

Hal Darbo would be my artificial limb.

XVI

Hal had few other resources but he did have quite a lot of money. Our first engagement was in a restaurant. If he had been just a little more clever, he would have learnt that two hours spent in a theatre or a cinema save a certain amount of effort. I felt that he was putting himself through some necessary though hardly pleasant system, almost as if in preparation for an examination. I was not sure whether I was the matriculation he sought.

For he wanted me, or performed the manoeuvres of one who did, though he was not privately lustful, which saved me, since I was entering a period of my pregnancy when all contact, even with my clothes or with soap or a towel, seemed violent. I was also keeping myself like a bride for Lucas Salik. I let myself do this, and would continue to do so, until Hal became importunate. Of this he showed no sign. In public, he mauled me, but only when people were looking. When he said goodbye to me, we kissed as though reciprocal insertion of tongues into mouths was the general method of signalling departure for all people, whatever their relation. He did not draw me to him.

He seemed not to enjoy being with one other person. He spoke of his friends, not in a way which suggested that they had any distinguishing characteristics but as though they were his chorus, providing reaction to his performance. Not a thing he did was done without consideration for its effect. Not its consequence, its effect. You felt if he were especially jubilant he would not sing or dance or make love, but quaff some jazzy liquor, purchase a powerful speedster and open up full throttle into an impossible blonde on an alp. Because he was a reflection of others' dreams, he was not so much insubstantial as so fashionable as to be very nearly dated all the time. 'Not even wind surfers, dear, can always be *dans le vent*,' Anto had once said to me.

Hal was the embodiment of modern cliché. He was not an eternal verity become a cliché, he was a nonentity with shrewdly mimicked characteristics. He was like reproduction furniture. I wondered if he had been born with no face and taken to a plastic surgeon. It would be a *plastic* surgeon. All these lofty conclusions about Hal excused me to myself. It is easier to forgive yourself for doing damage to a doll than to a person. As to who loved him, his friends and family, I did not yet know.

He was personable and he took me out a good deal. During this time, he asked me almost nothing of myself. This was a relief since I could not tell the truth, and also because it would be easier simply to use a person who had never shown himself interested, warm or vulnerable. I saw him at least once a day, and he telephoned me more often than that. I did not feel that he called to hear my voice but rather to check in, as one does before an aeroplane flight. I wondered if he realised that marriage was my destination. There was a comforting passivity for me in all this, which suited me as my body concentrated upon itself and its ward. While the word parasite is ugly, it is fine to be a host. In Greek, the word for host and guest is the same, and sometimes, after I had said goodnight to Hal or in the morning before dressing for work, I felt that I was the baby's guest, that he was entertaining me.

Of course it was a boy. It must be.

Tertius seemed delighted at Hal's pursuit of me. He frisked about his chambers, making sandwiches which he left among the highly coloured broken books. He asked me all the questions Hal did not ask me about myself. He began to show a side which it would be mistaken to call womanish. It was more tender and less competitive than that. He could ask the right question, again and again, like a kind torturer. I was starting to like him. I knew that he was a petty, easily bored and venal man, and a promiscuous homosexual. But he gave the impression, after you had observed him for some time, that these were the only sane things to be. He was spoilt, he had carved a waxy cell for himself among the drones, but he enjoyed what he did enjoy, properly. I was not able to imagine his most private enjoyments, but I had seen him crooning over his gesso, giggling over gossip, and spluttering his enjoyable anger all over a greasy but savoured feast. His vulgarity seemed like a tremendous headdress worn to keep marauders from something of very good quality borne inside his head. It might have been something as abstruse as perfect taste – that is, taste so good, rather than so exclusive, as to be almost a moral quality. Or it might have been that he was very kind and did not want to show that kindness to everyone, for not even that much kindness may help more than the very few intimates of a man.

It was at about this time that I learnt that Tertius was a friend of Angel. He was rigid with snobbery, I'd realised that long before, but I could see that it was at once professionally necessary and also a cure for his boredom. I also cannot see that snobbery is more of a failing than it is a source of pleasure. 'If *that* pleasure is not innocent, what is, now we are told that food and sex are toxic? That leaves snobbery and sleep as the last simple pleasures,' said Tertius.

But snobbery could not explain why so lively a man as Tertius, and one so at heart conventional, should spare time for my colleague and tormentrix from the charity shop, Angelica Coney. Reared in a palace with different time zones for each wing, Angel was one of those sirens whose pull is all towards destruction. She was of any age between twenty and forty-five and she was a witch. I feared her and was dashed when she withdrew her lovely smile and pretty favours from me. She had black eyes and surprising blonde hair. Much of her power derived from her not speaking, or infancy. It was so alarming that you would resume worship to bring the sun out from behind her wrath. Her power was over all animals, especially men, but she used this power over them mostly to advance the boundaries of her princesspality, the animal kingdom. As a tiny child she had begun her career of animal-sympathy by releasing the hounds, the ark of her class's covenant, the only animals invariably counted two by two.

Angel had ignorance. It clothed her impermeably. She had no Achilles heel where comparison and reference might strike her. Her attitudes were unqualified and unclouded by awareness of anything but her own feelings, and these were few but strong; there was no danger that she might bore her opponents with fact to support her statements. What Angelica loved was animals, though it was more and less than love, for it was not a human feeling. They were her familiars. She felt their pain. Human pain compared with it, she said, was a luxury fathered by time on speech. When she did speak, it was to say such things. Brought up where the worst pains were invisible or trivial, she had decided that all human agony was so. The worst she had seen was adultery and mismatched shoes. I suppose she believed in original sin without knowing it, and felt the animals were innocent.

She was dangerous because she had learnt disguise. She was considered human but the beast's eyes stared out. She was the only child of parents whose name would die with her and whose great house, if she could achieve her dream, would be turned over to the animals.

Her ambition was the restitution of animals to their proper place. I had laughed at her, imagining a sort of cheery reversal of roles, teddy bears conducting buses and giraffes delivering letters, or maybe just a wonderful party for creatures, elephants dropping their chains and cats letting themselves out for the last time. I said as much to Angelica, who blazed, no smile on her tiger's face. She had needed to say nothing about my misplaced anthropomorphism, patronage, indeed she did not know these words. Instead, she turned on me, and said winningly, 'They will eat you and all people like you and spew you out because you taste bad.'

Angel was so cool and charming in her bearing that the fact that she was a lunatic was ignored. Her nobility would in any case have protected her from incarceration. I was not sure in what direction she organised her animal ambitions. I was sure the charity shop was some sort of front, and sometimes half expected to see a black panther in a fedora slink in, talking out of the side of its whiskers. Most of the time Angel was quiet, like a cat, and used her almost dumb vocabulary to hypnotise and stun men. She did, curiously, a lot of work for charities, all to do with animals. Her name, her passion for the beasts, and her beauty made her an adornment. I suspected that she licked men all over with a rough tongue before killing them, and when I saw her little hands, I would think of them laid, immovable leaden velvet, on the neck of some poor white hunter, before she inclined her little neck to begin the imperative neat destruction of her victim. Angel was as it were a vegan carnivore; cheese, eggs and milk she eschewed, but I imagined her coughing up hairballs of expensive shoe leather and silk ties after devouring a toothsome banker. She did not need it for herself, but she did need their money for her causes.

Angelica lived near the charity shop, which was itself in Sloane Avenue, when she was not at her parents' house. I had not been to her London house. I did not much want to. I feared there might be people, stuffed, under tall cloches, like the kudu and jewel-footed eagles she had not been able to persuade her gentle parents to destroy at Wyvern. After all, their life was destroyed already. But Dolores Steel *was* a frequent visitor to Angel's London house. She was unable to describe things save in relation to prison, where she had spent two years. Things and places were thus better or worse than prison. Nothing was the same as prison, not even, she had said to me in the charity shop the day before she announced she was about to go in, 'Not even hospital. And I should know.'

Dolores Steel was Angel's lieutenant. No, more secretive than that, I suppose. She was her crack division for desperate measures, for the extraction of money by means more forceful than charm and connections. I was not sure that Dolores ever did anything wrong, but her bearing was that of a man over and over polishing his gun, weighing it, spinning it, polishing again. But her gun was part of herself, you could not take it from her. Dolores looked like Angelica, though how her parents, a Spanish stevedore and a male impersonator from Hornsea, had combined to replicate the product of nine centuries of aristocratic jerrymandering and landlinked marriage was a mystery. Where Angel was fair, Dolores was black in all but skin. I thought her black-hearted, too, but I came when she called.

Dolores's crackshot sex appeal and crazy past, whatever it was, left her with few friends, and I felt sad for her. I thought of her in hospital as I had seen her before, diminished by the little bed and six flowers in a jar next to the Lucozade, and told myself to remember to go and see her this time. So embroiled was I with my own interior, which made me not ill but not well, that I almost did not ask her why she was going to hospital. We were sitting, she, I and Angel, on the floor of the shop, sorting old clothes into piles. The room was badly lit, the paint stained, but beige anyway, like many of the clothes having been tinted for serviceability, not appeal. The clothes were improbably stained, as though they had been lent to a troupe of incontinents for amateur dramatics. The necks of the women's clothes were biscuit-thick in orange make-up. Before a laundry hamper of these clothes sat Angelica and Dolores, small, dark-eyed, high-cheekboned, and made up not with the rose colours of other women but with toffee and black, their four eyes doubled with black, their clavicles powdered with gold. I did not want to turn my back on them. Here, among the wool on the floor, they might be my kittenish friends, always curled together or definitely apart as is the case with cats, but they did scare me. Indeed, in spite of my comparative height, they called me Mouse, when they wanted to tease. Their natures were similar, not more than that. At some point in the future their relationship would end, I considered, though I could not say who would be the winner. For it would be a fight. At the moment their parity was almost perfect, though in the end Angelica's atavistic confidence must give her the ascendant. But they were infatuated with their physical similarity to each other and increased it by dressing alike. Their straight backs and poised heads, with beautiful dangerous tight throats, prevented their resembling expensive paired whores. Their doubleness did not look like a gimmick, nor did they appear to be sisters; as for being twins, it was not possible to imagine such a pair surviving childhood without the one drowning the other. At the moment, though, they appeared to live on some secret, erotic cream. Theirs was not a friendship; they were mutually completely useful.

'You love people for their weaknesses,' gentle sages say; Dolores and Angel loved their mutual and respective strengths. What might have been seen as weaknesses by a human interpreter – absence of imagination, of feeling, of gentleness – were inoperative in their world. But, as we folded the old cat-smelling clothes in the stained shop, I was concerned when Dolores mentioned that she was to go into hospital. When she said that it was for her heart, I hoped, while blaming myself for the selfishness of the thought, and realising that to preserve myself I must not appear too keen for information, that Lucas Salik was to be the surgeon in charge of Dolores.

'D'you know who you're under?' I asked, and let this awful idea literally twist my heart with jealousy.

'The great Front Wheeler himself.' Dolores was indiscriminately racist; she hated all humans. Can the word for it be humanist? I hoped further. There is, however, more than one Jewish surgeon of the heart.

'The one with all the publicity on account of his pretty face,' said

Angel, and her face was like a bad child's, sweet with hard eyes looking out. 'That might even be handy, Dolly, see what you can do.'

'The point of all institutions,' said Dolores.

'Is to find and destroy their immune systems,' continued, in chorus, Angelica. They had a line in barmy but plausible-sounding maxims. I was not much interested. I mostly ignore ideological recipes.

'And they transplant animals' hearts. I would not care about the people. They live on to drink beer and go jogging, but look at the creature casualties.'

I heard about creature casualties all day. I imagined them, rather quaint, a dachshund on crutches after driving heedlessly around a bend, a Louis Wain cat with toothache, far removed from the photographs Angel and Dolores purred over. These photographs were of split dogs and cats with their craniums neatly lifted off, replaced with glass and wire. I would sometimes see these photographs, blown up, fly-posted, lettered as though with a huge potato print, giving details of action to come.

'Would you like a visit in hospital, Dolly?' I asked, broaching the nickname as you might stroke a puma with a sick headache.

'Why not,' she said, with no inflection, as befits a royal person.

So, I went. It was Lucas Salik. After speaking to him on the telephone, I wondered whether I had succeeded in my attempt to make him jealous. I had spoken of Hal, who was after all a friend of Lucas's, as though he and I were a couple. I have never known whether this alarms or challenges men. But, with time running out, I had thought to goad Lucas into some committing gesture, just one, to leave me free to throw away and dedicate my life on and to Hal and the baby boy.

I had so little time in which to reach him. It was a desire to have known him, rather than to know him, which drove me, as though a glimpse would give me that for which to strive through the rest of my life. Sometimes, dreaming of him, I would remark his similarity to our idea of death – tall, pale, dark – and wonder if that was what I wanted. But, if so, I did not think I would be lucky enough to die in childbirth. I have never been that well organised, or how should I have arrived where I was?

So, it was curious to propose something as ordinary as dinner at my house, with Hal, to Lucas Salik. After I had spoken to him on the telephone, I thought of several ways I could have improved upon the telephone call. By praying to him, perhaps, petitioning him, throwing flowers in his way.

Where he worked, where he performed his miracles, a hospital, seemed to me scented with clean sanctity. To my queasy pregnant nose, the disinfectant was a delicious uncomplicated smell, and I connected it with medical infallibility in the service of life. Dolores was burning bright with rage in her bed, but she ate the fruit I had brought quickly, cracking the lychees like little birds' skulls.

To see him was not disappointing, but it showed me how unrealisable was my dream. He was a real, a busy, man. In a way, it was his colleague, a cheery doctor whom you could see mowing a lawn or washing a car, who made me feel that Lucas had a life which was ordered in a book, with a ballpoint pen, on lined paper. I had seen him only socially, at ease, where he was independent and unbeholden. Here, it appeared, that as much as his patients needed him, he needed them, to practise his skill. I felt that there was a system of ill health, which he required. I did not want to look at him in front of Dolores, for I knew she would see and use my naked self against me. Men's attention turns to Dolores as though she were hanging by her teeth from a trapeze, naked, but Lucas appeared to want to leave.

Dolores's glare may have unsettled him, for she looked at him not as though he had repaired her heart but as though he stank. I could not tell if this concerned him. I wondered if he noticed. Perhaps she was just a collection of faulty valves to him, as women are said to be to their gynaecologists. Or at any rate, by the wives of gynaecologists. But what of the gynaecologists of gynaecologists' wives?

I liked the big blue car by now, it was an emblem of his distantness and competence and power, but I was not sure how to speak to this presence by my side. How can you address an idea? I wished for a secular collect with which to address him. I was terrified of embarrassing him. Things had become not more easy, but more difficult, with time. My affair, if that was what it was, with Hal, seemed trivial. So enormous yet simple were the things I felt for this man that I did not want to be too close to him. I required a new, formal language in which to address him, not the vulgate.

And then I felt a soggy mass at my side, lifted and observed it. It had escaped from its wrapping. I was surprised that he could face the further treating with organs, having presumably been dealing with them all day, but it was a tongue, uncooked. He had said he would buy something for supper. I have heard of ways of cooking it which make it edible, but I would as soon eat a bull's eye. When I asked him, he seemed surprised. I wrapped the tongue in a newspaper which announced on its front page, yet again, Lucas's operation on the little Afghan boy, the tones of the article waiting for the child either to take up his bed and walk or to die. Such papers were everywhere. There was also a scrap of paper within the newspaper. It must be the butcher's receipt.

He said, 'Please don't tell Hal. He hates mess.'

Bloody, bloody Hal, I thought, and I thought the word in full, gory and sticky. Hal hates mess, does he, Hal who is not pregnant, not covered in tongue blood, not sitting here inextricably tied to a man who will have nothing to do with him? To hell with Hal, I thought. I wanted to spit.

But it was he who did that, on my doorstep. In the same second as I saw Dick and Gloria on the floor, making love in their basement, Lucas Salik was very sick. It did not affect my infatuation. Partly there is the divine degradation of serving the fallen idol, and then there is the simple pleasure of seeing that a person needs you, in the most direct way. I had wondered how mothers deal with their babies' disgusting milky sick and curdy bottoms, but I saw now it would be easy. All I wanted was to make him new so he could do it again. He was mine. Moreover, he fainted, only just inside the house, and only mad strength enabled me to haul this skeleton tree of man to a sofa, where I mopped and swabbed. It was like those dreams where you save your idol's life. It was all I longed for.

While he was unconscious, Dick and Gloria went off to their work at the opera. Like Angel and Dolores, but how unlike, they were entangled, but like contiguous root vegetables, not tangled animals. They were both pale and thin, but their tameness and their indifference to the darkness of the basement made them desirable subtenants. They thrived, indeed, in the dark.

When Lucas was recovered, I gave him a stiff shot of rum and felt like a seducer. Its scent of cane and molasses made me dizzy.

'There was a note,' I said. 'It said, "THEY CAN'T TALK".'

Certainly, those who could not talk must be the creature casualties, and some mercenary of Angel's must have done this. I was too vain to let him know my thoughts, and decided to make light of it. It was after all an isolated incident. Anyway, how did they get this great lolling tongue from an animal without cruelty, or was it from some beast not inconvenienced by the absence of its tongue?

Since he seemed unwilling to talk, I left him to cook his part of supper, which is how I should like to have been treated in the same circumstances. I had prepared everything I intended to cook beforehand anyway.

I love the feeling of well deployed time that having things done in advance gives. I suspect that it is really an elegant way of wasting time, but the dishes of cubed, diced, peeled, waiting components make me feel like a mosaic maker, placing colour on the table, which, seen from the critical distance of the diner's chair, seems to have form and shape.

I had not been prepared for his being able to cook. Had he learnt it from his mother, as men usually do not? All I really knew about him was that he was Jewish and Polish. I knew that this made him rare – a survivor, or, rather, the child of survivors.

When I returned to the kitchen, I felt like Mary *and* Martha: there he was, in my house, doing something quite ordinary, which he seemed naturally to endow with grace. I hoped that Hal would be eaten by sharks on the Bakerloo line. The occasion was separate and delightful, like going swimming at night or a first dance. As it occurred it entered my memory, not, for once, adorned, but clear and simple. The baby was apt in the domestic scene. The tall man in blue in my plain kitchen made the room replete. He lifted and poured batter from its blue jug, and he poured again. The noise of fat fizzing and settling, the blue fat smoke, the fritters as light and hard as sugar glass, though they were salt, but sweet to me, did not make me nauseated. It was as though my nerves themselves were being sealed. Time hung light. I seemed to take part in and to see the scene, two big people in a small room, a round and full scene shown in a round mirror, hanging still. He handed me the yellow C-shaped fritter he had made for me. I was happy.

After Hal arrived, the evening became ordinary again. I insulated myself more successfully than I would weeks ago have thought possible against Hal's digs, his resentment, his innuendo. I wondered how Lucas would feel when Hal and I married, as I was quite certain we would.

I wanted Lucas to go, so I could think about him. He was tired when he left. He seemed drunk, but I thought it must be the shock. The source of that shock, the tongue, I set to cool and jellify under weights overnight.

That night was the first night Hal stayed with me, and I found that I could remain courteous, even conversational, by thinking, as he moved, of Lucas Salik, pouring down from the blue jug a pale fluid stream.

XVII

After our first night together, Hal appeared to calm down, as though he had made the first connection on his journey, wherever it was taking him, but the checking-in telephone calls became more frequent. I had to leave the job where I packed jokes into matchboxes because he telephoned so often that the nuisance was no longer offset by the cheapness of my labour. So I was working more at Angel's shop, and, of course, I was still going to Tertius's chambers. Sometimes Angel appeared when I was cleaning there. Tertius would then look at me as though he could no longer recollect who I was, and I would know that it was time to go. He did not like to share Angel, at whom he poked no fun, whom he always called Angelica, 'So oddly vegetable a name, Cora, no?' I felt that, while he liked my cleverness, it did not to him, a clever man and a self-made one, have the integrity of what is born, the pure abstract contemplable beauty of immemorial money. I felt no bitterness about this. As long as you are yourself eating something fairly nutritious, the feudal food chain is quite ornamental and not desperately restrictive. 'Class,' Tertius would say, cutting off a section of Arctic Roll and eating it over the *Burlington Magazine*. 'Class, does it start in school or does school start in class? Or *does* class start,' here he would purse his lips like a monkey de-pipping a grape, 'does class start, as you might say, in class?' He needed class and was entertained by it; he was like a banana grower with the keys to the monkey house.

I began to hear an accent in Tertius's voice. He had always spoken in tones, astoundingly, unashamedly, camp-posh, which suggested he was entertaining after dinner, to the accompaniment of a desultory piano, a home-service audience. But, just occasionally, when he eased up, as he put it, in my presence, there was a fruitiness in his vowels, and he seemed about to swing quite the other way, to speak in a Northern accent unheard but in pantomime. The gusto of his pretentiousness was endearing; it was like his gung-ho queerness, so caricatured that it protected itself. Tertius was offended by the naturalist school of homosexuality, he liked it colourful and mannered and full of sickly tints and hectic colour. I think he was offended, aesthetically, by its current, fashionable ubiquity and barefacedness. Not that he objected to coveys of boys dressed to kill. 'Ooh look at those private partridges,' he would say when we went to deliver frames. He loved to see a kept boy. 'Real *poule de luxe*,' he would say, without jealousy of either keeper or kept. But I think that he liked the beauty of the cat in the bag, and now it was out of the bag he felt a certain thrill was lost. This may have been his age, a lament in him equivalent to a more conventional man of his age having regrets about the second post or proper cake at railway stations. It was entirely suitable for a pregnant person, I felt, to be around a queer.

Anne was away. I did sometimes want to speak to a woman, and a woman who had had a baby at that, but she was not approachable and I had not seen her since the night I had met Hal, when I had felt her eyes on me too coolly not to be coming to some conclusions. Was pregnancy visible even in its earliest stages to women who had known it?

And now, the baby could be felt. It was November, and he was to be born early in April. I could carry off the extra bulk, but I must marry Hal soon. Sometimes it seemed to matter a great deal, and then I would pull away as it were from my own life and perceive that it did not really matter, that the seas would wash us away anyway, that we were all protected from duty, responsibility and the future by what is called mutually assured destruction, which is the capsule the world keeps under its tongue for when the prison walls start to grow together. From these thoughts, which were I suppose the sin of despair, I would come into mad fits of gaiety when I could set my eyes on fire with looking at something quite ordinary. Stupid, optimistic, pushed towards light by the baby, I would sleep, and wake up, reality appearing dim when I awoke, hung-over from adrenalin.

For when hope was there, it was not small and personal but

enormous, ambitious, redeeming. It was an unreflective, biological, hope. I suppose it was the hope of hormonal change, sufficient to keep a mother blind to any rough truth till the baby is born.

I was feeling, for quite different reasons, something of the emotion and energy which were the medium of Angelica and Dolores. In me it came from the baby. Their ideology (it was as totalitarian as that) must come from something too. I could not think what drove them.

'Of course, it's sex,' said Tertius. I was folding shirts for the laundry, bending them really, they were so stiff with dirt. He had this trick of starting a conversation at its most salacious point, in order to reel you in to it.

'What's sex?' I asked. I thought for a moment he had been speaking of some new painter, Sachs.

'The secret of Angelica's amazing energy. She's like a really well run machine. Not something whimsical by Tinguely though, Cora, but a really big, cold one, going day and night, no frills. A crematorium, something like that. Pure, consuming sex. I mean,' he said, and he looked a bit sad as though his usually convenient proclivities had let him down, socially, by causing him not to desire her, 'even I feel it.' He made a long, square, face.

'Talking of which, darling,' he said, 'how's it going with the golden boy? Or is he a Golden Ass?' He pronounced it with a long 'a'. Tertius liked simple, two-ply jokes.

'We speak a lot.'

'You must do something more than that. He's made for you, my loss of course.'

'Oh Tertius, I'd always do for you.'

He gave me a purple-veined look. He was like Silenus, but in a mosaic, all composed of squares and violent colour, requiring distance to be apprehensible. His suit was brown from across the room, but as you approached it, it flowered into its constituent colours, a fearful orange, a winking turquoise, a gleeful purple. His tie was as solid as a block of chocolate, his cufflinks tablets of the Law. His teeth were the demerara brown of Kendal mintcake. I saw that Tertius could be a bad enemy.

He left the room, and returned, bringing a bottle, which he appeared to have lifted out of a Braque. It was square. It did not look like other bottles. He poured me a glass of white stuff.

'Sit down, love, I'll be back in a mo, I've got a surprise.' The drink was like icy supercharged marmalade. The baby began to dart like a goldfish but I was pleased with myself and liked my new burning heart and floaty head.

I heard the front door open, voices, and then in came Tertius, with, behind him, Hal. He seemed to have been neglecting the highlights in his hair. I thought, 'This is the first personal detail which has intrigued me about this boy I plot to marry. He dyes his hair.'

'Cora, baby,' he said. He was addressing only me, not itemising me and my contents. His face looked still handsome but neglected. It is not customary for a man's looks, unless he is much older than he says, so speedily to disintegrate.

'God I've been miserable,' he said. Not, 'without you', but I feared he might mean this, and it was lent regrettable credence by the pouched face. I did not want him to care for me, so much as to want to marry me.

'Come to lunch, won't you, Co, there's a doll.' No one calls me Co. No one ever has. Affronted, touched, sensing a crisis I could desire, I poured the orange fuel down my throat and said to Tertius, 'Can I go early?'

'Can she come, Thrice? Say yes, do.' Hal sounded like a woman asking for a geegaw. He had his name for everyone. It was a weary piece of his constructed charm. His charm was prosthetic.

'Go, children, go,' said Tertius. He saw what I could have told him was wrong, a young man and a young woman in love, arm in arm, going out into the autumn.

We ate at Hal's club off Clifford Street. It was unsuitable in every way. He had for some time been holding a meal there out to me as a treat to come but I had not realised quite what a treat it would be. I re-found him after a journey to the ladies ('Which if you need to attend you are not,' said the face of the breeched pederast at the desk) which took me under London and approximately to below the bandstand in the Park. Of course, we were eating in the 'ladies permitted' section. He was sitting at a small table with a dirty cloth and a menu so comprehensively coated in plastic that it looked as though it were adapted for benthic use.

'I've ordered wine,' said Hal. An older pederast appeared with a carafe of untranslucent wine, the size of the vinegar bottle at a chip

shop. At its neck was a tassel, like a very small jousting favour.
The bottle was set down. Hal seemed to be recovering. He was
rather impressed with himself and his club. Under the floor
were men drinking wine and eating meat which would satisfy
Lucullus.

I didn't look at the menu, but I had a shot at guessing. 'I'll have
egg mayonnaise and tongue salad,' I said. And in the kitchen, I
thought, it will be like those intelligence tests with matches, how
few need you move to change DEAD into LOSS? My guess was that,
if I did not eat the one lettuce leaf, half tomato and monocle of
cucumber garnish on the egg mayonnaise, they'd simply need to
swab the plate down and plonk on the rubber mat of pressed tongue
to convert EGG MAYONNAISE into TONGUE SALAD.

I had given *my* pressed tongue to Dick and Gloria for what they
described as a 'bit of a do' backstage. 'At least you can't skid on
tongue, or there'd be the hell to pay with cueing – "Oh, so sorry,
I just tripped over my tongue,"' they said.

My mind was wandering. This was, I was certain, to be the
luncheon during which I became engaged to the young man of my
contemplations.

Hal ordered smoked salmon, which unaccountably was not the
rectangular brown sort found in sandwich bars, but ragged rosy
slices of it with a big pithy half of lemon and proper untriangulated
bread and butter. 'They're partialish to me here in point of fact,'
said Hal.

Anything which followed would serve me right. But the baby
must have a father.

The prongs of my egg mayonnaise fork were connected with a
sticky web, as though the person before me had eaten shredded
wheat. I ate my egg (it was *an* egg) with my pudding spoon, one,
two, half ellipses. Hal did not notice. Would I be able to carry on
regardless in our marriage too? I started to develop the idea. But
my heart was not in it. That heartless stylish hypocrisy was gone,
killed by good intentions, romance, and the horrible consequences
of promiscuity. I ceased thinking of 'adultness', or 'going my own
way', and looked at Hal. If I concentrated on feeling drunk, he
looked handsome enough.

'You're beautiful, sweet, and you'd be a wonderful mother,' he
said, and I could have sworn he was addressing himself, ruddy now

after two glasses of Quink and the meaty salmon, as he saw himself reflected in the towering glass behind my head.

'Cora, will you marry me?' asked Hal, speaking to himself in the mirror. He clearly accepted at once.

I was so relieved that his question made me happy. After all, I would do my best.

'Thank you, Hal, but are you sure?' I could think of so many objections, it seemed strange that he could not. Perhaps he required to be married. But why would he then so touchingly, as though reading a script, have given me that conventional triple necklace of courtly compliments?

'Are you ready for the second course?' asked the older pederast. He addressed Hal. 'Was it satisfactory, sir?' He did not ask me. He knew the answer, but I was lucky to be there at all. I was not worthy so much as to gather up the crumbs from under the table.

We accompanied the tongue, and Hal's game pie, with champagne, which showed a complete conformity to the routine of almost every lunch Hal ever had. It would almost have been more remarkable not to have it. He might recall a lunch without as 'the lunch of the unhad champagne', something like the unbarking dog.

'Hair of the dog,' said Hal. 'I've been drunk most of the time since I last saw you.'

I could not think of much to say. 'I hope it wasn't to do with me?'

'Nope. Nothing.' It must have been something pretty serious, for he had the clammy look of one who has not been sleeping easily for days. I would hate to have put him, or anyone, through that.

He put his hands on the table as though to keep them under his eye.

'Nothing at all. D'you get?' and he looked at me with nasty eyes. He looked at himself in the glass again and modified his gaze to represent new love.

As we left his club, I saw, leaving from the entrance reserved for members unaccompanied by ladies, Johnny. It was a grey afternoon. Ribbons of fog stirred low against buildings. A flower-seller pulled change from his long green apron, as he stood among his schooled shoals of flowers. Hal put his arm around me. The champagne, the optimism, the relief, conspired to make me feel tender towards him. I smiled at him as though I loved what I found in his face.

I heard skidding feet at our backs. Soon we would be looking in the windows of a ring shop.

Do the proprietors see and believe all that fresh love, or do they wait for the probate valuations to see if it has endured? I was prepared to face anything now, me, Cora, and Hal. And the baby.

'Cora, Hal.'

It was Johnny. In front of his chest he held, as a bossed shield, a bouquet of white chrysanthemums, each like a head of coral.

'Let me be the first to congratulate you,' he said. Then, like a fish, he was gone, among the fluctuating crowd, which was tenebrous, grey, dark blue and black, parting now and then for the passage of a sleek car.

XVIII

I had seen engaged couples before, and there can be a spooky air of conjunction about them, but I was surprised that Johnny had seen our state so quickly. Can it be that a proposal of marriage acts upon the processes as conception does, setting in train a sort of beacon-relay of festival synapses? I had thought that I was fairly undelighted, and Hal was not perceptibly enraptured. But some solitaire corpuscles must be pumping through my veins, telling my heart to tie a ribbon around itself and display its soft centre. Little chips of happiness were coalescing in me, it is true, but whether they would fuse as a champagne hangover or as a three-carat drop of pure joy, it was too early, on the very afternoon of my engagement to Hal, to say. I expressly did not covet the signs of engagement. As I am a greedy girl, not merely swayed but waltzed into orbit by appearances, this might have been surprising, but I explained it to myself. The baby was there, the soon-to-be visible sign of more than engagement, and I had not the brio to display at once a pregnant belly and a blushing absorption in the cut and colour of diamonds, aprons, lower-ground-floor apartments, and going-away costumes. I felt like a pig, who, having been slaughtered, is keen to be made into collops, loin, blood pudding, head cheese, trotters, and ells of nutritious, quotidian, sausages.

I longed for the dailiness of life. Had I had a companion who knew about the baby, she might have told me that I would shortly be in receipt of the dailiness and the nightliness of life, but as it was the only sources of information were the magazines and baby books I read and threw away as a man might throw away pornography which can no longer work its magic. I threw away my baby books, though, in case they somehow contributed to, even enlarged, the crescent stranger within. I drugged myself with superstition, like a child knowing she will dodge the devil if she goes upstairs three at a time. I was certain that I was performing the correct actions to keep chaos at bay. I had been finding my unplotted life too shapeless to carry further and had taken steps to freeze its slippery form in order to bear it, in all three senses. Rather than attempt to carry alone a leaky vessel, overfilled, meniscus atremble, full of spilling, tricksy, watery, changeable life, I preferred to strike the water solid at a blow, like a hard frost, rendering it clear and portable as ice. I forgot for a time that ice burns are as savage as the burns of heat and steam. Ice also carries less weight than water, and displaces more.

I wanted things solid and clear and marriage appeared to me then to be the only means of achieving this. I was astonished that it was so easily come by. I had been lucky in finding Hal, physically so suited to be the father of a child of Johnny's and also, it appeared, keen to be married himself. The enormous gap, the certain absence of love between Hal and me, appeared an advantage. It made crystal clear the icy fact of our marriage. I liked, too, the way we did not discuss our love, or rather its absence. I felt modern, light. Where love for Hal should have been were the ether of my great true love for Lucas Salik and the fleshly love for my growing baby. Spirit and flesh, they joined to provide something equal to what another girl might have felt for the man she was to marry. In fact, very possibly superior to it. Hal and I, I thought smugly as we walked past the queue of people awaiting taxis outside Claridge's, had a very tidy beginning, uncluttered by illusions and undusted with fragile spun hopes. He must realise this. We were embarking on a minimalist life. I had been to the flats of people who believed only in black and white and uncluttered space. Used to the gluey clutter of Dick and Gloria, and to my own dusty trophies and tableaux of soaps and flowers and pots, I had wondered what they did with all their things. Now I knew.

They did not have them. No chest of drawers, no drawers, no wardrobes, no robes, no hooks, no hangings. A floor, a ceiling and walls are all that are required to contain light. This thought gave me a satisfying sense of weightlessness and purity. In a world silted up with choice and variety and brought to the edge of chaos by plurality, we would be starting our adult life uncluttered by emotions which would be certain to sag, to grow dusty, to be holed by moths of doubt and irritation. I felt light with the optimism of a person who has just completed a great job of cleaning. I felt a suffusion of almost renunciative brightness; I felt supernaturally tidy. That was that, I thought, as you might after taking the veil.

The queue of people outside the lighted entrance to Claridge's was marshalled by a tall doorman with the olive froggy face of a Spanish duke. His umbrella housed those nearer the front of the queue, sheltering them not so much from the light rain which was beginning to fall as from the vulgar gaze. 'Look at them, weighed down with commitments and addled hopes and transmuted or tarnished love,' I thought. 'Look at the couples who not only hate each other but have paid to accompany each other, over an ocean perhaps, in order to pay to share a room and a series of hollow outings, costly, shared and disappointing. How terrible that they hate each other; how much worse that they once loved each other. How fortunate we are to be without that indignity. Look at that old pair, holding gloved hands like children crossing the road. How can they face the disintegration seen in the face of the other, the betrayed desires, the secrets unspoken and left to curdle? How can they look at each other, leathery over breakfast in their sleeping suits, and face that once they could not bear to separate, that they said into each other's ears things which revealed they were afraid of the dark, or liked this or that.' How shocking to realise that you have given your time to an old stick with ordnance survey cheeks, when once you thought him a king. I would never be disappointed and nor would Hal: we had no high hopes, no low hopes, no hopes. We had acquired each other as you acquire a refrigerator, to prolong cold storage. Our life would be clear and unmetaphorical.

Hal was simply himself. It was reductive not metaphorical, his style. The only implications were the obvious ones of image. I was convinced he would straighten, by being only himself, my bent for complication, for fossicking out alternatives, for organising problems, for arranging difficulties. I felt as though he made me as he was. I would be his paper consort. When I was with Lucas Salik, it was true I was paper consumed in his fire, but now I had become engaged to Hal I must tame that feeling. Or at any rate when we married.

Anto had teased me about the way, given the coloured board of my life, I had fretted it about till it was a jigsaw with pieces which would rearrange in too many different ways. He had laughed at the complication. He liked things simple, he often said, they were complicated enough even then.

So he would be pleased about Hal. Who could tell, perhaps he would like him.

My life appeared to me now as one unending television advertisement, all appearance and flawless fitting of intention to function, untroubling of conscience, unstirring of those ambitions which lead to error and tragedy. Nothing could go wrong in a world where things appeared so perfect. The baby would be fitted for our century by this life, would never be disappointed, having grown to expect only food for the eyes and body. He would be raised without ideas. He would not learn the discrepancies and shifts which are there for those who see them and absent for the amoral, the enviably blind. Unburdened by religion, by knowledge with its implications of more knowledge, the child would be as blessed as an animal, untroubled by interpretation, unvisited by nightmares. And Hal, the father, would see to this.

'When do you think?' asked Hal. We had just walked through Shepherd Market. Not a tart in sight in these days of outraged nature. I'd heard from Anto that this was where the golden-hearted ones still had their beat, and I had been shooed off once by a mansized tart who had thought me a rival, but it was quite empty now save a notice, 'FAMILY BUTCHER: BRAIN'S, HEART'S AND GALANTINE', illuminated by a bluish light, raisined with dead flies. There was a dry-cleaner in whose window flashed a sign, 'FRENCH PRESSING'. Hal and I emerged opposite a bookshop where I had spent afternoons. I said goodbye to its bow window. Inside were towers of books; there was a chocolate-house atmosphere to the place which gave to the passerby who entered the feeling that he belonged to a literary group. Hal would not understand, and why should he? But I saluted it as I went by, for its not having moved with the times, and for what it had lent me. Like Albany, it had shown me an older world, one which was richer than the world *I* knew of carefulness and re-impacted soap and the car used only in emergencies. Some of the patrons of the bookshop could not read, some bought books according to the colour of their spare rooms, but even these had given me pleasure. I said goodbye to all this and turned to my modern lover.

'Very soon,' I replied to his question.

'I'd better tell Lucas.' It was Hal who spoke, though he spoke my own thoughts.

'Not your parents first?' I asked.

'Them too,' he said.

His voice was not that of a bearer of good news. I could tell he would fit in his telephone calls between those to clients in the morning. Thinking of the morning, I realised that we might, now bound to each other, have to spend the evening and the night together. I did hope not. I wanted to husband, if the word was the correct one, my resources, and now we had come to our conclusion I wanted time alone. I wanted to get it all done with as little fuss as possible.

'I've got to see a person this evening, baby,' said Hal. He moved his head like a pony, his palomino fringe momentarily covering his eyes. He pushed the hair back with his right hand and I saw the darker hair near the skull. I wondered what he would do when he was bald, then thought with some relief that he would probably not go bald but move with the aid of dyes from gilded youth to silver age with no bimetallic middle period.

'That's fine,' I said. 'I'd like to think a bit, too.' As if thinking were something to be done alone. Soon I hoped to be able to stop thinking for good.

'Leave the planning alone for a bit would you?' he said. 'I don't go for the idea of you doing it for yourself, not having a mother and things.'

Had I said I had no mother? Not as far as I was aware. People used to guess because of my domestic hopelessness, but I had rectified that. At school there had been a term of derision, then pity after I had sewn my nametapes on outside my clothes, like small civic awards. CORA GODFREY. CORA GODFREY. Cora, simply, even then.

Hal's face looked odd. He looked a little like a still from a film where someone is very slowly dying young. His eyes were filling with something moist which was gathering in their pink cills. He was a photogenic man, I was sure. A drop of Hal's eye moisture hung from one of his blue-black eyelashes. Hal was exhibiting sympathy. It was of course counterfeit, could well have been used to sell black tulips or those brogues which stretch with the dead foot after death, but I was tired and pregnant and could not risk exposure to sentiment that evening, for fear of melting down.

He faced me and leant his forehead till it touched mine, so our touching heads made a gable for our faces against the now heavier rain. Leaves lay yellow and flat on the shiny road, silent town leaves unlike the crisp country leaves of autumn. He made me thoroughly depressed about not having a mother, as though it were like ordering the wrong wine.

'It will be good,' said Hal, kissing me photogenically, and pushing me gently to meet a swiftly advancing taxi.

XIX

I was grateful to whoever had put the severed tongue in Lucas's car. The rawness of the shock had disarmed him and given him to me for that time he had spent in my house. Had we not passed that time together, I do not think that I would so quickly have decided to accept Hal's proposal. But that I had this occasion to pore over (I had seen him asleep. Can you go further than that?) gave me a dowry of felt life ('What other kind is there?' asked Anto. 'Underfelt life, I suppose.') to take to my grave or my manger. Besides, there was no need to look at it that dramatically, for I gathered that Lucas would always be there. He was fond of Hal. Perhaps, after delving into open chests trying to trap the life within, he was soothed by Hal's superficiality. I have noticed too that some men have a – completely unsexual – nostalgia which is frequently for a lost youth which they did not have. I imagined that Lucas had spent much of his youth isolated by books and by his work, and was nostalgic for a time of action and surface and success with girls which he had passed up. People feel such tenderness for themselves when young. Perhaps Lucas Salik had grown up in a town; Hal had grown up in the country, fed on bacon and Studland crabs and cream. Was Lucas perhaps envious of Hal? No one had told Hal's parents no longer to inhabit their part of Dorset, nor burnt their parish church. Hal's grandparents had not had to hide in the hills from Roman Catholics setting out on a pogrom from Wimborne. Yes, surely that must be a cause of envy.

Sometimes I even thought that Hal, as it were, came with Lucas, and I could not believe my luck. It was not that I envisaged a ménage à trois, but it was good to think that Lucas's life would be parallel to our own.

'I am delighted for you, of course, but Hal is really the lucky one. And me,' said Lucas on the telephone two days after I had become engaged. This confirmed my feeling that he would be there throughout Hal's and my marriage.

'Thank you. I hope I shall please you.' Whether plural or singular, he could never know.

'You will please me.' I felt my wrists grow cold as though they had been wiped with acetone. I rocked as I held the telephone to distract myself from the pleasure.

I did not want to say 'thank you' again or we should be stuck like two characters from Molière faced with a revolving door.

'And, Cora, are you working today or are you able to join me for a late lunch at home? I have to finish some work here but there are some things . . . '

'I am working, but can have lunch.' I was in the charity shop more and more. Angel and Dolores seemed to need me.

'I'll collect you, shall I?' he asked. 'You won't have time otherwise.'

'Oh, thank you, you don't know what a difference that would make.' I had had to start taking buses because the underground made me so ill, and I was not good at it. When I am on the tube I wonder where all the pregnant women are, or have they mastered the buses? They do not walk, for I never see them on the street, and they cannot all be indoors. I have seen only three other pregnant women exposed to the public eye. One was a big blue brigantine of a woman running an easting down Knightsbridge. One was an Indian in a mauve sari with a little boy atop the coming baby; she was trailing a tartan golf-bag full of shopping. The other woman was myself advancing in a shop window. And only I as yet knew I *was* pregnant. So perhaps I had seen thousands more than I knew, but I just could not tell. I look at stomachs now, to see if they shelter citizens of the future, parenthetic people.

'I shall collect you at half-past one. You do not know how I look forward to it,' he said.

At the shop, Angel was as still as a cat. She was stiff with electricity. She hissed down the telephone. She was in places without perceptibly moving towards them. She was dressed as an astral plumber, in dungarees and tennis shoes. In her ears were gold spanners and she wore a belt of gold, which showed that her waist was as narrow as a hand. Furs and feathers and leathers were taboo, but she felt no shyness of treasure and wore metal and gems like a savage queen. With her 'boring' real baubles, she wore false gems. Dolores shared Angel's ropes and manacles and shackles and cleats of minerals. Each of them invariably wore a gold handcuff, a split pair, Angelica explained, used by her great-uncle to civilise jealous mistresses. He would leave them cuffed together for the night, right hands linked. In the morning they would be brought tea – 'And the co-operation of the two thirsty ladies in their mutual desire for refreshment was remarkable to see,' Angel would say, mimicking the old man. Two ladies had stimulatingly displeased him by ignoring the tea. 'Pretty as a picture,' the great-uncle said, Angel told me. The chambermaid saw it too. And how did Angel know? 'Oh, Harding was with us for ever and she had a grey parrot with which she taught me to kiss.' I thought of the dark blue spatula of a parrot's tongue and Angel's pink triangle. 'The parrot had a dark pink crest which stood up when it was excited,' she said, and she looked through me to Dolores who was also rigged as a navvy. The studs at the front of Dolores's suit were haphazardly done up. The chains seemed to weigh her down. She looked trammelled with languor as she sat, little red cotton sandals on the bar of her chair, and legs tense and spread as a frog's, except that her right hand was busy, scratch, rub, writing in what looked like a diary. I assumed it was accounts for the shop. Her hair was caught up in pins to the top of her head so that her eyes blazed unobscured. Both she and Angel had eyes which were long, made to be seen, like those of a pharaonic slave, in sly profile, with a sweep of lid as long, like the undisplaying tail of a peacock. These four eyes looked like the hieroglyphs for fish.

As I grew more pregnant, I became more scared of these two. I had let the side down. I was sure that they had insides which would not be so inefficient as to be hostess to the issue of a man. As for getting married, I dared not tell them. When I did, they would simply replace me, and until then I wanted an income and somewhere to go in the daytime. It had become my only job beside cleaning for Tertius.

For there was money. I had none. When people I had come to know said they had no money, they did not mean what I mean. They meant that the extravagant step they contemplated might not at that moment be prudent. I meant that it was a question of looking to see if that Isle of Man fifty-pence piece I had found in my raincoat lining was legal tender or if it would be best to try it on a chocolate machine before handing it to the greengrocer. This moneylessness was starting to bite. In their middle twenties people start requiring all sorts of hardware; the game of being a student starts to pall. I was good at the appearance of money and hopeless about its principles. If I could make a day go by with the sustained appearance of solvency, I let the next day go hang. I had somehow not learnt the virtues of thrift and providence. More than that, I desired their opposites, though I had never gambled with anything but my life. For every day I just about got through on money from redeemed fizzy-drinks bottles, the lie (that I had money) dictated by my vanity was protected and sustained. The reason many of my contemporaries could play for so long so late and with such dangerous toys was that they could go and recuperate in houses whence nothing could be seen but green. Before their dinner parties they rang Nanny, nodding in her little room in Rye or Brighton, to find out the recipe for thick gravy. And, no matter how wild they were, they would have narrow feet and know how to tip and whom to address as Mr and whom as Esquire. They knew never ever to touch capital. The boys were the same. They changed their shirts twice a day and were neither familiar with inferiors nor keen with their seniors. They had few superiors. They passed out like gentlemen, having aimed the sick inconspicuously, and were impassive, even derisive, in the face of female nakedness. If at a party other women than the stripper were present – real girls, girls whom you married – they knew how to carry on. Treat it as dressage, and make cool and detailed comment indicative of expertise. Just in time, I was getting out. Lucas would take me and Hal under his wing.

'Address these, Cora, would you,' stated Angel. She was folding leaflets. Periodically we sent these out, appealing for funds. Why did Angelica not just auction a selection of golden tools?

No sport in that, I supposed.

So I spent the morning addressing glueless envelopes, glueless because the gum is made from the feet of cows, as anyone who has worked for a newspaper or lived near a knacker will tell you, and is therefore ideologically unsound. There was at my school a girl with such a seraphic face that she was unable to convince people that she had ever done anything wrong. She was poised and lovely. Her rosy cheeks seemed scented with sweetness. She was cruel and loved to tease ugly people. Her tribute was obedience without question and a constant flow of dirty information; if you kept her in these, she left you alone. I bought a term's peace from her with a corked test-tube full of cow gum. I told her I had obtained it not without difficulty from a boy I knew. The terrible smell of sealing that lie I cannot forget. She was in ways a perfect beauty, ethereal to look at and with a real enthusiasm for her subject. Perhaps she was my first Angel. I fall for these tyrannical beauties who are preposterous but a pleasure to please, like monstrous children. Once in possession of your abject devotion, they excise you. You cannot keep them happy for very long. They are, for girls educated only with other girls, not a lesson in one's own sex so much as an instruction in the ways of heartbreakers. From them, you may painfully learn what to beauties of each sex comes naturally, encouragement, evasion, desertion. The smell of cow gum always recalls that summer of meretriciously purchased peace. The licking of envelopes evokes its price.

Angel provided me with a list and a pile of envelopes. The names were the usual ones, the back two pages of most exhibition catalogues and all opera programmes, but this time with their addresses. Magnificent storekeepers, famous scientists, and a procession of older beauties, if you could categorise them at all, seemed to be the catchment area today. But I did not ask Angel how she had made her choice of 'victims'. I have thought before now that she can hardly differentiate between people. She does not see them as more than a herd.

Just before one o'clock, Dolores sighed, put down her pen and stood up. Then, like a cat washing itself, piecemeal, she admired herself, section by section. She walked over to the glass and strained on tiptoe until she could see her face. She smoothed her brows with licked little fingers. She smoothed the pearly brown long lids of her eyes with the middle finger of each hand. She tilted her chin at herself, this way then that, and caressed her own neck till it seemed to grow longer. Then, she tucked her right hand and her left into her dungarees and, as though she was touching icing sugar or talc, she remoulded her breasts. They stood out soft and hard-tipped, on either side of the range of press studs down her front. She held her hands away from her, of necessity at arm's length, and then flattened them slowly down her swerved back, African buttocks and small round thighs. To watch her do this was to watch a sculptress. She had re-made herself, in her own image.

'Wait a bit, Dolly,' said Angelica. 'We've got to wait till the Mouse's trap appears. Who is it Mouse, today?'

Should I feel guilty about allowing Lucas near these girls whose associates, I was fairly certain, had put that disgusting tongue in his car? It was not brave to have hidden that I suspected I knew where the thing had come from. Vanity again, I thought.

'It's Lucas Salik,' I said, and I was delighted to be able to say it.

I was pleased that these girls, who did not care about such things, indeed who despised them, would suspect, if only for a second, that the man I was besotted with was my lover. That they might think this made it a truth to me. I could understand why lies grow out of dreams.

'Oh-ho, and has he cut you about yet?' asked Angelica. 'And has he sliced you open to see what it's like inside?'

'He'd never find out the usual way,' said Dolores. This was a long sentence for her and seemed to bear some meaning which amused her, for she put her hand to her mouth, a human gesture for once. Dolores hummed when she was in her stride, a humming not from the throat so much as from her core. It was an almost soundless whirr like an idling machine or a cat too replete to purr. The noise may just have been the tension she conveyed, a tension not unpleasurable to its dispenser.

'What've you got that he wants, Cora, contacts in the organ world?' asked Angel, and she materialised at my side and pulled Dolores against her so they were like dancing partners, linked at the waist. They were as appealing as animals: that they were human gave them the vulgar but undeniable allure of creatures photographed for a newspaper, two frosty-whiskered leopard cubs. I even seemed to see them in a granular newsprint texture as though I were looking through a veil. This disintegration of what I see precedes tears for me. I hoped that they would not perceive this. I have never liked being teased.

They began to sing. Clues like this would sometimes encourage me to think that I had at last found out their age; but the only way to do that would be to hook them and tell over, as with sharks, their stomach contents, and that must wait till the Resurrection. As I would rise again with my son, so they would each produce the devoured souls of armies of fallen, rich, subjugated men.

They sang:

> Last night I dreamed a dreadful dream
> Beyond the isles of sky
> I dreamed I saw a dead man fight
> And that dead man was I.

Their voices were not thin like children's, but swooped like cats' cries.

'He's here, and we've got to split. We're seeing a man about a dog. Take the afternoon off.'

I was grateful and surprised. Angel took the keys of the shop from her cinctured waist, and we all went out. Before I could introduce Angel, or Dolores could show her surgeon how well she remained, they were gone, tails in the air, starry behinds twinned, and I, heavy with assumed nuptial glee, was in the car of Lucas Salik.

'Cora, it's very good news, I know you are doing the best thing.' Not, I know you will be very happy, I thought. Perhaps doctors are wary of such prognoses.

'Are you sure?'

'I've known Hal for six years and can promise you will always be diverted.' No sermons, no backbone of England references, then. 'And that is a better promise than almost any. The cardinal virtues can be learnt later.' I had a picture of Hal, red-hatted, buttoned into his covering gown, swiving, poisoning, machinating, as cardinals will. Mandrills and bishops have purple in common.

'I'm happy with the ordinal ones,' I said.

He turned to me as we drove. I do not like this, it makes me fear a slip, a skid; I prefer to speak to eyes in the mirror.

'I prefer the cardinal ones. The big ones, if advertised, are absent, and, if present, are like mountains, so great that you can't see them till you're away from them. I mistrust anyway what is larger than life. Saviours, statesmen, generals, saints, they would all be dreary at dinner. I like sinners with besetting virtues. Great big men are like constellations, their faults made fiery by night's blackness all right, but also rather humbling, and, on bad days, making you shake your fist at their splendid absentness.' He spoke to me as though I understood what he said, which made me happy.

'Do you love your patients?' I asked.

'Do you want to ask me that? I love them intensely when they begin to cease to depend on me. I feel as though I created them. Then they leave and they are as they were before, and I have been nothing but a cloud which fell over their life and moved off. It is like a mother, perhaps. I do all I can and I can't do more. But my hands can do more than my brain reports back to me, and that instinct is like love, it is blind but sees clearly too. Shall we eat at home? Do you have to go back? Those girls look like twin Siameses.'

'You know one of them.'

'Do I?'

'She was one of your patients. Dolores Steel.' Did he know she had been in prison?

'Your question is answered, then. I was as deep inside her as a person can be but I don't recognise her. Still, some love is like that.'

'What love? Surely not.' I could not tell what he meant. I would know you in a shaven crowd of skeletons, I thought, and then thanked God I'd not said it. I have seen pictures. I threw away a book I found in the public library. Not to save me, to save them. I felt thrilled by it and was terrified. The book had been borrowed more than any other I'd seen, papered with borrowing slips. The man who wrote the book had been in one of these camps, and now he lived in Wigtown. 'He was the last man in the Wigtown telephone directory,' said my teacher. 'It's one of those names you deny thrice, all zeds. But I expect he counts himself lucky to be there, even the last man in Wigtown. And if you look at that sort of stuff again you'll turn into a toad. It's pornography.' So I would just look at these books in the library, in between bodice-rippers and ballet books. Like most girls brought up in a town, I featured in a series of small violations, among them a sad dark man in a jumper and a duffel coat who felt my knees under the fabloned table in the library one smoky afternoon as I skipped through *The Rise of the Reich*, *The Diary of Anne Frank* and *The Scourge of the Swastika*, looking for pain. Then I took home *The Leopard* and was on the way to recovery.

'I thought you would like to eat in my secret room now that you are one of the family, Cora. I've put it all up there.'

I had not realised that his tall flat had another floor. It was big enough already. He led me upstairs, cautiously, as though he were going to present me to someone whose behaviour could not be predicted.

I took a liberty. 'Do you have a secret life in your secret room?' I asked.

'Don't be arch. I thought you were over that. And don't get hurt feelings. Women always have hurt feelings and it's all show. Wait till you are really hurt. There you are.'

He opened the door into a large warm room between whose high windows was drawn a bath. That is, there was a bath, the old-fashioned sort with feet and smooth flanks, full of water, fuzzed with steam. It was a real bath, though almost everything else about the room was not real, but painted. On all four walls were depicted dancers, tumblers, musicians. The room was a clearing in the heart of a crowd of pastel celebrants, all shown in noisy joy, and all flat and silent. Harlequin, masked and with his nose erect, clasped coy Columbine in her wafered chiffons to his grape-groined body, chequered with kites of cinnamon and bosky mauve. Pierrot mooned over his tortoise-bodied lute. Ribbons of lettuce green hung from it. Among these figures of the *commedia* walked, danced, embraced and drank real people, if you could call them that, the damsels and queens for a day of rustic picnic. It was stylised, yet domestic, unreal in the uniformity of the faces of the revellers, which seemed, like the faces of ballet dancers, to have more in common than simply eyes, nose, mouth, even the actual cast of those features. It was as though the painter had codified the faces, for what was variable and distinctive was the colour, pattern and texture of the limbs, clothes, tents, instruments and bowers of the figures. Swagged, paisleyed, pied, piped, tasselled, pelmetted, stippled and dappled with a lemony sun which was gently overlaid and contradicted by the real pale sun from outside, as it washed in, checked by the windows' astragals, the scene was as busy but orderly as an enormous textile. Appearance was everything. It was not a tidy room but everything in it appeared to be placed, not put. It was full of broken light. The shadows of the last leaves on the trees by the canal showed trembling over their still, painted counterparts. Painted clouds showed flocky underparts where the real sun fell. And the clouds of steam from the bath were not, as nothing was, what they seemed to be. The bath was foaming over, I saw as I came closer, moving past a shawled piano, with a deep head of baby's breath.

'It's customary for brides,' he said.

It was all too lovely.

I am an intellectual snob. In really lovely rooms, I have eaten canned ravioli and hairy toast, with great painters whose trousers are their painting rags. I mistrust loveliness unaccompanied by a little salutary privation. Battered beauties, ruins, were what I was used to. There was something too groomed, too purchased, about coexistent beauty and luxury.

'Don't be a prig,' said Lucas Salik. 'You are a young woman, and engaged to be married for the first time, so leave your high mind on the hatstand and have some of this.'

The feast was cold. It was like the meal which Beauty eats in the house of the Beast before he appears. This was clear delicious food unmixed, primary on the flat palette of the plate. There was red salmon, and red tomatoes dewy without skin; there were red plums and yellow plums and a bowl of green and purple leaves. These leaves were glossy, and there was a smell of oil and wine. Chinese white, four peeled eggs lay like decoys on a blue pond of dish. There was a loaf which was torn in pieces, of a white just warmer than milk but not as deep as cream; the top of this bread was shiny, its declivities and heights grape-shot with seeds. White butter, white cheese and red wine were wax and chalk and ruby in the sinking sun. The room smelt of one other thing, not smoke, or flowers, but something between, with the pervasive strength of the one and the sweetness of the other. On a glass dish flat like a lily-pad lay platelets of sugared carmine jelly.

It was a meal to be painted not eaten – but have you never wondered in what state still lives are by the time their beauty has been transposed into paint? The caterpillars on the plums must be chrysalids on prunes by then, and the game riced with grubs, its feathers long poached by the painter's wife for her hat.

Lucas appeared to be preparing himself to say something. If it was a bargain like Pluto's with Proserpine, I was already too late. I had eaten a plum, which must, in the barter of fruit with time, equal more than six pomegranate seeds.

'You eat,' he said, 'and I'll talk, for the moment. Not for the sake of it but because I've something important to say. Had you thought about the practical side of your life at all?'

I could not say that this wedding would not *be* were I not organising the practical side, a life for the baby, a father and a home.

'I mean where you will live and on what?' he continued. 'I hope you won't think me either interfering or underhand but I have discussed this with Hal and I managed to persuade him to accept a little help. I hope that you will be less reluctant than he. I wonder whether you would allow me to buy you a house. Nothing too demanding for you, but a little security for you both. As you know, Hal's family have land but land is not, as the island race remind one, liquid, and you cannot start your married life in a rented flat. That is, of course you can, but I would not like it and I can afford to do this for you. It will give me pleasure. And, now . . . ' He did not let me interrupt, but like a parent with a picky child buttered me a curl of bread and put it into the hand which was not holding my glass. 'Now you must let me talk about the baby.'

I was dressed much as most of the posed revellers about us; in cloth more patterned than shaped. The baby could not yet show, or could a doctor tell?

He went on. 'If and when there is a baby, when, I hope, rather than if, will you allow me to make it my heir? I have no family left. I am not old but I have no plans. Please say yes.'

'What did Hal say?' I had the surrender of will which overtakes as the anaesthetic floods in. It was at once pleasant and compromising. My motives in marrying Hal were not pure, but they were not as impure as this could make them seem. But who would know?

Lucas sipped his wine. His mouth made that noise, sip, and he looked like someone who very nearly remembers something well forgotten. 'I'll tell you what he said when you've guessed what this is,' he said, and passed me the flat plate of red sweets. I picked up a square. It had a pasty texture; it tasted of Turkish delight made not of summer's roses but of the tastes of autumn, smoke and leaves and apples, a sweet mulch. The sugar made a noise like frost in my teeth. It tasted like the smell in the room. The smell was like musk, and breath, and ash.

'It tastes like the smell in the room.'

'What is it? See if you can track it down.'

I set off about the room, my glass, again full, in my hand. It could be the baby's breath, but could you make a red jelly of the white flowers? Not unless the flowers bled. I pushed my face into the frothing tub, but it smelt only of green stalks and light powder.

'Go to the piano,' he said.

The shawl which covered the piano lid was the transparent red of the smoked salmon, paisley-eyed with almonds of green. It was held against slipping by a pile of sheet music, the pale blue of washed shirts, lettered in spindly Gothic black. At the tip of the fin of lid was a row of yellow apples. The scent came from them. When I picked one up, it was matt, like clean skin, and fluffy like a man's cheek, in towards its stalk. At school they said that I put things in my mouth before I thought I bit it as you might an apple. The flesh held my teeth like the stone the sword. My mouth parched.

'It's a quince. Put one in your sheets and you'll smell your wedding night all year. But not very nice in fact until boiled down to a pulp with a lot of sugar.' Speaking in his voluptuous room against the dying light, he looked oriental.

'I found it,' I said. 'About the house and the child. Thank you more than I can say. I'll try to deserve your kindness. What did Hal say?'

'You will earn it, never fear. Hal said, "Are you ever the fairy godmother?" Shall we discuss plans? Have some more wine.'

XX

I left the seeking of our house to Hal. It was his job, after all. I had not yet met his parents.

Hal and I chose the feast of St Nicholas for our wedding day, to give his family a space before they had to start Christmas. It was as though Christmas was a section of railway, arduously to be built of Yule logs and glistening ribbons of line, cut through the dark green forests of December by the poor Darbos, working in the heat of the snow.

Whenever I had thought of Hal's brothers, I had imagined the architectural orders. Could their parents have named their other sons Saxon, Norman and Roman without seeing their, no doubt, upstanding boys, turbanned in stone, flanking a small doorway into a hidden chapel, or grimacing in ammonite-haired glee from a boss of Purbeck marble? I played with the idea of three *pâtisserie*-coiffed daughters – Ione, Dorrie, and, what else, Corinthia? I did not tell all this to Hal.

'Six December, that's nice, does your mother think it's nice?' said Mrs Darbo over tea the first day I met them in their very warm sitting-room. She was nervous, pretty, shockable. I was perhaps twice her volume and spoke twice as loudly. In her ears slept little gold snails and her hair was like a party cake. She kept her knees together, pushed to one side, as though she were a summer chair, put away for the winter.

Hal had driven me to meet his parents. Parents are about as intimate as you can get, more intimate than sharing a toothbrush. They show you the past and the past is as tender as worn clothes or a mourning brooch. Meeting Hal's family was like meeting a nest of tables. They were separate, flat-topped, and fitted together by no more metaphysical means than by being of different dimensions. Saxon, Norman and Roman, certainly not stone-hatted, were like Hal but not as well-pointed. He was the first-born, the prototype. They did not possess his golden-silver colouring, but then, I was sure, nor did he, naturally. His mother, being a woman, was not of the mould. She was perhaps the smallest table, the one with the most ornamental legs. The father, Rex, was, naturally, the big table, big and brown and square. He was also made for carrying drinks.

They did not drink heavily, the Darbos, but they drank methodically, to mark time. Gin at eleven, sherry at twelve-thirty, something with lunch, a mantled puddle of something creamy afterwards, and starting again at six, with a different, more racy, routine on Sundays developed around what they called Bloodies. All this kept Mrs Darbo very busy with mats, because she hated rings on tabletops.

'Dead,' Mr Darbo was mouthing of my mother to his wife in the absence of my reply, without making a noise, but for the twin d's which leave little doubt.

'Mmm, dear?' said Mrs Darbo, at once pulling her skirt down and crossing her ankles. I said something to Saxon, to spare Mr Darbo realising that I knew my mother was dead, and he explained my trouble to his wife. My mother's death, however else I had thought of it, had never appeared to me as an unacceptable personal odour, but I was aware of its being thus classified by Mrs Darbo. She had a word for such things.

'How aggravating,' she said. She cannot have known what she was saying. In that room, refulgent with polish and glaze and calf and walnut and brass (a club fender like the jaws of a small hell) it was my swelling belly which was aggravating.

For the beat of two ticks of the rocking Dutch fleet on the grandfather clock, we were without words. Then we remembered the reason we were gathered together.

'It's nice you're tall,' said Mrs Darbo. 'You can carry it.'

What do I carry? The baby? She was a blameless woman but she made me want to yell.

I smiled. If I did it without showing my teeth, she did not shrink away.

'The dress. I love a pattern,' she revealed. I had decided, in order to give all the preparations some point, to allow Mrs Darbo to fulfil her dreams on me. I agreed with everything she suggested. Her ideas changed frequently, and she brought her menfolk into line with each hard-taken decision, but we were at the moment following through what Mrs Darbo called a 'motive'. Means were provided, I suspected, by Lucas, the concealed opportunity by the baby. When I thought about the whole business, I felt ashamed. I had to keep these thoughts away, for I was not taking anything serious seriously, except the desperate need for a future for the baby. And I could not even dare really to consider that. How soon would the baby's amiable and hoodwinked grandparents be bringing it a Perambulator, straight up, on the tray with the Sidecars? Would Johnny himself not have been better as a husband? The truth is, I thought, he wouldn't have had me. A blot on the escutcheon.

The 'motive' we were following through for the wedding was currently that of the holly and the ivy. We had had Jack Frost, the Snow Queen, and Christmas Roses. The objections had respectively been glitterdust in the church, artificial snow fumes and the fire insurance, and the terrible cost of fresh blooms. I had suggested that we celebrate St Nicholas's Day and have a big white horse and a little black boy and clogs full of chocolate, but Mrs Darbo costed it up and decided it would be effective but a bit unusual. I appreciated 'unusual', it was like different. It meant Jewish. It meant funny peculiar. It meant tall. It meant *not the same*. Had Lucas met Mr and Mrs Darbo? I thought I wouldn't ask them. We returned to the dress, which was to be trellised with ivy on the skirt, at the back. Not holly – 'Too full of pricks,' said Mr Darbo bravely, his wife's pinched lips daring him. I did not ask about the merry organ. All this was my own fault and if I looked like a west wall that was my fault too. Ivy, the fingery destroyer of houses and stealthy embracer of graves, crept over me. What about a nest with a cuckoo in it on my head, and two eggs?

I had two eggs, in fact. They were from Lucas and they were my engagement ring. They were two oval pearls, and they were the faint pink of the eggs of the Petran sparrow, which lays its eggs precariously on the ridges of the rose red city. The ring was thin and old, its metal gentle like old mirror, and the big paired pearls were held only by being caged from behind. How could Hal allow his friend to buy these things? 'I've no false pride,' he'd say, 'and I like things nice for you. Lucas didn't pay for it in actual fact. He had it knocking about.' I supposed it must have been Lucas's mother's and let it bind me further to him.

'With your height you can take this bold front,' said Mrs Darbo. She was a needlewoman of fearsome dexterity and output; undecorated spaces of colour were a challenge to her. She was planning to corset my torso in a casque of quilted ivy leaves. The poisonous black berries of the ivy were not to be omitted. There was nothing negative in Mrs Darbo's capability; her work, of which there were examples all over 'Cranford', had the hyper-reality of souvenirs. The black ivy berries to be sewn on my breast we had found in a craft shop, they were sold as eyes for soft toys. There were several boxes on a shelf below the clownish bolts of sheeny implausible fur; they were clearly labelled 'Eyes, teddy', 'Eyes, squirrel', 'Eyes, rabbit'. The eyes came in pairs, twisted on a single string. For one-eyed bunnies or Persian pussies with odd eyes there were no allowances in the nursery world.

Precipitated into intimacy with Mrs Darbo, I was grateful for her hobbies. They gave us material for conversation. She was kind to me, though I did not receive the impression that it was a kindness called up by sympathy between us. She was kind because I was Hal's, and if I had genuinely been so, this amnesty-bestowing love would have been enough. As it was, I felt shifty about receiving kindness from her. Her first-born was clearly her favourite and she showed no desire to have a daughter. She was the broker of feminine power in that house.

Sometimes in the days before the wedding, I found myself staring at some neutral particle of the complicated celebration about to take place, and would snap to, aware that I had been giving a cold ham or a ribbon or a list of names the evil eye. But there was also a pleasant sense of being just a leaf in the flood, as the days wound towards The Day. Mrs Darbo referred to December the sixth like this, which gave it a Last Trump sonority. Hal and I did not refer to the day between ourselves. Had I cared to think about it, he might have been a mystery to me, but a mystery implies a desire for solution and I certainly did not want to find a solution. Once or twice, I wondered why he had implied to Lucas Salik that the Darbo family sat safe among expansive lands in grand decay. But I was in such a hurry to be over with the entire business that I really just thanked God that for some reason Hal wanted what I wanted, and stopped my eyes and ears to almost everything else. I was not interested in him. I do not think that I thought of him as a person, with his own secrets and desires and bad nights. I was smug with solitariness. It may have appeared, buffed to a sheen by my pregnant glow, like rapt early passion.

Mrs Darbo kept the dress in tissue paper which was pearly on one side. She had what Rex Darbo, doting and virile, called 'Monica's room' and the whispering parcel was hung up in it, a calico-covered torso. 'God knows what she gets up to in there,' he would say. Rex had an equivalent room, referred to by his sons and wife as 'Father's study'. The word study is almost exclusive to people with awe of and distaste for books. Gloria had once asked me whether I had studied all the books in my room. 'No,' I replied. 'That's a relief,' said Gloria, fetching a stage sigh, 'I can't get around to studying a plain book.' A plain book is a book without pictures. Being a Roman Catholic, Gloria is used to holy pictures. Hal's father, Rex, had many coloured books, mostly concerned with stupendous feats of engineering, or what he called 'man's conquest of nature'.

There was bounty in that house. Warmth and food and drink induced a bovine content. Hot water flowed almost silently into deep baths whose sides were lapped in carpet. The walls never trembled with passing traffic, as did my walls in London. The windows showed a garden featuring a tennis court and a swimming pool, now laid down under taut blue latex for the winter. There was a patio to catch the absent sun, and a pair of urns containing small rubbery plants. The bird table had a porch, and its three chalets were of different sizes, to segregate the different classes of bird. I had seen no villainous crows in the taller trees about, hints of the old New Forest. It was as though crows were too obscure for this bright world. I wondered where Hal and his brothers had had their childhood in this secretless place? Had they had to escape to grow up? For all the security of the house, I was thirsty whenever I was there, as though my secret were parching me like swallowed pumice, and I felt like someone staying in a luxurious hotel, not to his taste, and not at his own expense, who can nevertheless not escape the fear of the bill. Each big cold unslaking drink would appear on the eventual tally.

A large tent was to be put up in the Darbos' garden. Mrs Darbo

selected green and white stripes as the most suitable colour scheme
to promote the theme of holly and ivy.

I told Dick and Gloria about the holly and the ivy. They were in
the basement room in our shared house. The room smelt of railway
tea. They were dyeing startling white lace in buckets of strong tea,
for the Marschallin's nightgown.

'Holly and Ivy,' they said. 'Sounds like a pair of queens.'

Seeing them together, I considered how easy things are for those
who have work which they love, and how happy twice over they
were since they worked and loved together. Gloria wrung out a
squeaking hank of lace over a bucket, doubled it and wrung again.
He was stronger than he looked.

'Jasmine tea would've been nice,' he said.

'Save that for *Butterfly*,' said Dick, and pulled another pin from
his mouth. He was crouched on the floor, pinning the hem of a
dress the ochre of old mixed mustard. It was frogged, like a
dressing-gown for a levee.

'Which grandee is that for?' I asked.

'Oh that's not for *Rosenkavalier*. It's a beggargirl's dress for
something else, but you have to do it in all this posh cloth. Rags
don't look good. They don't look believable. You don't believe the
real thing.'

'Not enough impact, the real thing,' said Gloria, and he dried his
hands before giving Dick a touch on the shoulder. Dick was so
accustomed to the affection and its source that he did not turn
around.

It was December the first. Dick and Gloria were very gentle with
me in these days. They took me out a lot. We were having a
valedictory honeymoon with each other. They cooked for me, which
they had not done before, nicer things than I would have made for
myself. Preparing food made me ill, anyway.

I had given my notice to Angel that morning, explaining that I
was to be married in five days' time.

'I know,' she said. 'I'm looking forward to it. I've not replied to
the invitation yet, I'm afraid. I've been busy.' I supposed Hal had
invited her.

Dolores looked up. They both wore collars of jewels today and
had come through the snow in serapes of bright wool. They wore
clothes in a way which made these clothes appear to be fetishes.

'Cora, I meant to say, well done, that's great. You've been really useful. We couldn't have done it without you.'

They kissed me goodbye, and I felt ashamed that I was flattered by them even as I feared them and let them roll me away, me and my floorbound domesticity, like a tired old rug made to be trodden on.

Never afraid of archetypes and symbols (they believed horoscopes, portents, tarot; they were always in the ascendant), they gave me for a wedding present a wallet of cooking knives and a pot of cymbidiums.

'They're just from the orchid house at home,' said Angelica with the aristocratic ungraciousness which gives its recipients a craven shot of gratitude.

Knives must not be given hand to hand. They bring bad luck, as Angel and Dolores would surely know. The donor must put them down. The recipient may then pick them up. But I took these knives as they were intended, directly. I was given over to destroying my own life.

Having put the knives carefully down at home, I gave them to Dick and Gloria, who were pleased and used them to cut vegetables for a stew. They did not think Angel and Dolores could possibly have intended them to cut meat.

'I think they meant them to cut orchids,' I said, and we all laughed. Dick and Gloria held their groins in faked pain. Higher now in my belly, the baby pressed against my heart.

XXI

I had four full days to go. Before going to bed in London on the night of the first of December, I had received a telephone call from Monica Darbo. It was clear that she found my passivity fitting. I wondered whether she felt the great contusion of will deep in my malleable manner.

'Some last things, Cora,' she said. I thought of last things: urns, caskets, cerements, the emergency rations of Egyptian graves, a few raisins and a slave. There is a congruence about weddings and funerals in Christian life; but for the hats, they are where we most nearly meet our Maker's eye. Christenings are more dangerous because the children, squibs who have not yet learnt good taste, keep lighting on things unmentionable.

'Fire away, Monica.' She made me talk as I strictly do not. As we grew older, would I speak to her through birth and bereavement as though she were someone pleasant enough whom I had met in a middle-class queue, at the butcher or the lingerie sale?

'The heaters go on in the church two days before to take the chill off, expensive but there you are, and it's not as though church was the living-room. But the flowers and foliage prefer a bit of an edge, so I've said to keep it parky in the vestry, where we'll be signing. You won't mind that, will you? Then the green stuff can stay in there till the last moment.'

'That sounds most reasonable. Thank you for doing all this, Monica,' I said into the receiver.

'It's what I'm here to do. It's not as though you could be here *with* Hal.' Her voice implied that we would somehow mark each other and appear as 'seconds' at our wedding.

'How is Hal?' I was just a good enough actress to ask.

'Out, he's so busy at the moment. Such a lot to do. But *you* must just get yourself as beautiful as possible for the day.' My looks were not in her style, nor were they at their best. Had it not struck her either, who had girdled my waist with satin leaves, that I was growing like a cuckoo, in the heart of her own nest?

'And Cora, I've got plastic bags to put over the bridesmaids' heads. You know, in case it rains.'

I thought of the three little girls, plump, oven-ready, behind plastic, no breath clouding the clear bags, the satin feet like little trotters.

'How sensible. What if there's snow? Or a hurricane? Won't the tent blow away?' But I must be careful not to be too satirical.

'On the whole early December is pretty still round here.' The air was like jelly all around 'Cranford'.

'I've had Mrs Hall do two identical cakes, so people don't feel fobbed off by the bottom layer.' Do you dream then of your husband to be only if you have a slice from the top tier of wedding cake under the pillow? Perhaps a slice from the second tier leads to dreams of adultery?

'And the bottom tier is already in the freezer for a christening.' Her voice was unprurient. A baby would be like a car, what one had. Which was lucky in the circumstances.

'I've made buttonholes of laurel and mistletoe for the groom and best man.' She was referring to her two elder sons, yet their rank must be mentioned. She was like a service wife speaking of her husband to an NCO.

'Mr Hall is going to wash the car, in and out.' The Darbos' car smelt of pine and new carpets. 'There's a new lavender fascia polish I like the look of.' The car was of a colour referred to as 'heather' by Mrs Darbo, who never called colours by their bolder, more general names. Her bath was lemon, her suitings aqua, almond, sky. There was a good dash of gouache-like white thickening her perceptions.

'Is there anything I can do?' I asked, a bit too late.

'No, love, as far as that goes, we just want you to look your best and say the right things.'

I was shocked to tears by the endearment. Like a deformed face touched, my heart swelled dangerously, and I said in a voice colder than I intended, 'Good night, and thank you.'

I slept very well, waking up with a child's appetite, refreshed by the hours of crying I had put in before sleep. Dick and Gloria had made black coffee in a jug and there was a pot of milk on the old stove, whose thorny trivets rattled when the milk approached the boil.

'The trick's to catch it while it's all froth and no liquid, and not spill a drop,' said Gloria.

'Tasty,' said Dick. He stressed the second syllable. He was quiet in the mornings.

'Was that Holly or Ivy reduced you to tears last night, then?' asked Gloria. Like a lot of untidy people, he was very neat in some ways, and one of these was to keep dirty talk in the bedroom.

'Could you hear? I am sorry.'

'It's only natural, four days off and counting.'

'Don't be nice to me, Dick, or I'll start again. Give me sugar, jam, honey, anything to fill me up.'

'You've got fatter. Don't overdo it. Brides are meant to melt away. Anyway, you've got love, you don't need sweets.'

'Does it show?'

'What?' they both asked.

'The fatterness.'

'Only to us. We watch waistlines all day, remember. Too much body in the corps and we're on to it. But yours isn't food, is it, or is it?'

'No,' I said.

They both spoke at once. From ferociously respectable homes themselves, they were faced with something they understood,– a shotgun-bride. Probably they had seen it dealt with before. Gloria anyway was often in touch with saints Anthony, Jude and Rocco, for lost things, lost causes and lost potency.

They fell back on kitchen witchcraft, warm drinks and old sentences.

'Two birds with one stone . . . '

'Can't cry over spilt milk.'

'Dry your eyes and drink up.'

They were incurious about Hal's attitude to the baby. Probably they assumed he knew. We were so near to the wedding that I felt I could ask them not to tell.

'I don't want to spoil it for everyone,' I said.

'But babies are the point,' said Dick.

'Don't back-seat drive, love,' said Gloria to him. 'We won't say. Now or never. It's not her fault we're experts. A doctor wouldn't know yet. Or does he?' he said, turning his head over his shoulder to ask me. They were both very curious about Lucas, probably on account of his celebrity in the newspapers.

'No he doesn't,' I said. The thought of him made me so empty I wanted to suck on a spoon of honey all day. I was viscous with self-pity. Like all lonely secret-keepers, I was near to telling everything. It was only fortunate that my discoverers were Dick and Gloria. It could as easily have been Stanley, the tramp who sang and masturbated all day on the bench outside. It could have been the woman in the supermarket, who had picked my leeks up, looked at them very closely, and told me her husband did not like foreign food.

'Will you be all right if we leave you till tonight?' asked Dick. They were taking more notice of me than ever before. It was horribly touching. There was one word I could not bear them to say.

It was their last word as they left. 'See you later, little mother.'

After they had gone, I made a loaf into sandwiches. I made golden syrup sandwiches. I made sandwiches with hundreds and thousands. I made sandwiches with strawberry jam, the cooked berries like anemones at low tide. I made molasses sandwiches, which smelt like horses in winter. I made them all before eating them, and I put them on a white plate. I was in my nightdress and by the time I had finished it was dirty with stickiness. I was not full, though my teeth tasted like seaside rock. But the ulcerous hunger was still there. Sometimes I could feed this emptiness with a bout of destruction. I walked to the bathroom, and looked at myself in the mirror, face only. I looked until I had made rivers of the red veins in my eyes, creeks of the lines on my forehead, rainforest of the roots of my hair. I blew up the image of my face like a photograph, until I saw it so grotesque and so enormous that I could imagine myself dancing around each black follicle on the waxy white floor of my scalp. I imagined nits grazing like sheep on these uplands. I blew the horrid picture up, till the grain was like a magnified photograph of a murder victim. I made myself dead.

Then I took the mirror and threw it into the bath, so that I could no longer see this ugliness.

The bits of mirror, white in the white room like seagulls in snow, lifted and settled like ice. After the one big noise, there was only the sound of settling. The white pediment of the mirror's frame was dusty with old powder, like a ruined doorway after shellfire.

I resumed the day.

Washing the white plate and my smutched nightdress and tidying the bathroom took most of the morning. I turned on the radio. It made me included once more, member of that family of unseen listeners. I felt it gave decency to me, so reasonable were the speakers who returned familiar as friends but not as personal. There must be other girls listening, girls in the club. Yet this was not the radio of contact and access and phone-in – I was nervous of that – but the radio of made jokes and prerecorded surprise. The only real surprises on this radio station were the big ones: wars, strikes, murders.

The programme was *Desert Island Discs*. 'And one book . . . ' I moved away from the radio to put my shards of mirror, now wrapped in newspaper, into the dustbin. The castaway is also permitted to take one luxury. I had often considered this. Lipstick, women say, but the clever ones know they can suck the red Morocco of their Bible for that. As it was, with the baby, perhaps I should ask for a luxury for him. A father was rather more than a luxury. Maybe the baby was my luxury.

I took a pot of cooling tea into my bedroom and started to pack my things ready to move to the house Hal had found. He had liked the idea of what he called investment property, which, as far as I could see, meant very expensive and bound to become more so. It was in a part of London I did not care for, Fulham. I was obscurely pleased about this, as it dissociated me further from my own life. He was welcome to fill it with sunken baths and kitchen peninsulas. Yet it was a present from Lucas Salik.

I felt that the house was from Lucas Salik to someone else, I did not know whom, not to Hal and myself. It was as though we were to squat in it, or at any rate I was to do so. The house was being fitted at unseemly speed with expensive things. There was nothing money could not buy. The garden, now filled with old paintpots and propped trestles, its pond stacked with discarded accoutrements of departed lives, too vulnerable for the open air – a clothes horse,

a carpet beater like a pretzel, a clyster perhaps for wasps' nests –
would, I was sure, be neat if unleafy on our return from honeymoon.

It is impossible not to feel a honeymoon as a holiday apart from
other holidays. I do not think there can be such a thing as a second
honeymoon, though perhaps it is different if you belong to a church
which can annul. But I think, like virginity, a honeymoon can come
only once. I did not know where ours was to be. 'Nowhere too
poor,' said Hal. 'But not too expensive either.' This did not leave
anywhere very much, and I imagined that real honeymooners would
surely like best the rich savannas of whatever bed in which they
found the other.

Towards four o'clock, I finished packing up my possessions.
They looked like stage properties. There was no menagerie of toys,
but the toy clothes of girlhood – shorts, little skirts, ballet shoes,
braces with redcurrants sewn down them – allowed themselves to
be packed small, as though they had shrunk. I boxed away the shoes
like snakes in which I had first seen Lucas Salik. They, like the
shoes with telephones at the heel, were products of afternoons of
prototype-making, when I thought that I must be able to make and
sell shoes. There is a market for gimmicks, as long as you are not
too original, or so I told myself, sent away by shoemakers, and
having left no glass slipper at anyone's threshold. 'Imaginative, but
unwearable,' they had said. I was determined to prove them wrong.
But, of course, they were exactly right.

My books looked smaller, and the dust lay on them like ash.
Green Greek and red Latin, the parallel texts packed neatly into a
single box. 'Dead languages,' Hal had said, and I felt very tired as
though I might crack of boredom if I heard myself reply. 'What use
is Classics in today's society?' he said and I resented the singular
verb and bit my tongue.

I left out from my packing a sponge bag. My nightdress was
drying round the tun of the immersion heater. A small suitcase
packed for the unknown destination of my honeymoon – our honeymoon – stood like a hod of bricks at the side of my fort of boxes.

I went to the now mirrorless bathroom and pushed the bathplug
into its socket. It was a universal plug, such as travellers to Russia
use, and it would not fit snug. I tipped a mogul of blue salts into
the tub and turned on the taps, which called a seabird's cry from
the heater, and a dim roar. There was a smell of matches as the

boiler ignited. The water rose, blue and troubled, up the sides of the bath. I stepped in, thinking, if I was thinking at all, about making a cake for Dick and Gloria. Perhaps I could even bake something into it as the prison visitor bakes in the file, two bachelors' buttons maybe. I rocked. The baby rose to the top of me as I lay. It rested like cream over milk.

I awoke, and heard Dick and Gloria themselves. The bath was not quite cold. The wind was getting up outside, flapping like a sail going up. The gusts were caught among the masses of the city, an inconsistent, interrupted wind.

Dick and Gloria sounded quiet, like nurses.

'She's not in the bedroom, only a lot of boxes,' said Gloria.

'Cora, are you about?'

I pulled myself out of the bath as out of a rocking chair in sand, my pregnant body off its centre, and put on a towel.

'Hello Cora.' They looked embarrassed.

'I'm sorry I've not got any clothes on. My nightie's wet and I'm afraid the bathroom mirror . . . '

'Get a drink,' said Dick to Gloria, and he pulled me into their room which was like the parlour of an out-of-season house in Chekhov, the furniture covered with the dustsheets of the tea-impregnated lace.

We had brandy from thick glasses. Had they not been thick, I would have cracked mine into my palm.

'We raced with the telephone. We thought Hal might get you first. Something rather bad has happened to Lucas Salik.' They were that good. They did not draw to themselves the glamour a bearer of bad news can claim, with suspense and banner headlines.

I felt three things. One was a sharp deep pain, as though I had been sliced. One was guilt, at not having loved him enough to provide a protection. The third, as involuntary as a smile at a funeral, was relief. There could be no wedding now.

ANNE

XXII

I was not looking for it. I saw it first in the paper. The only reason Tertius did not get in with the news beforehand was my insomnia, which had held off till about four in the morning and then arrived and faced me out like a clock whose hands will not move. I opened my shutters and watched the London darkness change beyond the balcony. It changed from deep festive blue to cupreous green to rusty red. There was a wind which came from no fixed quarter. The leaves had been swept away by a giant with dust in his hair and a stiff besom. His coat was shouldered in reflecting plastic which was as proclamatory as a white stick; it said, I am very slow, do not run me over while I sweep up leaves before your car. His cart was made of some base metal like zinc, frosty with arcs of fanned shimmer. Metallic too, the moon showed sharp in the changing sky. I moved to the other, cold, side of my bed, and took up my book. I could as well have written letters or cooked a small feast, but there is a night-shift loneliness to these things, done alone; with the one other, of course, they are transformed.

I read my book by turning its pages. I had no presentiment, for I could not feel time passing. I jerked to complete alertness with rough eyeballs and a snapped neck when the papers came slapping through the letterbox like fish.

I receive all the newspapers in case there is one I feel like reading. There is no nonsense about ironing them, but at Stone the tabloids go into the low Aga for ten minutes and in London I wear white cotton gloves which get black on Sundays. If you read one of those tabloid papers without wearing gloves and then went out and killed a man, the police would have you by the evening edition.

Today there was no time for gloves. I am used to pictures of Lucas in the newspapers, but these pictures were cropped. I recognised the photograph; it had been taken at a party. His face, repeated in various sizes on the front page of each paper, looked facetious without the body, at ease, one hand no doubt holding a glass, from which it had been separated. I was used to seeing photographs of Lucas with children tented up in bed or parents looking like lottery winners. But these reproductions of this personal photograph suggested not the saintly surgeon the papers as a rule promoted. He looked vulnerable and exposed. I did not read the words till I was back up in bed, where I had dropped the papers from my bundled nightdress. If I don't read the words, they will go away, I thought. I'll phone him and he will be there.

He had been attacked, it seemed. He was not dead, though he had been left for dead. An attendant had found him; attendant of what, the papers did not say. Like the street sweeper, there must be people who sweep up corpses. I wondered if the attacker realised just whom he had been assailing, if he had read of his victim in the paper the morning before, if he connected the surgeon and the falling, bloody man. He had been robbed. He had been beaten and cut about in what the police were able to describe as 'a brutal fashion'. Show me the kind cut.

None of it was at all unusual in these violent times. Sir Lucas was a well-dressed man, distinguished looking. The implication was that the streets are not safe for those of this description. Only the poor and already halt should go out; let the others stay in their well-appointed quarters. Some papers implied that he had simply conducted lightning, that fame has its black side. Some spoke of the ingratitude of a society served by these – immigrant was the word – healers; there was a declamatory piece of hysteria about blood for blood.

It was, like all news, a game of ambiguity. Read one way it meant one thing, read in the other way it meant another.

There was a fog of implication about the whole thing, which suggested that the papers were going to see which way things went. If he died, he would be honoured richly. If he was kept alive by heart surgery, all well and good, rather a coup for the biter bit school of thought. If he mended very quickly but there wasn't much else in the way of news, well . . .

I supposed it must have been a boy. The newspapers would not be unaware of this but it was not yet of any use to them.

I could see him in my head. He was calling. He was very pale and he was bandaged. He lay on his side as though in a painted deposition. He looked stretched. The blood was very clear, not brown, and it kept coming and coming. It came in a regular seep and surge, seep and surge, as he grew whiter. This picture left me and I thought back to the actual time of the attack. What I could not bear to think of was the moment when, as I assumed it must have, desire had changed to fear. At some split, sectioned, second the fear which was part of the desire must have eclipsed it. It was the touch of the inorganic knife which must have done it. I did not know, but thought he must be used to cuffs and kicks, of a regulated kind, held within bounds. I do not understand his need but I do not fear it or dismiss it on his behalf and I knew that Lucas did need it.

I could not stop thinking about him, about his last moments. He must have passed out. I thought of his head, low in dirt. I knew, as I knew at Mordred's death, that this was something which would not leave me. Not that it would haunt me, nothing so insubstantial. It was a positive constant, like love. I thought of him as I arose and washed and dressed. It was not a gentle folding of thoughts about Lucas, as though preparing him for the gradual washing-out we accord even the dead we have greatly loved; it was that nothing did not remind me of him, dirty and broken and bloody. The dawn was late. There was a magnesium brightness low under the fading wheel of moon. The sun came came up like revenge, red.

But, look, I had him dead already. He might not be.

Tertius's telephone call was a relief. To talk about it was for a second to abscond from the fearful cinema of blood in my head. It was clear that he had not yet worked out a way of distancing himself from it; I was not sure of Tertius's own tastes (do you know if your neighbour sucks oranges or cuts them up or just eats the smiling pieces as they come?), but he must have felt a guilty relief that it was not he who had been cut down. Later, if Lucas lived, Tertius would be the first to say, 'Lucky old you, I've never managed to get them to go that far,' and look around the room to see the effect, but now he was all officious spokesman and helpmeet. He was crying. I blessed him for it. He sounded like someone who is swallowing blades. My tears started to come; they were cold. They would not stop. I was disgusted at my own unbloody, clean state. I wished it could have been me. At least then I should not have to think about it, I could just die.

'Can I come to you?' I asked.

'Are you all right on your own?'

It was as though murder was catching. I would be murdered if that would make him out of pain. I hated the slits in his body. Entrance into the body is private, not for strangers. I hate clean cuts, they make cheese of flesh. I hate the glimpse they afford of within, shiny and meticulously packed. A sharp knife to my finger, and I am holding it aloft like Liberty, to bring the blood back to my heart.

How would they hang this whole man aloft to retain his blood?

'I'm not all right on my own. I'll be better with you. I'm coming,' I said.

'I'll ring the hospital.'

I could not drive myself, I was shaking too much, in irregular spasms, as though my body were trying to throw off a weight, which it could not. People jerk like that when they are exorcised. It seemed unfair to me as the taxi drove through the awakening streets that I was free to do as I wished with my body, but Lucas had had that taken from him. The taxi was surprising and beautiful to me, a barouche of leather, glass and steel. Its several blacks, of rubber, hide, paint, were too much for me to take in. A bunch of flowers would have slain me with colour and variety. I felt like someone whom a bullet has missed in war. I could see nothing but the futile beauty about me, for the bullet had hit my beloved friend, but its sharp trajectory had been enough to make me see how bright life was and how close death.

'I feel like the shit who pushes his way into the last lifeboat,' said Tertius at his chambers. 'I doubt I'll ever forget this day.'

'December the third. Oh my God, worst of all, the wedding,' I said.

'What do you mean, worst of all? Can't you ever let up? Please, Anne, have a care. He's not a social problem, he's our best friend.' I saw that Tertius was pleased to carp at me. It was restorative. His last sentence was not convincing.

'You know what I mean, "worst of all". There's nothing so

dreadful as calling-in festivities. It's bad enough when the bride decides she's got to join a cult in Devon, but as for this . . . '

Tertius began to laugh. 'How would you suggest the wording went?' he asked. '"On account of the untimely demise of the groom's – ahem – benefactor at the hand of a warrior unknown though to be honoured in a white wedding world where boys and girls live happy ever after, we are holding not nuptials but obsequies"? I'm certain in these enlightened days, Anne, you can get them ready printed.'

Bitterness is wanton, like showing the hangman the gauge of your neck, even wearing a pretty silky slip-knot around it in readiness. It also comes easily to lazy sentimentalists; it bestows an articulacy which sounds like thought and fires up the clay of sentiment till it resembles a vessel which will hold water. Mostly the bitter ones started with little sweetness, anyway. But Tertius's sexual-guerrilla talk *was* caused by something, I was sure; he seemed very upset at the thought of the cancelled wedding, and the upset was coming from him in shocks of irritation quite apart from his grief about Lucas. I felt it from him as you might feel the irritation of a man who has missed a plane in an earthquake. The unheroic side of life continues. That is one of the hardest things to face, the banal form of life after death.

'What did the hospital say?' I asked. There was so much emotion in the room that I wanted to bring it to heel before we had a fight, just to stop it swallowing us. I sat in the window seat. A shute of sunshine ended in my lap, full of motes. I had no idea at all of what to wear; oh God, let him get better so I can tell him that he has discovered the occasion of my not having a thing to wear.

'They said did he have any parents? I said that *they* were his employers, did they have no records? They said that I was clearly overwrought and that they advised two Disprin and a book but no, at the moment he was serious, not out of danger.'

'It makes him sound like a little ship. Can we see him?'

'Certainly not, unless he gets worse or better. To put the pennies on his eyes or in his mouth or wherever, or else to take him round adult games and deli food, I suppose.'

'Have you spoken to Hal?'

'I can't find him. I have tried Lucas's own flat, Hal's parents, the *nid d'amour* in Fulham . . . '

Like his boisterous clothes and cubic cufflinks, his expression seemed tactless but gallant, as though his show must go on.

'He's not at his work?'

'No one seems to be able to find him. And I don't want to be the first to tell Cora.' He pondered for a moment. 'Do you really think the wedding should be called off?' This seemed to worry him a good deal.

'I think we should all think about it seriously. I suppose we should try to do whatever Lucas would want us to do.'

Tertius looked shifty, like someone blaspheming in his sleep on a train, who has awoken to find his carriage full of nuns. He did not seem able to stop his face assuming a barker's jovial untrustworthy expression. Poor thing, here he was, miserable, but his big red face could not accommodate it.

'I'm sure Lucas would want us to go on,' said Tertius. He made the marriage sound like the attainment of a summit. He was an incongruous man of action.

As Lucas's oldest female friend, I felt that the ordinances and stratagems of the next few days would be up to me. Like cleaning sinks, organising rites of passage falls to the women. Lucas's own mother I knew was dead, his father too.

'Very well. This is what we'll do. We shall decide nothing about the wedding till we have spoken to Hal and Cora. We cannot visit Lucas in hospital, but we must make sure they have each of our telephone numbers and we must call them every hour if we are not at home. We have two days clear before the wedding. Either he must die quickly or he must show a big improvement soon.' I felt very strong and completely breakable, tense as frozen metal.

It was as though I had pushed Lucas out to sea. Life and death were too great for my control. I was left with the trivial and comprehensible, a party which would or would not take place, its provider either rocked in the deep or sunk beneath it. I prepared myself not for the first time in my life for a midwinter spring of assumed competence.

Radiant with self-control, I kissed Tertius's red face with my cheekbone, and went out into the wind. I knew what to wear.

I would keep him alive with my will.

XXIII

I took a short-cut home past the shop of Mr Virtue, in its mews off Bond Street. As a rule, there is in the window one slung masterpiece of vair or blue mink, the restraining chains against robbery unconcealed. At night the window is screened with mesh as solid as the marble fretwork in a mosque, though Mr Virtue would not like that comparison. It was on grounds sartorial rather than religious that he was suspicious of Mohamedans, making for them as he did coats of great splendour which might never be publicly seen. But their taste must have given him some variety in his work.

I have been to synagogue with Lucas, though he told me he preferred church with me since it was less personal (but what could be more personal than that bleeding man on the cross?), and the upper level where the women stand was all sheeny dark fur seamlessly stitched by Mr Virtue and men like him, every coat the same – though without the effortless uniformity of the original contents – being tailored, cut and fitted for the new but secondhand wearer.

Today, the shackled trophy was not in the window; the grille was down as it should not have been during the daytime. Like a star, but not the evenly pointed star of David, was a crazed burst in the glass before the grille. A policeman dignified the door of the shop, giving it almost diplomatic status. I pitied him in the bitter cold; he was not wearing gloves, which seem to be the preserve of the enemy. Burglars, stranglers, aristocratic Nazis and collaborative wops may wear gloves; junta leaders, despots and dictators wear gloves, and the Guardia Civil; but bobbies do not. While they may not have cold feet, they must have cold hands.

Today it was not a shock for me to see this ugliness and indication of violence. They accorded with how I now knew the world was, unless I could outwit it.

The unreal self-control made me able to think about the policeman's gloves at the same time as I grieved for my friend. I decided that I must investigate what had happened here. I had trained myself to stay sane in the face of horror. By dissociation and observation, I reminded myself that in the midst of death we are in life.

Robberies at furriers' premises are not uncommon, though it is more usual for the workrooms or the storeroom to be chosen. I approached. Haloed, as in a war comic, by the starry hole in his window, was the face of Mr Virtue. He was wailing. His wailing seemed to come in cantos, as though he were telling an old story.

'Please let me in,' I said to the policeman.

'Sorry, lady,' he said, 'the premises is not open to customers today.'

'I should think not,' I said, 'but Mr Virtue is my friend.'

'Who shall I say then, lady?' he said.

'Can I not just go in?'

'Security. We must obtain the names of all people who go in and come out.'

'Lady Cowdenbeath,' I said.

'Not a friend, then,' said the policeman.

But he let me in with a new resentful deference. Uniformed security forces fear the aristocracy. Plain-clothed detectives in fiction merely defect from it.

Mr Virtue could not stand still; he was walking about the room picking up and letting drop the pieces of glass which lay across each other like ice. The grey room was foggy with fur, as though enormous cats had been fighting; the surprising thing, one felt, was that there was no blood, when the scene was so clearly that of the aftermath of violence. The impression was that of those perverse poised photographs of beautiful young women in red underwear and icy gems. The shocking thing about the wreckage of Mr Virtue's shop was the elegance of it. Sheeny caterpillars of monkey fur and snowy lianas of fox-tail crawled down the walls. A silvery grey conversation seat the shape of the symbol for infinity stood in a drift of smoky mink pelts. The grey walls, covered with a damask which changed with the light, fitful, as the wind blew clouds over the white winter sun, had been cut open. Through these fraying gashes were visible panels of some insulating material; the purchasers of very expensive goods like not only warmth but quiet.

Mr Virtue was making a noise like the breathing of a large unwell animal in its earth. He stepped over a heap of mauvish and lavender skins; they had the grey bloom of grass tussocks near the sea, and where the skin showed it was bleached like drift-wood. It was as though the animal owners of these reassembled skins had returned and spent the night fighting, reincarnated inimical species in a tame setting. The mess looked like none that humans could make.

'Look at the paper behind the sound-proofing,' said Mr Virtue. He had a strong accent. His ears and nose grew black hairs and where he shaved was blue. Over each ear was a long curl of black hair and his eyebrow was a line over his khaki-pouched eyes. He wore the white overall of a butcher or a scientist, but it was sewn at the breast with his own name. From his pocket protruded a folding ruler. His hands were white with French chalk. He was a small man with tiny feet. He kicked, not so as to hurt, the soft mauve pile of fur. Beneath it, face down, were fans of papers. His accounts, I supposed, whose figures were to tally with the mending of his burnt child's skin.

'Mr Virtue, what is this, do you know, why did they not *take* the furs they found here?'

'Look at the paper behind the sound-proofing,' said Mr Virtue. He was still making the noise as though he had breathed burning gas. I thought that I must do as he said, just to keep him from strangling on his indignation. He moved about the room like a dog with nowhere to go, shaking, dainty on his feet, having a care to his back. He looked unbearably cold.

'The paper?'

'Where they have split the panel. Look behind it. Just snap a bit off. It doesn't matter.'

Polystyrene snaps like rice-paper. I broke off a long triangle and dropped it among the splintered glass. It landed without sound.

'I thought so,' said Mr Virtue. 'But I did not want to discover it on my own.'

'What is it, Mr Virtue? Can I help?' I felt unable to touch him but was sure that that was what he needed. 'Where is Mrs Virtue?'

I asked, feeling useless and out of place. I wished he were a stranger so that I might embrace him.

'Mrs Virtue, thank you, is at the hospital with Tomas. Look at the paper, now, be so kind.'

'It is ordinary striped paper, about fifteen years old, nice enough.'

'And I worked for twenty-five years to afford it and twenty more to afford to cover it up and who cares at all?' My Virtue began to cry without any help from his body. It seemed to be fighting him. 'I think it is a perfectly nice paper as you say and I wish I had perfectly nicely left it on the perfectly nice walls so that this perfectly nice person could come and perfectly nicely put their knife into it. Why did I waste the time? Why did I improve myself whatsoever? The police say this is what I must expect. I tell them that it is what I have learnt not to expect, and it has taken me my whole life to learn not to expect it.' In between his words, Mr Virtue's breath was sawing in his chest. He looked not violent but ashamed. There was a trace of something very alarming to me. He was indignant, frightened – and unsurprised.

'Who, and why, Mr Virtue, and what do the police say?'

'The police say . . . the police say' – Mr Virtue drew breath – 'that this sort of thing is to be expected where things of great value are found. I tell them that the people who have been here are not thieves or they would have gone to where the things of great value *are* found. This is my workroom. They think I do not speak English properly. I explain again. They say your thief nowadays is just after a few bob till the next fix. I say he is not my thief. He is theirs. I say they read too many bad newspapers and why don't they listen. Nothing has been taken. And they say they will leave this baby outside with his bare hands and big feet while they notify a lady Inspector who will come and speak to me when I am myself. They cross the road and buy some coffee at the sandwich place and go away.

'Eating on duty,' concluded Mr Virtue.

'Should I stay with you till the woman comes?' I enquired. I wondered whether this would insult him. The policewoman might think that this frightened small foreign man had asked one of his snooty clients for protection. I did not mind; I have seen the police antagonised by an officerial male, but they are flummoxed by a woman treating them as upper servants.

'No, but thank you.' Since our new relation, bestowed by the crime, he had not used my name. Before it had been a fender, protecting us from each other. 'But will you help me tidy up?' he asked.

'Did the police say you could?'

'And you too see too much television. I am tidying up. I am not sitting here, thinking. As a matter of fact, they did say I could tidy up. They have done the notes and the prints as they put it.'

'They wore gloves?' I asked.

'Gloves,' he replied, 'though I do not somehow think leather. Rubber gloves.' Could he honestly be so consistently interested in his profession?

'Oh, what do you mean?' I didn't intend him to reply. I was thinking of the next thing. The thought of Lucas was never away; it was like being pregnant, a state of vicarious being. The next thing for Mr Virtue was clearly a cup of tea. 'I shall go over and get you some tea. Can you drink on duty?' Mr Virtue ignored my pleasantry; he did not shrug off his grief as English people can, with a joke and a cuppa. He reassumed it as though it were an illness from which he had had remission but which now repossessed him. He had been for years without external persecution, with only the private concern for Tomas, but its reappearance did not surprise him.

As I waited for the tea in the steamy shop opposite, I looked at the star of breakage in Mr Virtue's window. The policeman outside had probably only heard of the war from his father, who probably himself recollected it in terms of rationed chocolates and *his* father's flimsy demob hat.

'Plenty sugar for Stan,' said the Italian woman behind the counter. She had gold hoops in her ears and had resigned her beauty with grace. 'It's wicked what these boys will do to get a bob for their next fix.' She would not let me pay. I was not clear how relieving one very rich woman of paying forty pence was to help Mr Virtue – 'Stan' – but there was a restorative feeling of warm, curious, concern, and I was sorry to leave the sandwich bar for the awful disorder of Mr Virtue's shop. The policeman looked most unofficially at my two plastic cups of tea. I gave to him the one I had intended for myself.

'You're a pal,' he said, contradicting his previous conclusion.

Mr Virtue had swept the glass into a corner where it lay in a heap of blades. He had collected as many of the pieces of fur as possible and lain them on the dainty infinity seat with its gold feet. He turned off the Hoover which had been leading him over and over the carpet in grey lanes.

'The Hoover is not used to swallowing whole animals,' said Mr Virtue. 'I have emptied it twice. It makes me sick. I am right about the gloves. Not leather.'

'Get this down you,' I said. I was not sure of how to deal with him. He had pulled himself together considerably. He looked less haunted, as though he had identified the source of his nightmare, and this knowledge had reduced his enemy. I turned to look out of the broken window while he drank. I was in time to see the boy policeman throw away my milkless tea; of course. I am kind, but inconsiderate, as Oppie says, and that's worse than no use. Kindness requires imagination. Imagination alone is not kindness.

'Look, Lady Cowdenbeath,' said Mr Virtue. With the tidying of his shop, he had recovered his respectability. Or had he laid some ghost? He certainly appeared calmer. He took off his white coat, and hung it from a hook on the door which led to the back room. He was dressed as always for a decent funeral. He moved the furs aside, turning out his left arm to bid me sit. His unbelievableness was returning, the stagey little man who had made a solid living of fleeting beauty in creatures and in women. I liked him more when he was sad.

He sat, both small feet on the grey carpet, on the other half of the conversation seat. I had to twist round to address myself to him. He had used this intimacy before to induce women to order; it is hard, when seated like confidants together, to resist the atmosphere of intimacy and collusion attendant on the planning of extravagance. It is not hard to imagine the stealing of kisses on these little seats. To see the other's eyes, you must move your body, and all that is between you is the miniature balustrade, its S a compromising knot. But Mr Virtue lifted a squared-off pile of paper, and turned it over like a chef turning out a terrine.

'Look, I was correct about gloves. These people are the mad ones who think lettuces have pain and set tigers free from zoos. They would never wear leather, oh no, but they will break up the life of an old man.' He looked much better now. Being able to identify whoever had caused this trouble made him quite chipper.

Aggression and certainty were working their revision. He had been a scared old man, the fear of the star on the shop mocking his diligence and blowing out all his light-filled years. But now he had an enemy – and a mad one, he seemed to imply, at that – he looked better. 'See, they would wear surgical gloves, rubber, while they were at their dirty work,' he said. I thought of Lucas, operating, in his surgical gloves. Automatically, I looked at the block of coloured paper in Mr Virtue's lap. He had no waist. He was all of a piece, like an egg. I could imagine his clownlike short braces, no more than loops over his stooped shoulders.

'Christ,' I said. Mr Virtue looked terribly shocked, though surely the blasphemy is worse for a Christian. 'Oh God,' I said.

Printed very crudely, the colours bright and unaligned, was a calf in a harness, braced into an apparatus which appeared to combine a rigid balaclava helmet and a set of stocks. Turquoise blots indicated approximately the eyes of the creature. Crude orange letters announced 'I DIE THAT YOU MAY HAVE LIFE'. The last word was crossed out and the word 'lipstick' was written in an educated and ornamental hand.

Broadsheet across the next page (Mr Virtue was showing them to me with the grim commitment of one who shows off family photographs) was a pig. Wigwam-eared, with Scandinavian eyes and the pained regard of a fat boy, the animal was caught in some kind of tumble-drier, which contained, presumably, its body. The suggestion was of some monstrous rectal gavage. The effect of these pictures was to turn the animals into people. I was afraid to look at too many like this for fear I should become inured to torture. In atonement, or to comfort myself, I did not know which, I picked up one of the strings of fox-tails from my side and stroked it. It was the colour of apricots and it smelt of nothing meaty. It had been denatured. There were no masks or paws in the tumble of skins about me.

The pig picture also said 'I DIE THAT YOU MAY HAVE LIFE'. Again the last word had been crossed out. The substitute word this time was, inaccurately in the case of Mr Virtue, 'sausages'. The next picture was of a new-born child with a long, bony tail, on a rack. The commodity provided by this creature's death was said to be 'serums'. Green and cerise bracelets of an ethnic style were about its wrists and ankles and it had a complicated hollow crown, tied with colourful ribbons. The baby was a monkey and the jewellery well connected, I suspected, to an electric source. I hoped that none of these broadsheets would remind Mr Virtue of Tomas. I was unprepared for what came next. It was a big beagle.

I have had the same old dog since Mordred died. He is a beagle. I leave him alone for long periods because he does not like the town. He is well looked after at Stone. I like animals. I am inconsistent about them. I eat meat, wear fur, yet feel the day blest if I see a fox through the window. My dog has spent more time listening to me than any other being has. He was the repository of my mourning when Mordred died, because Alexander was too young, and when Alexander died the dog noticed and would not let me go anywhere alone. I was reared on Beatrix Potter, who makes her animals venal, so one accepts them as companions not toys. We share a cruel world, though I suppose our cruelty to them is even more systematic than our cruelty to each other.

The beagle was open. Its ribs were shown like a grate, with scarlet winged lungs, the heart overlaid in deep crimson. Hoses, ice-picks, a selection of explorer's gear, staked out the beast, with its sorry face a replica of my dear stiff old dog at Stone. The words for this horror were 'I DIE THAT YOU MAY HAVE A HEART'.

I thought of Lucas, who was very possibly dying. Had his research and operations on people depended upon this sort of thing? I did not care to know, for I could not think of anything but the horror of knowing too much; and the complete unoriginality of sin.

'I'm here, Mr Vertle,' called an effeminate policewoman, with blonde hair and mottled legs, coming in on a wave of cold air. 'Virtue,' said Mr Virtue, 'or are you unfamiliar with it?' He was much better now.

I set off once more for my house. A low early dusk was rising towards the sinking sun. I walked into it, staring until I could see two suns, one dull orange, and the other, misaligned and bloody, to the west.

XXIV

I was pleased to arrive at my house and find everything in place. I did not consider it home as Stone is home, but after Tertius's tip and Mr Virtue's poor dishonoured shop, I was refreshed by its order. I tried to keep it as unidiosyncratic as a modern hotel. I do not pile up little still lives as clues to myself and the tables are not modestly petticoated. Widowhood has not drawn me to bandage my rooms with chintz. Ribbons and bows hold dust and I dislike their womanly bustle and billow. The most overt clue to my sex are the muslin curtains which hang flat over each window. They give a wavering tropical light. They are washed often and dry as they are wrung out, so must be ironed sopping. The smell is delicious, like spring flowers, or the better smells of a new baby in the house. Even the flowers I keep could be the choice of a man who has been brought up well by his mother. I like phlox, lilies, white hydrangeas, orchids and tall anemones. In London, I put one stem or head in a tall vase and let it react to the dry heating and bleak urban air. I do not have the heart to fill the room with bins and sinks of flowers as at Stone. In the wet Borders air they live and develop. In London I feed and tend my town flowers but they are unrobust blooms. Tubbed outside, only camellias thrive in the phthisic air. On this day, I had a staked tub of datura in the fireplace, some forced hyacinths and a fringed white orchid, *Habenaria radiata*, rooted in sharp sand. It appeared today to me to have the texture of a reptile's neck, white hairbrushes and the face of a white bat. Had I been happy it would have resembled trumpets, bells and a butterfly. If I ever had suddenly to leave, it was only these plants which would require anything to be done. When I am not there, it is possible that the plants' personalities expand and their whims develop in order to occupy the servants who are patently bored by my widow-hood. Once, more drunk than usual, Mr Vang the butler told me that they all missed a man in the house. Such an absence is really more convenient than not for him, for it allows him to drink, as he believes, unobserved. I do not think he realises that I can count as well as Mordred could.

I have the paintings moved while I am away, not to surprise myself, but to amuse Lucas. He likes all evidence of riches. It makes him feel more secure. Only insofar as it bestows order does money comfort me. For every manifestation of this there are self-seeded shoots of disorder pushing through the heavy bland paving. The only proper grout is love and I lost that. But I am in the habit of my way of life, and Stone gives a purpose. As does the giving of pleasure, even if it is an illusion, to others, most particularly Lucas.

Four o'clock on the third of December; had I really spent all that time with Mr Virtue, with Lucas hanging, slung about with machines like one of the vivisected animals? Vivisected indeed was what he had been, cut while yet living. I must use the telephone before it dared bring me bad news. I spoke to a nurse who was amiable and helpful, not the monster matron of Tertius's fable. Hospital, like prison, is always there. I crossed my fingers as she said that she would just go and find out what the position was on Sir Lucas.

'No visitors yet, but he is out of danger.' Fingers crossed, these simple words were all that mattered. 'Is that his wife?'

'He has no wife,' I said.

'Oh, that's funny, I could've sworn I spoke to a woman who said she was his wife earlier today.'

'She must have known she wasn't,' I said.

'Sorry? Who shall I say called?'

'Anne Cowdenbeath.' I prepared to spell it.

'A friend?' What did she think?

'A friend,' I confirmed.

'I'm sorry, but we've had a lot of press all day, and the phone hasn't stopped. If only they'd give blood like they give grief on the phone we'd be getting somewhere.'

'How would you say he was?' I asked. Her jolly, brisk idiom was catching.

'Well he won't be out on the golf-course just yetawhile but he should mend if only he lets himself. It's very largely' – and I knew what she was about to say – 'an attitude of mind.'

Of what else could there be an attitude? Surely he had a will to live? It was a delicate web. If he appeared to be about to die, the press might make much of the nature of the attack. Would he then be too humiliated to live? Did he mind people knowing? I had never thought so, but there is a difference between his narrow social world and his broad parish of patients, who might well be afraid if they knew, superstition about disease being strong if hysterical, theories about offended nature easy, comforting and currently ubiquitous, the sexual worm turning. Self-righteousness replacing righteousness, all the champing adulterers waving their tracts and flashing their QED at the poor offenders against public health. Health as a metaphor for virtue, is that the reason it is hard to meet the eye of the sick? Was Jesus ever ill? Surely the usual baby poxes, or was His Crucifixion His first illness? Then, He was not a queer, or do we make something of the soldier's lance?

'How is he?' I asked the Irish nurse, but she was losing patience with me. I could not remember whether or not I had spoken aloud my thoughts. My attitude of mind needed a splint.

'As well as may be expected. I'll tell him then when he wakes up that Angela called.'

It was too late to put her right. The telephone was making its dry crick of disconnection.

Next I rang Tertius. He was quite drunk. I did not blame him. It was not as though he would be required to give the kiss of life to Lucas later in the evening. The telephone reveals drunkenness as sure as a tongue-twister. The added self-consciousness it induces pushes the carefully controlled drunk over into prissy burlesque, but you hear all the fouled juices close by, betrayed by the receiver. I could tell that he was not alone.

'Annie, darling.' I heard the hand come down over the receiver, and his boisterous voice call, 'Won't be long,' to whomever was with him.

'I'm sorry I've been so long in getting in touch, Tertius. Mr Virtue had a robbery.' What was I making excuses for? For not having Lucas, healed, unpierced beside me here on the sofa, complaining a bit about the evening ahead, turning his drink and putting his feet on the white cloth? I repealed in my heart all the nagging laws I had laid down for him. He could walk over all the undinted snow of my cold house, if he could only walk.

'Anne, you are hysterical. I can hear it.' As drink is audible, magnified by the telephone, so is mood.

'Not hysterical. *Not* hysterical,' I said, and thought, I really am. It will not help.

'You really are and it won't help. Get old Mainstay to get you something for God's sake. God doesn't take bribes. He won't make Lucas well just because you go hungry.'

'Vang,' I corrected, sucker, since Tertius finds new misnomers for the butler daily. It is one of the many small games whereby he staunches his boredom.

'Vang. And who can Virtue be? Such names. Have you spoken to the hospital?'

'He is much better. Mr Virtue is my furrier. Though the funny thing is, not funny a bit really since as you say they employ him, a person calling themself Lucas's wife has been calling.'

'Calling *her*self, presumably,' said Tertius, a leer in the voice. I could imagine his anchovy-coloured face, to one side like that of a chewing cat. 'Though in a sense Hal could be seen as the wife. Same awful inescapability.' Someone laughed and Tertius made a noise as though he had been pinched.

'Which reminds me, I'm now going to call Cora. She is certain to have heard, and she and Hal must have come to some sort of conclusion,' I said.

'There's never one of those. I mean there's only one sort of conclusion and that's the sort friend Lucas has just missed by a whisker. What gives anyway with the furrier? Animals come back to fetch their coats? I wouldn't like to see that, a rush of little raw rodents. Very Bosch.'

'It was something like that,' I began, and I told him. I did not have the energy to make a tale of it. I told him as simply as though I had a verbal quota, as though I were choosing the plainest possible words to fit into the stop-press section of a newspaper.

'Cranks? Must be. The big-deal thieves come and go talking of . . .'

'I know, I know,' I said. He was showing off to another person in the room. 'Who's with you, Tertius? And will you be in if I call back after I've spoken to Cora? I just wanted to tell you exactly how Lucas is.'

'Angelica Coney is here. And I stand rebuked. Or lie, at this rate. I'm sorry. Drink and being noisy are my way of being subdued and introspective.'

'It doesn't matter. I'm a prig. Give her my love. No not that. My regards. Is she talking to herself? I thought I heard more than one.'

Before telephoning Cora, I asked Mr Vang to bring tea and toast. He did not advance his condolences about Lucas. I was grateful.

Shunning autumnal whisky or brandy, I poured a tumbler half full, or half empty, with neat vodka. I swallowed it as a car takes in antifreeze. I merely felt prepared to take on the next frost or skid encountered. The spirit was surgical in its prophylaxis.

Cora was in. When I heard her voice, I was surprised not to feel jealousy. I did not have the energy, I suppose. I was aware of affection towards her.

I had liked her at first, when I met her at Kew. I had not been sure what her relations were with Anto Cranley, and I did not very much care for her to know that mine with him existed. I lied to Lucas when he asked me where I had met Cora. I did not want him to guess that I, as he did, required comfort enough to take it from someone I would rather not invite into my house. I liked Lucas to think me more virile than that, I suppose. Nor did I want him to be too interested in Cora for her connections. She too had been Anto's mistress, I gathered. They took trains to meet each other and coupled in hotels, a romance for missing persons, though I supposed that, being young, she considered the rootlessness romantic, not perceiving that it was a painted desert, with a mirage for an oasis, and those colourful prickly times with Anto as bad to grasp as cactus.

It was safe for me to take Anto, which I did as I had just drunk the vodka, for I knew that I was thirsty sand, not slakable, but briefly held together by quick moisture. I had no further expectations. What to Cora was fleet glamour was to me the most practical means of meeting a requirement in the minimum of time. It suited me that Anto was a nomad, because I hate a trace of another now Mordred is dead. Except, perhaps, for Lucas.

Cora said, 'Hello, Anne, I've been ringing the hospital all day. It's wonderful that he is alive.'

It was sweet to pretend the main worry for her was Lucas. Surely she must be thinking of her wedding, the festival chores either to take place or be cancelled?

'Isn't it? Alive isn't enough though. We want him living, do we not? And what of you, Cora? What have you decided, or have you thought at all, about the wedding? Are you able to discuss it on the phone? What does Hal say?'

'Hal.' She sounded as though she had come up with the answer to a dull crossword clue. 'Oh Hal. He's in a bad way,' she said. It was a direct quote, I guessed. The strange thing about Hal's inarticulacy was that it suggested no secret, no inexpressible. He expressed entirely the sum of what he felt; his language was adequate to the thing which occupied his brain. If he had a mystery, I had once observed to Lucas, it was where he kept his battery. One felt no interest in what he left unsaid.

Lucas had looked sad. I said, 'Well, he doesn't appear to plug in anywhere. Or you've never found the adapter.' Lucas had left in a sulk.

Perhaps if I had been nicer; what if I had welcomed Hal, encouraged them to live together? Would Lucas then not have been stabbed under ground, perhaps by someone whose walk or hair had reminded him of Hal?

'Hal,' continued Cora, 'wants to go ahead with the wedding. He seems very keen. Keener if anything. Oddly enough, I'm not. It's not even the main thing, either, that puts me off. It's really the grotesqueness of a whole occasion paid for by someone who might be having his funeral the next day. I kept thinking,' she was rambling, 'that the cress rolls would keep for the funeral and I did not like entertaining those thoughts. And it's all become too serious to get married.'

'I thought that was when people did marry,' I said.

'Oh if they love each other, yes. Then I dare say it would be like a fairy story. Getting married would fight off Lucas's death. A good deed in a wicked world. But it's not like that. It's a bad deed in an indifferent world.'

'Have you spoken like this to Hal?'

'What do you think?' She evidently found me less formidable on the telephone.

'I think that he is pulling one way and you the other, and someone will slip, and by chance you will find this extraordinary decision taken just because of expedience and that won't do. Besides, what do you mean by, "*If* they love each other"? Don't you love Hal?'

'I needed Hal. Or I thought that I did.'

'Now what do you need?' I had forgotten the puissant selfishness of the young. Only someone as young as Cora could ascribe this importance to her feelings. She had not yet learnt that event and plot are unaffected by them. She had not yet learnt to give in, and conserve strength.

'I need to come to your house and confess,' she said.

I did not question her meaning. 'Take a taxi. I will pay. Spend the night. It's easier to spend the night not alone when you are afraid.'

XXV

Since meeting Mordred and marrying him, which is to say ever since I have been familiar with Stone, I have trusted a presence in my life, which watches me, and as it were narrates my life to me. I am not in thrall to this presence, though it is like a system of discipline; neglected even for a day, it exerts pressure, asking to be respected. It is wiser and calmer than I am. It appears to have more time. It is more than the unexpected strength drawn from even the weakest person when death occurs. It is not in me, nor from myself, as such a thing could be. It has increased with the years. It has taught me things with which I was not born, like patience. It has taught me to be surprised by nothing. While its source may have been Mordred, its location is now Stone, but when I am not at the house it accompanies me. When I am exasperated with someone, the thing which is greater than I am will show me that person biting their hands with grief in a closed room. Of course I betray this balance frequently, feeling I owe myself a tot of malice. It is not a personal gift to me, but by accident it is mine. It has settled on me because I live in the house where it is living. In its gift are a rich impartiality and a stamina which grows as it is used up. This sense may be religion in the lives of believers; some dwellers in very old houses have it. It is a fit sense of one's own unimportance and a dignity which is not of fabric or of history, but held up by the soothing knowledge of temporariness. It is like custodianship, or a vocation. Because everything at Stone surprises me still, surprise is my habit. I might walk out into a different century, but there the house would be, sheltering lives, indifferent to whose they were, human, arachnid, noble, ignoble, or the fragile life of a house martin's egg. And while I am fond of the border country around Stone, it is not a landowning pride to which I refer. At night, I often feel that the house is a ship, that I do not know where it will be in the morning. The thing is grace I suppose, a magic worked by the household gods of this particular house; it is like an enlightened haunting.

I knew, as soon as I had her in my drawing-room, that I must take Cora to Stone. She looked deserted, half dressed, and knocked about, like a half-clothed mannequin from a shop window at night, elbows bending at the same angle as knees, blouse buttoned awry, dressed only for modesty, not for display. Even her hair looked like a wig whose rooted cap had slipped. She could not hold anything. I gave her a cup of tea – Mr Vang brought a fresh pot – and her hand, pretty and undextrous, held it for a coincidental moment only before it was spilt on the carpet; then there was the steamy smell of sheep and compost, of carpet and tea. This made me pause, and the saving grace which shields me stopped me, for another coincidental moment, from speaking. I obeyed its prompting to think before speaking, and then, having thought, I did speak.

'It made me drop things too. When is the baby to be born?'

I am not a woman who invites confidences of this type, but as I asked I felt a reassertion of motive in my days stir like something hatching. I am not a maternal woman. I came to love Alexander like life, but did not instinctively do so, not at once. I do not think I loved him because he was a little Mordred, or because he was little. The physical youth he had, while it touched me and I found it attractive, was not one of his main charms to me. Perhaps this was because he had been my only companion during my widowhood, and this had made him, I thought, less of a child, completing him, making him what Lucas once told me his mother called an old soul.

But I did feel towards this girl a desire to protect and shelter. It was selfish too. I wanted to concentrate on making something live, with hope on my side. I was like a woman who has been sewing mourning weeds all day and who rushes out to water her flowers, thinking of how they will be when spring comes. I was delighted with the sense Cora's being pregnant – surely I was guessing correctly? – gave me of conforming and of being without will in some unorderly but fertile plan.

'Early April. You and two others are the only people who know.'

'Hal?'

'No.'

'But he wants children, I know, Lucas told me.'

'I know, that's why I'm, I was, marrying him,' she said.

'Which came first?' I was listening again to my prompter, and letting it keep the pace very slow. In between her breathy sentences, I was feeding Cora tea. I put my hand under her hair, bracing the neck, to do this. I had to regulate the amount of tea she took, or she allowed it to run from her mouth. She was like an old woman or a baby, not a young girl.

'The egg, if you follow. What I mean is, I decided to get married to someone because I was having him, the baby.'

I said, 'We'll leave gender for now. Aren't you at the anything so long as it's black stage?'

She looked worried. Perhaps my joke was to the point. But then surely she would not have selected Hal as the father.

'Why Hal?' I rushed.

'Time and his looks. Not how good they are, but how like they are to someone else's, someone else tall and blond.'

'Why cannot the father be the father? You have stolen a man's child.' I was outraged.

'I do not think we could make what we had a basis for a baby's life. The baby would be raised in a restaurant.'

'There are a number of worse places. You are secretive and spoilt and wilful. And there is no time. Would you like two eggs and toast? Boiled, I mean.' I was touched by this daft girl, who should not have owned a chemistry set let alone a reproductive system.

'What about your parents? What do they say?' I asked her later once she had been fed the eggs and ten fat toast soldiers. Mordred fed me this double treat throughout my pregnancy with Alexander. It is soothing to a body taken up with growing older to be reminded of its own extreme youth with baby food.

'What about the wedding, hadn't we better plan that? Or not plan it?' she asked.

The controlling voice told me to be patient, about her parents. And had Hal felt the baby? Did he know that there was such a limit to the whiteness of their wedding? Had they really not slept together?

'It is really up to you and Hal. Though I am sure you want me to take control and boss you about and take all the decisions, I cannot, because there is another person involved. Another two, counting Lucas, oh, and the baby. And how many hundred guests, for the day after the day after tomorrow?'

'Hal, who seems astonishingly busy at the moment . . . ' she began.

'He *is* getting married . . . ' I upbraided, though I would not be that particular devil's devil, never mind advocate.

'But his mother hasn't seen him. Which is funny. And when I ring him he's not at Fulham. Or the other numbers. Though he has called me. The funny thing is that he hasn't suggested we meet to sort it all out. His mother seems to be carrying on regardless, an expression she has. It would be a real improvement if I didn't appear for the wedding. They could have it anyway. I've felt like that all along, as though it was something like the change of life or moving house for Mrs Darbo, another challenge to her capabilities.'

'Those women are very good with babies,' I said. The prompter had nodded, just for the instant. 'Anyway, Cora, never mind where he is, what does he say?'

'It's all on. He's sorry about Lucas, but these things happen.'

'Well. This thing happened. Rather dissimilar. Unless you believe everything you see in the hanging and sagging press they do not happen all that much, no. I think that Hal, by saying that he wants it to go on, is either showing terror of his mother or a fondness for you which he is having some difficulty showing in a normal way. I think we must go to great efforts to find him. But tell me your side of it first. What would you like to do? What do you think you should do?'

'Until this happened to Lucas I would have got married if I'd had to wear thorns. All I've been able to think about is giving the baby a house and a father and fixing him somewhere in life. I dismissed all worries about not getting on with Hal and just thought of the baby and how safe he would be, with three of everything and his own toys and no sitting in libraries waiting for me to get home, and wearing his key under his cast-offs.'

'You are not describing the childhood of your own baby,' I said, and was moved to leave that, too, till later. 'Did you consider what time spent with Hal would be like? What it is like? It cannot be changed. A baby, whose growing is drugging you with all these nesting dreams, will not make Hal more truthful or more kind or more funny or less like a . . . '

She interrupted me.

'I think he is rather like those cars which stretch round corners, with a great flat eagle on the nose and a whole torture chamber of silver pipes and prongs and a horn like the last trump and a man in a moustache leaning out. The whole car is built of enamelled toothpaste tubes around a musical box engine, and the driver is one of those boy dolls children learn to do up poppers on and make short wars with till they are bored – only bigger. But on the whole I do not think of Hal.'

'You are going to marry him on the sixth of December. You are then going on the last complete lotus-seek of your life, during which time you will see no one but him because you will tactfully be left alone by everyone who observes you are on your honeymoon. And everyone will observe that you are, because you will respond with enthusiastic conversation to every rug seller and waiter. The only time I ever contemplated infidelity to Mordred, whom I adored, was on our honeymoon, because I was frightened that the happiness would run out if I kept on taking it from him, but also because he was always there, his voice, his signature, his opinions, his past, his presence. It is a great change and all people are terrified of a beginning, as opposed to its potential. Once the beginning comes you have actually started walking across the unmarked snow, and you cannot stop. So now you know what I think. There are other things which I begin to think you should know, though it is breaking a promise.' And if he lives, Lucas will be entitled to tell *my* binding secret to whomever he pleases, I thought. But he could not have foreseen his death, though God knows he took steps to court it. He must have left his card with death's footman often enough.

'What other things?' asked Cora. She appeared less disjointed. I had seen her lift her hands over her stomach as though it was a bowl of suds. The baby was kicking. I was again surprised at my own early interest.

'What do you know about Lucas?' I asked her.

'I know that he is good and beautiful and true.'

'No one is all those things, Cora, it's not a fault to be bad and ugly and untrue.'

She interrupted me with the vehemence of a fanatic who will not hear the rumour of a whisper without calling treason. She was twenty. I did not know her well. Lucas was beautiful, for sure. Goodness and truth seem to little girls to come with beauty. The fairy tales she had read about him must have fanned it to what seemed to be a crush, so much more sore than love. There was no need to be rough with her. I had had the same once, for a choirmaster with a red beard. I thought the cathedral grew from him like wings as I watched him sing. I must not demolish her necessary infatuation, but transplant it respectfully.

'I love him I love him I will make him well,' she declaimed, standing up, shaking, shrieking like a burning witch, belly out.

'Sit down. You'll wake the baby,' I said, and she did sit down, before the preposterousness reached her. Her body was practising obedience to motherhood. I wondered whether Lucas would be pleased about the baby. It would be something to live for, something surely greater than seeing his own passion twist the lives of it and its mother, and, of course, that of Hal himself. Had this not happened to Lucas, would there have been the same urgency to Hal's marrying? Lucas might live, but crippled perhaps, or maimed, and then the pleasure of perhaps seeing Hal eventually disillusioned with the girl Lucas had pimped for him would be a bitter one. I could not tell what Lucas really wanted from Hal – to know that he absolutely needed him, perhaps. And why was Hal so very keen to marry Cora? Was his saving grace love? Had I judged him cruelly? It is of course a mistake to say the shallow cannot feel; they can, to their depths. But Hal was without lovableness. He had no charity. What did he want from this particular girl? Why had he not purchased a shrink-to-fit girl who would not mark easily? I had felt an uninventive sadism in him from the first, an uncerebral and effective cruelty.

I have never explained sex to anyone. Mordred explained it to me, not only with words, and Alexander died. I summoned the courage. But did this girl, so modern, so free with bad words, know about Lucas?

'Did you ever think Lucas would . . . ?' I asked. I had not intended to finish the sentence.

She left the silence for a while, then replied, 'I hoped. Then I realised that it wasn't possible. The baby. And he's old enough to be my . . . '

I spoke quickly.

'Mordred was old enough to be mine.' Where was the benign censor? In all this emotion, I was welcoming any opportunity to be as I had not been for years, female, reminiscent, soft. Weak.

'Nothing else crossed your mind?' I went on, forcing her to find out on her own. It was not hidden, after all, nor even that shocking. 'About Lucas? His friends? Hal?' I said, digging out the buried bone and handing it to her, daring her not to find the poor skeleton in the cupboard.

'His friend Daniel had married very late,' she said, proving that we see what we will, not what pokes us in the eye.

'Lucas will not marry. He is not the sort of man who will marry.' I refrained, thank God, from saying, 'Unless he marries an old rich woman when he is bound to his wheelchair.'

I have never before seen someone suffused with temper, like a small child. She went black with affront. Apparently so easygoing, in fact so afraid, she showed insult, rage, fear. Something which could not be changed tomorrow had stood in her path. This alarms the very young. They start to see fences, walls, cordons, providing not shade, allotment, discrimination, but exclusion and exception. Then there are the newspapers, which are a now daily journal of the plague year, the poor sad gay men their pariahs. Children of Cora's age are more conservative than we were at that age. I wondered what she would say.

'At least no other woman can have him,' she said, and I wondered whether my household god had adopted Cora, abruptly so well-mannered and gentle that we might have been discussing his taste in music. Then she looked angry again, not black, but exasperated as though she had caught St Jerome with an alleycat, having thrown out the lion. 'Does he really love *Hal*?' She said 'Hal' now as though the word were a hair she was taking from among her teeth. 'Anyone but that. I suppose that was why he was going to pay for the wedding? How odd not to notice. I was in the middle of my own life. He keeps Hal, really, I think. I thought it showed not his lust but his goodness.'

'His lust isn't bad, Cora.' Oh God, I would shortly be explaining to her about the little seeds. 'It's bad for him in the case of Hal,' I went on, 'because Hal has cunningly diverted it so that Lucas expresses it in every way but the only way. It is very painful to see.'

'Something has always prevented me from revealing what I really thought of Hal,' she said. 'Vanity, I think, as much as anything. I did not think I could be seen to marry someone I had advertised as a nasty bore, but when I first saw him I was stunned. I thought he was like a tart, flash and curves and jut and paint, and my face must have said it all, but then I saw he was what I needed . . . '

'You sound like a mad eugenist,' I said.

'I am one, I suppose. The father of the baby is hale and hearty, even quite nice . . . '

'Who is he?'

'John Croom.'

The prompter at my shoulder acknowledged another royal flush.

'He is my nephew. My son was his age, a little younger. Your baby is my great-something,' I said.

'Great nuisance,' she said.

'I am so pleased. I want to tell Lucas. Oh God I'm so pleased. Can't you tell John? He is nice. A bit of a cold fish.' The child's relation to me gave me yet more strength for Lucas.

'I call him that too. He doesn't like it. I don't know. He wouldn't have me. I'm soiled goods. Leavings, as well as pregnant. And Hal and I haven't yet called off the wedding. It's all far too complicated.'

'It may be far too complicated, but it is a deal simpler than the other way. Anyway, leave it for now.' I was being hypocritical. I was filling with resplendent middle-aged energy, but I knew not to nag the girl.

'I haven't really explained to you about Lucas and Hal.'

I had decided not to tell her about Lucas's fearful drag-hunting at night; I had not the words, everything sounded arch or brutal, as though one was describing a disease. It was in any case the kind of thing it is easier to understand once you have learnt some analogous bent in yourself. Nor would I tell her, pregnant, recently disembarrassed of her blind filial – I supposed – passion for him, that Lucas had selected her as Hal's wife because she was malleable, a rag doll who could be tossed away.

'Hal was desperate to marry, quite suddenly, and Lucas was so hurt and downcast that he wanted at least to have a say in the choice of bride. And that's you. So you see he likes you.'

'It's odd to want, suddenly, to get married, isn't it?' she asked.

'You did.'

'Hal can't be pregnant.'

The talking was tiring me, though my brain was full of emerging tallies and rallying hopes. I still had the sense of being pregnant myself, with Lucas's state, and felt the deprivation of his actual presence, but I knew he would be all right, now that there was so much to live for.

'Let's ring the hospital,' I said to Cora, who seemed even a bit lively.

'Fingers crossed,' she said, and she crossed all the fingers of each hand over, so they looked arthritic.

'Not the left hand, Cora, it's bad luck,' I cautioned.

I got through to the hospital and spoke to someone whose voice called down a corridor and relayed an echo-foreshadowed dispatch.

'There is hope,' the voice said.

We had been through weeping and laughter, love and desire, and now, from the hospital, that strange unclosing bank of life and its irreducible overdraft of illness and injury, came hope. Cora and I each took half of it to bed on the night of the third of December.

XXVI

I cannot sleep unless I have made some sense of the day. I like to shake it out and fold it, arms to sides, collar straight, no marks unexpunged. I should like to see my time as a cupboard, the days, colourful, pale, bright, in their places, individually of use, collectively beautiful and bright. But this was a white night.

My immanent narrator is for me as the sea can be. It takes no decisions, comes to no conclusions, although it can help me to do these things. I lay in my bed, on watch for Lucas's life. The wind was unresting. It pushed through the white iron of my balcony as through the deserted bridge of a pleasure craft going into the wind. Ribbons of draught insinuated themselves between the window and its frame, lifting the muslin of the curtains.

I have always spoken aloud. It is not the same as talking to oneself, which elicits no answers and is the first sign of madness. Talking aloud, I can hear whether or not what I say is true. It is like reading aloud. False quantities and loose thinking make themselves audible. Declaiming, it is hard to deceive yourself, perhaps easier to deceive others. Though I do not doubt that the perfect voice with which to wash people's brains is their own. The wind was loud, but its noise firmly without. The curtains, sieving out the last drift of the wind, moved in high but silent waves. I talked on. Once, when I stopped for a time, I heard someone else talking. It was the trace of my own voice, like a star drawn on a misted window, with a finger. When the wind was again the only thing I could hear, and, though wild, abstract behind glass, at last I slept.

I awoke again, the sky no paler, my eyes flinching in their sockets. I was guilty, not with the superstitious guilt I had grown used to over the past hours, of having allowed Lucas to be hurt, but with ordinary social guilt about Tertius. I had not telephoned him, as I had promised, to tell him what I had discovered of Hal and Cora's decision. Strictly, I supposed that I had come no closer to what it was, and I had learnt some new complications which I knew it would be rash to confide, as he would instinctively turn them into a divertissement to the grand drama of blood and death. Tertius must have awaited my call, drinking till he could not have heard it had it come, I was sure. Unless Angelica Coney, who has self-possession like a skin, had stopped him. But I thought that she enjoyed seeing people behave like animals. Or, as she had it, like people. She enjoyed the humiliation of men with the Homeric ruthlessness of a goddess, and seemed frequently to be mysteriously present when it took place. I had watched her grow up and seen her stand, uninvolved cause of the rout, by knots of bloody, muddy, boys. When Alexander was small and they played together, she would make him drink and drink then tie him to the banisters at Wyvern and leave him to soak himself. I learnt this later, or I would have hit her, but he told me only when that was no longer the worst thing he could remember.

She told him bogus facts of medicine, was quite scholarly about it. I found a vivid little book she had bound herself in yellow buckram and given him. It smelt of size, from the hand-marbled papers. It was illustrated with flat cross-sections of mustardy paunch and lumpy swags of gut. Crude red arrows nibbed points where, the ill-spelt text explained, most pain would be felt. The pictorial style was knockabout and free with blood, like block-printed medi-aeval marginalia. The words were convincing and literal. The certainty of children, as of very few grown-ups, is undeniable. To see these pictures was never to forget them. Who is to say that children make things up? Perhaps we just cannot make the same things out. Angelica told Alexander more than I can know, since he took the knowledge with him. I am sure that she made of the stork a vulture and of the gooseberry bush a thorn tree. They played together, all the usual games. She took his innocence. When I think of my boy, I don't think of him with his lashes dry. He was always laughing or crying. And then he drowned, and they were wet again.

The morning came only slowly, and to occupy myself I went into my cupboards and lifted and tended and rebedded my shoes.

I then went through scarves, folding them in layers of colour like soft sand. Touching the cloth, I thought of Penelope unmaking her weaving by night. The surprise of it was surely that she was not found out by a drop in standards, a slack weft, an unmatched tint, for why should you care if it is all to go? But one does, and as I thought of Lucas and Mordred and Alexander, I held and buffed in my cupboard, preparing it for the day of judgment, sorting and selecting, finding wanting, disposing. Unlike Penelope, I had no suitor and the only persistent gentleman caller appeared to be death, waiting to collect Lucas, having been satisfied in his appointment with the other two.

A tentative dawn was announcing itself not with birds but with the sibilant awakening of the house. Which part of the body is first attacked by grief? The heart breaks, we are told. But I felt that whatever was water in me was returning to itself. I heard voices in the conduits of the house. Pipes chuckled their malice. I heard the murmurous concern of the taps, requiring a single twist to bring them to copious weeping. I was all lymph. I wanted tears.

I awoke elastic and restored, with empty eyes. The house seemed to have been consoled. It was late. Cora was by my bed.

Cora was by my bed; we were past the protracted courtship of women. It had been accelerated by emergencies of life and death. I was happy to see her.

I liked myself more when she was there. My having had a child was of use to her. It was not embarrassing, because inevitably recalling his death, as it was with other friends. She restored to me the more ordinary side of my past; without this ordinary past what was extraordinary would have been so much costume drama.

'We are going to see him in an hour. I thought you might be someone who dressed for occasions,' she said.

I do not habitually ask girls into my cupboards. They take it all too personally. They perceive it as an unfair advantage, of course. Then they look at me and realise that all this contemplation and cut gives me something which is not their careless appeal, which is not beauty, and they see that it has taken time, and they are impatient. Like active men who cannot see the pondering point of Plato or his lucid beauty, they want to deny it. I do not make such grand claims for clothes, naturally, but there is something so civilised in their necessariness, when it is made beautiful, that I am suspicious of those who dismiss them. They are generally people who cannot make time for whatever it is of which time is the point.

But I could hardly keep my new child out. She herself was dressed in what she had been wearing the night before. The garments were arguing less than they had been, and were buttoned to the neck. Her shoes, unsuitable but for once unvulgar, were the grey slippers which we had bought on the afternoon I had tried to get her to be tempted and clothe herself to hide her shame. She had won that skirmish, and I had no heart for more.

'What did the hospital say? Is he that much better? Are we going to meet his secret wife?' I asked.

I was allowing her very close to me.

'I wonder who it was? Not Hal, with a conscience. God, his conscience must be more than pricking him, it must be cutting him up.'

I didn't need to point out to her what she had said. Language is a case of knives.

'Tell me. The only thing that matters is how is he? Last night there was hope, today we can see him. So what's the difference?'

'They never say, they can't or they'd be priests, but what has happened is apparently that he has turned the corner. He is out of danger.' Again the little boat, this time tacking, leaving the reef behind, waiting for the wind.

'I think it's more comforting that they talk like that. It draws the thorn. We would not understand the medical words and could not bear the emotional ones.'

'It's like a police state, only told what we should know.' She stuck her chin out.

'Nonsense, Cora, if pain isn't an official secret what is? Privacy is a democratic privilege.'

But she was messing about in the cupboard.

'I never thought anyone did it so carefully,' she said. 'You must be worried you'll get run over by the State Coach, not just a bus. I have never seen such things. And they are clean as though for inspection.'

'I like that,' I said. 'It makes me happy. It stops things going out of control. One for wash and one for wear, and then you can turn the other cheek knowing that there . . . '

'Are three more cheeks,' said Cora. I like cheap jokes when I am overwrought, but not many people see this part of me.

'I was going to say knowing that there is another cheek.' I put her down, but I was laughing.

'I knew,' she said. The I was long and indulgent. 'But you have had to turn so many other cheeks you must either have several faces or be black and blue.'

'I cover it up. Choose me some clothes.' I did not even say it wanting to see her attempt to find something to her taste among my monotheistic vestments, and that a gloomy god. She put me into what she had chosen, zipping me up and hooking me in like a mother before a party. It was a piece of blue cloth which committed itself to the bones of the body only at the wrists and knees and in between flirted with the flesh. Until it was worn, it looked like a dead raven.

'Lovely on,' she said, making the 'on' as camp as a belted marquee.

'Try this for size. We always say the nicest things come in the smallest parcels,' she said, continuing the vendeuse game. I had not played like this since Alexander. She had handed me a really enormous coat. It was as heavy as a packed chandelier. It had been Mordred's, and was far too big, black, with the shawl of beaver fur traditionally worn by capitalist oppressors. It was out of the question for me to wear it.

I am small.

'You can wear that, Cora, if you don't mind being taken for my girl.' I meant it in the twilit sense, Oppie's niece, and she took it in the maternal and gave me the uncoordinated type of embrace which must be reperformed neatly at once or be the cause of shyness for a long time to come.

'I cannot think of anything rather, better, more, nicer. And you put this on. I wouldn't like you to get a cold.'

Mordred would say that the English, inhibited inhabitants of a cold country, express family love with enquiries about weather-proofing – Are you warm enough? Will you be cold? Take a jersey. I was alarmed and pleased that Cora and I were expressing our love. I was afraid it might be rained off. Mordred and I had wanted a daughter. As a small boy, Alexander had asked if he might have Angelica Coney for a sister.

'The devil you may,' said Mordred. He was an old-fashioned man, who could invoke nothing worse than the devil. God and his adversary had not yet been moved on by the words in Angel's little buckram pamphlet, blasphemy dethroned by pornography.

No one since Mordred had worn the coat. I did not want her to feel odd about this, but I self-indulgently wanted her to know the privilege she was enjoying.

'It must be your husband's,' she said in the car on the way to the hospital. 'I am very lucky.'

'It doesn't do to make a fetish out of things,' I said.

'I believe you, but not many people who have seen your cupboard would.'

'And why do you?' We were approaching the hospital. On the tiles under the original windows, green-gowned pre-Raphaelite sawbones stood about with their curly lips and lily-white hands. The modern part of the hospital, Lucas's part, stood up like a tusk.

'Because I know that you care for what you have lost and cannot bear to lose again, more than for all that treasure trove.'

'Here we are. Watch out for the granite gorilla, or do you know her?' I have never been good at declarations. I elicit them and then do not know where to put them down.

We were both, I think, as excited as children about to claim a reward. To get what we want, to retrieve a life, we will make awful bargains. But I had done no trading with the devil. I had sworn to my prompting power that I would use only will. And he was well enough to be seen, after only a day and a night, proving that either my will was indomitable – or that it was quite immaterial.

We went in past the granite mother and child, a small bobble hat by the stone apple. The hat had flaps, as small as a puppy's ears.

He had a room to himself. Cora motioned to me to go in alone. Then I saw her thinking that what I saw might distress me, so that she had better come too. She stood at my back, in her long wool and sombre fur, the grey slippers making a Sienese courtier of her. Her big face had the smoothness of fresco. Its features had an absence of radiance to be seen on the faces of worthies attendant on a painted crucifixion. She was young, but then, in the fifteenth century, twenty was middle-age.

Lucas was pale and bandaged so his body in the bed made a long barrow. Bladders of liquid depended from tall metal trees at his head and feet, and to each side. There was no red, anywhere. I had prepared myself for it, and there was none. I had practised, thinking of all the most bloody things I had seen. I had even thought of the thing which I do not think about, Mordred's dying.

'Anne,' he said, 'don't be scared. Or are you disappointed?' He spoke slowly, as though he was thinking something out. His face, with its prominent bones, resembled the false heads placed in their beds by prisoners escaping, built of papier mâché and the will to live. I could think of no word to tell him how the sight of him affected me. What we had said to each other over the years was composed of the same twenty-six letters which I wanted now to be able to shape into a perfect sentence of love.

'We didn't bring you anything,' I said.

'Nothing would have been enough to thank you for what you have given us,' said Cora.

'You look as though you have got something for me,' he said, looking at her. She had taken off Mordred's coat, and had sat down beside him in a chair on his right, between his bedside and the thin silver tree with its serous fruit and hanging tubes. Seeing him alive, and with the resilience of her state, she had blossomed. Robed to the neck, and with her hands in her blue lap, Cora looked at him. Her hands were empty, her lap full.

'I may not be God but I am a doctor,' he said looking at her. 'A life for a life is it? How long till this baby is born?'

XXVII

I noticed then that Cora, now she had told me her secret, was blatantly pregnant. Because I had considered her as a bride to be and as a pretty but unedifying face at parties, I had not included pregnancy as one of the characteristics I allowed her. But now, I saw that it was not to be overlooked. She appeared to have grown since even that morning. She was sitting like a boat low in the water. She even rocked a little.

'Do you get backache?' asked Lucas. She nodded. I thought of him spatchcocked on the ground.

A profession can protect a man. There he was, every inch a doctor, while in fact a patient.

'If only I could. Heal myself,' he said. He had less voice than usual. Had they cut his lungs? When I cut up the lights for the dogs as a child, that breath leaving the pink sponges under my hand reminded me that this dogs' food had been sheep's life. The lungs had the airy mass of that jelly made with condensed milk which settles into layers, the top opaque and oxygenated, the middle translucent, and the bottom layer as clear as strawberry plasma. When cut, the lights were delectable but repulsive, sweetly pink, susurrating, airy. They smelt of blood and stale air.

Not many of my friends have yet fallen chronically ill. Those who have died have done so in a selection of more or less voluntary ways. Oppie tells me that I am reaching the age when, tired out by all the divorcing, they will begin to go. But I have not refined my hospital visiting (prison visiting is another matter) much beyond talking over the sick friend in the bed while drinking the champagne I have brought. I was uncertain of Lucas. This was unfair, as it placed social obligation upon him, but I could not see how to talk

220

to him. My natural instinct was to embrace him, but I feared the drips entering his body under the sheets, which were too small for him, and clearly nametaped with the name of the hospital, as though he had been in that bed growing since he was a little boy. Though of course, he did not go away to school. I was shy of him. Even before this his inheritance of suffering had made me shy. My suffering, so different and so much more comprehensible, made me not more but less forbidding. Unable to touch him, I felt myself about to say something emotional to him. I knew that if I did it would be momentously tactless.

'My visit to India put flesh on the bones of my concept of poverty,' I had heard a bishop announce on the wireless once. (Unlike Lucas, I cannot bear music in a car, it makes me introspective and lunatic, because it is so demanding.) I knew that if I made a less than neutral remark to him it would curdle. 'Fall-out,' Lucas calls it, when I leave a particularly wrong sentence to settle. He speaks the language better than I do; he tells me this is the case with Poles, look at Conrad. All I *can* do, I say, is look at him, I can't read him. All that hidden metal and the incessant sea.

Not that there was an awkward silence. I sat now at his other side and stared at him. He and Cora were discussing, no, he was giving her a consultation. With some slowness, and stopping occasionally to rest, Lucas was enquiring about the progress so far of the pregnancy. Was she anaemic?

I wondered if he had contained much blood when he was found.

Did her ankles swell? Did she know peaches contained a natural anti-nauseant?

'Spring baby, then?' he said.

With her baby not yet born, she was unfamiliar with mortality. People with children live with it. She may well have considered Lucas indemnified by the narrowness of his escape. She had no idea that death is not only there when he leaps through the trapdoor with his invitation to dine. She had not observed him conscientiously paying his respects to the virtuous, the healthy and the brave, who invariably meet him as he slips in uninvited.

'Spring baby, just about an April fool,' said Cora, looking at him with the trust women reserve for doctors. Most of my friends fall in love with their gynaecologists; one or two had large numbers of children in order to re-experience this passion. Had Cora fallen in love with Lucas only because she was pregnant and he was a doctor? If you asked me, it must have something to do with her childhood. That capacious psychoanalyst's toybox full of dolls with lifted skirts and one-legged soldiers, what a lot it is made to hold.

'But no winter wedding,' said someone. The voice was mine. I had uttered my first sentence of love and commiseration to my best friend who was lying before me, irrigated and drained artificially, having undergone a violent attack under ground not long before. My best friend who was just not dead.

'Thank God someone has a proper sense of scale,' said Lucas. 'Lying here, you have no idea what it's like, they think that life and death are matters of life and death. All along the small things are more terrible. Like buttons,' he said, and looked suddenly very tired. His eyelids lowered for a time. I honestly think that his body did not contain the power to keep them raised. Where his head lay, at an angle to his body, bandages began. They were covered with a pyjama jacket. The cloth was coarse. It was striped, blue and white, the pyjamas of farce, hospital issue, worn like the burglar's t-shirt and the pirate's patch, to identify him – he was an ill man, a man in bed. Why was he wearing them? Were they holed for the ingress of tubes? Were they a dickey, like the evening shirt of a corpse, off to meet his maker? Those striped pyjamas had a grim levity which reminded me again that Lucas was not only alone but in a foreign land. Those photographs of sexless pyjamaed people are a tragedy in the dress of bedroom farce. I suppose the stripes were for visibility if the skeletons tried to move.

We looked at each other, Cora and I. I was pleased with her. She had done nothing at all remarkable, she was simply having a baby, but I saw it, quite as surely as the sacs aloft on aerials, transfusing pleasure into Lucas. The creature knitting together inside Cora, fed by its thin nutritious cord, was a reason for Lucas to let himself be nourished back to life.

I think he slept for five minutes. We did not speak for fear of disturbing him. The silence between us was not uneasy. Up to this last time together, Cora had an edgy relation with silence, I had thought, as though it were a waste of time, time during which she could be putting herself over. I have always thought this a vain exercise, since a character will reveal itself anyhow, and only a great actor, a great spy or a truly guileless soul can neutralise the truth-telling of the face in repose. Cora looked down at Lucas.

Hero-worship, I suppose it was. We are asked to feel it for our leaders in war, and in peace people who sing or are beautiful are raised up for the young to worship. God takes a back seat, letting himself be driven by bad but brightly uniformed chauffeurs. The intense desire to emulate and to follow, which is there from birth, is a dangerous one. She looked at this sleeping pale man with a regard of fierce obedience; she did have a look of a religious fanatic. She had chosen him as her personal despot, or at least master. Was I jealous? Of either of them? I think not. I was certain of his affection, and from her I did not want hero-worship. It would have been in more danger of becoming a romance than I cared for. Oppie is right when she says that these things between an older and a younger woman sooner or later degenerate into fights about bangles and face cream. Besides, I was coming to care for Cora. I wanted to behave well to her and see good done her. Private education, private health, why not, for Cora, a private hero? Even God, I notice from those colourful wayside pulpits (a prayer for the morning, Lord make me crisp and ready to serve), has gone private, though the soft word used is Personal. I suppose this means that we no longer need to go round to His house when we want to speak to Him. Myself, I have found Him a jealous God, and not fond of going out.

The room where we sat at either side of Lucas's bed was white, and uncurtained. Its blinds were a razor of grey. A description which would fit many of my London rooms, the difference being only deployment of resources. Where I had paintings, the bagged liquor of priceless life decorated this room. What I spent on flowers in a week could have purchased the aluminium cot, with its black feet, and the two chairs covered with mossy cretonne. The thin small sheets I have mentioned smelt of bleach. I could see they were rough as cheap paper, the sort of paper they wrap delicatessen food in on the Continent. Everything was washed, none of it looked clean, because there was no time for the refinements which draw attention to cleanliness in the lives of the rich; redundant napery, unneeded whiteness.

A black face and arm came around the door. The flattened hand beat twice on the flush wood, showing a pink underside sudden like a cat's yawn.

'Tea, ladies?' asked the nurse. 'The sleeping beauty is living on kisses only just at the moment.'

She indicated that she meant Lucas, and in the same moment, like a soldier who is afraid of protocol the instant after saving a life senior in rank to his, she looked wary, as though we might tell him that she had gone too far.

When he woke up, or came round, we were doing a dumb show of thanks to the nurse, whose legs were darker than her stockings, shining through like some beautiful patinated wood. Cora was indicating that the biscuits were just the thing for feeding two. In the very short time since she had told me about the baby, she seemed to have come to the state which is to be desired for pregnant women. She was enjoying it. She was even showing off about it. Perhaps the baby had taken over. Unborn, we are full of common sense.

'There is a chemical to stop me being thirsty,' he said. 'Undistinguished vintage, but acceptable.'

'Do you get a dry mouth?' I asked.

'Anne, how nice you are. Yes, but they don't give me stones to suck. Did you get burning ears? I thought about you a lot.'

'Is it like drowning?' I asked. I was not thinking of my Alexander, but I saw him flinch, as though for any pain *I* might have felt. I wondered whether he could be a saint.

'I wouldn't know,' he said. 'I mean, I have never drowned, but I expect drowning's nicer, not so confusing.' The nurse came in and they spoke. Because we were there, from tact I think, she addressed him in very technical language and he responded in the same way, as though they were adults and we children, not let into the secrets of pain. She reached in under the light blanket and short sheet, both arms braced at right angles to her body. As though she were a fork-lift truck, she lifted and raised and redeposited Lucas, more comfortably, in his bed. He flinched when she withdrew her arms. It was done as though he weighed nothing. She smiled at him with the fat beneath her eyes and her pleated lower lip; it was a collusive smile; it congratulated him. He must have been in pain. I thought of what Lucas had said to me once about the stiff upper lip. 'The stiffness spreads to the brain in most well-bred Englishmen, but never reaches the one part where it might be useful.'

Cora had eaten the biscuits. Each had borne the words 'Healthy

Life'. Healthy Life biscuits are like Five Boys chocolate, a food which makes moral claims, not the Fabian claims of muesli but the empire-building claims seen as a rule only on over-vividly revived advertising hoardings of the Edwardian summer. Made in Scotland, these biscuits must be part of some deal of the government. Perhaps a few biscuit workers were staying in work on account of having to supply a big London hospital? Or maybe Healthy Life biscuits had been bought by a conscience-stricken tobacco company? They look like old impacted horse-droppings, a good stalky chew. I have them at Stone.

'*Was* it confusing?' asked Cora.

'You sound like the police, keen to know but terrified to ask. Very. I still do not know what to think.'

'What do you mean? Surely you can only think "Thank God I am alive",' she said.

'I haven't reached that stage. I am not yet sure I am. But seeing you two has made me want to be.'

Did he mean that he still might die? Did he mean that he would be crippled? It sounded as though he considered himself as good as dead. He was polite, like a man of substance going into exile.

'The baby most of all,' he said. 'I can't help wondering what it will look like.'

I was alarmed at this. He was clearly expecting a new little Hal, who could be nurtured and groomed. Had he not been laid so low, I would have said something to fight this. There is something sinister in the grooming from birth of sexual playthings; it can backfire. I am sure that the inventor of the stoneless peach choked to death on a cherry stone, and the thornless rose's breeder very likely fell on his sword. Since he evidently assumed that the baby was Hal's, I also assumed that he wanted the wedding to go on.

'Can you answer me about the wedding?' I asked. I sounded shrill, but Cora was so obviously honeymooning with her idol and her baby that I felt I must nag.

'It won't happen,' he said.

'But,' I interrupted, though my heart was not in the objection, 'postponing it will just cause twice the work, all the cancelling and revoking and reinviting and . . . ' There is a plateau reached by the nagging voice when any words may be used at all because the hearer has ceased to listen.

'It's not to be postponed, darling. It won't happen,' he said.

I would reserve my anger for later. He had lit this feeble candle for Hal and Cora and now he snuffed it out. I was pleased at the extinction, angry at his godlike way of achieving it.

'What if they want it?' I almost shouted.

'It is clear why she wants it and he may not have it. That is that. Trust me. I have asked my secretary to be at your disposal while you dismantle it. The little Afghan boy is mending well. I have had to put off my own work until later, the new year. She will have some spare time. Please do not have the wedding flowers sent to hospitals. They will be too funereal. I am so sorry, Cora, if you love him. But if, as I think I see, you just wanted to shelter your baby, take shelter with me. I am sorriest for Hal's mother. But she may like the fuss. You must be the villainess, Cora.'

'I'll have to be, I can't find Hal, so we've no villain.'

'Oh,' he said. Around his mouth was a white line, and he swallowed. His Adam's apple was like a swallowed elbow. I saw again the jovial and institutional pyjamas. 'Very dehydrated people cannot spare the water to weep,' he said, 'so I can tell you that you won't see him for a while. None of us will.' He spoke as though Hal were dead. I did not like that idea. I did not care to enrol Hal among my glorious dead. See, I am even exclusive about death.

Cora yodelled – 'What do you mean, I'm marrying him, I'm not marrying him I mean, in two days? *Where* is he and how do you know?' She could not make her curiosity resemble concern for Hal.

'I don't know where he is and I haven't the heart to tell you how I know. I'm sorry to be mysterious, but I am in the dark.' I saw the undone button of his blue and white pyjamas. Outside the hospital window was the blue sky, violet at its height. One satellite hung, too bright to be a star.

'Prisoners and people in hospital call it the sky,' he said. He had seen that I wanted to leave. 'I am unused to so much natural light. Perhaps I'll go green.'

His joke went wrong. I could imagine him, having suffered a loss of heart, giving up the ghost and commencing to glow sickly green while the sky changed its signals through the window.

'Leave me now,' he said. 'I'm all at sea. Thank you for coming. Come again soon.'

I dreamed of him in the next night, buried at sea, wrapped in his bandages, the striped tent of blue and white sky above, too late for the unconfusion of drowning.

XXVIII

I have seen, at the Tattoo on Edinburgh's Castle Rock, soldiers erect and dismantle military encampments within minutes. Surely wedding brace with socket, handling articulated metal and fields of tarpaulin as though they were so much balsa and tissue, often in a high wind and always under floodlight, which bleaches out detail, they perform what is to the civilian observer a marvel. They know that they are doing nothing more than exhibiting what discipline has taught them. The advantages these soldiers had over Cora and me and Mrs Darbo, in the dismantling of the wedding, was practice. I have, the deaths being sudden, organised at short notice my husband and my son's funerals.

Weddings are not wholly another matter. There are the same dull necessities, provision for the intake and evacuation of food. Funerals demand more spirits and richer meats. In this case, because there was no love involved, the process, while demanding, was not painful. The most intense emotion was in the end the chagrin of Mrs Darbo. What reason could we give to her for cancelling this occasion towards which she had worked with such blind zeal? I thought that the least we could do was go to see her. It was the day before the wedding. Cora and I and Lucas's secretary had made many hundred telephone calls. The responses were various. Very few people asked why this had happened. The men mostly said, 'Better now than later I suppose.' Young women evinced the poignant disappointment of those who have planned exactly what they will wear; even the most unromantic young girls believe they will meet their future husband at a wedding. I placed one of those sad announcements in *The Times*.

I had spoken only briefly to Mrs Darbo on the telephone, telling her that I thought the wedding, for various reasons, could not go ahead. I was aware that I should have been Cora's parent, but Cora had told me some things which made it clear this was hardly possible. I introduced myself to Mrs Darbo and asked whether Cora and I might come down to see her. She was polite. Control had been wrested from her and she gracefully conceded it. Cora had exaggerated Mrs Darbo's managing way.

I buttoned and braced Cora into clothes which made her look not gravid but porky, as though the bulk of the baby were distributed over her frame. We had risen early, and I stopped before we left London for Cora to buy newspapers, ours being as yet undelivered. She came out of the shop with a bag of sweets and the papers. She stuffed the papers down by her feet, and we moved off. The traffic was not heavy, and I was happy to be in the car, using my brain to take small decisions, letting the worry feed itself for the time being. I had not wanted Mrs Darbo to be intimidated, so I drove the smaller car. Tony, my driver, will not ever leave the Bristol, and this creates what Lucas calls the Sandwich Problem. He is a Gurkha who was charged with grievous bodily harm. There is a growing demand for disgraced military men among those who employ servants; it is the combination of obedience, competence, and shame. He waits for me for hours sometimes, but he will not eat a sandwich, if brought out to him, nor take a mug of coffee, for fear of making a mess of the car. The car he keeps under a sort of prepuce of flannel in its garage. In the glove compartment are his teach-yourself books. Some weeks he is learning how to run a large company, other weeks he is conning *Easy but Elegant Recipes for a Family*. In the glove-box behind these pamphlets is a directory of whores, in a yellow clothbound book entitled *Around the World in Eighty Ways by Phallus Fogg*, by which title the author reveals something of employment prospects nowadays for graduates; there is of course a section on 'Reform'. I cannot imagine when Tony is visited by the girls he finds herein, unless they come to the car, and, as Lucas says, *that* can be messier than sandwiches.

The smell of white chocolate and penny nougat filled the air. I was glad we had not taken the big car, or I should not have been able to face Tony. Cora had a bag of pink sweets shaped like shrimps, and a clutch of white chocolate penknives. She was chewing wetly with her molars, abandoned as an American beauty chewing gum. She was getting careless and sloppy, as pregnant women may.

In my pregnancy, I had become immaculate. She seemed to have moved on, to have floated adrift from the wedding and its methodical disembarkation. She had left it as a ghost ship, and was there in her life raft, women and children first, confident of rescue. I was less afraid for her than when I had known she was to marry Hal. Yet I loved her now, and with love goes fear, so the buoyancy of the baby was having to sustain me too.

'What a disgusting smell,' I said. 'It's like the essence of boiled-down dolls. What's in the papers? Do you have to put them on the floor? It can't be clean and then you'll pick up the papers and wipe all the prawn and chocolate over them and your face . . . ' I was enjoying the intimacy of nagging. You cannot nag people for whom you do not care.

Unlike a real child, she took it as it was intended, lovingly. She began to read the papers.

'Little ones first,' she said. 'I'm getting too thick to read the others.'

'If only it were just morning thickness,' I said. She liked these simple puns. I've learnt not to speak them aloud invariably when they occur. Not everyone understands that words have sandwiched meanings, and others, dictionary people, do not like the mess these sandwiches make. I prefer the sideroads of speech. The main roads are too direct. Besides, it is on the byroads that you come upon the important things, closed houses of despair, undiscovered copses of delight just at a dwindling road end.

None the less, today we were actually driving down the unrelieved motorway, going south by the most direct and least lovely route. It was a day of double weather, just the day for a fox's wedding, black sky and bright light promising rain in large drops.

'There is rather a lot about Lucas here,' said Cora, 'I'm sorry to say. It's opposite the pin-up. He wouldn't like that.'

'He's used to it. Life-and-death babies and big breasts have always gone together.'

'This one looks like anything but a wet nurse. She's got boxing gloves on which look like her bosoms and it says "OUR CHRISTMAS BOX". You wouldn't dare call cute Lyn a little right-hooker in case she gave you one there and then . . . shall I go on? Oh Christ!'

'Cora, what is it? Remember the baby, don't talk like that.'

Nursery fears about thinking bad thoughts crippling the baby came to me.

'I wasn't reading the stuff about Lucas till later, but you know how you read this sort of stuff like an eye test just by looking at it, the letters are so big? Anne, has there been anything much about your furrier in the papers? I've got so lazy about reading them. Did you know they thought that it wasn't robbers, but animal rights people?'

'Anyone could have guessed that. And what is this to do with Lucas?' Sometimes when you ask a question it is answered by your own re-dealt pack of memories, a straight solution, the patience out in one.

'The police have got Dolores Steel.'

'Dolores Steel? Tell me she's real, with a name like that.' I was driving fast. It was not a pleasant outing we were on, and I grudged our pursuit by the hounds of bad news.

'She *is* real. I know her. She works in the shop. She is a friend of Angel Coney. She's been in prison before for assault, but I thought she had put it behind her.'

'And now d'you mean she's put it behind Lucas? What are you saying?'

'She changed her name. At school she was Consuelo Sharp. She kept it Spanish sounding, to please her father.'

'Not something she can always have had an eye to. Spit it out, Cora, we're off to have a very uneasy day already.'

'She has been charged with the attack on Mr Virtue's shop. Apparently there are accomplices who aren't named. "She distributes leaflets . . . " Oh Anne. I've been addressing envelopes to distribute her stuff. "She distributes leaflets from the exclusive Sloane Street address of a charity shop where she works with the beautiful Lady Angelica Coney, who says, 'I feel sorry for Dolores. She had a chance and she has blown it. These people are no better than animals.' The leaflets are printed by a press called ART which stands for Animal Rights Terrorism."'

'More rat than art I'd say. I would give these people a piece of my mind,' I said. I was alarmed by her fear. It was the infatuated fear Angelica Coney had aroused in Alexander.

'They'd take a person, Annie, and eat them raw like monkey's brain. They are merciless.'

'Go on. What else does it say? Do you want to look it up in one of the big papers?'

'Not really. I can't help feeling sorry for her – Dolores,' she said.

'For her, for her, what about Mr Virtue? And for the love of God, what about Lucas?'

'"Some ART leaflets were found beside the near lifeless body of Sir Lucas Salik, who had been left for dead by attackers in the King's Cross area of London. Police are pursuing enquiries. They are not answering questions from journalists, but our man with his finger on the pulse" – it says that – "says that animals are extensively used in the type of research needed to support work like Sir Lucas's." And now the paper hedges its bets. "Who are we to say, when we look into the suffering eyes of a child or of a seal pup, who suffers more?" Make it a nasty smelly old man and a warthog and maybe we could think straight. Oh, the unfairness of appearances. "Police are requesting that anyone who can help them with their enquiries please come forward.

'"If you know about ART, have a heart for brave Sir Lucas." The thing is, I do,' she finished.

'What?' I felt the difference in our ages.

'Well, I didn't know I did, but I must have, I worked there. Also, something happened, at the very beginning, but I didn't want it to be anything. I mean, for me in a funny way it was a good thing.'

She told me a story about a raw uprooted tongue lying in Lucas's car. I felt sick and was silent.

'And for me in a way it was nice because he had to be looked after,' she said, poor fool.

'Did you think that Cupid goes about putting the tongues of dead animals into cars? For goodness' sake, Cora, what were you thinking of? You must have suspected something. Oh love, don't worry. I am just frightened by the way these things get out of hand. When I was young it was nations not notions.'

'Now I see it, but then I did not, because I didn't want to. If I am utterly truthful I think that I did not want anything to have any connection with me. I wanted, even though I knew it wasn't possible, him to think me as perfect as I thought him.'

'That's not love. It's calf love.'

'I'm only just not a calf. We're all half calf. Wasn't that what the dreadful tongue was saying?' she asked.

'Except *they* can't speak. And I think that it is that in the end which makes us different.'

'Anne. That's what the note said, in Lucas's car, there was a note saying "They can't speak". I'd forgotten that.' She sounded as though she spoke the truth.

'I would say that that was less an excuse for what they do than a reason for how we are – lords of creation, I mean. Though I suppose the people – ARTists, do they call themselves? – are human too, and that must be a bind for them.'

'Dolores and Angelica are in human guise. They are cats. More beautiful than humans. But is that beauty enough to make them better than humans? And *you* borrow the coats of beautiful animals to make yourself more beautiful.'

'Hardly borrow. And even though I have often thought of killing Angelica Coney I cannot imagine wearing her. She herself does it too well.'

We were past Basingstoke. We were driving through the Wallops, Over, Middle and Nether. I thought again of Stone, and longed to take Cora, the baby and Lucas home and away from all this.

Cora said, 'I didn't know you had strong feelings about Angel?'

'Well, I've known her all her life; I feel as though I've known you all your life but in fact I *have* known Angelica. She played with my son.' If that is playing.

'*Was* she ever a child?' she asked.

'Always, still is, amoral and powerful. Brilliant at manipulating men. I think that she must have more to do with this than we will ever know,' I said.

'But then she has betrayed Dolores.' Naïve child.

'Cora, that's nothing. She probably liked Dolores because she smelt the blood from her wounds, having been to prison once, certain to go again if the need arose.'

'But they were friends.' She bleated like a pet lamb who sees the rosemary tied in its little bunch, and the knife lying by it.

'Angelica has no friends. It's why she's so popular. She is feared. People are at their best with her, because they do not dare not to relax, or they'll be sent to the knacker, or the exterminator will be called.'

'I thought Dolores was like that too.'

'Girls like Angelica always have a consort, whom they ingest. They are kingmakers. They pretend it is rule by two kings like in ancient Sparta, and then they kill the other and raise up a new one, green and fresh, from the old one's fresh blood. I've never known Angelica without her other half, and it has not once been a man. Men narrow the possibilities so, they don't travel light,' I said.

'What do you mean?'

'With them comes love, or babies at least. And they are bad liars. They do not understand that everything is true when it is spoken or performed, even though it is a contradiction. Women do not have to explain this to each other. Or not Angelica's sort of woman. Her strength makes her seem straight, but she is twisted, she is a hook, no matter how you struggle the barbs dig deeper.'

'Was your husband in love with her?' Cora asked this, though I think she cannot have liked doing so.

'Absolutely not, funnily enough. I think the reason I dislike her so is that she took Alexander's childhood from him. If it had been a childish love affair, I would perhaps by now have been pleased that he had that, at least. But she misinformed him unpleasantly, she turned him against himself, and she made him see that nothing, not home, not family, is safe. With Mordred dying, he would have seen it anyway, but she did it in such a grubby way. She smuggled the serpent into his garden. I am certain she has a lot to do with all this. Has she ever asked you about Lucas? Or did Dolores?'

'Dolores came to hospital. I visited her. He was doing something with her heart. He mended it. They did ask about Lucas,' she admitted.

'If a heart can ever be mended. And did you notice how she was with him?'

'Very cold.'

'You see, Cora, Angelica would have been charming. Poor Dolores, she is obviously the saddest kind of fanatic, the one with his heart on his sleeve who loses his shirt. Are we getting near?' I did not know whether I was pleased or not that there was some suspicion as to who had hurt Lucas. I did want to know who had disfigured Mr Virtue's shop. I wanted a straightforward penalty for the person who had done that, but I did not like to face that if and when Lucas's attacker was found, I would want him or her to undergo terrible pain. I did not like this in myself. I hate to see animals in pain. I put rabbits, bats, foxes, beautiful screaming hares out of their misery. But I did wish to see whoever had done this suffer protracted pain. Not even animals have this desire. Except, perhaps, the cat playing with its mouse. My desire was not an animal one, it was intellectual. It was all that makes us, supposedly, superior to animals, it was a civilised, refined desire to see another human being suffer. It gave me cousinhood with the worst people who have lived and I was ashamed. I was also exhilarated, like a hunter on the scent.

'We are getting near. It's called "Cranford",' said Cora.

'I have seen that on your invitation, fool. You were to have been married tomorrow, remember? Is it this one? You can't imagine getting homesick for it can you? Poor old Hal.'

A woman was running towards the car. She must be Hal's mother. I regretted my snobbery. She looked so wretched. I wound down the car window. She was turning and turning her hands at the bottom of her cardigan. Her clothes were the rubbery texture of scrambled egg, the synthetic tweed uncreased. A small marcasite brooch, a sailing dinghy, rocked on her breast. The colour she wore was a colour reserved for bedjackets or re-usable picnic items, a green unreminiscent of grass or trees or sea. It probably washed like a dream. I prefer my dreams dirty. Or is the truth that I do not do my own washing? She was speaking, and making gestures of welcome and apology. I did not see that she should apologise. The years of being a widow have made me able to assume the astringent tone of a man in an emergency; I extended my hand to her, and smiled, calm and slow like a politician with bad news, but not so bad that it cannot be talked out.

'Bad news, oh bad news, oh, oh,' she was saying. But my firm frostiness reached her and she calmed down enough to ask us in.

'The boys are out. All day.' They would arrive after we had gone to drink strong drink and speak of a merciful release.

'Cora, dear, how are you?' Mrs Darbo looked almost happy when she contemplated the scruffy fatso who had almost been her daughter-in-law.

'As well as can be . . . ' began Cora.

' . . . expected,' said Mrs Darbo. We were in the sitting room.

It was so comfortable that there was nowhere to sit without being compromised by the chairs' embrace. I wanted air.

'A coffee?' asked Mrs Darbo. I felt as though Cora and I had found ourselves on the set of a television quiz show. The room was full of appliances. Nothing looked old. All the wood that was intended to look old had a vivid, unconvincing richness, like a suntan. There was one flower arrangement, for arrangement it was; it resembled a cauliflower, painted by a Persian, turreted pompoms embowered in straps of green. The ribbons flowing from it had the lemniscous curve of Arabic letters. It was, I was sure, Cora's wedding bouquet.

'Some coffee would be very nice, thank you, Monica, let me help,' said Cora. She looked, thank goodness, more depressed than I had seen her for two days. The expectant radiance was gone.

They returned with a tray of coffee.

'Biscuit, Cora?' asked Mrs Darbo. There was a selection. A pink wafer and a custard cream with a ruby drop of jam in its navel would, I knew, tempt Cora.

'The thing is,' said Cora, 'I don't really like biscuits.' I wondered to what, then, Mrs Darbo would ascribe her fatness.

'Horse-radish is what you need,' said Mrs Darbo to Cora.

I wondered if it was like mandrake. What was its use to those with child? Was it an abortifacient? Could Mrs Darbo see the truth?

'It does wonders for fluid retention.' Poor Mrs Darbo, her eyes mauve from crying, she must have been keen to retain some fluids.

She began to chat. Illness and complaints are an area of amnesty in women's conversations. We boast a little of campaigns waged and won, of corners defended, of ambushes repelled. We were on neutral ground. We did not discuss children, whether on account of some tact for my sake from Mrs Darbo I did not know. Surprisingly, she did not mention Hal, whom Cora had told me I would hear described in hyperbolic terms.

We made play with coffee, milk, sugar tongs. Mrs Darbo gave us each a small mat, embroidered with a posy.

'French knots for the hollyhocks, quite hard to do but rewarding. It was to be for their' – no need to ask whose – 'new home but I thought waste not . . .'

' . . . want not,' I said. It was not difficult to converse with Mrs Darbo. One performed an antiphon of platitude. She appeared calmer. Perhaps her coffee had calmed her down, but I smelt menthol on her and it reminded me of a governess who drank, steadily and without subterfuge, during afternoons of teaching me stem stitch and birdsfoot hemming. When she went out for a nip, I sucked the silks. Purple was most delicious. At the roots of Mrs Darbo's teeth was a ridge of primrose yellow and a red thread of blood. I wondered if her husband drank too. I thought of Hal, again, with something which was not sympathy. It was a willingness to share his apprehension of his cosy, airless home and his unhappy mother.

At times of great disaster, there is invariably one get-together which is rich in funny possibilities. When Mordred died, I suppose it was going to the local conservation society meeting that evening. No one knew of his death, and I could not let them down. We passed paste sandwiches and discussed the susceptibility of cowslips to loud noise. Stone, like the rest of Scotland, is often under exploration for oil. The seismic records show that this is knocking the kangaroo of Britain all askew from the waist up.

'I like to think of the cowslips nodding away long after we are all pushing up daisies,' said Mr McIver.

'Uh huh' – which is the scots for 'Yes, but', meaning assent with conditions – 'speak for yourself,' said Miss Erskine. 'I prefer cut blooms. More in keeping with a bereavement.' And the Scots, so neat in death, do prefer cut blooms, placing them against the weather in glass bells on flat discs of white marble which are handy later for the fresh keeping of the creamier cheeses.

This coffee ceremony with Mrs Darbo was not funny now, but I could imagine, if Lucas lived, laughing about it with him. It was not she who was funny, nor the house, nor the garden, furled up now but potentially as garish as a golf umbrella. There was cotoneaster spidering over the slabs, which were weeded, as clean between as dominoes. It was just that we had reached the overspilling point where nothing more of a terrible nature could be borne, so the slightest thing was funny. I wished there had been an animal there, a dog, to give us innocent fun, to give us a reason besides hysteria to laugh.

'I have decided to save the dress in case one of the boys marries someone statuesque,' said Mrs Darbo. I had been curious about this.

'And the flowers,' said Cora, 'where have they gone?'

'Well, it was most awkward that they couldn't go to a hospital, but then I had a brainwave, really.' Perhaps, sensibly, they were going to keep them and give a party anyway?

'My husband has connections in the afterlife and we are allowing them to go to the undertaker at Poole. It's most respectable.' This is what she said.

As we left, she took the bouquet from its vase, wiping all unsightly dampness from its stems with a pink cloth which was immediately wet through. She sought an invulnerable surface on which to place the damp cloth, and gave the flower-cauliflower to Cora. 'Thank you for coming,' she said at the door. It was cold. She wanted to be inside her house, to shut out strangers and the wind.

'Amazing she's taking it so well,' I said as we turned left on to real road, and away from their golden conifers and pink gravel.

'It's not that amazing. She feels guilty.'

'*She* feels guilty? When for no very clear reason her son's wedding is called off and she has to sort it out two days before. Guilty? Have a heart, Cora, do.'

'She told me something in the kitchen. I never quite believed her and her family. I've never considered them seriously. But Hal has done something which makes you take her seriously.'

'What's that?' I asked, asking as much on account of her tone of voice as from a desire to know.

'He's given himself up to the police. He did it this morning, just before we arrived. She told me in the kitchen. And she said that I would never be good enough for him, so perhaps it was a blessing . . . '

' . . . in disguise,' I chimed, as we swung north up the direct route to the city's broken heart.

XXIX

I t was March before I could get them to Stone. It took so very long because Lucas had to be well, not, as he had indicated, to resume his work, but to see Hal tried for the attack. The trial was incidental. The tragedy was not there in the cold court but long ago when Lucas first saw him. He fell in love with his own angel of death. But, perhaps because it was dark, perhaps because he was afraid, Hal had not completed his task. He was not even Lucifer, though I am sure Lucas thought him the bearer of light as he saw the golden head he loved before the knife struck. But angels are messengers sent by higher authority, and Hal's message was a garbled one.

A jury does not find the desire of men to embrace each other in lavatories simple. There is a new righteous wrath, a new nosology of morals. The man who just used to *suspect* he did not like chaps in cravats drinking gin-and-it now has a flaming sword to bar their entrance into happiness. These creatures of disease, thinks the heterosexual, so tenuously preserving his right to promiscuity, had it coming to them, for the way they looked, for the way they spoke, for the way they were. Pox comes from llamas, AIDS from monkeys. He's all right, he never sleeps with either. Boys who had entered the decade pioneers, with innocent brio and a taste for the design and redevelopment of the inner city, were leaving the decade lazars, and the cities ghost-towns. That the disease is shared by users of drugs, prostitutes, yes, and black men, puts power fair and square in the reins of the horsemen of the apocalypse. Like all plagues, it gives work to liars and cowards and power to the bullies. A scourge of the unrighteous, a blessing in disguise. The disease is a news vendor surpassing babies with new hearts, surpassing glandular freaks of womanhood, surpassing even crowned heads. A great game of Russian roulette for us, who do not touch the gun, to watch. It is of course a matter of time before the sickness is available to us all. And then there are the innocent, how do the righteous explain the babies and the mothers and those whose blood will not stop running out of them? Is it the god of wrath accelerating the apocalypse? Or is it just as sad and without point as war?

It has a name, innocuous, helpful, AIDS, a succubus not succouring. I was reading an article in French about something I imagined must be a new cult: 'SIDA. Ça va evaincre le monde?' Like all religions, it is catching. I have read, indeed, that there is fear among Communicants that the disease may be passed by chalice. It is like someone who has just left the room, everyone is talking about it. Like a secret which is out, it is killing trust and splitting groups. It is also evoking new and fearful braveries. Could you have imagined a world where it was brave for a restaurateur to serve his clients, for a forensic scientist to perform an autopsy? Even if there is nothing to fear, the fear is there, and it calls up courage. Tertius is growing thinner. Is he on a timely diet? Did he see himself in the glass and feel a little worried by his sea-lion bulk? Or is he wasting away? The dangers drawn by Lucas's black trysts were once rejection or attack. There was, he has told me, a thrill in the closeness to danger. It was a melodramatic, erotic danger, to be feinted but not fulfilled. There is no such frisson to the consideration of a more lingering and more painful danger. Yet Lucas and men like him need the anonymity, the lovelessness, like a fighter the fight. Should isolation hospitals become brothels? AIDS is grand with metaphor, like all plagues. The lists of love become trenches of horror; this new germ warfare is thoroughly modern, though it is attired in the mediaeval dress favoured by death and his troupe. Leeches will come back, and embrocations of rue, as this new disease, decked out in the theatrical dressing-gown handed down to him by fear and bigotry, walks abroad, putting his hourglass into the hands of boy lovers in cocktail bars.

I am determined to ignore it. It is simple enough for me to do this, naturally, since I am not in utero, intravenal, haemophiliac or homophile. It is easier for me not to take all this illness and dying too personally. But it is starting to touch the people I love. It is like attending a masked ball; the one in your arms may be Venus, or a lifetime of mercury. But AIDS is without the energy of the pox; its acronym makes it hard to nickname. It lives with us but will not be treated familiarly. Careless talk is costing lives again; a whisper about a man leaves him alone out on the turret, being offered the third cigarette.

So, the jury were suspicious. They smelled a ship of rats, but were put off by Lucas's repute, his frailty and by Hal's cut and dried story.

The press were waiting, pest-control officers with a taste for gassing. Their weasel words have learnt since Wolfenden many tricks of omission and suggestion. Lucas was made much of, but his stock epithets were now, as well as 'brilliant, pioneering, brave', 'never married' and 'childless'. His foreignness was stressed more than it had been. Once delighted to boast of his parents' choice of domicile, the newspapers began to suggest that perhaps he, Sir Lucas, should have kept himself to himself a little more, not become quite so Englished. Whether they wanted him to wear a gingham blouse and weep into his black bread after stitching up their children all day was not clear. The bolder newspapers suggested that of late he had been favouring the heart problems of other people not always of British extraction, and that this might have something to do with money. The Afghani boy became 'the son of a prince we cannot name', suggesting great riches and the, in the end, peculiar unspellability of foreign names. Lucas's full name was read out in court. 'What a mouthful,' said the papers, over a photograph of Hal looking like a girl, taken at the seaside long ago. The copy was dull enough, just Lucas's full name, and a little piece about his father having been a seller of gherkins. I do not believe they spelt his names correctly: they just snored zzzzzs through a blanket of Catholic names.

Hal explained that he carried a knife for digging into the lath of houses he was selling. It was like tasting a cheese. The judge looked up. Not all stupid, then, this boy.

Of course, Hal was not telling the truth. I knew that Lucas, unable to speak to Hal, to tell him what to say, was miserable at the stupidity of his lies. Lucas would have made a neat case which as nearly as possible exonerated Hal. His love would have grown in protecting him. As it was, he saw him accused. I think he may have wished Hal had killed him.

Hal spoke like a child saying his tables, and getting them wrong. He appeared to think that repetition and vehemence might compose truth.

After one day which had been very long, dull and frightening, like being shut in with a snake, Lucas said to me, 'I wish it was an inquest on me and Hal had skipped off to a life of ease.'

'Did you see him when you were attacked?' I asked.

'How not?' he replied. 'I even see him when he isn't there. I was pleased to see him. But it wouldn't have come to anything, not sex, because I know him. By now I have him too deep for thrills. With him the thrill is the distance, the holding off. The only way it could have come to something would be if he had finished me off. I should have died happy.'

'Would you tell everything, to save him?'

'Nothing can save him utterly,' he said.

The trial was cursory. Fear kept us silent. We were all compromised by what was unsaid. Hal did not reveal that he knew Lucas more than casually – socially, he corrected. Sex and money, attendant on the meanest trial, hung about oppressively outside, but never got in. It was as though the immune system of the established order was enclosing this symptom of things being different to how they seemed, and breaking it down, to immobilise it. The establishment, well inoculated, was safe so far.

I am a Scots Calvinist, so used to the idea of there being unjustified sinners, and I did not take Hal's conviction hard. He was to be away for three years. I felt sure that good behaviour was not beyond him, and his time would be correspondingly tailored. I know prisons, and was pretty certain that Hal would adapt well. He was good with fear and used to authority; he understood hierarchies and was comfortable with deceit. He was a solipsist and he could write joined up. He would therefore, I imagined, plan the perfect crime and write love letters to the wives of his subordinate colleagues, for a small payment of tobacco, drugs or chocolate.

But Lucas suffered. He knew that punishment is not equal to crime, that somewhere there is short change. He would have died for Hal, without question, long before that became more than a figure of speech, in December. He knew that much remained unsaid. He would have spoken to save Hal, but he saw that it was best to act simply, to be the dignified physician. He saw that it was a smaller crime for Hal to attack a rich man he hardly knew than for him to attempt to kill a man who had him toiled about with love, provision, money and even a bride. He cannot have helped wondering why Hal had done it, but he did not speak of this.

Cora was a character witness. Huge, she stood and dared the men in wigs to question her. Her status as the defendant's almost-bride was made clear. She spoke well of him. Her state was allowed to speak for itself. To advert to it, since the baby was not Hal's, would be to lie, but in order to allow the silent witness to speak below its mother's bland face, the defence made sure that she wore tall heels and a dress tight as an arum's packed velamen.

Lucas had recovered in body; his walk had changed. I saw his back once when I visited him in hospital and they were moving a dressing. Rods of white cicatrised it, disorderly as kindling; I thought of the first pain he must have felt.

What gave him hope was the baby. Though I did not ask him, I could tell. It may have been because it was a life so far untouched by all that had happened, indifferent as the moon. Sometimes I was afraid to leave him in a room alone. I did not think he would kill himself. I feared he would die of shame.

'Though why *he* feels like Judas, I can't think,' said Cora. 'He never even said anything.'

'It's the containing of a secret,' I replied. 'He had hoped to get the whole lot off his chest, I suspect. It never works. People hear what they have ears to hear. If he had stood up and shouted his secrets, he'd only have been ignored. Then everyone would have cleaned their ears out and he would be relieved of his job and he'd've got old suddenly and turned this flat into a doss for refugees. But they wouldn't've been real refugees, they'd've been lazy scams who know a milchcow by its guilty eyes.'

'You are very sure.' Cora was in Lucas's upstairs bath. Not much water was required to fill it deep about her. She could no longer get out on her own. The soap was a pink oval, transparent. There was blossom frothing by the canal and the sky was a pale blue which lay reflected on the top of the bath-water like a floating pennant. I was pushed on by spring. It does not forbid mourning, but it gives it white underskirts.

Since the trial, we had been with Lucas almost every day. I sometimes stayed in his white spare room and sometimes went home. Cora turned his upstairs room, which I had always found too much of a good thing, into her bedroom. So she lived with me and she lived with him, like the child of a happy divorce, and other modern fairy-tale princesses. Together, the three of us had made of the upstairs room a nursery for the baby to come.

Lucas found a cradle which resembled a small skiff. I asked Mrs Virtue, on one of my visits to their family, whether she would sew curtains for the cradle, voile sails. I spoke to her with fingers and thumbs and smiles. Tomas, her boy, was at ease across her knee. He wore shorts and a jumper with the sleeves pushed up, and he stared up at the underside of his mother's chin as if in wonder anything could be so old. He flicked at the strap of her watch. He was hardly scarred. His face was smooth as a petal, his arms and legs merely boy-bruised. Mrs Virtue was a keen sewer, she told me. 'Or my hands worry,' she sighed. Her English was growing.

She and I began to spend grandmotherly afternoons planning mist, snow, cloud and all other conditions of whiteness and wool and cotton, to be made into small clothes. She had a book of needles the shape of a crinolined lady, the needles kept in her petticoats, needles which were so thin they bent. They were thinner than the thread they drew. The box of white clothes grew in Lucas's room upstairs.

Cora sat with Lucas a great deal. I did not hear them talk much, but she read to him and she made him food. When he first came home, he took a long time to get upstairs, but he spent more and more time there now. He was working again, but the newspapers were neglecting him. He had so nearly destroyed the black and white of their categories. Read all over it would have been indeed, had the truth come out.

On occasional Sundays, I took them both to Kew, and we sat, like a family, and walked, and sat again. Because they both moved more slowly than I, they walked together and I went on. He leant on her. He might have been her father or her husband.

She had told me about her father the night before Hal gave himself up. He and her mother were dead. I should have guessed. It was no doubt why she had fixed on Lucas, or the idea of him, cold, skilled, unfleshly, controlled. We talk easily of falling in love, but we allow the process only to lovers. It happens all the time, among the family we choose for ourselves, the family of friends. I had fallen in love, perhaps, with Cora as a daughter, she with Lucas as a father, and all three of us again with each other when we saw the tangle between us resolve itself into a knot. Cora had invented her memory of her father, her sources books, *Sara Crewe*, *Daddy-Long-Legs*, *The Thinking Reed*. School holidays were spent with the families of other children, so she had picked up several vocabularies and a palette of protective colours.

Sometimes I wondered whether her story was all true, if she thought her life was not interesting enough, if she prevaricated to keep my love, and this made me sad. But she proved it was true one day when she brought out an old pale blue box. It had once contained chocolates, and had that thick scent. When she opened it, a tight fit on account of the purple-brown paper and perforated-paper lace lining it, it contained her few certificates. They added up to what she had told me. Dead parents, and a very little money of her own.

'I wasted that. I'm sorry for it. And for wasting time,' she said.

It was as though she were giving me the deeds to herself.

'You are very sure,' said Cora in spring from the bath in Lucas's upper room. Lavender and the yellowless green of lichen, the dancers made flat merry on the walls. Her hair was up in a scarf, pink like a tulip, and the sails of the cradle hung in the light air. She soaped her feet with effort, bending over herself, separating her toes with the equivalent fingers, making the water play against the enamel.

I had bought a few toys for the baby. It would not like them until it was older, by when they might well have been lost. I treasured a teething ring of ivory; was it made of the milk tusks of elephants, or have they only one growth? I find it harder than ever now to find logic in our dealings with dumb creatures. The age of the teething ring made guilt difficult. Am I sorry about the evicted polyps from the baby's coral necklace wasting in the drawer? I can make no more sense of it all now than I could on the morning when I found Mr Virtue lamenting his savaged shop.

All I can say for sure is that an animal in pain must be put out of its pain.

I did it to Mordred, as I do to any animal. I put him out of his misery. It was at point blank, and it was strange to go to the conservation meeting afterwards. He fetched me to do it, a wounded

245

creature trusting to my courage and cold blood. I do not know how he made it to me. He had come, dragging his gun, from the hothouse to my writing room. He had shot himself in the hothouses from considerateness. Water for sluicing, and nothing to be stained. The white wrought iron could be hosed and orchids do not mind blood, even prosper on it though they prefer it unfresh. But he missed. He came, pulling himself, to my room. The carpet has a pale, silvery nap, like the poll of an olive tree under the breeze. As he pulled himself over the floor, he left a double trail of blood and of light-lessness where he turned the carpet's nap against itself. I put him out of his misery and made arrangements. Fingerprints are invariably taken, but not the prints of lips. I kissed him and kissed him. I had not heard the first shot from his gun. Ours is a house not of mercuric brick but of secret-bearing stone.

Of course, Lucas knew.

In March we went home to Stone.

XXX

For the last month before the birth of the baby, we lived at Stone. Both of them knew it, though neither had spent solid cuts of time there, unless that time had been taken carefully off the bone, made light and untaxing by careful, practised, hostly division.

I had not been home for four months. It was the longest separation from my house since my marriage to Mordred. I had never before spent Christmas away from Stone, but this last one before the baby I did spend with Lucas and with Cora in London. We ate preserved foods from jars and went for a walk in the afternoon. There was no one in the streets. Fountains had frozen, exuberant and still, like storks' wings. The high-smelling tramps were indoors, entertaining their benefactors, who are often more lonely than they. When we got home, I gave Cora her present, a Roman mirror I had bought from Tertius, who was so pale and thin now that his clothes looked like an Auguste's pyjamas.

'My appearance? Anno Domini at my back,' Tertius said. 'Sounds like a delicious little Caprese, but I can tell you it's nothing so fitting. That's it, cross my palm with silver. I think I'll be away next Christmas.' Whether he was contemplating heaven or Elba I couldn't say. He was too polite to me nowadays, and I felt I could hurt him with a word.

'Join us,' I said, not wishing him to.

'I rather thought I'd do a bit of your thing,' he said. 'Prison visiting. It can't be all beer and skittles for Hal in jug.' Jug sounded so friendly. I wondered whether Tertius had any idea of the grimness of prisons.

'It's not beefcake in chains,' I said.

247

'I've been,' said Tertius. 'Here's your mirror. Who knows what it has seen. Have a Christmas, I can't say happy after all this, and joy to your babies.' He did not mention Lucas, nor did Lucas any more speak of him. There had been a lapse as though someone had stopped seeing a joke.

Tony drove us up to Stone. Cora and Lucas slept. We drove through the night. I awoke, as I always do, as we crossed the border. I have never outgrown that. The first small towns, with bannock in the windows and hosiery shops with the word spelt out in red and white stockings, the ugly villas with names tooled into the keystone – 'Ardrishaig', 'Kinphail', 'Sgreadan'; even the foodstuffs have celtic names – 'Glenwheat', 'Tobermac Fish Bits'. No other country has fallen so hard for its own image in the funfair mirror. Tartan rock, and a Scottie dog for every pot. But it is to me the only serious place to be. The road opens out into rearing country after the border, and the coarse grass and blue roads shiver under the grudging, then hospitable, sun. Nowhere dirties the air quicker than Scotland with all its swearing, drinking, cigarettes and dying factories. The gas towers over Grangemouth hold sulphur orange and a copper green up into the sky like brushes full of poster colour. But there is more air to dirty than in the rest of Britain, and each morning is new, the old day having cleared its throat and gone during the short night of the north.

Past the green flocking hills, always between the walls of dry stones which are clapped together at the top like hands, and past big harled houses with too little window and slipping turrets at their shoulder, and with not flowers but green vegetables on the south walls. If any of it were to disappear, I would still see it, for I see, of course, with sentimental eyes. What would another make of it? I am partial.

The car snicked between the Crook Inn and its walled garden on the other side of the road. The gate into the garden, against the freshly colouring sky, was flat as a nursery frieze, two woolly lambs flanked by two shepherds' crooks, white flat iron, white as milk and wool. There are those words used by tourists to Scotland – 'beauty spot', suggesting contrivance and falseness. The Lowlands have nothing of vain beauty though; they are protective, gentle, reliable, nurse to the rakeheaven grande-dame of the Highlands. Those mountains put on black and diamonds at night. Down here in the

Lowlands, there is a shawl of mist in the country and a good rabbit fur of fag-ash over the towns. We may omit the Lion of Glasgow and the Unicorn of Edinburgh. Each of those is singular.

Stone lies between the two, and is approached by an irregular drive. To arrive, it is necessary to pass the house, which is entered from the side. It has two fronts and two climates. In the douce summer I live in every room; in winter the wind makes the eastern face of the house too brusque for papers and too cold for sitting. In the winter I have found flowers, matured to their fruit, left from the autumn, in ice, held in the vase like Fabergé's gemmy berries in crystal. Asleep in one of these rooms, you might put out a hand in sleep and in the morning find it gone quite white. The only way to foil the cold is to be in love, and even that is not sure. The house is plain. It is not squinched or pepperpotty, it recollects no French alliance. It is of grey stone, unfaced, and the stone is black when it is wet. There are hills to the west and hills to the east, but they are small for hills and the house is big for a house. It has twenty-seven windows on each side, three rows of nine, their glass of the type which spins all light that hits it. It tells the sky to itself. In the sills of the windows tortoiseshell butterflies hatch too soon and need daily rescuing. There is an attic room where the flies go to die. It fills your hair with noise. To east and west there are porticos, that to the west with a pointed pediment, to the east with a curved pediment. These are supported by unfluted columns to the east, fluted to the west. The columns are Doric. There is no suggestion of romantic vegetable matter anywhere in the architecture of the house. It looks as it sounds, stone.

When the sun rises, it fills the arc of the eastern pediment and the tubes of the columns with light. The smoothness of the portico looks pale against the grey house, and larger, as though it were another house itself. These steps end in a terrace. The terrace is lapped by a lawn shaped like an almond. The man who built the house had lost his heart to India, and found there rich compensation for this loss. The tip of the almond drops to a ha-ha. Cowslips grow in spring at its ashlar foot. A long field of leaning trees moves out to the heather. What the wind began, the trees' disease has completed. Scotland seems to favour brushy trees, hazel and rowan and gorse, over the English givers of contemplation and stealthy veiling shade.

A lozenge within the eastern pediment, of earlier date than the house, and lettered in pothooked lower-case, not the Trajan capitals you might expect, says:

> It hath and schal ben evermor
> That love is maister wher he wile.

To the west, which is the side a newcomer first sees, the sun falls down the chutes of the columns, and sinks; the pale portico holds the colour in its severe frieze, a simple cornice of mortised panels. The confident motto, spaced evenly within the base of the portico's isosceles, is 'The brother of death exacteth a third part of our lives'.

The steps down from this portico debouch into a courtyard, almost filled with a lawn, which is elliptical in shape, the broadest part of the ellipse being exactly at the centre of the house. In the centre of the lawn is a tall pedestal. It supports a statue of an old man with a tortoise at his feet. I no longer speculate about the tortoise. The man may be Aeschylus, who was killed by a falling turtle, or he may be the inventor of the lyre, or he may be simply a clue that the sculptor was exhausted by carving staffs, snakes, lions. Ever since I received no reaction when I told a table full of visitors, struggling to amalgamate oatcakes, butter and honey without messing their fingers, that it was Darwin with a young Galapagan turtle, I have ceased to speculate. No one laughed, and I missed Mordred so much I could have run away.

'Most acceptable honey. Is it your own?' had asked Miss Erskine. I all but stung her.

I brought my friends home in time for breakfast. The rooms at Stone are large and very numerous. Unusually for a middle-sized Scots house, it is a unit, not an accretion. The bottom two storeys of the house have rooms of great height. The top floor's rooms are just tall.

None of the rooms has curtains. The windows are shuttered with finely made wooden shutters which fold and lock as snugly as big Bibles. Each of the shutters folds away in two parts, so you can allow into the rooms whatever fraction of the light or weather you wish. On days when the light is too strong for the old chintz and large pale furniture, the shutters are closed. It takes one person an hour to close them all, and the arms ache. Seen from the furthest point of the almond lawn with all its shutters closed, the house looks not deserted but full of pleasant secrets. Each set of shutters has one oval hole, about a third of the way down the left-hand shutter's outer fin; through it you can watch the sun and moon and stars' passage. A line of sun comes through the hole on summer days, a beam whose Copernican rulings over two centuries may be traced on carpets, walls and wood, where they have faded or where the veneer is just beginning to bridle. There is a pale diagonal of books in my bedroom, showing how orderly or how unreading have been the ladies of the house, and a beam of bleached books, paler even than their faded neighbours. Taken from the shelf, these books, the sun-paled and the merely old of spine, show bright sides. Some of them contain letters or flat flowers, a surprised embrace.

When I was waiting for Alexander to be born, I lay in my room with the shutters almost closed, and watched new colours appear in the three high portholes, green dawn, orange daybreak, and a lilac afternoon changing later to dark blue. There is never the fear of a face at the window. Through these holes only birds can look.

Under the eaves, in what Scots call the rhones, live martins in spring. Their nests are neighbours to the plain white acorns which look like enormous eggs, hanging from the cornice below the roof. Like nomads camped in the Sphinx's paw, the swifts seem indifferent to any menace which might hatch from these great white wooden eggs.

Rarely, but then as orderly as a weft in tweed, the geese will mount up and over the house, and an unreeling of their elegant repeated pattern will be seen, up the west face of the house, and slowly down the east side, landing slowly in a slope again like cloth on the loch beyond the field. Herons nest there. The geese make a noise like people, and they have two watchmen which give the alarm when there is danger. When they go, they leave ivy-green droppings, white chalk at one end. At rest in the field, with the leaning trees, and their two look-outs, they have the beaky brown faces of the Bayeux soldiers.

The glasshouse is on the south side. It fulfils the purpose of a lemon house, but at Stone we bring into it not lemons, but almost everything which will not take the winter. It contains within itself an orchid house. It is all very sturdy, not lacy; nevertheless, stones should not be thrown. The door into the stone house from the glasshouse is a good hurl away. The kitchens and my day-room are all at this end of the house. Incorrectly known as the back door, this is the door to which people come with boxes or for boxes.

It is the door to which Mordred dragged himself, and then on through it. That last corridor is hung with dreary photographs. These show men and tigers, men and trains, men and men in turbans, men in pearl ropes to their knees and whiskers out past their ears. There are several photographs of yachts, ablaze with a wardrobe of sail over the brown Bay of Bombay or the brown Solent.

When I am at Stone, I do not know why I ever go away. I do, however; and become more familiar with the house as you do with absence. As I have said, it in some sense accompanies me. It sets no officious standards of scale or beauty, but it gives me the inestimable qualifications of being certain that I have at times been perfectly happy. How many people have that, or know where it has been? It is where the two worst things happened, but, more important, many thousands of good. The fountain in which Alexander immersed his concentrating face has gone. Fountains are things of changing but repetitive beauty which reward long contemplation, and I could not have contemplated that one without seeing the backs of his legs with their green veins, and his wet eyes. I have kept other fountains, since I had no further children to lose. His grave is at Stone. It says:

PAUPER SUM EGO
NIHIL HABEO
COR MEUM DABO.

For Cora and the baby – who was to be born in hospital, and brought home – I had chosen two rooms on the first floor of the house, looking out to the hills and the morning light. Lucas I put in the equivalent rooms at the other end of the house, with windows also towards the glasshouse. From his windows the dovecote was visible, a helmet of pinkish grey bricks in the field beyond the glasshouse. The doos, which is how they are called by the Scots, are the ordinary eating kind, with black eyes and iris necks, not the red-eyed pouters with their pantaloons. Sometimes a cinnamon-fronted turtle dove joins them in their brick roost. In the evening, the sounds from the dovecote make it a hive of lullabies.

Corbies, Aesop's cheese-eating dominie birds, and the guzzlers of dead men, come rarely. They are to be seen after heavy rain, trying to pick off wet shrews. The main scavengers are foxes. I encourage them more than I discourage them. They dance along with their chrysanthemum-coloured tails out straight behind. From the east face of the house I have seen fox pups play tag over heaps of warm grass clippings, and then flop down, trembling and eager, ticking their tails, biding.

Nabob would lie like that as a puppy. Mordred knew him as a pup, and I am sometimes terrified of the dog's death. It will bring it all back. We know death is inevitable, but we go on having dogs. George and George, who with their wives run Stone when I am not there and when I am, persuaded me to find another puppy. I imagine this is against the death of Nabob. He is going white, and his legs sometimes fail him, but he is as devious, greedy and wheedling as he ever was. He thoroughly dislikes books. Unlike a cat, which will come and sit on a book its master is reading, Nabob just interrupts. But he listens well, and, like a grumpy old man, he has soft spots. He is disciplined about meal-times. He relishes vandalism for the attention it brings, enquiries into his puppyhood and so on. His ears have tears from wire and from teeth, but they are still silky. He does not smell and his nose is a surprise of black in his hungover old face. Without the braceleted ankles he had as a pup, his feet are still amusing. He will cross his forepaws to hold his chin or to watch television, which he does from a chair. The puppy is still on probation. She is a Sealyham and her feet touch her pink stomach as she walks. When Cora's baby is born, the puppy will have grown to be about the size of the child. At the moment, she is about the size of a bottle of milk. She spills easily, still. It is up to her to win Nabob over with more than her appealing looks. He has not had his day; he is just not interested in puppies. Her name is George too. Nabob had better develop an interest in appealing small bundles clothed in fluffy white. Nabob has a grand way with the house. He knows it all well, but no longer frequents the rooms which are of no use to him. He looks ducally on at George as she fossicks with enthusiasm in the corners of another new room. He is like an old grandee who has retired to his club in advanced age, and is able happily to deride morning-rooms and gun-rooms and still-rooms, having had them and discovered the amenities of bungalow living.

I like to arrive home in the morning in order to have a day of the ordinary shape and size, which will in its turn initiate others. The appeal of order is the sense it makes of time. No regret, no dropped stitches. It is like my cupboards.

Tony stopped the car. As children are, Lucas and Cora were woken by the silence. As I like, there was no one to greet us. Tony would stay for an hour of talk, some food, and three hours' sleep. He would then go back to London. He does not like Scotland. 'Too slow,' he said once to me. I took them to their rooms, through the hall whose floor is black and white, in sober alternation, and whose ceiling is corniced in plain but gold-leafed beading, uncomplicated and decorative as mimosa.

'I didn'a ken gold came in books,' said one George, after the beading had been redone by a sad man from Dumfries. 'Except mebbe pension books.'

The staircase is of stone; it is not carpeted. It ends in a coved barrel vault as high as the sky, pale blue, and the banister leads the eye like a tree to the top. I put Cora into her white room. The wives of both Georges had made a pile of Alexander's old baby clothes in her dressing-room, whose walls were stencilled faintly with ribbons. The cot waited, not yet set up, like a toy gate, and a basket full of shawls lay on the dressing table.

'No doubts about why I'm here. What if it's just biscuits making me big? No baby?'

'Then I shall retire and breed pigs,' said Lucas. He gave her a kiss. It did not touch her, but the air over her head. He kept his arm about her. The stairs had taken a stitch in him. I took him to his room.

He seemed delighted with it, the room he always had. He looked out through the curtainless tall windows and over to the hills. The light was so strong that he became a silhouette only. He held up his hand to his eyes as though against light from the sea, a salty light, not our soft London light.

'What a wonderful place for Cordelia to grow up. I'm sure she will be a girl,' he said.

'Who is that?'

'Mother and baby. It's her inheritance, her name. Cora is for short. You can't have read her papers very closely.'

I walked to the other windows, with the view over to the dovecote. It was like a bell, the silver bell shaped like a breast which is rung for lost ships. A list of things I must do came to me. For the first time in months the list did not need to be analgesic. I looked down through the roof of the glasshouse to its firm latticed walkways, made to hold us with firmness and beauty between water and glass, affording us time to see the green things about.

I lifted the door a little to set it closed in its frame behind me. It had been a cold winter, the doors were just unwarping.

They would come down, all three, in their own good time.

HAL

XXXI

They have found each other. They will be fine.

When Tertius gives me gossip, across the table over which we cannot touch, I don't really listen. I loved him so much but now I am afraid I ever touched him. He looks bad. He has a thin plucky look to him like one of those ventriloquist's dummies men in blue dinner-jackets stick their arms up and talk through, mouth shut for the duration of the act. He put on all this snobbish business, but he was never cold. We got drunk together after I'd done it, and by the end of the evening you couldn't hear a single vowel that knew the M1 from the A1. He panicked a bit and told Anne Angelica was there and didn't mention me. Angelica *was* there for a while, but then it was midnight and she had to go and change into her wolf suit, or whatever she does. Besides, she's not one for drink, she's just disorderly. Her kicks, while Lucas was in hospital, she got from ringing up pretending to be his wife. It's as if she liked them dead. I know she wanted him to be dead, but I sometimes thought she fancied him dead, as though that would give her more pleasure than anything else. Different, very.

She made me do it. She had more than a peck of dirt on me and she has the trait I've learnt in here is tops for a successful criminal; she knows all the weak spots, just by instinct. She knew how Lucas got his jollies, I guess from her cultivation of poor old Tertius. Is cultivation the word? She more like ploughed him up, but he was too chuffed to see he was being had, richly. The thought of her father's place I suppose; more than a few frames down there. She was hard to resist, by the time I confessed I was more afraid of her than of anything the police could do. I think she could get in anywhere, she's like smoke. I strictly am not a muff bandit but I could not stop thinking about her for all that bad autumn and winter and now I'm here I think I would cry if I saw her. I see pictures of her sometimes and I want to say, 'There's another notch I've carved,' but I don't think they'd believe me. I'm not as pretty as I was. I'm fatter, and my hair is just brown, like my brothers'. But she wouldn't have looked even when I was like Eros. I'm just not on her level, which is way, way up. She's so high up, she's like God. Life is cheap to her and she'd think nothing of smiting, or drowning, or sending in the locusts. Perhaps she really does like animals only because they can't answer back, like in all those mother-in-law jokes about bitches.

So Tertius told Angelica about Lucas's not so angelic side. He probably thought that she'd like him more, the bigger the ball of dung he rolled her way. But she's not like that; she'd've been more likely to eat him up. I'm getting my beetles and spiders mixed; it's amazing how you remember things in prison, stuff you'd forgotten, almost as though you knew you were going to do time. So, for instance, I can remember *The Ladybird Book of What to Look for in Winter* and any number of manuals. I wish I'd read more, now.

She wanted him to look like any old cruiser with his number up on the great fruit machine, three plums, and then I was to tuck all this literature under him, so the police got a surprise but could never be sure. It's quite possible the police think queers and people who think animals have rights are one and the same. Or Lucas could have picked up a hunt saboteur with his regulation spray of 'Antimate', the fragrance which is a must for putting people off the scent. It's a joke, really.

Angelica was ready for an act of violence like some girls are ready to get married, and it was as though she'd settled on Lucas for the lucky man. She thought about it a lot, and when she talked of it her face went soft, as though she heard the footsteps of her lover. Tertius wouldn't believe it, that I'd actually done it, and he thought it was his fault. Perhaps that's what he's got, guilt, not the other thing, the disease, about as easy to cure as each other. Unhelpful, AIDS.

The saddest thing is that Lucas liked being hit and my particular forte is hitting. A perfect match in a way, but the thrill goes with the same person, and knowing what they had for breakfast is just not romantic. Even knowing the other one's name can kill the thrill.

Actually, Lucas never did know my name. It's Harold. My father converted when I was two; we are called Deerbergh really and the other boys' names come out of a book called *Pillars of the Church*. My father got it wrong; he thought they were like Elders of Zion. It makes me sad. Those meals of pickle and piles of cheese and salt beef Lucas would make reminded me of something back before I got my big teeth. He was mad about me for being blond and English and all that and it was all a lie I was in the habit of because my mum and dad hid everything to do with the other thing. Not many Jewish criminals, so here I am. Lucas loved my blue eyes and they meant a whole lot to him I didn't need to say. He supplied his own romantic crap. I didn't have to do more than push a few gentle hints, and he had me born and bred flaxen on rolling acres. My mother pushed my father to convert. It can't be a dramatic faith to enter, Anglicanism, more like a nursery pool after the real thing, with its waves and the great Red Sea parting like a cleft palate.

The other business came over me in a rush on account of a severe bit of facial readjustment I'd administered. It was because of that I'd got to marry – and chop chop. That's the trouble. When a guy says 'No', it doesn't always mean yes.

I'd've married anyone to get silence. It might have reached Dick and Gloria's four little ears, and, what's more important, all their little friends' ears. They are not the same as me, with their plans for a shared mortgage and their doing the ironing with *Tosca on Ice*. So I will admit I was worried, and so was Tertius, who has always said that he liked to think he was the queen in my life. That is odd, he was much less good-looking than Lucas, but I did love him all down my early twenties, and still had a soft spot. I think it was that he was kind. Like Anne says, ad bloody nauseam, being thoughtful, having imagination, they aren't the same as being kind.

I picked Lucas up. An afternoon and a decent watch, I thought. But he was like ice, and by the time he got around to accidentally on purpose touching my hair I was well past interest. Not to bother. I quite liked him, and he was a cheap charm school for me, not to say a host of contacts. The pathetic thing was, he was taken in by my bit-part posh English, coat for jacket and glass for mirror, and button flies, not realising my dad had got them from some kind of phrase book by P. G. Wodehouse. He was a snob, but romantic, Lucas. I wouldn't be surprised if he thought *he* was English. He taught me more than the knifework at table (from the outside in, a useful tip when approaching a grown man in a topcoat with a view to stabbing, too, I may say). He taught me some of the lipwork. I've got a wide vocabulary and I know quite a few folk with stiffish handles, which could be useful. I met Anne Cowdenbeath. I liked her. I liked that her clothes needed a lot of people to keep them on the road. There was more than a suggestion of big running costs to her and I go for that. When I was growing up, we went to Harrods like church (the converting was all to do with standing, my mother would say, and I could not get what she was driving at); then Mum realised that the real class use Harrods like God, to have an account with but not to discuss, and not to mention at all available times.

We started going up in the world so fast you could see the greasemarks. I liked the things side of it. Mum took to it like a duck to water. Then she was taking to more than water, little glasses of gin and cin which she would hide behind the curtains and knock over fetching the next one. We had been to Spain a few times by now. I was happy enough at school. Boys like big cars. I started to learn the pleasurable side of being a mother's boy. I never got like the brothers. 'A good soft mouth,' I heard Saxon say one day, and he was talking about a dog. I've kept my hard mouth, I think. He went and believed it all.

Being an estate agent was a doddle. Castles in the air, houses in the air, unfurnished semis for rent in the air, I can get a punter to pay. I met a few expensive guys like that. What expensive means in the context is free, and with substantial tips. I found you could get anything out of them not with actions but words. As for women, it's the same. It is all a lie about women wanting men, they want a taped message of soft porn telling them they are different. I learnt one or two poems to use on them and they drive me mad now after closedown here, when I hear the lines come back in my head, all those roses, hearts and flowers and I will love you still after all the seas ganging up. It makes you weep.

When Cora was wheeled on, I quite liked her. I got fond of her in a way. She was a bad liar and blind as a bat and talked too much, but she did have what the visitors here call a low self-image, and I love that. It's something to stand on, it gives you a little rise. I put off bed for as long as possible, Johnny had told me what to expect, a grapefruit amidships at least, but that wasn't as bad as the scar she had which he *hadn't* warned me about. That did make me feel a bit rough, till I thought of the backhander Johnny gave me. I hate scars, or anything like that.

A monkey, he gave me.

He's married now, so the papers say (all my friends are in the papers one way or another, it makes you wonder where the real news is), to a bird he met in Rio. Tertius said Johnny bumped into her in the street. She was dressed as a naked girl at the time, it being carnival, and they upped and off, and some time later got married. He had gold glitter all over for a month, he said in a note he sent me with a piece of cake in a box, and he'd swallowed so much of the gold stuff he could've laid a golden egg. And what a surprise I do not think when she turns out to be a miss bred like a greyhound with a couple of big ones, two castles, a grouse moor and more. No kid yet, but then he's had a dry run, so they should be OK.

It's not love that matters, or family ties; it's money. Cora's little bastard will have enough of that to keep it a love child for life, and to stop people thinking it's a bit dodgy an old queer like Lucas setting up with two women, one as rich as greasers and the other old enough to be his daughter. I saw he'd married one of them, I can't remember which, but I hope she is in for a white marriage and a big bandage-wash once a month. The baby is a girl.

Angelica saw I wanted to beat him up, I guess. She's a witch, as such. It wasn't love I got for her, it was obedience, like she controlled me. All the things I'd had to learn, trying to make them look natural, she had grown up doing and chucked in. She was like all the freedom I get from the bashing up. And the forays, as Tertius called them, were losing their charm. After the big announcement, me wanting to settle and all that, and meeting Cora, all set up naturally by Lucas and Johnny, not knowing they were both at it and thinking, She'll have to do, I went out and trifled with Lucas's umbrella for an hour or two.

It was a fumy night, and I touched the boy quite radically, but I kept having this severe feeling he had parents, you know, a mother and a father, and I couldn't make it, hardly at all.

The money I got from Johnny to make an honest woman of Cora

went on shushing up the boy I'd carved up. He was very polite, lived at home, about forty. He was quite nice about it, and I felt bad when he said, 'I just told my mum and dad I was mugged.' I wondered if he had a dog just so he could go out for walks and told his mother every week hers was the best chicken à la King he'd ever tasted. I gave him a smile, and he gave the money to his parents. He smiled as though he had some teeth left.

When Angelica started me off doing errands, it was nothing physical. I had to do a bit of writing ('Imperative Graffiti', she called it), and a couple of interferences. I did not like carrying that tongue in my bag like a big old snail. How the ox carries it in his head I will never know. It had black patches, and I wondered if it came from a spotted cow, the sort city children learn the country on, those cows which are always picking their noses with their tongues.

She had told me before she started getting me wired up about Lucas, told me about her and Anne's son. She told the kid his mother killed his dad, and that he had better kill his mum. Lucas always said the father committed suicide on account of having cancer, but you can never trust a doctor.

Angel told me about the kid, and how he would moon about after her wanting a kiss, never leaving her alone, pestering her, all eyes and teeth and a place at his father's school.

The animal stuff mostly passed me by, but Angelica was working on me about Lucas. She could see so clearly. She told me about how he had taken me from myself, killed my spontaneity, and I could get back in touch with myself with this one single act. She'd send Dolores out for these chats, to get the food and drinks. Angel's a feminist, you see. Angel told me my heart was in the right place and I felt good. Then she started seeing me a bit less, being a bit less nice, and the wedding was coming and I felt bad like those timberwolves shut in their cages sloping about watching the children sucking Mivvis and wishing they could suck the children's little red legs with the white marrow. I felt shut in. I wanted to be like her. She was beautiful and free like that little dish in the opera Lucas took me to, a boy who is a chick and gets the best of everything, bed, champagne and all the attention. I began to dread the wedding, the house in Fulham, the sneaking out to pick up a boy.

The day we went to Chatham, I did feel nervous about hurting him. I thought about the time we had had together. I had a sailor in the ropery that day. The corridor is about half a mile long, and this dirty great hank of rope is getting twisted and twisted till it's as tight as death, steel and sisal in a twist like hair when you drag a man's head back and turn it. It was heavy and dangerous and under control. Released, it would have knocked the heads off a line of men. I watched it spin, under eight wedges of light from the eight dusty windows, and I touched the neck of the boy, just above the blue edge of his square-necked shirt, with my mouth. I had made up my mind.

I drew the line at the little fur man's shop. Dolores was put on to that. I don't know if it was something racial. I drew the line, but Angel stepped over it. She had feelings about Jews, she said, about how they run the money and the arms and all the fur shops and the law and how they put bad stuff in oranges to give to monkeys in the zoo. 'You're talking buckets of eyeballs,' said Dolores, a bit cheeky, and I saw trouble coming her way, though I couldn't get why. Angel said she had it in for Jews more than for even all other people. She says these things which aren't pretty but they make you want to do stuff for her, and bring her things, heads on plates, or on big thin knives.

I knew where Lucas went at night. After all, I went to the same places. The problem up to now had been avoiding him, it would've been like asking him to marry me, meeting him in all that shining white. Angel posted all those not too good pictures of animals staked out to all kinds of people and I kitted up.

She'd told me she'd get me away for my alibi and she said – she knows all the social stuff – that the wedding would have to be cancelled. No wedding guest, no wedding, she said.

What did for me was I listened to him. She had said, 'Do it for me, do it, do it,' and her voice was like a little girl's. I felt good and strong, and I knew I could give her joy. I went for him, that was easy. I was quite interested to see him without his manners. But I got carried away and I began to bawl, as I cut him, 'D'you get me, d'you get me, d'you get me?'

'Don't let those be the last words I hear,' he said, but I was well on the job, cutting away like a doctor on the television.

He started raving about undoing a button. Disgusting, really. I suppose it shows how far some of these oddballs will go.

I looked at him. His eyes showed sections of brown under the lids, which moved very slightly. I had no heart to go on.

I could not cut out all that stuff I had learnt. And it's not as though I asked to learn it either. I can't forget about starting from the outside with the knives.

LEWIS SHINER
DESERTED CITIES OF THE HEART

Finally, being a rock star just wasn't enough for Eddie. He used booze, sex, smack, 'ludes, anything to help forget his need to know it all meant something. Then he went crazy and disappeared.

The sacred mushrooms at Na Chan kept calling Eddie, and while he dreamt among circles in time, lots of crazy things started: His brother Thomas and his wife Lindsey caught up with him; Carmichael, a journalist for Rolling Stone tracked down Carla, the charismatic leader of a guerrilla outfit struggling for survival; and the fighting 666th, a US private army – funded by Irangate profits and CIA-backed, fighting under a fanatic quasi-religious banner to save the world from communism – is about to overtake them all. All of them at Na Chan – just in time to see the beginning of the end of the world.

Lewis Shiner brings us face to face with the paranoia and confusion of a nuclear age; dragging hidden longings, guilt, fear and passion protesting into the open in one violent thriller of politics, ancient civilization and twentieth-century corruption. DESERTED CITIES OF THE HEART is an extraordinary achievement, exciting, erotic and totally fascinating.

0 349 10001 2   **FICTION**   £3.99

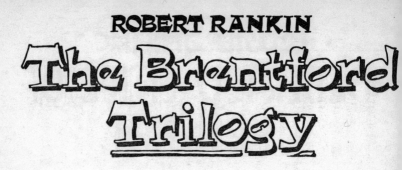

ROBERT RANKIN
The Brentford Trilogy

Can that be Jim Pooley himself? Layabout, bookies' best customer and dedicated pint-of-Large-fancier? Yes, unquestionably, it is he.

And by his side, isn't that the professionally unemployed ladies man, Flying Swan worshipper and bike rider, John Omally? Indeed. It is that lad.

Once more the dauntless double-act must outwit the fiendish Unknown Powers of Darkness, and defeat alien superpowers, crushing the legendary ancient Evil which, from time to time, crawls out with a new game plan, intent on nobbling life On Earth As We Know It! But the plucky Brentonians are never alone – even when facing the Big One. There's back-up from Professor Slocombe, Norman, Neville and Soap Distant – throw in a camel, some magic beans, Penge, the Great Pyramid, Norman's Morris Minor, a fleet of robots and a uncanny feeling for atmosphere – with expert consultation and guest appearances from Edgar Allan Poe and Sherlock Holmes . . . it all makes you wonder why Evil ever bothered to have a go!

'A born writer with a taste for the occult . . . Robert Rankin is to Brentford what William Faulkner was to Yoknapatwpha county'
TIME OUT

0 349 10028 4   FICTION   £3.99

Donn Pearce

COOL HAND LUKE

Lloyd Jackson was caught red-handed, abusing the system. So he was brought before the wrath of the Law. And he left an anguished chorus of forlorn voices praying behind him, and danced his way heel and toe right into his cell and on to the chain gang.

Donn Pearce's own experience on a chain gang in central Florida created COOL HAND LUKE and later the screen play to the classic film, starring Paul Newman. This story of one man's refusal to let the prison system grind him down has a poignancy and vitality which immediately caught the imagination of everyone who read the novel when it was first published in 1965. It remains just as powerful today.

'Rhythmic prose, tragic drama, and realism made larger than life'
PUBLISHERS WEEKLY

0 349 10004 7   FICTION   £3.99

S·U·M·M·I·T

D. M. Thomas

Age and soggy brain cells are not a safe combination for a US president, and 'Tiger' O'Reilly's got a big helping of both. Let's just say he makes a big blunder and impeachment looms. In the circumstances, a summit meeting with the new Soviet leader, Grobichov, seems a good thing to go for.

Quickly, the two world leaders take protocol into their own hands, dismissing the ranks of fawning advisors and second-rate interpreters, deciding to hold discussions on a private man-to-man basis, to cut the cackle and really get to know one another. And it has to be admitted – Alexei and Larissa, 'Tiger' and Wanda make a great double-date. A coup of Class A misunderstandings *do* slip through the fine mesh of presidential intelligence . . . something to do with twenty million contraceptive coils and California being presented to the Soviets . . . but world leaders are only flesh and blood, after all . . . anyone can make mistakes!

'With its canny political satire, its hilarious insights into the sex of politics and the politics of sex will delight and amuse even Thomas' most devoted readers.'
Erica Jong

0 349 10024 1   FICTION   £3.99

A DARKNESS
IN THE EYE
M.S. POWER

Seamus O'Reilly, 'Godfather' of the Provisional IRA, was a ruthless, vicious man. But he found the times demanded such an attitude. He was also thoughtful, humble, and tired. Tired of always losing in the struggle for peaceful, political solutions. Now the British Army is determined to infiltrate and exploit an angry new splinter group rising up within the Provos. O'Reilly's superiors make their decision, and the pale image of a settlement fades out of his grasp again.

This final novel in M. S. Power's haunting trilogy about Northern Ireland takes O'Reilly closer to defeat than he had believed possible. It carries us directly to the heart of an eerie world of shadows, ghosts and muddled beliefs, where another war is fought: against the stupid, misunderstanding the very nature of power, and against the ignorant, unable to value a future beyond the thrill of their own violence and revenge.

Also by M. S. Power in Abacus:

THE KILLING OF YESTERDAY'S CHILDREN
LONELY THE MAN WITHOUT HEROES

0 349 10024 1   FICTION   £4.50

Also available in ABACUS paperback: